Other Anne Stuart novels from Bell Bridge Books

Historical Romance

Lady Fortune

Barrett's Hill

Prince of Magic

The Demon Count Novels

Romantic Suspense

Nightfall

Shadow Lover

Now You See Him

The Catspaw Collection

Catspaw and Catspaw II

by

Anne Stuart

Bell Bridge Books

This is a work of fiction. Names, characters, places and incidents are either the products of the author's imagination or are used fictitiously. Any resemblance to actual persons (living or dead), events or locations is entirely coincidental.

Bell Bridge Books
PO BOX 300921
Memphis, TN 38130
Print ISBN: 978-1-61194-599-7

Bell Bridge Books is an Imprint of BelleBooks, Inc.

A mass market edition of *Catspaw* was published by Harlequin Intrigue in 1985
A mass market edition of *Catspaw II* was published by Harlequin Intrigue in 1988

We at BelleBooks enjoy hearing from readers.
Visit our websites
BelleBooks.com
BellBridgeBooks.com
ImaJinnBooks.com

10 9 8 7 6 5 4 3 2 1

Cover design: Debra Dixon
Interior design: Hank Smith
Photo/Art credits:
Man (manipulated) © Anatol Misnikou | Dreamstime.com
Bridge © Lovescene | Dreamstime.com

:Lcvf:01:

Catspaw

"HAVE YOU EVER made love wearing only an emerald necklace?"

"No," Ferris responded.

"Well I have," Blackheart replied. "Of course I wasn't wearing the necklace—I'm not that kinky. The lady in my life at the moment obliged. It was very uncomfortable. I don't recommend it."

"That's fortunate, because I have no intention of attempting it," Ferris snapped.

"You mean, it's just going to be skin to skin when we make love?" he inquired, a thread of laughter in his soft, warm voice. "I thought I was going to have to be very inventive the next time I got you into bed."

"You're going to have to be fast on your feet when you try," Ferris shot back.

Blackheart flashed her a disarming smile. "Don't worry about it, darling. The thrill is gone. The challenge has been met. I make it a policy never to steal the same thing twice. Unless it's a kiss. . . ."

Chapter One

FERRIS BYRD DIDN'T want to be in that plush, silent elevator carrying her inexorably toward the top floor of the San Francisco town house that held Blackheart, Inc. She'd argued—oh, so gently—manipulated, dragged her heels and flat-out refused. And still she was here.

The elevator doors whooshed open, exposing a small, charming hallway with white plastered walls, stripped oak woodwork and several doors. All belonging to Blackheart, Inc. and they were all closed. No one had seen her arrive—she could turn around and head back down to street level and tell Phillip Merriam and the Committee for Saving the Bay that someone else could deal with their chosen security firm. God knows why everyone had insisted on Blackheart, Inc.

No, Ferris knew very well why everyone had insisted on Blackheart. He had cachet, he had charm, he had a sly sort of fame that most people found irresistible and Ferris found offensive. She hated feeling judgmental, disapproving, stiff and pompous. But she also hated what Blackheart represented.

What she hated most of all, however, was cowardice, particularly her own. Phillip had talked her into it; the committee had insisted and here she was. She had no choice but to carry through.

"May I help you?" The office was a perfect example of San Francisco remodeled, with antique oak furniture, masses of plants and the obligatory stained-glass window. The only thing that didn't quite jibe was the receptionist. She was young, in her mid-twenties at the latest, with short-cropped red hair, distrustful blue eyes, a pugnacious tilt to her chin and a small, compact body dressed in modified army-navy surplus. The polite greeting had been uttered in a surprisingly hostile tone, and the look she passed over Ferris left little doubt as to her opinion. As if to emphasize it, the receptionist, whose desk plate identified her as Kate Christiansen, sniffed disapprovingly.

Ferris had no doubt what the woman would see through her flinty blue eyes. She'd see a woman of elegance, her custom-made leather shoes worth more than Kate Christiansen's entire wardrobe. Ferris's soft wool suit was Liz Claiborne, and it draped artfully to conceal the rounder parts of her figure. Her long legs were encased in real silk, her dark hair was clasped in a loose bun at the nape of her neck in a style that showed off her elegant bone structure. And the face itself wasn't bad, Ferris thought dispassionately. She knew her green eyes were cool and assessing, her mouth, with its pale-peach lip gloss, had curved in a polite smile, and the discreet gold hoops in her ears added just enough color to her warm skin tones. She looked rich, understated and well cared for, from generations of such pampered elegance. And only she knew how hard it was to come by that look.

The thought pleased her into widening her smile. She could afford to be generous; she was so close to her goals. "I'm Ferris Byrd," she said, her pleasant, well-modulated voice another triumph. Its slightly husky note was the only part she'd left of her original mid-western twang. Now she sounded bored, upper class and slightly naughty—and it was this voice, over the telephone, that had first charmed Phillip Merriam. "I have an appointment to see Mr. Blackheart."

Kate Christiansen did not look pleased, and Ferris wondered whether it was jealousy that caused that glower, or something else. She was almost tempted to inform the pugnacious young lady that John Patrick Blackheart was the last person she wished to entice, but then she controlled herself. That had been her worst trial, overcoming the sudden, unbidden urges to do something outrageous, but she had conquered the temptation, and now it was only a passing fantasy, quickly dismissed.

Kate Christiansen scowled. "He'll be with you shortly. You can go on in." With a jerk of her head she indicated the door on the left, then turned back to the sheaf of papers on the oak desk in front of her, effectively dismissing the upstart.

Ferris allowed herself her first real smile of the morning as she settled in a low-slung chair by John Patrick Blackheart's empty desk, her long, slender legs stretched out in front of her. Here she'd arrived, determined to disapprove, and instead she'd been made to feel the outcast. It served her right, but it didn't make her any more comfortable. Why hadn't she been able to talk them into hiring someone less . . . less unorthodox?

There was nothing about the office to suggest the history of the man who ran it. The walls were the ubiquitous white plaster, the woodwork and oriental rugs as discreet and tastefully anonymous as Ferris herself and probably manufactured with as much care. The only sign of personality was in the choice of paintings. They were a strange mélange: a romantic watercolor of the bay, a passionate oil of a storm at sea, a rigidly logical geometric painting that just might be a Mondrian. And most surprising of all, a Roy Lichtenstein silk-screen comic strip, with a cigarette-smoking, beret-clad lady holding a machine gun that went, according to the balloon, "crak-crak-crak." Ferris looked at it for a moment, a reluctant smile curving her deliberately pale mouth. It was an odd, jarring combination of artistic styles that somehow worked.

"Ferris Byrd?" The smooth, friendly voice made her jump, and the body that went with it was just as much of a shock. He was an immensely tall, almost ridiculously handsome man, with a mop of blond curls atop his high forehead, steely blue eyes, a thousand teeth shining in a tanned face, and the broadest shoulders Ferris had ever seen. He held out a hand the size of a small turkey that easily enveloped hers. "I'm Trace Walker, Patrick's associate. How can I help you?"

Ferris immediately decided that the toothy smile was charming, the steely-blue gaze warm and friendly. It was only Blackheart himself that she distrusted. With luck maybe she could deal with this affable giant entirely. "I represent the Committee for Saving the Bay, and we're in need of security consultants."

He smiled that dazzling smile of his. "How convenient. We just happen to be security consultants. I talked with Senator Merriam yesterday—he said it has to do with the Puffin Ball?"

Ferris controlled the little spurt of irritation that sped through her. Phillip never did trust anyone else to get a job done. His hands-on approach aided him immeasurably in his political career, but it irritated the hell out of his administrative assistant and brand-new fiancée. She smiled again, a little more tightly. "Exactly. We've added a new touch this year. The Von Emmerling emeralds, to be exact. The raffle last year was such an astonishing success . . ."

"You're raffling off the Von Emmerling emeralds?" Trace Walker echoed, aghast.

"No, of course not. They're not ours to raffle—they're only in San Francisco on loan. We're raffling off the chance to wear them at the Puffin Ball. The first prize winner gets to wear them for two hours, second prize one hour, third prize half an hour."

"Oh, Lord," Walker groaned. "And you want us to protect them? The most famous emeralds in the world, and you're going to be handing them out to just anybody to wear in a crowded ballroom?"

Ferris smiled. "Crazy, isn't it? But people seem to be going wild about it. We've already sold a huge amount of tickets, and the committee's had to order up another printing. It was an absolute brainstorm."

"Yours?" he questioned glumly.

She shook her head. "I'm too conservative. I'd be just as afraid as you are that someone might decide to keep them. Originally we were thinking of auctioning off the wearing time, then decided against it. If someone knew ahead of time, they could have copies made, and it would be simple enough to make an exchange in the bathroom or something. We thought with a raffle it would be safer—the winners won't know until they arrive at the ball."

"You're going to end up with a lot of women dressed for emeralds," Walker pointed out. "You realize this is going to be practically impossible?"

"I imagine it will be difficult," Ferris allowed. "But not impossible. At a thousand dollars per guest the list will naturally be limited, and we'll have our own security there to make sure there are no gate-crashers. Your only worry will be the emeralds. As long as Carleton House is secure and someone's on the scene, I expect it will be all right."

"Carleton House!" Walker groaned. "On the point? That rambling old mansion will take weeks to burglar-proof."

Ferris smiled sweetly. "You have one week. The Puffin Ball is next Friday. I'm afraid we only just decided we'd need extra help for the jewels themselves. Of course, if you don't think you can handle it . . ." She was no longer certain she wanted him to give up. On the one hand, it would certainly make things easier for her, dealing with the firm that handled the regular security for Carleton House. On the other hand, Blackheart, Inc. had a certain appeal. Fortunately, it didn't seem as if John Patrick Blackheart busied himself with the mundane details of the workaday world, and Trace Walker had a puppy-dog charm that even a securely engaged woman like Ferris could appreciate. It really might work out very well indeed.

"Don't browbeat him, Miss Byrd." Another voice entered the fray, and Ferris cursed the silent doorways and the even quieter footsteps of the man walking toward her. Obviously her hope had been in vain. The man walking toward her with that amused expression on his face could only be the heretofore absent John Patrick Blackheart. The most famous living cat burglar in the world.

BLACKHEART HAD been cursing quietly under his breath as he climbed the steep hill toward the town house that held his offices. Not that the hill was bad for the dull ache in his leg, but the dampness of the San Francisco weather certainly didn't do it any good. The knee had tightened up again, and it took all his willpower not to favor it. It had been three years since he'd conquered the limp, three years since the last operation and the physical therapy and rigorous exercises. And now his right leg was as good as anybody else's, could do what anyone else's could do. He could dance, if it was a slow one and he had a nice rounded body to hold onto, he could walk briskly without any sign of strain, and he could even manage a sedate run along the beach south of the city when the mood hit him. The one thing he couldn't do was scramble up the side of buildings and over rooftops, couldn't cling like Spiderman to the back walls and sneak into fifteenth-floor windows. Not anymore.

He paused long enough to admire the discreet brass plate on the brick front of the town house, a wry smile lighting his face. It still amused him, two years later, that he'd be making his living from the same people who'd served him in the past. He'd taken his considerable experience and talent in the field of breaking and entering and used it to keep other people from following in his footsteps, and he did a damned fine job of it. Unlike the more traditional security firms in the city, he understood the mind of the thief, knew how his thought processes would work and how to circumvent him. If his job didn't net any disappointed felons for the city jails, neither did it come up with any valuables missing. Blackheart was never completely sure if it was his ability or honor among thieves that kept his jobs successful. He imagined it was a little of both.

He was late for his appointment, and Kate would give him hell. He viewed that certainty with not the slightest chagrin. From the very beginning he had been deliberately lax about appointments. His change in lifestyle was too radical as it was—he couldn't be expected to be punctual on top of everything else. Most of his wealthy clientele viewed it as a lovable foible, one they'd never accept in any other employee.

It was a woman, a friend of Senator Merriam's, who was coming in. From his knowledge of Merriam, he knew the woman was bound to be good-looking, so there really was no need to hurry. Trace would be sniffing at her heels, all but drooling over her. He'd be just as happy if Blackheart didn't show up too promptly.

They made good partners, Trace Walker with his handsome, open face and friendly manners, Blackheart so much the opposite. He had no illusions about the image he presented to the world. Just slightly devious, with secrets lurking in his shadowed face. Women seemed to find him irresistible, which was an added bonus, and the ones who didn't lean toward him were just as entranced with Trace's beefy good looks.

Trace would have never made it as a cat burglar, or in any form of breaking and entering. For one thing, he was too big, for another, he was too good-hearted. He could never hear the tales of Blackheart's illustrious career without worrying about the victims.

He'd been one of the victims himself, long ago. The one attempt Blackheart had made after his fall was Trace's apartment, and it had been a fiasco all around. Blackheart had made it a practice only to prey on the extremely wealthy and well-insured. Trace put up a good front as an antique jewelry dealer, but his openness and good-heartedness had proved bad for business, so that by the time Blackheart fell clumsily in his bathroom window he was on the far edge of bankruptcy. There were no jewels in the large apartment with its rent overdue by three months; there were no expensive artifacts. There wasn't even a camera or some portable stereo equipment, not that Blackheart would have stooped so low. There was only Trace Walker, glowering at him, more than happy to have someone on whom to take out his financial frustrations.

In retrospect Blackheart realized he hadn't needed to be so rough with him. Sure, Trace outweighed him by forty pounds at least, towered over him by five inches, and had fists the size of hams. But he would never have gone far in such an uneven fight. Unfortunately, he didn't realize that the fight was uneven in Blackheart's favor. Blackheart had some frustrations of his own—not the least being the sloppy attempt at burgling Trace Walker's apartment and his nagging feeling of guilt—so in less than a minute Trace was flat on his back, breathing heavily, staring up at Blackheart's fierce face with an expression of complete amazement on his open features. And then, slowly, that amazement had broadened into a grin, and he'd held out one of those hamlike hands to his would-be thief.

They'd been friends ever since. Trace seemed to think Blackheart needed looking after, and Blackheart felt the same about Trace. The two of them had an uneasy alliance that had served them well in the last two years, both professionally and financially. Blackheart was more than willing to let all the pretty young debutantes of San Francisco end up in Trace's office and eventually Trace's bed. He'd gotten tired of perfect bodies and empty souls.

"There you are," Kate grumbled. "Trace beat you to it."

"Any need for me to go in?" He gave the proffered mail a cursory glance before attempting a winning smile in Kate's direction. As usual, it failed to get any response.

"Probably. Trace had that love struck look in his eye last time I saw him, and she's more than the usual type."

"How so?"

"I can't really tell. Everything looks right—the Rolex watch, the suit, the discreet little gold touches. There's something more there, but you know Trace. Everything at face value. And he sure seems to like her face." If her voice was slightly disgruntled, Blackheart was kind enough not to notice it. He knew what was going on with Kate's chronic bad temper, even if his obtuse associate didn't, and he knew there was no way he could interfere.

"Where are they?" he said, sighing.

"Your office. You can't miss 'em. He's the one looking like a lovesick calf, and she's the one that stepped out of *Vogue*," Kate grumbled.

He moved with the silence that had gained him access to a hundred hotel rooms. Kate was, as usual, right. Ferris Byrd looked as if she stepped out of *Vogue*, and yet there was something that wasn't quite right. Maybe it was in the glint of humor in those incredibly green eyes, maybe in the scarcely disciplined curve of her pale mouth. Too pale, Blackheart thought critically. And the hair should be loose, flowing, a brown-black cloud around that arresting face of hers. She wasn't really beautiful, at least not with a pink-and-white prettiness. She had something more than beauty, and he wondered whether a predictable man like Senator Phillip Merriam could appreciate that something. From the look of the diamond ring on her left hand, it appeared that he did.

But the very last thing he expected, watching her bait Trace with the lightest of touches, was the look of hostility in her green eyes when they turned to his. Miss Ferris Byrd did not like John Patrick Blackheart one tiny bit. And despite his general indifference to the opinions of his fellow man, Blackheart found himself intrigued.

Chapter Two

HE WASN'T WHAT she expected. Which was silly of her, since she'd seen photographs of him, heard enough to have a fairly accurate expectation of what he was like. But it was all shot to hell the first time she looked at him.

John Patrick Blackheart had to be somewhere in his mid to late thirties, and he'd lived every one of those years to the fullest. He was above average height, probably about five feet eleven, but next to Trace Walker he looked smaller. There was nothing particularly remarkable about him. His eyes were cool and brown and assessing, his dark brown hair a little too long, not styled, but rather like the hair of someone who hadn't managed to get to a barber recently and didn't give a damn. He had a light tan, and he was dressed all in black—black denims, a black turtleneck hugging his lean torso, black leather boots on his feet. He didn't look like a world-famous criminal, but he didn't look like an ordinary mortal, either. It might have been that genuinely amused curve to the sensual mouth, or the glint in the cool brown eyes. Or it might have been in the slightly tense way he held his lean, muscled body, poised for flight, poised for attack, poised for something. Ferris came to the unhappy conclusion that he was remarkable indeed, and she knew she was in trouble.

"Patrick!" Trace greeted him exuberantly, with only the faintest expression of guilt marring his open features. "I didn't know whether you would make it in this morning, so I thought I could get started . . . that is, Miss Byrd was here, and I . . ."

Ferris watched the smaller man take pity on his partner, smiling at him with a charm that was nothing short of dangerous. She decided then and there to be prepared if he chose to use it on her. "Don't worry about it, Trace. You know I'm always late." He turned to Ferris, and for the first time she felt the full force of those tawny brown eyes. They weren't cool as she had thought, they were warm and subtly caressing, even as that mobile mouth of his curved in what was definitely a mocking smile. Ferris didn't like to be mocked.

"I'm Ferris Byrd." She rose, holding out her hand with determination, carefully putting this man in his place. She'd had to deal with men trying every sort of intimidation; she'd faced sexual intimidation often enough to recognize it and fight it. She waited for him to take her hand, and when he did she realized her tactical error. His hand was rough with calluses, strong and warm, and it caught hers with just the right amount of pressure. Like an equal, none of that pumping, caressing stuff that always made her skin crawl.

"I've already explained the problem to Trace, and I—"

"Senator Merriam spoke with me this morning," Blackheart said gently. He had a soft, low voice that nevertheless commanded instant attention, and the quiet tones that should have been comforting were instead unnerving.

"Senator Merriam's been busy," she said, unable to control her start of irritation. "Then you know the problem?"

"The Puffin Ball, the Von Emmerling emeralds, and Carleton House? Yes, I know."

"Do you think we can handle it, Patrick?" Trace asked eagerly, obviously more than happy to try.

"I'm wondering what Miss Byrd thinks," Blackheart murmured.

He must have sensed her disapproval. She certainly hadn't gone to any pains to hide it, but the thought of his reading her so accurately bothered her. "I think the Carleton security staff would be just as capable," she said coolly, meeting his dare.

"Do you? I have the impression that Miss Byrd doesn't approve of us, Trace."

"Oh, surely not, Patrick," Trace protested, looking like a very handsome, very wounded moose. "We've been getting along like a house afire."

"I stand corrected. Miss Byrd doesn't approve of me," Blackheart said with a gentle smile. "Isn't that so?"

Damn him, he was playing with her like a cat with a mouse, a fat, succulent little mouse. Well, she wasn't going to cower away from him. "Quite true, Mr. Blackheart," she said in dulcet tones.

"You've never heard the saying, 'It takes a thief to catch a thief'?"

"Certainly. The question is, what does the second thief do once he's caught the first one?"

Blackheart smiled. "I expect he splits up the booty, like any sensible thief. Is that what you're afraid of? That we'll run off with the Von Emmerling emeralds ourselves?"

"Oh, no, Patrick!" Trace's protest was explosive. "She wouldn't think that we—"

"Yes, I would," Ferris said sharply.

"Yes, she would, Trace," Blackheart said, clearly amused. "So the question is, how do we get Miss Ferris Byrd to trust us enough to enable us to do our job properly?"

"Are you taking the job?" Ferris questioned. For a moment she'd thought she'd driven him off.

"Oh, most definitely. I never could resist a challenge," Blackheart said, his laughing eyes running over her, and Ferris had the melancholy suspicion that he wasn't talking about the Von Emmerling emeralds.

"That's just as well," she said briskly, squashing down the strong sense of unease that washed over her. "The Puffin Ball is only a week away, and we'd have a hard time making other arrangements at this late date."

"In that case, why don't I accompany Miss Byrd out to Carleton House to get a good look at the place?" Trace suggested eagerly. "I haven't anything on for this morning, and I'd be more than happy to make the preliminary study."

"Have you forgotten your report on the Winslow collection? Kate's going to have your head on a platter if you don't let her close the files."

"I'll close my own files." It was the closest Trace ever got to sulking, and he did a credible job of it, but Blackheart was unmoved.

"I can wait," Ferris offered helpfully. "I have some errands to run in town. I can come back in a few hours when you've finished the report and take you out there, Trace."

Trace's face lit up for a moment, then darkened as he cast a beseeching glance at his partner.

Blackheart shook his head slowly. "You're undermining discipline, Miss Byrd. Trace has got a full day's work ahead of him. Besides, he usually concentrates on the physical side of the job, not the planning stage. He's got too much energy to be a mastermind."

"I've got too little patience, you mean," Trace said sheepishly. "He's right, Ferris. Anything I did would just have to be done over by Patrick. You're better off with him."

Ferris controlled her disbelieving snort, turning her gaze to Blackheart's. She expected smug triumph, not the very real humor that lingered there. "All right," she said, knowing it was graceless and not really caring. "I don't suppose you'd rather go there by yourself?"

"I don't suppose. Senator Merriam assures me you know more than anyone about what's going on with this benefit. He promised me you'd be invaluable." Blackheart smiled sweetly, but Ferris wasn't fooled.

"Let's go then," she said, caving in. "We may as well get it over with."

"Charmingly put," Blackheart replied, almost purring. "Let me give Kate a message and I'll be ready. Soothe Miss Byrd's ruffled feathers, Trace, and tell her I'm not half as bad as she thinks."

"Patrick's great," Trace said earnestly, obeying unquestioningly as Blackheart's lean figure disappeared out the door with the same uncanny silence with which he had entered. "Really, Ferris, you have nothing to worry about. I'd trust him with my life."

"But would you trust him with your jewels?" she drawled.

"If he agreed to protect them, I would."

"And if he didn't agree?"

A frown creased Trace's broad, handsome face. "I'm not sure," he said honestly. "But I wouldn't work with him if I didn't trust him, and didn't think other people could trust him too."

"And I'll just have to take your word for it."

"I expect you'll have to," Blackheart had returned, damn him, still on silent cat's feet. He had pulled an ancient Harris tweed jacket over the black turtleneck, and Ferris remembered belatedly that he was half British. He didn't sound it—he sounded soft and menacing and American. But the coat looked as if it had belonged to some country squire. He probably stole it, she thought cynically.

"I expect I will." She rose, ignoring the hand he held out to her. She couldn't help but notice it was a well-shaped hand, with long, dexterous fingers, the better for plucking jewels out of someone's bureau drawer; strong wrists, the better for hanging off buildings; and broad palms, the better for vaulting over rooftops. It also looked warm and strong and more than capable of caressing a bare shoulder. Damn, but the man was trouble. "Let's go," she said.

Blackheart only smiled.

"We'll take my car." It was a challenge, one Blackheart didn't rise to.

"Certainly," he murmured. "I walked to work anyway."

Ferris gnashed her teeth as she yanked open the low-slung door of her vintage Mercedes 380SL. The navy blue had pleased her discerning eye, the classic lines enhanced her image—and if she had a hidden craving for a red Corvette, she suppressed it admirably. Corvettes were tacky.

"Nice car," Blackheart said, gripping the seat as she tore into the traffic without looking.

"I worked hard to get it," she snapped, tires screeching as she rounded a corner and started down one of San Francisco's precipitous hills.

"And I wouldn't know anything about hard work?" Blackheart questioned softly.

"I didn't say that." She yanked the wheel sharply, the tires skidding slightly as she turned another corner and headed out toward the bay.

"The inference was clear. Tell me, do you always drive like this, or is it simply for my benefit?" He was completely unmoved, watching her with that damnable half-smile on his face.

She pressed harder on the accelerator. "A bit of both," she said in a disinterested tone of voice. The Mercedes had far too much power, and they were speeding full tilt down California Street when his boot-clad foot slid over to her side of the car, hooked under her ankle and pulled it back off the accelerator.

She swerved in surprise, almost losing control of the car. Skidding to a stop, Ferris turned off the key with shaking hands. "What the hell were you trying to do?" She demanded in a rough voice. "You could have gotten us both killed."

"Not if you hadn't been driving so fast. I don't like speeding in the middle of the city. It attracts a great deal of unnecessary attention, and I have an aversion to the police." It was all said in the most reasonable of voices, and her lip curled.

"I just bet you do," Ferris snarled.

"We're not going to get very far like this, Miss Byrd," he said gently. "I think we should call an armed truce, at least for the next week. Senator Merriam is counting on you to give me every assistance."

"He is, is he?"

Blackheart's smile widened, opening up that dark, shuttered face. "So he told me this morning. You wouldn't want to let him down, would you?"

"I have no intention of letting him down," Ferris snapped.

"Then you'll be giving me every assistance?"

"To the best of my ability." It galled her to say it, but she had no choice.

"And I give you leave to disapprove of me all you want," he added magnanimously, that wicked smile lighting his eyes. "As long as it doesn't interfere with my work. I have my professional pride to consider."

Nobly Ferris swallowed the retort that rose to her lips. That left her with nothing to say, and she stared straight forward at the busy street ahead of them.

She could feel Blackheart's eyes on her, and they were far too astute. "A truce, Miss Byrd," he said, holding out his hand. She had no choice but to take it, dropping it as quickly as she could.

"A truce, Mr. Blackheart. And you may as well call me Ferris, since we'll be working together."

"I might. But I don't like it. Do you have any other names?"

Ferris controlled the unexpectedly nervous start. "Frances," she said sullenly.

"I don't like that, either. I'll just have to make do with Miss Byrd until I find something that pleases me," he murmured.

"Do you mind if I continue driving?" she asked pointedly, but Blackheart was unruffled.

"Please do." Leaning back, he shut his eyes, but Ferris could see his hands clenching the leather seat as she pulled back into traffic. She drove sedately enough, and finally his eyes opened, those warm, all-knowing brown eyes that constantly unnerved her. "Are you going to tell me what you have to do with Senator Merriam? And the Committee for Saving the Bay?"

She wasn't quite sure if it was a peace offering, but the subject was innocuous enough. "I'm Phillip Merriam's administrative assistant. He's trying to move up from the state senate to the U.S. Senate, and I was working on his election campaign when he decided to lend me to the committee to help them with the Puffin Ball." She was quite pleased at her even tone of voice. Even the observant Blackheart couldn't guess how disgruntled she was at being out of the action, shepherding a bunch of bored debutantes and society matrons. But she couldn't allow herself to think like that. If all went well, if things went her way, she could be one of those society matrons, safe and secure in her giant house in the heart of San Francisco.

"Administrative assistant?" he echoed. "In my experience, administrative assistants are either people who know nothing and do nothing, or know everything and do everything. Which are you?"

Her foot began to press down harder on the accelerator again. "Guess."

"Not so fast, Miss Byrd," he said gently. "We aren't in any hurry. We have plenty of time to get to know each other."

She took the corner too fast, but then made a concerted effort to slow down. She wouldn't put it past him to put that strong, rough hand on top of hers and pull her over. "That's what I'm afraid of," she said gloomily.

Blackheart laughed.

IN THE BRIGHT, glaring light of the small, secret workshop hidden behind the false wall of a closet in the basement of his jewelry shop on Geary Street, Hans Werdegast admired his handiwork. The Von Emmerling emeralds had to be his greatest creation, his masterpiece, his chef d'oeuvre, and there was no one to appreciate his genius, his craftsmanship.

Sighing, he shook his head, rubbing his lined forehead with a wrinkled linen handkerchief. That was the problem with his chosen avocation, he thought. No audience.

However, the money made up for it. He earned a comfortable amount from the small, elite jewelry store above him, supplementing it with a few custom-made pieces in the upstairs workshop where his assistants had free access, but the secrets of his hidden workshop did more than pay the bills, they bought him the luxuries and pleased his soul at the same time. He could no more give the workshop up than he could fly.

He was getting to be an old man, though. And he wouldn't like to be caught. There was no way he would ever submit to being imprisoned again, behind bars and barbed wire, locked away. He glanced down at the faded, almost unreadable tattoo on his wrist. Months went by without thinking about it. Maybe he should stop being such a foolish old man and think about it more carefully.

The Von Emmerling emeralds were admittedly magnificent, the replicas so close to the real thing that anyone without a jeweler's loupe would be fooled. Maybe it was a good place to stop. His customer was paying through the nose—the Von Emmerling emeralds were a fitting swan song.

Sighing, the old man dropped the glittering almost-jewels into a plastic bag, sealing it with a twist tie. It wounded him to treat his prize creations so shabbily. They deserved velvet as much as their authentic counterparts. But that would make the package too bulky, and he had to be ready to pass them to his customer later that evening with a minimum of fuss. A shoddy fate for a masterpiece.

He climbed down off the stool and shuffled back toward the hidden doorway to his storeroom closet. He'd miss his workshop, miss his secrets. But it was time to retire, and best to retire at the top of the game. For a moment he wondered what had possessed his customer to tackle such a monumental job. But he knew. As enamored as he was of the phony emeralds, he knew the real ones would be far more enticing, particularly once you held them in your hands. No, he didn't blame his customer. And he would make sure that he profited by them, just in case the elaborate scheme didn't succeed. Elaborate schemes had a high risk factor, and Hans Werdegast had almost been burned too many times.

Yes, he thought with a sigh, shutting the back wall of the closet behind him and shuffling into the deserted storeroom. It was time to retire. He'd spend his time in the upstairs workshop from now on, and look back with satisfaction on his memories. Particularly the Von Emmerling emeralds.

Chapter Three

CARLETON HOUSE was an impressive old mansion overlooking the Pacific Ocean on a point of land to the west of the magnificent Golden Gate Bridge. Once, years ago, it had been a private residence, until the bankrupt sea captain left it to the Daughters of the Pacific. In the last decades it had played host to any number of charity balls, garden fetes, debutante dances, ladies' luncheons and even a discreet conference or two. The multitude of cavernous, elegant rooms, the expanse of beautifully maintained gardens, the dozens of bedroom suites on the third and fourth floors made it an admirable facility for any kind of social affair. It also made it utter hell to protect. That thought pleased Ferris no end.

"There you are, Ferris, dear." The blue-haired lady in the elegant tweed suit greeted her with a warm smile. "And you've brought Mr. Blackheart. How good of you to come, Patrick! I knew we could count on you."

Ferris had her first look at Blackheart's celebrated charm as he kissed Phillip's mother's hand with a panache that would have done Errol Flynn proud. Had Errol Flynn ever played a cat burglar? He would have been good at it, Ferris thought dismally. This explained, in part, why Phillip had been so insistent on Blackheart, Inc. Regina Merriam was clearly entranced with the cat burglar.

Ferris knew an escape when she saw one. "Regina, why don't you show Mr. Blackheart around while I check on the decorations committee? You know Carleton House as well as anyone."

Regina smiled at her future daughter-in-law. "I'd adore to. I had to sneak out from the flower committee—the air was getting a little thick in there. Too many boring old matrons. Come along, Patrick, my boy, and I'll show you what an impossible job you have ahead of you. How's Trace? Will he be coming later? Olivia has been pestering me all day."

"Trace will be here."

Ferris could feel those eyes of his following her as she made good her escape.

"Later, Miss Byrd," he called after her, the words a warning and a challenge.

She hesitated for a moment, contenting herself with a cursory nod before disappearing into the nearest reception room. She could hear Regina's amused voice drifting after her. "Heavens, Patrick, call her Ferris. She's the dearest girl. Far too good for my son."

Ferris stopped dead still just inside the door, straining to hear his answer. But they'd moved away, out of reach, and only the soft murmur of his voice carried to her ears.

God, she was in trouble. Blackheart was far more dangerous than she'd imagined. The only thing she could do was call Phillip and beg him to let her come back and work on his campaign. He'd thought the Puffin Ball would be good experience for her, outside the political arena in the social world where a politician's wife spent so much of her time. She was getting to know the major names in San Francisco society, and she was becoming good friends with her future mother-in-law, but all those benefits seemed to pale next to the seemingly very real threat of Patrick Blackheart.

Not that there was anything he could do to hurt her.

He couldn't read her mind, know the deep, dark secrets of her soul that she trusted to no one. He was no threat to her, she had to remember that.

In the meantime, she was too busy that day to think much one way or the other about John Patrick Blackheart, apart from avoiding him whenever she saw him coming. He had the uncanny habit of sneaking up on her, his booted feet silent on the marble floors of the old mansion, that damned, bland smile on his face. She would find him waiting patiently behind her shoulder as she listened to a thousand and one questions, complaints, and impractical suggestions from the busy ladies of the Committee for Saving the Bay, and the only clue that he had reappeared would be the sudden, fatuous expression on the speaker's face.

She couldn't get through to Phillip till late in the afternoon, when most of the members of the committee had drifted away. The sound of his deep, mellifluous voice had its usual effect, soothing and warming her. It was one of his greatest political gifts, that rich, mellow voice, and Ferris was no more immune to it than his besotted constituents, especially when she knew what a basically decent, nice person resided behind that warm voice and those patrician good looks.

But the soothing tones offered her cold comfort indeed. "It will only be a week, Ferris. Surely Blackheart can't be so bad—my mother adores him, and I trust her taste implicitly. After all, she thinks you're too good for me.

"Blackheart isn't bad, Phillip. I'm just not comfortable around him. Things are coming together beautifully—your mother knows as much as I do about everything. Couldn't I please come back?" She let her voice sound mournful and pleading, hoping she might appeal to his protective instincts.

Phillip was too smart for her. "No, Ferris. There's nothing you can't handle, be it a hostile constituent or a retired cat burglar or the combined forces of the Committee for Saving the Bay. I'm counting on you, darling. This is the kind of experience for you that money can't buy, and it will all be over by Friday. I'll be there to take you to the ball, and we might even consider making our formal announcement."

"I thought we were going to wait till after the primary." Why was she suddenly reluctant to have her triumph made public knowledge? Enough people had seen the diamond on her left hand and given her a knowing look; it was no longer a secret.

"I was considering it, but I've decided you might bring me more votes," he said frankly.

That was the problem with their relationship, Ferris decided suddenly. His election always came first, for both of them, and their engagement was more a useful adjunct than an emotional commitment. The thought was suddenly depressing.

"Let's wait and see," she temporized. "Will you call later?" Her voice was no longer mournful, it was brisk and efficient.

"Sunday at three, same as always. You'll stick with it, won't you, Ferris? Mother's capable, you're right, but I don't like putting so much responsibility on her after her stroke. You can do it, can't you?"

Ferris sighed, well and truly trapped. She may as well acquiesce gracefully. "Of course I can, Phillip. I just miss you."

The deep, rich voice, like chocolate custard, breathed a sigh of relief. "I knew I could count on you, Ferris. I love you." The last was hurried, almost by rote, and Ferris repeated it the same way.

They would deal well together. She would be the perfect politician's wife, charming, reserved, very clever, with just the right amount of public deference and private encouragement to aid Phillip in attaining whatever office he was seeking. The public acclaim was not part of her own particular fantasy—she'd be just as happy if Phillip had remained a lawyer. But Phillip was an ambitious man, it was an integral part of his nature, and she wouldn't have him any other way. It was ambition that had gotten her where she was now, and she wasn't going back if she could help it. She would support Phillip completely, follow him . . .

"What's that determined look on your face?"

Ferris dropped the phone with a nervous shriek, cursed, and rounded on Blackheart. "Must you sneak up on people like that?" she demanded indignantly.

"I can't help it." He favored her with that charming smile that melted all women within a ten-mile radius. Ferris did her best to remain stonily unmoved, but it was an uphill battle. "I can't change years of habit overnight, Miss Byrd. Are you ready to leave?"

The last thing she wanted to do was get back into the cramped quarters of her car with him. That lethal charm was beginning to work on her, much as she fought it. Why did that smile of his have to be so damned infectious? And why did his brown eyes glint with hints of amber as he looked at her? And why couldn't she trust him?

None of that really mattered of course, with Phillip in the picture. "I'm not quite ready to leave," she said coolly. "Perhaps you could get a ride with someone else."

He seemed to have the uncanny knack of reading her mind. Slowly he shook his head. "That won't do, Miss Byrd. Everyone's gone. I'll just have to wait here, all alone with you in this big old house, while you finish whatever you're doing."

"I'm ready," she snapped, interpreting the smiling threat correctly. "It'll take me a few minutes to lock up. I'll meet you at the car at ten past."

"That'll give me just enough time to check in with my office," he said sweetly.

"Why?" Her suspicions were instantly aroused.

"To see if my burgling tools have arrived," he drawled. "Go ahead and lock up, Ms. Byrd."

She hesitated for a moment, watching as he picked up the telephone. "If I'm the last one to leave, I have to lock up, Mr. Blackheart. Once I do so, you won't be able to leave without tripping the alarm."

He laughed then, a rich, full laugh that was even more attractively unnerving. "You really think so?" he questioned gently. "You do underrate me, Ms. Byrd." For her dubious peace of mind she could be grateful he was waiting at the car for her. She had little doubt that he could leave the house with its locks intact, but her sense of responsibility would have insisted that she go back and check, and Blackheart would have been bound to follow, smiling that damnable smile of his. What she wouldn't give to wipe it off his face for just one moment, she thought with wistful violence.

It was a foggy day in late February, cool and chilly and distinctly unfriendly. She couldn't wait till she was back in her small, cozy apartment, her shoes off and her long legs curled up underneath her, a real fire in her working fireplace and a snifter of brandy in her hand. *God bless gourmet frozen dinners,* she thought with a blissful sigh.

"What occasioned that erotic moan?" Blackheart drawled from beside her, and she jumped. For a brief, heavenly moment she had almost forgotten he was sitting beside her as she raced haphazardly back into the city.

She allowed herself a short glimpse at him, and her tense shoulders began to relax a trifle. In less than five minutes she'd be free of him, in ten minutes she'd be home. A tentative smile lit her face. "I was thinking about food," she confessed.

He was staring at her, his expression arrested. "Do that again," he said, his low, drawling voice suddenly husky in demand.

"Do what?" She couldn't summon more than a trace of irritation as she screeched around the corner toward his office.

"Smile. I didn't think you could."

It was with a great effort that she kept another, answering smile from her mouth. "And you, Blackheart, smile too much. 'A damned, smiling villain,' Shakespeare said. He must have had you in mind."

"You think so?" He seemed genuinely pleased at the notion. "And who are you?"

"Lady Macbeth," she snapped, pulling to a stop in front of the old brick town house that housed Blackheart, Inc.

He made no move to leave the car, just looked at her out of those translucent eyes of his. "No, I don't think so," he murmured. "I haven't got it yet, but I will."

"Be sure to let me know when you think of it," she said sarcastically.

He smiled at her. "I will. You really detest me, don't you, Miss Byrd? Think I'm the lowest of the low?"

She said nothing, neither denied nor confirmed it. "Good evening, Mr. Blackheart."

Reaching for the door handle, he pulled himself out of the Mercedes with a graceful swoop. Leaning down to close the door, he looked in at her. "I'm not really that bad, you know," he observed gently.

"I'm sure you're not," Ferris said, sure of no such thing.

He grinned, a glint of wickedness in those tawny brown eyes. "At least I always go by the same name." This was said in the softest of tones, and the door closed before she could respond.

There was nothing she could say. There was a sick burning in her stomach, her hands were clammy with nervous sweat, and she felt a nasty headache coming on. Without another word, without a look in his direction, she screeched the car away from the curb, directly into the traffic. Horns blared in protest, and then she was gone, tearing down the hillside with a blithe disregard for traffic and stop lights.

HANS WERDEGAST handed the plastic baggie over with a sense of real regret. He would never see them again, what he had fondly come to think of as *his* Von Emmerling emeralds. They were even prettier than the originals, if he were any judge, and he was. To be sure, the stones were fakes, beautiful ones. But he'd executed the delicate filigree settings with an even lighter touch than the original master who'd designed them. And now they were being shoved into the pocket of someone who'd done nothing more than glance at them through the filmy plastic.

The old man took the creased envelope stuffed full of old bills and shoved it in his pocket with all the care it deserved. Money was nothing, compared to art. "This is the only time," he said heavily, hating the sound of the words, knowing he had to say them. "No more. Tell the man who sent you."

"Why?"

"I'm getting too old for this sort of thing. You'll have to find someone else for your next job."

"No one else is as good as you."

"That's true," the old man agreed sadly. "But that's the way of the world. There are no craftsmen left, only technicians."

"You won't reconsider?"

He shook his head. "You have in your pocket, my friend, my last hurrah. Treat them with respect."

His customer grinned. "I'll put them to very good use."

HE COULDN'T HAVE known, Ferris thought as she undid the three locks and let herself into the maze of rooms that constituted her apartment in the marina section of San Francisco. There were six of them, with steps up and steps down, a small terrace with an impossibly windy view of the bay, the tiniest kitchen this side of a Winnebago and a bedroom so small it only held her queen-size bed and the television set. The largest room in the mélange was the bathroom, with a marble bathtub the size of a small swimming pool, a double marble sink, mirrors that would put a whorehouse to shame, and a towel rack directly over the radiator that gave Ferris deliciously heated towels in the morning. She loved the hodgepodge of space, but nothing pleased her that evening.

It must have been a shot in the dark. He knew she went by the name of Ferris, but she'd openly admitted her first name was Frances. And that was the truth, or mostly the truth. Her first name was a variant of Frances. And it was none of Blackheart's damned business if she chose not to use it. She didn't have any criminal reason for wanting to hide it.

There was no sign of her disreputable gray alley cat. Blackie must be out on one of his sabbaticals, wreaking havoc in female feline hearts. He might not be back for days. She kicked off her shoes, her bare feet padding comfortably over the hardwood floors as she trailed through the living room, dining room, kitchen and bathroom, finally ending up in the cramped confines of the bedroom. She took a delicious dive, ending up in the middle of her unmade bed, a trail of clothes leading toward her destination. She'd pick them up later. For now all she wanted was a moment of peace.

It was hours later when she opened her eyes. Blearily she peered at the digital clock residing on the floor beside her bed. Almost twelve-thirty. Damn! She'd never get back to sleep, not for hours. It was always a mistake when she let herself nap before dinner.

With a groan she pulled herself from the bed, scampering across its wide length to the bathroom. A long, hot shower would help, so would the glass of brandy she'd forgotten all about. It was too late for dinner. She'd curl up in front of the television and watch an all-night movie with her favorite vice.

Her flannel nightgown had seen better days, but the cotton was so thin that its comfort was practically transcendental. She poured more brandy into the Waterford snifter than was proper for savoring its bouquet, but once she got settled she didn't want to have to scramble back to the kitchen again. With a desultory attempt at housecleaning, she picked up the trail of clothing and dumped it in the hamper, then allowed herself the delight of opening her freezer. Oh, blessings, there was Heavenly Hash.

She must have made a ridiculous picture, tromping across her bed to the mound of pillows at the head, an overfull snifter of brandy in one hand, a small mixing bowl of ice cream in the other, mismatched socks on her narrow, chilly feet. With a sigh of pure pleasure, she collapsed against the pillows, spilling a tiny bit of the brandy on her nightgown.

Setting her goodies carefully on the floor, she dived under the bed in search of the remote control for the TV set. She had misplaced it for two weeks once, lost in the welter of clothes and papers and magazines and single shoes that lived and multiplied under her

She loved her remote control. She could only be thankful she didn't live with some man who would commandeer it, a man who had the right to complain about her life-style, which could only charitably be called casual. Her sisters had told her she was a walking disaster, but she liked it that way. At least if the earthquake that everyone had been promising came, no one would know the difference in her apartment.

Aiming the remote control, she settled back, reaching for her ice cream. If hot milk was supposed to help you sleep, cold cream should do almost the same thing, she thought righteously, digging in. Peter Sellers was on, the movie was just starting, and she settled back with pleasure to enjoy the travails of Inspector Clouseau. A moment later she sat back up, a low wail of anguish emitting through the Heavenly Hash.

"Oh, no!" she moaned, as a black-clad figure edged his way over the rooftops. She didn't need a movie about a cat burglar, tonight of all nights.

Quickly she flicked through the channels. Talk shows, John Wayne war movies, Betty Grable musicals. Peter Sellers was unquestionably the cream of the crop. With a sigh, she turned it back to the *Pink Panther*, reaching for her ice cream again. Some of the chocolate had melted and spilled onto the sheet, and she made an ineffectual attempt at rubbing it away. She'd have to remember to sleep on the right side tonight.

Finishing the ice cream, she pushed the bowl under her bed and reached for the brandy, settling back to concentrate on the movie. Maybe she'd learn something about how to deal with Blackheart. Taking a contemplative sip, she let the liquor burn through the ice cream coating on her tongue, swirling it around with absentminded pleasure. And maybe Phillip would change his mind and rescue her before Blackheart stumbled any closer to the truth. Somehow she doubted either of those things would come to pass.

"*A votre sante,*" she toasted the good inspector, raising her brandy glass high. "And heaven help me."

Chapter Four

THE ALARM RANG obscenely early. Ferris opened one eye, groaning as the sunlight beamed into her curtainless bedroom from the terrace. She fumbled around on the floor for her alarm clock, pulling back in disgust when her hand encountered the empty ice-cream dish. She had no choice—she opened the other eye and levered herself off the side of the wide bed to search for the recalcitrant alarm clock.

It was under an issue of *Time* Magazine at least six weeks old. How the magazine could have migrated over to cover the clock after she'd set it last night was beyond her imaginings, but she shrugged her shoulders, pulling herself upright with a weary sigh. She had long ago learned not to worry about what was where in her apartment.

There was one major blessing to this day. Nothing was going to be happening at Carleton House. It was Saturday, the ball wasn't until the following Friday and the jewels weren't due to arrive until Monday. The flowers had been argued over and ordered, the decorations planned, the security hired and left, thank God, to their own devices. The only duty she had to perform today, other than the onerous weekly task of mucking out the accumulated mess that was her apartment, was to run over to Carleton House and retrieve her briefcase.

Not that she'd forgotten it in the first place. She'd left it behind on purpose, part of her distrust of Blackheart extending to her personal papers. She loved Carleton House when it was still and silent, its cavernous rooms spacious and secure in wealth and status. She would wander through those rooms this afternoon and pretend she was Grace Kelly, cool and patrician, born to the purple.

As usual, the mess took longer than she expected. It was her weekend to do the full job, even taking a broomstick under the queen-size bed to roust out the dead panty hose, week-old *Chronicles,* empty boxes of Yodels, a silk blouse she'd thought she'd lost, and three Nikes, all for the left foot. She was a strange housekeeper, she thought as she washed the dirty dishes that had an amazing capacity for reproducing like rabbits. Like a secret eater, it was a case of binge and purge. Every night her clothes would be strewn over the apartment, the kitchen would be littered with every pot and pan, even when she utilized dear Mr. Stouffer's concoctions, the papers and magazines grew in piles that threatened to topple over every available surface. And every morning she would wash the dirty dishes, straighten the piles, hang up all the clothes that hadn't somehow snuck under the bed, just as she transformed herself.

At night she wore fuchsia silk kimonos, impossibly soft flannel nightgowns, skimpy French underwear, designer jockey shorts, anything that took her fancy, and her thick brown hair that was almost black hung in a wavy cloud around her face. In the morning she shrugged into her Armani and her Ralph Lauren suits, fastened her hair back in a loose bun, and became Ferris Byrd, young urban professional. It was an amazing creation, considering what she started out with, she mused. It was a shame no one but her sisters could appreciate it. And some of them were more offended than appreciative.

With a sigh she withdrew her hands from the sudsy water, letting it drain out of the tiny sink that could hold a service for one. It was fortunate that her messiness wasn't downright dirtiness—if she ever got so lax as to let the dishes pile up for days, it would take her a month to wash them all.

Stripping off the chocolate-stained sheets, she tossed them in her overflowing hamper. Making the bed was her one holdout against compulsive cleaning. When she was gone all day, the only appreciative audience for a neatly made bed was Blackie, the peripatetic alley cat, and much as she loved the stubborn feline, that was going too far. The bed was made when clean sheets were put on it, and that was that.

And where was Blackie this morning? He'd been around just yesterday, demanding kitty gourmet goodies as she'd tried to dress for her fateful appointment at Blackheart, Inc. She should be used to his travels, occasioned by feline randiness or a case of the sulks. Blackie had very strict standards when it came to food and attention, and Ferris had fallen woefully short yesterday. It would take nothing less than creamed herring or his particular craving, overripe Brie cheese, to get him to forgive her.

With a sigh, she emptied a tin of Seafood Supper and set it by the open door to the terrace before getting dressed. Sooner or later he'd have to return, even if it meant settling for cat food. Blackie, like all good San Franciscans, was a true gourmet.

On the weekends, when Phillip was off on the early campaign trail and Ferris had no one to answer to, her wardrobe was more her own. Always keeping in mind that she might run into someone who mattered, she allowed herself jeans and sweaters, braided the thick hair in a loose plait that fell just below her shoulders, and returned to her Nikes, granted she could find a matching pair. She dressed that way now, in faded Levi's rather than the Diesel jeans Phillip admired, leaving off the discreet gold jewelry that was her mark of caste. The apartment was clean, Phillip was out of town, and she was free, blissfully free.

She stifled the quick wave of guilt that washed over her. Neither she nor Phillip would want smothering togetherness. Any woman with a mind of her own would need time to herself. She wasn't about to contemplate the unpleasant fact that she seemed to appreciate that private time more than she did the hours she spent with Phillip.

A reluctant grin lit her face as she sped her car along the drive toward Carleton Point. Blackheart had been so determined not to be fazed by her driving. She'd made strong men weep before, and no pleas or threats from Phillip had made her improve her headlong, headstrong pace. Her driving style was the one thing that still belonged to the twenty-nine-year-old woman who hadn't been born Ferris Byrd, and she held onto it stubbornly.

The fog had lifted somewhat by the time she pulled up in the empty circular drive in front of Carleton House, but it was still a gray, chilly day, typical for late February in the Bay Area. She'd left her briefcase in the downstairs cloakroom, but she was in no hurry. Nothing much would be growing this time of year, but she was especially fond of the grounds anyway. The formal Japanese garden overlooked the Pacific, and she headed straight toward it, glad that she'd pulled a thick wool sweater on over the lighter cotton one. She shoved her hands in the pockets of her jeans, tucked her head into the stiff breeze and strode past the tall windows that overlooked the flagstoned terrace.

She never tired of looking at the ocean, even from a high perch like this one. The ever-changing variety of the ebb and swell of the blue-green waves fascinated her, the never-changing vastness of it soothed her soul. A wide, four-foot-high stone wall separated the wide expanse of lawn from the rocky cliff beyond, and she leaned against the cool, damp stone, staring out dreamily into the windy day. There was a sleek yacht out there, slicing through the rough water with silken ease. For a long moment Ferris had the surprising wish that she were on it, sailing away from everything that surrounded her and weighed her down. And then she pushed away from the wall and headed back across the lawn to the French doors.

The ring of keys weighed close to five pounds, and it could unlock every single one of the thirty-seven outer doors of Carleton House. It took her twelve minutes to find the right one for the French door off the ballroom, another two minutes to rattle the rusty catch loose. And then she was inside, in her magic kingdom, with the wind and the constant hush of the ocean shut out behind her. With a sigh of pure satisfaction she surveyed the empty ballroom.

Ferris had fought the idea of using Carleton House for the Puffin Ball, fought it with all the considerable logic and wit at her disposal. Olivia Summers had been on the opposing side, determined that the Puffin Ball would take place nowhere but Carleton House. Ferris had been more than irritated when Olivia had prevailed, but that irritation had changed to delight when she first wandered through the old mansion. Her only wonder was that a cold-blooded bitch like Olivia Summers could appreciate it,

As a matter of fact, apart from the uncomfortable presence of Blackheart, Inc., Olivia Summers was the only cloud on her horizon. And she could thank Olivia for Blackheart, too. It was Olivia who'd first mentioned Blackheart's name, eagerly seconded by Regina Merriam and voted by the Committee for Saving the Bay with an almost lustful enthusiasm. She supposed she couldn't really blame Olivia; Blackheart was the obvious choice. He was society's darling, his checkered past only adding to his desirability. She should have known any argument would have been quashed completely.

It still didn't help her feelings toward Olivia. Granted, Olivia had once been engaged to Phillip herself, before breaking it off to marry Dale Summers, and Olivia had her own political aspirations, coveting Phillip's senate seat with her blue, blue eyes. She never for one moment forgot that she was the granddaughter of Ezra McKinley, one of the founding fathers of the city, who was in turn the descendent of Abraham de Peyster, one of the founders of New York centuries earlier. Despite the fact that her family's money had long ago run out, her indisputable blue blood, her racehorse-elegant body, her patrician bearing and WASP blond hair kept her firmly in the forefront of any social gathering. She also had brains, charm, ambition and a seeming regret that she had dismissed Phillip three years ago. Ferris hated her.

Olivia had always been unfailingly polite, and the blue-haired ladies doted on her, her peers vied for her attention and even Phillip seemed bemused in her presence. It seemed as if only Ferris could see the calculating look in those perfect blue eyes, could watch her clever manipulations with awe and dislike. Olivia Summers had the indisputable talent for making Ferris feel like an employee and the interloper she knew she was. It was all done with admirable subtlety—a tone of voice, a condescending smile, a graceful gesture. If and when Olivia did run for office, Ferris was determined to work for the opposition, even if it was some Tea Party fascist.

There was no hurry to get the briefcase. She'd tucked it down beside the radiator; it had doubtless survived the night and would survive a few more minutes. With her own careless grace, she sank down cross-legged in the middle of the empty ballroom floor. They were talking about white roses, Regina said. They'd do the gilt and rose-colored ballroom proud. With baby's breath, and just a hint of pink somewhere . . .

"Fancy seeing you here," Blackheart drawled from directly behind her, and Ferris screamed.

When she could breathe again she jumped to her full five feet four, never as tall as she would have liked, and her eyes were blazing. "Don't you ever," she said furiously, "do that again. Clear your throat, stamp your feet, fart, belch, I don't care what. But don't sneak up on me."

Blackheart looked completely unmoved by her rage, and for a moment she could see why the combined force of the Committee for Saving the Bay had fallen beneath his spell. The black denims had been replaced by blue Levi's so faded they were almost gray, and the khaki field shirt rolled up to reveal strong forearms made his brown eyes almost amber. Ferris had always had a deplorable weakness for field shirts, with their epaulets and their myriad pockets, and she had to steel herself not to react. He was wearing running shoes, which would account for his silent approach. Except that he'd been just as silent in leather boots.

"What were you doing, sitting there in the middle of the ballroom with that erotic expression on your face? I wouldn't have thought a chilly room like this would arouse your fantasies."

"They weren't erotic fantasies," she protested.

"I was watching you wandering around the gardens. You're much more of a dreamer than I took you for, Ms. Byrd," he continued in that low, warm voice of his. "You seemed so coldly practical yesterday. Today you look much more—" his hand reached out and gently tugged her braid "—much more human."

She batted at his hand, but he'd already removed it. She didn't like the phrase, *coldly practical*, but she was damned if she was going to call him on it. He just wanted a rise out of her, and she wasn't about to give him that satisfaction. And then the meaning of his presence there in the deserted mansion struck her, and she cheerfully jumped to the attack.

"What are you doing here, anyway?" she demanded fiercely.

"My job."

"How did you get in? The Carleton House security team was supposed to let me know if they gave out any keys."

He smiled that devilish smile, and her heart gave a little moan at its remembered effect. "I didn't need a key."

Her lip curled. "Of course you didn't. How could I have forgotten?"

The mockery bounced right off. "I asked about you," he said conversationally, and immediately she was wary.

"I doubt you found out anything very interesting." She managed an admirably cool tone of voice. "I haven't led a very exciting life. Who did you ask?"

"Phillip, for starters."

She didn't like that phrase, "for starters."

"He told me all about your glorious career at Stanford," Blackheart continued, "your rapid rise to your position as his personal assistant, your wit and charm. I had to take his word on the latter, of course."

"Of course."

"And he told me the touching story of your life. How you were raised by your patrician aunt on Beacon Hill in Boston after your parents were killed in their private plane. How you excelled at the exclusive little boarding school but were always just a poor little rich girl who had to throw all her energies into her studies, missing the comfort a real family could offer. It was very touching."

She held herself very still, hating him. "I'm sure you're not about to offer your sympathy."

His mouth quirked upward. It was an attractive mouth, she had to give him that, even as she longed to punch him in it. "And I'm sure you wouldn't accept it if I was."

"Very astute. What do you want from me, Blackheart?"

"You know, I rather like the way you say that," he mused. "Most people call me Patrick."

"Blackheart suits you."

"What's in a name?" he quoted softly, that devilish light in his eyes. "Ferris Byrd doesn't suit you one tiny bit."

"I like it," she said stubbornly, refusing to give an inch.

"Of course you do. I'm finished for the day, Ferris Byrd. Let me take you out to dinner and I'll pry all your secrets from you."

"Go to hell." She had turned to leave, consigning her briefcase to another night in the cloakroom, when his hand caught her arm. She had noticed the perfect beauty of his hands before; the gentle force on her arm burned the impression of it into her flesh. If she yanked, he would have released her. She stood still.

"Come away with me, Francesca," he said, and his low, sweet voice was a silky caress along her nerve endings as he used her real name. "Your secrets are safe with me. I'll even tell you a few of my own."

"Blackheart," she said, and she never thought she'd plead with any man, particularly this one. But she was pleading with him. "Let me go."

Without a word, he dropped her arm. Without a word she turned and left him, her Nikes squeaking on the polished dance floor. She closed the French door quietly behind her, turned into the windy afternoon, and ran like hell, leaving Blackheart to stare after her, thinking God knew what.

NOW THERE WAS nothing left to do but wait till the Von Emmerling emeralds were delivered, thought the thief, wait that interminable length of time until the night of the Puffin Ball. It was a shame the old man had finished with the copies so soon. There was nothing left to do, nothing left to plan. Everything was ready, all that was needed was for the time to pass. And it was passing damnably slow.

The old man was right, the fakes were beautiful. They'd look stunning against a silky white neck. Their glow was almost luminous—there was no way the originals could be any more glorious. It was a shame the Werdegast emeralds would have to be sacrificed for state's evidence. An ignominious fate for such craftsmanship, but now wasn't the time to be sentimental. Too much was at stake, it had taken too long to get to this point, with this perfect opportunity. Rank emotion couldn't be allowed to enter in at this late date.

The plastic bag with the emeralds was resting prosaically between the mattress and the box spring. So far it hadn't interfered with a good night's sleep. After all, "The Princess and the Pea" was nothing more than a fairy tale.

Ferris Byrd was a nosy complication, but she could be dealt with. That net of circumstance could drag her down, too. The thought was amusing, infinitely satisfying. The poor girl would never know what hit her.

Maybe it would be a good idea to check on the Werdegast emeralds. It had been hard to resist the temptation to sit and gloat over them. Maybe just for a moment, before anyone came in. It wouldn't do any harm—in another week they'd be gone, and the real ones would be in their place. Such a soothing, pleasant thought. And one more peek wouldn't hurt.

Chapter Five

IT HAD BEEN *Raffles* last night. Ferris had told herself she wasn't going to watch. The last thing she'd needed was to be presented with the spectacle of David Niven cavorting as a debonair cat burglar in London of the 1930s. What she did need was to lose herself in a long, fascinating book, forget that Blackheart ever lived, forget that name that he'd uttered so charmingly. Francesca, he'd said, and she could no longer hide from the fact that he knew far too much about her.

But *Raffles* had been irresistible, and she had given up the pretense of ignoring it after the second dish of French vanilla. There was still no sign of Blackie, and the apartment had seemed curiously empty. She drifted off just as the virtues of exfoliations were being extolled by an Australian pitchman, her lush body stretched across the queen-size bed wearing purple satin boxer shorts and a matching sleeveless T-shirt, her clothes in a tangle at the foot of the bed, the sink full of dishes. And when she woke the next morning, the first thing she saw was Patrick Blackheart, leaning against the doorjamb, surveying her sleeping form amidst the clutter with great interest.

Ferris usually awoke slowly, in stages, each successive cup of coffee bringing her into the real world. One look at Blackheart, however, and the adrenaline shot through her veins and she was suddenly completely awake. She sat bolt upright, ignoring the fact that she was wearing nothing at all under the thin satin undershirt and her full breasts were heaving with outrage and indignation. Blackheart's gaze dropped to their level, however, reminding her, and she quickly pulled the sheet around her.

"I hate to be redundant," she said in a voice strangled with rage, "but what the hell are you doing here?"

"Demonstrating my expertise. I thought I should convince you just how good I am at my job. I can get in or out of the most burglarproof apartment. If it passes my inspection, no one can get in."

"Apparently my apartment didn't pass your inspection. How did you get in?"

He gave her that cool, almost angelic smile. "You aren't hiring me, Francesca. Phillip is. Check with Kate for my rate for apartments." He moved out of the door, heading back down the three steps to the kitchen. "Want any coffee?" he called out over his shoulder.

She was after him in a flash, the huge sheet wrapped toga-style around her body. "I want you out of my apartment," she warned him, trailing him into the kitchen. "Now."

It had been a mistake. She had forgotten how very small her kitchen was, not much larger than a closet. There was barely room for the two of them to stand, much less without touching. Blackheart seemed amused by her predicament, but she stood her ground. She wasn't about to let Blackheart drive her out of her own kitchen.

"Do you take it black?" He reached overhead for one of her mismatched mugs, filling it from the pot before she could protest. She'd forgotten she had that pot—she usually made do with Starbucks. And damn him, he'd washed her dishes! They sat in the drainer, clean and shining. Ferris gnashed her teeth.

"No," Blackheart mused, "you'd take too much sugar and too much cream. Except that your cream is sour, and you're out of nondairy creamer. You'll have to drink it this way."

He held out the mug, and she had a hard time controlling the strong desire to splash the steaming liquid all over him. He was wearing jeans and a faded flannel shirt, and it would have hurt very much. With real regret she accepted the coffee.

"Thank you," he said in that gentle voice. "I wouldn't have liked having a bath in hot coffee."

"It's nothing less than you deserve," she grumbled, taking a sip for lack of something better to do. Even without the gobs of cream she usually added, it was surprisingly good. "I still want you out of here."

He reached out a hand and touched a strand of her thick cloud of hair. "I like it better loose."

There was no room to whirl away from him—she would have come slap up against the refrigerator. One hand was holding the cup of coffee, the other clutched the sheet around her, and she had to content herself with a warning glare. Her regret when he dropped the hair and levered himself up on her kitchen counter, away from her, was inexplicable.

"So tell me, Francesca Berdahofski, what are you doing today?" he inquired casually. "I need some help, and I thought you'd be the perfect candidate to assist me."

"You bastard. If you think you can blackmail me into helping you steal the emeralds you must be out of your mind," she spat at him.

The force of her noble outrage was weakened in the face of his astounded amusement. "You really do have a vicious opinion of me, don't you? How am I going to convince you I've given up my sordid past? I assure you, I no longer have what it takes to be a cat burglar, more's the pity. I have to get my jollies where I can, stopping other people from doing what I used to do so well."

She suddenly felt like a complete idiot, standing there clutching the sheet around her like an outraged virgin. Except, of course, that she was. What else did he know about her, besides her name? "What do you need help with?" she said, stalling.

"My first step is to make sure that no one from the outside can get in to steal the emeralds. If I can narrow it down to the four hundred and some ticket holders, it will be a minor improvement. There are alarms on every window on the second, third and fourth floors, except for the Palladian window in the back of the second floor hallway. I presumed no one bothered because only one narrow section opens, and the entire thing is in full view of the downstairs hallway."

"And?"

"And, I'm not convinced that someone might not be able to manage it. I don't think the view is unrestricted at all, I think there's a blind spot. I want to see whether I can get in without you seeing me."

"Why don't you just have another alarm put on that window, too? Why go to all that effort?"

Blackheart shook his head. "That's my reward for working a nine-to-five job. I get to try a little B and E in the name of business."

"B and E?" She took another sip of the wonderful coffee, and the hold on her sheet relaxed somewhat.

"Breaking and entering, it's called by the men in blue. A very unimaginative term for what can be a form of art. Of course, most B and E is crude and unimaginative. Junkies in search of stereo equipment and the like."

"You're really proud of yourself, aren't you?" she demanded, outraged. "You see yourself as some sort of hero, better than some poor junkie."

He shrugged. "I had standards."

"Standards!" she scoffed.

"I never robbed anyone who wasn't obscenely wealthy. I never kept anything that was uninsured, and I never kept anything that was overinsured. I only stole gems, beautiful, shimmering jewels." His voice had taken on an unbearably sensuous thread. "I never touched money or any of the other glittering toys rich people tend to have lying around. Just jewelry."

"Very noble," Ferris mocked, leaning against the refrigerator.

"So you'll come with me, Francesca?"

"Stop calling me that! My name is Ferris."

"Your name is Francesca. You never changed it legally," he retorted calmly.

"I don't like the name."

"Tough. It suits you, with that cloud of midnight hair and your magnificent breasts heaving in rage. What in the world are you wearing under that sheet? Those scraps of purple satin certainly look enticing, but not at all the sort of thing one would expect from the future Mrs. Senator Phillip Merriam."

"Damn you, you *are* trying to blackmail me."

"No," he said, the smile leaving his face. "I'm not."

"Then why did you check up on me?" she demanded.

"I could tell you I had Kate run a routine check on all the major people connected with the Puffin Ball and the Von Emmerling emeralds, and that would be true. When you're dealing with something worth that much money, you check out all the angles. But I didn't tell her to rush the others."

"And you told her to rush mine. Why?"

In that tiny, confined space, with him perched on the narrow length of kitchen counter and she as far away as she could be, leaning up against the mini-refrigerator, they were still within touching distance. A dreamy look came into his warm brown eyes, and a smile curved that mouth that looked suddenly quite irresistible. He was going to reach out and touch her again, he was going to pull her body against his and kiss her senseless, and she was going to let him. The sheet was going to fall at her feet, and she'd be standing there in the circle of his arms wearing the ridiculous purple satin boxer shorts and she wouldn't care at all. The thought made her slightly dizzy.

"Because," he said finally, and his voice was a seduction, "I thought you were my prime suspect."

She stared at him in absolute amazement, and then he did reach out one of his strong, beautiful hands, placing a long finger under her chin and closing her mouth. "You'll catch flies, Francesca," he murmured, that devilish light in his eyes.

"I—I—" Her outrage was so great that words failed her, a fact that seemed to please her uninvited visitor.

"Since you're feeling so modest in that sheet, why don't you go get dressed? I brought some croissants, too. Once you feel you're safely attired, we can discuss what we're going to do at Carleton House."

"You're going to get Trace to help you," she snapped.

"Trace is otherwise occupied; so is Kate. Sorry, lady, you're drafted. You wouldn't want Phillip to hear you've been uncooperative, would you?"

"There's a lot you could tell Phillip," she said gracelessly.

"But I wouldn't," he said, and she trusted him. That far, at least. "Go get dressed. And don't wear one of those damned suits. We may need to scramble a bit."

She took as long as she possibly could, even making her bed - an unheard of occurrence. She was sorely tempted to wear a suit anyway, but gave up the idea. Blackheart was outrageous enough to take it off her if he so chose. She settled for jeans and a silk and wool sweater that barely hinted at the ripe curves underneath. Scraping her thick hair back from her face, she pinned it into a ruthlessly tight bun and shoved Phillip's tastefully large diamond on her left hand before rejoining Blackheart in the kitchen.

He was munching a croissant, managing it with far more neatness than she ever could, but at the sight of her a frown creased his brow beneath the long dark hair, and he put the pastry down, advancing on her with a determined air. It took all her willpower, but she stood her ground.

"Very nice," he murmured, his long arms reaching behind her head, "except for this . . ." With speedy dispatch he removed the hair pins, and the hair tumbled to her shoulders. ". . . and this." Tossing the hairpins on the counter, he caught her left hand and took the ring from her finger before she was even aware that he'd touched her. She stared at him with reluctant amazement. The ring was still slightly tight that time of month, and yet he'd removed it as easily as if it had been two sizes too large.

He gave the ring a dismissing glance before dropping it on the counter with as much care as the steel hairpins, and Ferris felt compelled to defend it. "That's a very nice ring," she protested. "You needn't sneer at it."

"Completely unimaginative," he said. "But then, Phillip Merriam has never had the reputation for creativity. You should wear emeralds to match your glorious eyes. Or rubies."

"Diamonds suit me just fine," she said repressively, part of her getting caught up in the fantasy against her will.

"Then a huge yellow diamond, the size of a robin's egg," he mused. "But not a damned bland white diamond any banker's wife would wear."

"Did you want me to come with you or not? Because you're treading on very thin ice, Blackheart."

"Because I think you should be showered with precious jewels? I'd better watch my step."

"You'd better." She turned away, but not before a reluctant smile lit her face, and he caught her shoulder and turned her back, very gently.

"You can smile," he said softly. "I find that very reassuring."

"Then I'm no longer on the top of your list of suspects?" she said lightly.

The hand tightened for a moment on her shoulder, and she felt him lean toward her. And then the moment passed, and she breathed a small, uncertain sigh. "I'll trust you, Francesca," he said, "when you trust me."

"And that will be a cold day in hell. Let's go if we're going."

"I don't know, Francesca," Blackheart mused. "There are times when I think you're cold enough to freeze hell, and then some. Don't glare at me—I'm coming."

Chapter Six

DAMN, BUT HE was getting himself in trouble, Blackheart thought. Deeper and deeper, eyes wide open as he walked directly into the mire. At thirty-six he should have known better. It must be his restless streak acting up again. If he couldn't risk life and limb scrambling over buildings, he could risk the far too secure tenor of his life by messing with the bundle of contradictions by his side.

When it came right down to it, he disapproved of Miss Ferris-Francesca-Byrd-Berdahofski as much as she disapproved of him. He disapproved of her uptightness, of that proper image she'd created and wrapped around that surprisingly luscious body like an invisible cloak, of the snobbery that made her hide her roots, and most of all he disapproved of the fact that he wanted her so much it was a constant ache whenever he was around her. Of course, there was an obvious answer to the problem—stop being around her. But he couldn't resist—the danger pulled him like a magnet, and that cool, to-hell-with-you expression on her face was a challenge he couldn't resist.

"This isn't the way to Carleton House." He also liked that husky note in her voice, and the snotty way she called him "Blackheart," as if she thought the name suited him.

"No, it's not," he agreed, glancing at her averted profile as he continued heading toward the bay. She'd taken one glance at the disreputable-looking Volvo station wagon that had seen many better years, and the disbelief in those green eyes of hers had been worth it. She sat now in the front seat, seat belt firmly fastened, hands clasped loosely in her lap, trying to convince him she was at ease. Her knuckles were white.

"Are you kidnapping me?" she asked lightly.

"Would you like me to?" he countered. She appeared to consider it, then shook her head, the cloud of black hair swirling around her fine-boned face.

"We're stopping by my favorite deli to pick up something for a picnic." He took pity on her.

"It's too cold for a picnic. And I didn't say I'd eat with you, I said I'd help you with . . . I don't know that I actually agreed to a damned thing," she said crossly.

Damn, but he liked her. He liked the way she struggled to keep angry with him, he liked the ramshackle apartment with its piles of books and magazines over every available surface and the clothes tumbled on the floor, still smelling of Cabochard. It was a fitting perfume for her—it meant "pigheaded." And that was one thing that could be said about her; she was definitely a very pigheaded young lady.

Kate had warned him. She knew him and Trace like the back of her hand, had recognized that speculative look in his eyes and taken him to task for it. It was her thankless duty to try to keep Blackheart, Inc., running reasonably smoothly. Given Trace's susceptibility to the pretty debutantes and beautiful matrons that abounded in most of their jobs, given Blackheart's determination not to adhere to timetables or rules, she had her work cut out for her.

The last six months had added a new fillip to her problems. Kate had, apparently, always been uninterested in romantic entanglements, preferring to keep to herself. Until last year, when she'd suddenly become extremely secretive. Blackheart had suspected a married man, but he'd done nothing to verify it, respecting Kate's privacy. Whatever it was, it seemed to cause her more grief than sorrow. First there was a two-week period of swollen eyes, sniffling, and heart-felt sighs, and then Kate had pulled herself together, back into her usual pugnacious competence. And it had taken Blackheart months to notice that her usual bullying maternal attitude toward her co-workers had undergone a change. In Trace's direction.

Blackheart had been too respectful of Kate's privacy to inquire into it. He knew Trace had taken her out drinking a couple of times when she was recovering from her recent troubles. But he also knew that Trace thought of her as a buddy, one of the guys, having been lectured early on that she wasn't interested in him that way. But it looked to Blackheart as if she'd changed her mind, and Trace hadn't the faintest idea.

He pulled himself back to the present with no difficulty at all. There was nothing he could do about Kate's tangled love life, and he didn't think he would interfere, even if he could. Years of being a loner were hard to break. In the meantime, he had his own tangled love life to work on right now. And that was just what he wanted it to be. Tangled—in her sheets, in her limbs, in the cloud of hair.

"Speaking of erotic daydreams," she snapped, "stop looking at me as if I were a piece of strawberry cheesecake."

"Cannoli."

"I beg your pardon?"

"I see you more as a cannoli. Rich and Italian and full of sweetened ricotta cheese," he mused.

"You may as well go all the way and call me a blintz. I'm half Polish as well as Italian," she said sharply. "So I look like something stuffed, do I?"

"You look," he said quietly, "absolutely delicious."

"Get that rapturous expression off your face, Blackheart. We're going to break into Carleton House, I suppose we'll eat something, and then you'll take me back home. And that's it."

"Yes, ma'am," he said with mock humility.

She turned those magnificent green eyes on him. "Why do you always try to goad me, Blackheart?" she questioned in a deliberately calmer voice. He could guess how much that effort cost her, and he applauded it silently.

"Because I like to make you mad."

"Why, for heaven's sake?"

"It shakes you up and keeps you from looking down that very pretty nose at me. It also makes you forget that you're trying to be Regina Merriam or Olivia Summers."

"Not Olivia," she said sharply. "And I don't look down my nose at you."

"Sure you do. I'm still not quite sure why. Just a law-and-order complex, or is it something deeper? Were you molested by a cat burglar when you were a child?"

She turned to look at him then. "You're the one who's so knowledgeable about my past. Didn't they tell you about that?"

"A molesting cat burglar? No, that somehow slipped past my informants."

"What did they tell you?"

"That you come from a very large, very poor family from a small farming community outside of Chicago. Your father was Polish, your mother Italian, and you're one of eight children. There was never much money, but it sounds as if there was plenty of love."

"Maybe too much love," Ferris said slowly. "And I'm one of nine children. I had a younger sister who died when she was twelve. Of kidney failure."

Black heart was silent for a moment, digesting this. "Do you think if you'd had money she wouldn't have died?"

He was astute, she had to grant him that. "I don't know," she said. "I think if we'd had money I wouldn't have to wonder about it."

"Do you blame your parents?"

"Of course not. I loved them. They worked themselves to death before they were seventy, Mama from having too many children too fast and Pop from a form of emphysema called farmer's lung. Maybe money would have helped them, too, maybe not. It wouldn't have hurt." She looked at him then, with a sudden, savage pain in her green eyes, turning them from a distant sea color to a deep forest hue. "Do you know how many nieces and nephews I have? Twenty-two. Twenty-two from seven brothers and sisters. And one of them's a priest. And every single one of them either had a baby on the way when they got married or had one within a year after the wedding. My older brother Paul made it through one year of community college before he had to quit and get a job in a factory to support his three children. And he was only twenty-one years old."

"And you decided that wasn't going to happen to you?"

"You're damned right. I wasn't going to be trapped in that cycle of babies and poverty like everyone else. I finished high school a year early, got a scholarship to Stanford, and haven't looked back."

"Do you ever see your family?" he asked lazily.

"Of course I do. You think I'm ashamed of them? I'm not, not at all. But when I see how they're weighed down by poverty and too many children and no ambition, it makes me even more determined not to let myself get weighed down the same way."

"So there won't be any children for you?"

"Of course there will be. But they'll be wanted, they'll come from choice and not by accident," she said with great certainty.

"That makes sense." His voice was cool, nonjudgmental. "That still doesn't quite explain why you disapprove of me so heartily."

She looked at him for a long moment, considering something, he wasn't sure what, and then she leaned back in the seat, eyes straight ahead of her. "When I was eleven years old," she said slowly, "I wanted to be a Spanish dancer. I couldn't take lessons—even if we'd had the money, there was no one in our small town who could teach it. So I'd watch every movie I could, and practice out in the barn, humming to myself. I even made myself a costume out of one of my older sister's party dresses. All I needed was the shoes. I didn't even know what kind of shoes I should wear, but I knew they were important." There was a dreamy note in her voice, bringing back a nostalgic, painful past, and Blackheart listened intently.

"One spring afternoon I'd walked into town, and there in the local five-and-dime was a pair of red shoes. They were made from a sparkly, shiny kind of stuff, they were two sizes too big, and it was the only pair they had. And I wanted those shoes. I wanted them so badly that it made me ache inside, I wanted them so badly that I stood there in the store and cried. Every day after school I'd go in and look at them, every day I'd try to figure out how I could find the money to buy them. And then one day I went in and no one was there. The grain store had caught on fire, and everyone was out watching it burn. I was alone in the store with my book bag and no one to watch me, and the shoes were sitting right there, waiting for me," She closed her eyes, the lashes fanning out over her lightly tanned cheeks.

"I didn't take them. I stood there, rooted to the floor, staring at them, and all the while the fire engine was racing down the street outside and people were rushing toward the grain store, and I didn't even touch them, much as I wanted to. I just stared at them, and then I turned around and ran out of the store, ran all the way home."

He didn't say anything. He didn't know what to say. The sound of pain in her voice was fresh and new, from a wound that had never healed.

She opened her eyes again, turning her head against the seat to look at him. "No one, in the history of the world, has ever wanted anything as much as I wanted those red shoes. No one. And if I didn't take them, if I turned around and left without touching them when I wanted them that much, then there's no excuse for what you did. None at all."

"Did you ever regret not taking them?" he questioned curiously.

She sighed. "Every day of my life for the next five years. Until my baby sister died, and I had something more important to think about. Getting out."

"And you got out. Very effectively." She hadn't even noticed that he'd pulled over in front of the deli and was watching her, had been watching her for the last few minutes. "What does Merriam think about this?"

"I haven't told him. I've never told anyone about it."

"Apart from your family."

"Not anyone," she said distantly. "It didn't concern them. It concerned you." She closed her eyes again. "I'm going to take a nap. Go in and get the food. If I have a choice I like Beck's dark."

He wanted to lean over and kiss her on those soft lips, like Sleeping Beauty and the Prince. God, he must be going crazy! "Beck's dark," he agreed. "At least we have something in common." Sliding out of the car, he closed the door quietly behind him, careful not to jar her. If he had any sense, he'd turn around and take her straight back to her apartment. Francesca Berdahofski was going to interfere with his carefully made plans, and if he wasn't a complete idiot he'd stop the involvement that was entangling him before it was too late.

But he wasn't going to take her back to her apartment. He was going to get a six-pack of Beck's dark beer and a feast, he was going to wine and dine her on the floor of the empty ballroom at Carleton House, and then he was going to do his absolute level best to strip all those layers of clothes and defenses and armor away from her and make love to her on that hard, shiny floor, make love to her until she wept, till she cried away all the years of hurt that kept her heart locked away behind Ralph Lauren suits. And then he'd make love to her again, slowly, achingly, until. . . .

Damn, he must have that look on his face again. What did she call it? Rapturous? Maybe they'd have cannoli in the deli.

THEY WERE AN unlikely partnership, the three of them. Not what one would have expected, to pull off a caper of this magnitude. But their very unexpectedness would work to their advantage.

It was hard being a mastermind. Being responsible for your assistants' weaknesses, having to foresee every possible disaster when there were so many that could befall them. But it was a high, an ego boost unlike anything else. It was only unfortunate that no one would ever know the depth of the brilliance behind this particular little jewel robbery. It would be chalked up to Patrick Blackheart, others would be implicated as accessories, and the three of them would get off scot-free. And very, very much richer.

Quiet, self-satisfied laughter echoed through the room. *Yes, I am very clever,* the mastermind thought. *Very clever, indeed.*

Chapter Seven

THIS WAS A ridiculous thing to be doing on a chilly, rainswept Sunday afternoon, Ferris thought, leaning against the newel post on the long, curving staircase in the front hall of Carleton House. She should be home, watching old movies on TV, eating Double Rainbow ice cream and waiting for Phillip's phone call. Every Sunday afternoon he would call her, precisely at three o'clock, and every Sunday afternoon she would be there, waiting for him. But not today. She hadn't even thought of it until Blackheart had left her alone, and then it had been too late. She had contemplated the notion of having him take her back home and then she'd dismissed it, without trying to figure out why.

She hadn't even had a chance to look at a clock before he'd dragged her out of the apartment, but she figured it had to be sometime in the early afternoon. Not three yet, but there was no way she could get back in time to answer the phone, and no way she could get in touch with him—he could be anywhere from San Diego to Santa Cruz. So why wasn't she more worried?

Maybe it was the usual restful effect Carleton House had on her. She always preferred it when it was empty, no chattering magpies born to the purple cluttering up its clean architectural lines. And it might as well have been empty; after stationing her midway up the winding staircase, Blackheart had disappeared out the front door. He'd been unnaturally silent the rest of the trip out here, and Ferris had kept her eyes firmly shut, pretending to sleep. There was no way she could sleep with that lithe, slender, jean-clad leg inches from hers in the rattling old Volvo, no way she could relax so close to him. Why had she told him that embarrassingly story about her childhood? She'd never told a soul before, and a retired cat burglar was hardly the choice audience for such a confession. God, she was a fool.

Well, now she could relax. Blackheart was supposed to make his way through the windows with their elaborate alarm system, pilfer a scarf he'd placed in a second-floor bedroom, and end up back in the ballroom without her seeing him. There was no way he could do it—she'd watched the upstairs hallway like a hawk, determined to catch him, and there'd been no sign, no sound, no hint of his presence. Plus he had to get down to the ballroom without leaving the house—he couldn't just exit through the window.

Ridiculous, she thought dismissively. He was a little boy, playing at a game he couldn't possibly win, but she was content enough to humor him. Nothing would please her more than to catch him—

A quiet sound caught her attention, and she whirled around, ready to flash him a triumphant smile. He was standing in the doorway of the ballroom, the silk scarf in his hand, that damned smug grin on his face.

"How did you do it?" she demanded flatly.

"Never ask a magician to reveal his tricks."

"You must have cheated. You went back out the window and came in through the French doors. Though I can't even guess how you managed that."

"I didn't leave the house once I entered it," he said calmly.

She moved slowly down the steps. "This is supposed to reassure me as to your trustworthiness? You've now demonstrated just how easily you can burglarize a burglarproof house, you won't even tell me how, and yet you expect me to trust you."

"No, I don't expect you to trust me. That, it appears, would be asking too much." He held out his hand. "Come and have some lunch."

Ignoring his hand, she moved past him into the cavernous ballroom. He'd started a small fire in the huge fireplace at the far end, spread a blanket on the shiny wood floor, and set the goodies from the deli in place. "Where'd you get the blanket?" she questioned suspiciously.

"Same place I got the scarf—the upstairs bedroom."

"And you carried it back down here without me noticing?" She didn't know whether to be infuriated or awed. Perhaps she was a little bit of both.

"I'm very light on my feet."

"You and Dracula." She sank cross-legged onto the blanket, reaching with resignation for a beer. "If I didn't trust you I wouldn't be here, Blackheart."

Sitting down a decent foot or so away from her, he took the chilled bottle from her hand, opened it and handed it back, his tawny eyes sober. "Up to a point."

"Up to a point," she agreed, tilting back her head and swallowing a quarter of the beer. "Since you know all about my less than patrician history, I suppose I have to." Stretching her legs out, she leaned back on the blanket, a suddenly carefree smile playing about her lips. Phillip was out of touch, the echoing silence of the deserted ballroom seemed a magic place and the man opposite her a magician, a creature from some elfin world where people appeared and disappeared at will. And for a brief moment she was willing to be enchanted. The dark, rainswept afternoon let little light through the row of French doors, and the small, crackling fire sent a small pool of warmth into the shadow-filled room. "What are you going to feed me?" she questioned, that slightly husky note in her voice more pronounced.

"Knockwurst and blintzes. And Beck's dark."

Ferris laughed then, and once she started, she couldn't stop. Rolling onto her back, she let her delighted laugh ring out in the room, wrapping her arms around her waist to hold in the pain. Tears were in her eyes as the mirth bubbled forth. "That's . . . the most . . . ridiculous thing I've ever . . . heard," she gasped. "I thought you were on the make. Everyone's warned me about Blackheart, Inc., and its reputation for keeping bored ladies busy. With all that experience you should know that you can't seduce a woman with knockwurst and blintzes."

"You can if you pick the right woman," he said, levering his body forward. And then his mouth stopped her laughter as he covered her with his lean, lithe frame.

He couldn't have picked a better time. She was soft and vulnerable and relaxed from her laughter, with the warmth of the room around her, and his mouth on hers was right and natural, delicious with the taste of the dark beer. She started to put her arms around his neck, her mouth softened and began to open beneath the gentle pressure of his, and then sanity returned.

"No!" With a convulsive start she shoved him off her, rolling away to end up crouching warily, staring at him as if he were the devil himself.

He'd landed on his back, and he made no move to right himself, just lay there looking at her out of enigmatic eyes. "You needn't act like a Sabine about it, lady," he murmured gently. "It was only a kiss."

"I don't want you kissing me," she shot back, and he politely said nothing, the small, eloquent quirk of his mobile mouth signaling his disbelief.

"All right," he said finally, pulling himself upright and catching her abandoned beer before it toppled onto the blanket. "Come here and eat knockwurst and I won't even be tempted."

Ferris felt the tension drain from her body, felt the absurd disappointment flood it in return, like the ebb and flow of the Pacific. She hesitated for a moment, then, with a wary look in her eyes, rejoined him on the blanket, a good two feet away from him. "Is that why you bought it?" she questioned, accepting the beer from him again. "As a medieval form of birth control?"

"You don't get pregnant from a kiss, Francesca."

"Is that all it would have been?"

His eyes had darkened in the shadowy room—as they looked at her they were warm and gentle and subtly promising. "If that's all you wanted."

Ferris swallowed. He was so damned attractive, sitting there, and that infuriating smile of his was half the attraction. It was no wonder the female half of San Francisco society was at his feet. "And if I wanted more?" Why the hell was she asking such a question? Was she out of her mind?

Blackheart's smile broadened. "Why then, I'd be happy to oblige. Ever the little gentleman, you know."

Ferris gave a snort of disgust. "Hand me a knockwurst, Blackheart. I think I need all the protection I can get."

"We're going to need something to roast them with. I forgot to bring any sticks."

"I thought you were on top of everything." The moment the words were out of her mouth she could have cursed herself.

Bless his heart, he didn't even smirk, though the light in his eyes showed his appreciation. "I try to be. Things don't always work out that way."

"I know where the kitchen is. I imagine they have skewers of some sort." She rose swiftly. She could feel her cheeks were flushed, she could still feel the warmth of his mouth on hers, his bones pressing into her softer flesh. She needed to get away, and fast. "You build up the fire."

She got as far as the door to the hallway when he caught up with her. His hands were gentle but so very strong on her shoulders as he turned her back to face him. "Don't be afraid of me, Francesca," he said softly. "I'm not going to hurt you."

She met his gaze steadily, making no move to break free. "Then let go of me," she whispered.

"Oh, love," he murmured. "I can't do that." He pulled her against his taut body, slowly, giving her plenty of time to escape. She made no move to break free. His head dropped down, his mouth catching hers in a slow, searching kiss as his hands slid down her shoulders, down her back, molding her body to his. He kissed her with deliberate expertise, his tongue teasing her lips open, the rough texture exploring her mouth.

She didn't dare move, didn't dare react, or she would be lost. She stood passively in the circle of his arms as he kissed her, willing her mind to think of other things, willing her body not to respond. But then his head moved away a fraction, his eyes were blazing down into hers with a slumberous, intense passion that she could no longer resist.

"What's the matter, Francesca?" he whispered, a note of laughter in his voice. "Cat got your tongue? You're supposed to kiss me back." His mouth caught hers again, she was lost. Her arms slid around his waist, holding him close against her, and she couldn't tell if she was trembling or he was. Maybe they both were. Her tongue shyly met his, sliding along the rough-textured intruder with a shudder of delight. His narrow hips were pressed up against her rounder ones, and she could feel him hard against her. Those strong, beautiful hands of his were gentling her back, soothing her fears, just as his mouth was melting her brain. She couldn't think, couldn't fight, couldn't do anything more than react to the overwhelming sensual stimuli he was using. She could feel the last restraints begin to slip away, her conscious thought fading before the sensual onslaught of his mouth and hands and her sudden, overwhelming, unbearable wanting, and she wanted to sink to the hardwood floor and pull him with her, pull that strong, lean body of his over her and into her and around her and—

"My, my, we seem to have come at a bad time.' Olivia Summers's coolly amused tones broke through the haze of passion like a bucket of ice water, and Ferris tried to break away in sudden horror. But Blackheart held on to her, allowing her only a few inches distance as his strong hands caught her arms and held her there.

"What are you doing here, Olivia?" he questioned, and as sanity rapidly returned, Ferris could appreciate what he was doing. Guilt and panic were exactly what Olivia wanted, and she had almost made the mistake of giving them to her. She took a deep, calming breath, and Blackheart gave her arms a subtly reassuring squeeze before releasing her.

"Actually, I had a few measurements to make. I appear to have lost my notes, and Dale was a perfect lamb and offered to bring me over. It appears I interrupted a . . . conference?" she queried delicately, and it was all Ferris could do to control a snarl. "And such a charming spot for one," she added, her patrician nose raised in amused disdain. "Honestly, Patrick, you're up to your old tricks again. Do you and Trace always have to have a new conquest with each job? You really shouldn't pick on poor Ferris. She isn't as sophisticated as I was—she might think you mean it."

Ever the little gentleman, he'd called himself. He proved it then, Ferris thought, with that distant, polite smile. "Maybe this time I do."

"Oh, Patrick, I doubt that." Olivia's laugh was soft and faintly condescending. "And if you have no pity for poor Ferris, think of Phillip. You really mustn't play fast and loose with people's emotions. You should save yourself for someone who's better able to handle you." There was little doubt who Olivia meant, and not for the first time Ferris wondered how someone who looked like Grace Kelly could act like Attila the Hun.

"Olivia, I think there's someone here." Dale Summers's rich, fruity voice came from the hallway, preceding his lanky form. "I don't think we ought to—" Spying Blackheart and Ferris, he came to a halt, and a blush came over his long, bony face.

His obvious embarrassment only made Ferris more uncomfortable, but there was no way she was going to leave Olivia with the upper hand. "Go ahead with whatever you were planning, Olivia. Blackheart and I were just finishing."

"Really?" Olivia raised one exquisite eyebrow. "It looked to me as if you'd just begun."

"You do have a mouth on you, Olivia," Blackheart said softly. "You might consider washing it out with soap every now and then."

"So charming," Olivia purred.

"I do my best. What are you two doing here? I can't imagine you needed any measurements that couldn't wait till tomorrow. And why do you have a key? You aren't one of the people listed as having one."

"Dear Patrick, you are becoming so professional all of a sudden. Well, you've caught me, I'm afraid. I borrowed Regina's key last week and had a copy made. I didn't really relish going to dear Ferris every time I needed to get in. It smacked too much of boarding school." She cast Ferris an appraising glance out of her china-blue eyes. "Though I must say you're looking a great deal less schoolmarmish than usual, Ferris."

"You still haven't answered my question, Olivia," Blackheart persisted, that deep, quiet voice of his embedded with steel. "Why did you and Dale come here today?"

Dale had blushed even a deeper red, and his prominent Adam's apple worked convulsively. Ferris watched him with distracted fascination, almost missing Olivia's indulgent little laugh.

"Why, Patrick, you taught me about the erotic possibilities of empty mansions. I'll never forget the costume ball at San Simeon. I thought I'd bring Dale along and see if I could recapture the old magic." Her perfect lips curved in a smile. "I figured anything was possible."

Ferris had finally reached her limit. "Then I think we should leave you two to your privacy," she said quietly. "We were just about to head back to town anyway. I'm expecting a phone call from Phillip." She said it defiantly, eager to show she had nothing to hide from Olivia's beautiful blue eyes.

"Does he call you every Sunday? How sweetly predictable of him," she cooed. "He used to call me every Sunday when we were engaged and he was campaigning. Of course he used to call me earlier. Three o'clock, every Sunday afternoon. I'm glad to know he keeps in touch." She took a step toward Ferris's still figure, leaning forward in a confiding fashion. "Listen, darling, I'd never realized that we had such similar taste in men. Why don't we trade men for the afternoon? I've missed Patrick's—shall we say, enthusiasm. And you'll find Dale can manage a creditable performance when properly inspired."

Ferris's hand clenched into a fist. She would have given five years off her life to have driven that fist directly into Olivia's perfect little teeth, but the strong hand on her back would have moved fast enough to stop her. She gave up the notion with great sorrow, promising herself that sooner or later she'd have her revenge. "I'm going out to the car now, Blackheart," she said calmly, congratulating herself on her even tone of voice. If she couldn't have revenge, she could at least have dignity.

With a cool nod at Dale, she strode past them, ignoring Olivia's amused smile. By the time she reached the broad front steps she was shaking with rage, by the time she reached the car she was swearing and cursing in words taught to her by her brothers in deepest secret. Yanking open the car door, she slid inside and sat there, waiting, counting until Blackheart joined her.

He got there by seventy-three, and the surface of Ferris's white-hot rage had cooled to red. He slid into the front seat beside her, turning to look at her before turning the key in the ignition.

She met his gaze accusingly. "How could you?" she demanded in a furious undertone.

"How could I what?"

"How could you sleep with that slimy bitch?"

Blackheart shrugged, and she could see the amused light in his eyes. If it had reached his mouth, he would have been the recipient of her fist instead of Olivia. "I had nothing better to do at the time," he replied. "You want to tell me about your past love life?"

"I would have thought that would be part of your report."

"It should have been. Kate couldn't find out anything of interest, apart from a high-school football player."

"Damn you, Blackheart, leave me alone!" she snapped, enraged. "Tommy Stanopoulos has nothing to do with this."

"Nor does my past affair with Olivia Summers," he said calmly, starting the car.

"You're right about that. Your affairs have absolutely nothing to do with me. As long as you have the energy left to get the job done you can sleep with every single socialite, married or otherwise, that you can get your hands on. I won't say I don't admire your prowess, but—what are you doing?"

Blackheart had started out the driveway, but as her words escalated he'd slammed on the brakes, turning to her with the first anger she'd seen from him. Part of her was gratified she'd goaded him beyond that smiling calm, part of her was terrified. He put those strong hands on her, yanking her against him, and his mouth effectively silenced her.

It was a long kiss, deep and searching, and she was helpless to do anything but respond. When he finally released her, they were both breathless. She fell back against her seat, staring at him as he slowly put the car in gear and started back out the driveway. His breathing slowed, the hands clenching the steering wheel loosened, and the tension in his wiry shoulders relaxed. "That seems as good a way as any to shut you up," he said meditatively. "For your information, I don't happen to want to go to bed with anybody but you. Not right now, at least. My reputation is based more on rumor than fact; Olivia Summers was an unpleasant mistake that I don't care to make again. And if you want any more excuses, you can damn well do something to earn them."

The rest of the ride was finished in complete, absolute silence. He didn't bother to turn the car off when they arrived outside her apartment, and he kept his face averted. Without a word she climbed out of the car, without a word she grabbed her purse and without a word she slammed the door as hard as she could. She heard the tinkle of glass with real delight, and ran into her building before Blackheart could respond. Forgetting that when he was ready, locked doors weren't about to keep him out.

The angry squeal of the tires as he drove away was balm to her outraged soul. "Take that, Blackheart," she murmured, climbing the flight of stairs to her second-floor apartment.

Dale Summers turned to his wife, the high color fading somewhat. "That was close."

Olivia was staring out the window, watching the Volvo start, stop dead, and then start up again. "Too close," she murmured. "But every cloud has a silver lining. I've just had the most delicious idea."

Dale looked at his wife's serene little smile with worried doubt. "You wouldn't . . ." he began, but the icy expression in her blue eyes stopped him. "I just hope you know what you're doing," he said plaintively.

Olivia smiled her tranquil smile. "Oh, I do, darling. I know precisely what I'm doing. Come along."

Chapter Eight

ROUGH CUT HADN'T been enough to hold her interest past one that night. She clicked it off with a determined snap, burrowed under her tangled covers, and tried to will herself to sleep. It hadn't been the best day of her life, starting with Blackheart's appearance in her apartment and ending with Phillip's querulous phone call. Even Phillip's sulks were gentle and charming, and Ferris felt like every kind of traitor as she soothed his ruffled feathers. A traitor because she'd responded to Patrick Blackheart's kisses far more enthusiastically than she ever had to Phillip's restrained necking. Of course, Phillip respected her, planned to marry her. Blackheart didn't respect anything or anybody, whether it was someone else's diamond necklace or someone else's fiancée. And he probably went after both for the same reason—the sheer, mischief-making challenge of it.

Ferris was still trying to sleep when she heard the restrained batting against the door that opened onto her terrace, and she dived further under the covers, trying to escape the determined daylight and that nagging little sound. But consciousness had taken hold, and as the tap-tap renewed, she tossed the covers back with a glad cry to survey the fierce-looking gray beastie outside on her terrace.

"Blackie!" she cried, flopping across her bed and reaching for the door handle. It only opened a scant three inches against the oversize bed, just enough to let the furry creature slither through, hop onto her bed, and survey her with his usual haughty disdain while she slammed the heavy door shut again. "Where have you been, old man?" she demanded, stroking him on his grizzled gray head. "I thought you'd left me for good this time."

Blackie the alley cat expressed his thoughts with a feline sneer, batted at her hand, and headed for the kitchen. Ferris, knowing her duty when she saw it, headed after him, shivering a bit in the early morning chill. An ice-blue Victorian teddy wasn't the warmest of sleeping apparel.

"You've been gone three days this time, Blackie," she informed him as she opened a can of cat food. "I'd almost given up on you. I met your namesake while you were gone." Blackie sniffed at the can, gave her a reproachful look and sat back on his haunches. "I know, you'd prefer herring in sour cream, but I ate it last night. I'll buy you some more if you promise to stay around."

Blackie continued to stare at her, unblinking. "No, I don't suppose you will. Any more than your namesake. He's far more elegant than you are, old man. And far quieter. You sounded like a herd of elephants outside the door this morning. Come on, Blackie old boy. It's Dixie Dinner, your favorite."

Blackie considered this, his gaze alternating between her beseeching face and the dish of Dixie Dinner. Taking pity on his poor mistress, he bit daintily into the food, slowly enough to show his disapproval. Ferris knew full well that the moment she turned her back he'd scarf it down in record time. "I should have left you in that alley," she said ruefully.

And that was just where she intended to leave Patrick Blackheart himself. She must be out of her mind, to risk everything she'd worked so hard for, jeopardize her relationship with an undemanding gentleman like Phillip Merriam. She was going to be a senator's wife, and with Phillip's genteel ambition, who knew where that would end? Short of the White House, she devoutly hoped, but not too far short of it. She'd have wealth, security, and her own kind of power. Why was an amoral felon having any effect on her whatsoever?

It took her longer than usual to whirl through the apartment, straightening the mess she'd made the day before. Blackie followed her, weaving between her legs and doing his best to trip her. He seemed to take exception to the white linen suit she was wearing, and even Ferris had to admit it was a little severe. Just the thing to keep Blackheart in line, to keep herself in line. Although she may have accomplished just that objective when she'd inadvertently smashed his car window.

She made it to Carleton House at more than her usual breakneck speed, frightening even herself once or twice. She had almost forgotten—the Honorable Hortense Smythe-Davies was arriving that very morning, with the Von Emmerling emeralds in tow. They were being kept at a local bank until the night of the Puffin Ball, but the elderly Honorable wanted to see for herself that the emeralds would have the proper setting. And the ladies wanted to see the emeralds.

Ferris couldn't remember whether she'd informed Blackheart, Inc., of the occasion. It would be just too bad if they didn't know. Maybe it would be enough to take them off the case, and the major problem in her life would be resolved. Then all she'd have to do would be to change her cat's name.

The parking lot was filled with cars. Predominantly Mercedes, with a Bentley, several Porsches, and a Ferrari mixed among the Hondas, Cadillacs and Range Rovers. There was even a Volvo station wagon or two, but none of Blackheart's vintage. Ferris smiled triumphantly. He wasn't there.

None of that mitigated the fact that she herself was late. She scampered up the steps two at a time, entering the ballroom in a rush. Thankfully no one noticed her arrival—all the women were clustered three deep around an immensely tall, immensely skinny old lady with a crown of white hair, an aristocratic nose and an extremely British accent. Regina looked up and caught her eye, giving Ferris a broad wink before turning her attention back to the Honorable Miss Smythe-Davies, and Ferris allowed herself to relax for the first time that morning.

She made no move to get any closer to the famous gems—she'd see them soon enough, and she didn't fancy trying to elbow past Olivia Summers's regal figure, which was blocking almost everyone's view. Leaning back against the white-and-gilt paneled wall, she prepared to listen to the old lady's lecture delivered in tones loud enough to reach Oakland. And then she recognized the short, sturdy figure of Kate Christiansen, clad in modified combat wear, and her spirits flagged somewhat.

Well, she should have known Blackheart would be more efficient than he appeared. He was probably wandering around right now, preparing to pop out at her when she least expected it. That was resignation she was feeling, not pleasure. *Do you hear me, mind?*

"The Von Emmerling emeralds changed hands several times during the last three centuries," Miss Smythe-Davies was declaiming. "My great-great-grandfather, the Earl of Borsbury, won them in a game of whist, and they have been in my family ever since, with the exception of a two-week period in the early nineteen-seventies."

"What happened then?" Ferris could recognize Olivia's sculptured tones.

"My dear, they were stolen. The only time in their history, as a matter of fact. My father was livid, of course—it nearly brought on a fatal apoplexy."

"How did you get them back?" That was Regina's voice.

"We paid a king's ransom for them. I told my father we shouldn't, but he was adamant. Fifty thousand pounds we paid the miscreant, far less than the actual worth of the gems, but steep enough. Since then we've been more careful."

"It was only fifteen thousand," Blackheart whispered in her ear. "And it was dollars, not pounds."

She turned to stare at him, for once more startled by his words than his sudden appearance. "You didn't!"

He smiled that charming, self-deprecating little smile that seemed to have the most insidious effect on her stomach and its nearby regions. "I did," he confessed.

"Oh, my God."

"Don't worry about it, darling. The thrill is gone, the challenge has been met. I make it a policy never to steal the same thing twice. Unless it's a kiss."

"Keep away from me," she warned in an undertone.

"I wasn't talking about right now," he said, much aggrieved. "You know, you look like a nun out on parole. Isn't that outfit just a trifle severe?"

"I am a trifle severe. I don't dress to please you."

"That's for sure." His gaze turned back to the old lady, and Ferris gave in to temptation and studied his profile for a moment. It was a nice profile, with a strong, straight nose, good cheekbones, warm, deep-set eyes, and that demoralizing mouth of his. The khaki shirt hugged his wiry torso, stretched across his shoulders, tapered into his faded jeans. "Have you seen the gems?"

Guiltily she pulled her eyes upward. His pants were too tight, she thought grumpily. Or maybe she had that effect on him. More likely it was his proximity to jewelry that was turning him on. "Not yet," she said. "I'll see them soon enough."

"They'd go beautifully with those eyes of yours."

"No, thank you. Bland diamonds are more my style." Of course she'd forgotten to wear her ring today, blunting the effect of that particular barb. She clenched her left hand, drawing Blackheart's attention to it, and he smiled.

He was leaning against the paneled wall beside her, entirely at ease. "I'm afraid I disagree. You'd look magnificent wearing the Von Emmerling emeralds and nothing else. Have you ever made love in nothing but an emerald necklace?"

"No."

"Well, I have. Of course, I wasn't wearing the necklace—I'm not that kinky. The lady in my life at the moment obliged. It was very uncomfortable. I don't recommend it."

"That's fortunate, because I have no intention of attempting it," she snapped.

"Of course, pearls might be a different matter. I can just see you, draped in yards of huge baroque pearls. We could try that. I'd have to find the pearls, of course, but I imagine I could put my hand to some."

"I imagine you could. No, thank you."

"You mean it's just going to be skin to skin when we make love?" he inquired, a thread of laughter in his soft, warm voice. "I thought I was going to have to be very inventive when I got you in bed."

"You're going to have to be fast on your feet when you try," she shot back. "Or you'll be walking funny for a week."

"Such a romantic. Humor me, Francesca. What's your most memorable erotic encounter?"

"Don't call me Francesca," she hissed.

"Then answer my question. I could always raise my voice, you know. Olivia would be fascinated—"

"You wouldn't!"

"No," he said regretfully. "I wouldn't. But I'm tempted. Come on, Fra—Ferris. What did you do the last time you made love?"

Things were getting out of hand, as they always seemed to when she was around Blackheart. "I told Tommy Stanopoulos that I wouldn't."

"I beg your pardon?"

"I said that the last time I made love, I didn't. I'm wearing white on my wedding day, Blackheart. Well-deserved white." Why in God's name was she telling him, she wondered.

Blackheart went very still, and she couldn't read the expression in those beautiful eyes of his. It looked like an odd combination of amazement, wonder and belated anger. Why was he angry? It was a long moment before he said anything. "So if you can't give Phillip Merriam a patrician background you can at least give him an honest virgin on his wedding night."

"You bastard."

"Actually, I was never certain of that," he said calmly. "My father never told me, and I didn't want to pry, out of respect for my dear departed mother. I hope you enjoy your fairy-tale life, Ferris. You may find it's not quite what you expect." And without another word he turned and walked away from her.

So why did she feel bereft, watching him go? No, she wasn't bereft, she was relieved. She'd seen the last of Blackheart, heard the last of his taunting comments, and she was well rid of him. But why was he so angry?

"What'dya say to him?" Kate Christiansen had ambled away from the group of entranced women. "Must have been something good. He doesn't often lose his temper."

"What makes you think he lost his temper?" Ferris questioned coolly.

"The way he was walking. He must've lost his temper last night, too. His car window was broken. I had to give him a ride out here today."

"Then I can thank you for getting him here on time."

"No, you can't. I don't want your thanks for anything. I just want you to leave him alone."

"What?" It came out a little too loud, and Olivia turned her regal head to glance at them, a smug expression in her blue eyes.

"I said, leave him alone. He doesn't need you playing games with him. You're going to marry Merriam, aren't you?"

"Yes."

"Then leave him alone."

"Did it ever occur to you that it might be the other way around?" she questioned coolly, still aware of Olivia's fascinated gaze.

"It occurred to me. But you're not his type. I don't think he needs a broken heart." That was pain in Kate's flinty eyes, and the pale mouth in her freckled face trembled slightly.

"Are you in love with him?" Ferris couldn't quite believe it, but neither could she fathom the emotion she was eliciting from Blackheart's assistant.

"Don't be ridiculous," Kate snapped. "He and Trace are my buddies."

The light dawned. "Oh, it's Trace you're in love with," she blurted out with less than her customary tact.

She was rewarded for it. Kate sent her a look of such murderous hatred that it made Blackheart's temper seem mild in comparison. "You go to hell, Miss Berdahofski." And she stomped out in her boss's wake.

"What have you been doing, Ferris?" Regina glided up with the unconscious grace that had taken Ferris months to perfect. The Honorable Miss Smythe-Davies had ceased her lecture; the magpies were chattering and Olivia was still watching her.

"Winning friends and influencing people," Ferris replied morosely.

"Don't worry about it, darling. Did Phillip manage to track you down yesterday? He called me hoping I'd know where you were."

"He got in touch with me a little after seven," Ferris said.

"Phillip was very upset that he couldn't find you. I told him not to be such a baby, but I'm afraid he's a little spoiled. I must be to blame, though I don't know how I let it happen." Regina's lovely brow wrinkled in worry.

"Everyone spoils him, Regina. He's so charming and so handsome that people can't help it, both women and men."

"Well, don't you do it," Regina recommended. "Your married life will be hell. I suggest you make a habit of not being around when he calls. It doesn't do him any good to be too sure."

"Regina, we're engaged. Don't you think people should be sure of each other if they're planning to marry?"

"Are you sure of Phillip?" Regina asked gently. "And your feelings about him?"

When it came right down to it, there were times when Ferris thought she liked Regina Merriam even more than she liked her very likable son. She liked her too much to lie to her. "Regina, I have a miserable headache. Do you suppose the entire Puffin Ball will collapse if I go home?"

"I think you're so marvelously capable that you've ensured that things will run smoothly even without your presence. Go ahead home, darling, and take your phone off the hook," Regina said.

"Bless you, Regina."

"What should I tell Patrick when he asks?" she queried slyly.

"Blackheart won't ask," Ferris said grimly, her head pounding. "If by any chance he does, tell him I've moved to Siberia." On impulse she leaned over and gave the slender lady a hug. "I don't deserve you, Regina."

"Nonsense. It's the Merriams who don't deserve you. I hope for our sake that we get you, but I want to make sure you know what you're doing."

That was too loaded a statement for Ferris to question. With another squeeze she headed back out into the cool San Francisco sunlight.

OLIVIA WATCHED Ferris go, a cat's smile curving her perfect mouth. Things were looking very promising, very promising indeed. It always helped to be open to possibilities. Ferris Byrd would provide an admirable scapegoat if her first choice didn't work out. The more possible culprits the better.

She took another longing look at the Von Emmerling emeralds. When it came right down to it, the glass and gilt reposing beneath her mattress was prettier. Perhaps that yappy old lady would appreciate the substitution. Perhaps not. That was scarcely Olivia's concern.

She liked the choker the best. That one central emerald was really magnificent. The old lady said it had come from a Hindu idol and had a curse on it. Perhaps. Olivia had the notion that it would prove cursed indeed for several people. But lucky for her. Very, very lucky.

Chapter Nine

BLACKHEART STILL couldn't understand why he was so mad at her. If he had any sense at all, he ought to be pleased that Ferris had resisted the countless importunate young men who must have thrown themselves at her magnificent feet. There was no doubt, no question in his mind that he would have her sooner or later—why wasn't he obscurely pleased that he'd be the first?

Part of him was. Part of him reveled in the fact that whether Francesca Berdahofski knew it or not, her first lover was going to be a retired cat burglar and not the society blue blood she'd set her matrimonial sights on. Quite a comedown for such a ruthlessly ambitious young lady, and better than she deserved. Without any conceit on his part, he knew that he'd be a far better lover than someone of Phillip Merriam's limited imagination. Besides, there was no way in hell that the good senator could want her any more than Blackheart did. He must want her a lot less—if Blackheart was engaged to her, she would have long ago left her pristine state.

Maybe it was the very fact that she'd clung to her virginity for so long that bothered him. A part of him wondered whether she was holding onto it for bargaining power—forcing Merriam into marriage if he wanted to have her. No, that didn't seem likely. If Merriam was that hot to trot, he could have found a score of willing young ladies with more easily traceable pedigrees. He wouldn't marry her just to get her into bed.

So why did the thought of her still being a virgin bug him so much? He had the unpleasant feeling that it was because he was afraid. Afraid of Francesca, of the depth of her feelings, of the entanglement that would result if he broke through twenty-nine years of defenses as he knew he could. If he was willing to go through all that trouble, was he willing to pay the price likely to be demanded? He still wasn't quite sure.

He hadn't come to terms with his abrupt change in life-style yet, and it had been years since he'd made his living out of rich men's pockets. Well, no, that wasn't completely true. He still made a very handsome living from the upper classes—the only difference being that now they had some say in the matter. It hadn't always been so, he thought as he let himself into his apartment without turning on the light and flung his body down into the overstuffed sofa, stretching his stiff leg out in front of him.

There were three things his father had taught him, three things that were basic to the precarious profession of jewel thief. One: Never pull a job by the light of the moon. Two: Never feel sorry for the people you steal from—they can afford it far more than you can. And three: Never get caught.

He'd broken the first two prime rules, that night in London, and that, of course, had led to his breaking the third. His father later added a fourth rule to that list of sacrosanct commandments. Never trust a woman; they're seldom what they appear to be. It was the breaking of that particular rule that had set the seal on his fate, and one would have thought he'd learned his lesson. But here he was, five years later and five years smarter, about to do the same thing all over again.

Francesca Berdahofski was a bundle of contradictions, as far removed from his varied lives as anyone could be. And he had the uncanny feeling that she could bring him down as effectively as Patience Hornsworth had.

Patience hadn't been bad-looking, in a long-toothed, receding-chinned, sharp-eyed British sort of way. And of course, the diamond necklace her elderly husband had bestowed on her on the occasion of their seventh wedding anniversary, not to mention the tasteless but quite valuable sapphire and ruby collection belonging to Lord Hornsworth's socially ambitious and extremely ugly sister, only added to Patience's myriad charms. She hadn't minded cuckolding her husband in his own house, indeed, had been doing it on a regular basis since the end of their honeymoon, and Blackheart had done his best to tire the energetic creature out before he set off on his nightly rounds.

It was one day past the full moon, and Blackheart knew better, but the opportunity was too good to miss—the Hornsworth town house was chock-full of friends and relations, there for some boring but mandatory charity ball. Among the both elegant and seedy guests present in the rambling old mansion there were at least three other likely suspects when the jewels turned up missing, and Emma Hornsworth had been far too tight and far too smitten with a rather myopic young fortune hunter to remember to see about locking up those hideous pieces her maiden aunt had left her. They would be lying on her dresser, and even if she were in the same room, accompanied by young Feldshaw, they wouldn't see or hear him. He'd had too much experience to be more noticeable than a shadow or a breath of wind.

No, the damning light of the moon could be dealt with. The odd diffidence that had been attacking him more and more frequently was another problem. He'd been brought up to steal, brought up to think of the idle rich as nothing more than ripe and deserving victims for a poor man's son. His father had thrown a whole lot of Irish nationalism at him at the same time, half convincing him, when he'd started out, that robbing the fat British upper classes was a political act for the oppressed minority. It had been a while before he'd noticed that the only oppressed minority who benefited from the influx of priceless jewels were his father and himself. By that time it was too late—he'd grown accustomed to the rich life, and the last thing he wanted to do was to turn his back on it. The fact that the precarious profession he was in had killed more than one member of his family made little difference—it even added to his self-justification. He'd risked his life for the jewels—the greedy owners had done nothing more, in most cases, than inherit them.

But even that constant litany wasn't helping anymore. He was beginning to feel sordid, sleazy and, worst of all, dishonorable. Honesty and honor were two different things to him, and always had been. He'd tried to keep the latter in mind, while consigning honesty to perdition as a luxury he couldn't afford. But honor was beginning to slip away, leaving him feeling like the lowest sort of criminal, and his self-proclaimed image as a latter-day Robin Hood somehow vanished beyond recall.

He'd have to give it up, he'd told himself as he'd shoved the tacky ruby and sapphire necklace and earrings in the black velvet pouch he'd inherited from his father for just such a purpose. Or find some way to rid himself of these absurd feelings of guilt. Because what in hell could he do as an alternative profession?

The rooftops of Hornsworth House were crenellated, gabled, full of interesting little twists and turns. He always preferred plying his trade in Europe—the boxlike structures that held most of moneyed America made it far too difficult to maintain an adequate hold. He'd done it, of course, and reveled in the challenge, but for pure esthetic pleasure you couldn't beat the stately homes of England or the chateaus of France.

He'd shut the window behind him with a soundless click, leaving Emma Hornsworth happily entwined with a snoring Feldshaw. Blackheart had taken a moment to grin heartlessly at the happy couple. *Better him than me,* he thought wryly. Emma had been after him for more than a year now, but he drew the line at skin and bones and wrinkles. If he'd wanted to support himself with his talent as a swordsman, he might as well just be a gigolo. For one last time he tried to tell himself that what he did had more class, and for one last time he failed to believe it.

The moon had risen as he made his way back across the steep expanse of slate to Patience's bedroom, and his silhouette was black and mercilessly visible against the silvered roof. He moved as swiftly as he dared, not giving up an iota of silence for the sake of speed. If it had only been two weeks later, he could have made enough to keep him comfortably for a year or more— the amount of jewelry adorning the wattled necks of the Hornsworths' guests was estimable even in those overtaxed days, with a surprisingly small percentage of copies among the real thing.

But that wasn't to be. He'd already risked far too much on a moonlit night, and he wasn't as sure of Patience Hornsworth as he'd like to be. When he got back to the safety of her bedroom, he'd have to wake her up and make sure that she was too besotted to even think he could have left her bed for a rooftop stroll to her sister-in-law.

It was with a rough start that he realized that for the first time in almost seventeen years of making his living he must have made a mistake. The window that he'd left open just a tiny crack was solidly locked. He must have miscalculated—Patience's room must be on the next section of roof.

But the moonlight made it more than clear that there were no wide dormers over there, nor were there any back the way he had come. He wouldn't have, couldn't have made such a mistake on such a brightly lit night. This was definitely Patience's room, and the window was closed and locked.

He was used to thinking fast, and this time he didn't even hesitate. He'd go back the way he had come, sneak out through Emma's bedroom and . . .

And then what? Should he take his chances that Patience didn't suspect anything, had just woken up with a chill on her soft white shoulders and shut and locked the window? He could tell her he'd gone for a late-night brandy and take the chance she'd believe him. But then, he'd had the foresight to grab those very pretty diamonds that had been sitting in plain view on her bedside table. He hadn't taken the time then to check the rest of the room, planning on doing so at his leisure. Would there likely be enough to warrant the risk of going back? It wouldn't take him long, once he made his way back there through the rambling old house.

Or should he just get out as fast as he could? No one would see him go—he could be out of the house and out of the country before anyone realized that John Patrick Blackheart wasn't quite who he appeared to be. It would be an abrupt end to his career, at least in the British Isles, but he could always pick a new alias, a new identity, and start again. Or he could retire.

Suddenly, that thought seemed so beguiling that all hesitation left him. He spun around, planning to head back toward Emma's room and, through that, to the sort of freedom he'd never really known, when he heard a clicking at the window.

He was fast on his feet, and tonight was no exception. But Patience Hornsworth was faster. The casement window crashed open and Patience shrieked in fury, lunging out after him, her pale blond hair hanging around her white face, making her look like one of Macbeth's three witches. He could have withstood that shock if it hadn't been for Emma by her side, her improbably red hair a tangle, screaming imprecations. And for the first time in his remarkable career, John Patrick Blackheart fell.

IT HADN'T BEEN a pleasant time. He might have wished he'd suffered more than a smashed knee—unconsciousness would have been a great relief. As it was, an enraged Patience had directed her servants to drag him inside and lock him in the cellar, to await his fate like an eighteenth-century servant. And it had taken that bitch three days to bring in the police.

There were still times when he remembered what it had been like down there. The ghastly pain in his leg that had him rigid and sweating in agony, the hunger that began late the first day and was a gnawing in his guts by the time they let him out. The thirst had been worse—when the minions of the law had first shone their torches down at him, he'd been unable to do more than croak at them.

But worst of all had been the darkness. He had no idea where they'd dumped him—even the Hornsworths didn't possess dungeons in their London house, though he wouldn't put it past them to keep a covey of skeletons in the house in the Lake District. But that damp, impenetrable darkness had shut in around him, leaving him alone with his pain and his hunger and his fear, and only the sound of some curious rodent penetrated the thick silence.

In comparison, prison had been a snap.

There wasn't a whole hell of a lot they could do to him. After the weeks and months in the hospital, the operations just to enable him to walk, a goodly amount of time had been spent. And even if the entire British judicial system knew that John Patrick Blackheart was a burglar par excellence, even if they knew he'd been thumbing his nose at the police for more than a decade, and his family before him, there wasn't enough proof to do more than slap his wrist with a six-month sentence.

Emma and Patience Hornsworth did their best, of course, elaborating on the hideousness of his crimes so that, if they'd had their way, he would have been on trial for rape, sodomy, grand larceny and bestiality besides. Fortunately, the little velvet pouch had never materialized, and the witnesses for the prosecution were taken severely to task for their foray into vigilante justice, not to mention creative testifying.

And at the end of his six-month sentence he had limped through customs and entered his mother's country and site of half of his own dual citizenship. There was no way the United States could refuse to take him, much as it would have pleased the customs officials to reject a convicted criminal. The proceeds from the combined Hornsworth jewels would at least go far enough to pay for the best orthopedic surgeons on the West Coast. It would have pleased his sense of justice to have thrown it all away on wine, women and song, but finally he had his priorities straight. First he had to be able to walk straight again, then he'd see about making a living. He'd be far too busy to think about any kind of revenge, subtle or otherwise. The loss by Patience Hornsworth of her diamond necklace was revenge enough.

The only thing Patrick resented, the only thing that still grated against his sense of tentative well-being, was that it hadn't been his idea. He'd been on the verge of renouncing the life as it was—he hated like hell to let infirmity and the British judicial system make that renunciation for him. His anger at fate's manipulation had driven him to breaking into Trace's apartment so long ago, it pushed him into afternoons like yesterday, when he had to test his expertise against the solid bulk of supposedly impenetrable houses. A part of him always wondered whether sometime he'd have to do it just one more time, succeed at it just once, before he could let it go forever.

Well, he hadn't listened to his father, and he was still paying for it with his peace of mind. He'd robbed by moonlight, he'd identified with his victim and he'd gotten caught. And worst of all, he'd trusted a woman, Patience Hornsworth, who wasn't the trusting, randy socialite he'd expected her to be, but an avenging Valkyrie.

And here he was, about to trust another woman who made it clear she wasn't to be trusted. If he had any sense, he would keep as far away from her as possible. *It was Monday now,* he thought, getting up from the sofa and moving across his darkened apartment to pour himself an amber whiskey, the ache in his leg slightly more pronounced than usual. If he showed any trace of self- control he wouldn't have to have more than a few words with her in the next couple of days. The question was: had he lost his self-control along with his ability to climb around on roofs? He was rather afraid he had.

OLIVIA WAS PLEASED, very pleased indeed. Things were falling into place with delightful ease. If things went as they should, she would be able to close up that little room, get rid of all that electronic equipment, and live the life she wanted.

Of course, enough people would remember her lucrative sideline. Distribution of certain damning videos and the high prices commanded by them would be bound to leave an indelible memory in certain embarrassed gentlemen of wealth and power. Which was all to the good. When Olivia made her move, ran for office, there would be plenty of people who still owed her. The paying off of huge sums to cover up a recorded indiscretion didn't wipe out one's memory, did it? And she knew all their wives so well—a deliberately careless word here or there could do untold harm.

No, she would have a lot of people eager to help her, and all the money she needed, once the emeralds were liquidated. If things just continued to go her way.

Olivia smiled dreamily. Fate wouldn't dare do otherwise.

Chapter Ten

IT WAS PROBABLY just as well that Blackheart was keeping such a low profile, Ferris thought. He seemed to have had an uncanny knack of avoiding her during the past three days. Every time she walked into a room he'd find a reason to leave, every time she had to seek out a member of Blackheart, Inc., Trace Walker would appear, a beaming smile on his affable face. Patrick was there in an advisory capacity—if she had any questions, Trace was more than happy to answer them. He was more than happy to drape one of his heavy, muscled arms around her slight frame, more than happy to invite her out to dinner, more than happy to flirt outrageously while a stricken, sullen Kate Christiansen looked on.

Fortunately he took no for an answer with equanimity, his enthusiasm not the slightest bit diminished by her constant refusals. She only wished there was some way she could steer him in Kate's direction. At her one mild suggestion that he feed Kate instead of her, Trace had stared back at her in honest shock. "Kate's my buddy," he protested. "Besides, she's got a broken heart and she's not interested in men right now, except as friends. Did I tell you about this little Vietnamese place I know . . . ?"

Thank God it was almost over. It was Wednesday night, late, when Ferris fumbled through her keys. The ancient locks were more recalcitrant than usual—she had enough trouble using a key. How had Blackheart managed to get in so easily on Sunday morning? She should talk with her landlord—see about getting the antique locks replaced with something a little more reliable. Something hefty, burglarproof, fireproof, bulletproof. But could they find any that were Blackheart-proof?

It was well after midnight—she'd had a late supper with Regina and several of the other stalwart members of the Committee for Saving the Bay, she'd had one brandy too many and she was tired, just slightly tipsy and edging toward depression. The only consolation was that it would soon be over. Phillip was murmuring something about announcing their engagement at the Puffin Ball, and in another four months Francesca Berdahofski would be Mrs. Senator Phillip Merriam. Damn it, no. Ferris Byrd would be Mrs. Senator Phillip Merriam. *God, Blackheart, what have you done to me?*

Success was finally hers. The last key clicked into place in its lock and she stumbled in the door, closing it quietly behind her and leaning her forehead against the cool panel. She fumbled with the locks, with the latch and chain, feeling weary, depressed and very sorry for herself. In her current state even

Double Rainbow ice cream wouldn't help. She was going to go collapse on her bed and sleep the sleep of the just. She wasn't even going to turn on the television. They were still running those damned caper movies, and night after night she watched cat burglars and their kin romp through millionaires' homes and museums, and when she fell asleep she would dream of Blackheart. Last night it had been *How to Steal a Million,* and she'd been awake till four in the morning. Not that she was ever going to be Audrey Hepburn. And Blackheart was no Peter O'Toole in his prime. But God, she'd love to be kissed in a closet.

Slowly she raised her head from the door. Her blouse and jacket were off, her skirt a pile on the floor, when she heard the thin, distant thread of sound in her rambling apartment. There was also a pool of light coming from her bedroom. She stood very still, the last traces of the brandy leaving her brain, her hand on the locks. Didn't they tell you that if you came home and surprised a thief in your apartment you weren't to confront him? You were supposed to run as fast as you could.

Of course, the purveyors of that sage advice hadn't taken John Patrick Blackheart into account. She wasn't going to find some drug-crazed junkie looking for her cash. She was going to find what *San Francisco Nightlife* had termed one of the area's most eligible bachelors. It was that article that had prompted her to christen her cat in his honor. But it was a very righteous indignation that prompted her to storm down two stairs, across the hallway, up three stairs and into her bedroom.

He was lying stretched out on her bed, a pile of pillows propped behind him. He was barefoot, with faded jeans hugging his lean, muscular legs, a white cotton shirt open and loose about his chest. In the middle of his chest was a large patch of fur. Better known as Blackie, the wandering alley cat.

The human cat smiled up at her lazily. "There you are. We wondered when you were going to get home. Out with dear Phillip?"

"With his mother. What—"

He joined her in perfect unison, "—the hell are you doing here, Blackheart?" he mimicked. "Watching *Topkapi* and waiting for you. Does Phillip know you wear sexy underwear next to that virginal body of yours? What color is that? Peach? It's very erotic next to your skin. But I suppose you still wouldn't be so pure if the good senator did know. There are some things that can't be resisted."

It was too late for her to run screaming for a bathrobe. Besides, the hip-length silk chemise covered more than what she wore on the beach. "Blackheart, get out," she said wearily, leaning against the doorjamb.

"Not on your life, kid. This is my favorite movie, and my TV's broken. I'm watching it here. You can join me," he added generously. "We won't mind."

"I'm going to call the police."

"No, you aren't," he said. "It would make too big a scandal, and a clever lady like you knows better. You're going to climb on the bed and watch *Topkapi* with me. And I promise on my honor not to make a pass at you. I doubt your feline friend would let me."

He was right, of course. She couldn't call the police, much as she wanted to. She couldn't even call Phillip—as usual she had no idea where he was. She only knew he would arrive at her apartment in less than forty-eight hours to escort her to the Puffin Ball.

"Please, Blackheart," she said, hating the sound of pleading in her voice, unable to help herself. "I'm tired, I had too much to drink and I don't want to fight with you. Please go home and let me get some sleep."

Smiling, he shook his head, patting the bed beside him. "I promise, Francesca. I won't try to have my wicked way with you."

Was she demented in her old age? Or drunker than she thought, to be actually considering his suggestion. "Can I trust you?"

That mocking grin twisted his mouth, and she wanted to kiss it away. "For tonight you can," he said. "I can't promise you more than that."

She believed him, or was too besotted to know the difference. With a sigh she flicked off the overhead light and crawled across the huge bed on her hands and knees till she reached him. Blackie took one look at her, a disgruntled expression on his face, and left, stalking with all the dignity of either a Winston Churchill or a very old alley cat.

Ferris ended at the top of the bed, just within reach of her unwelcome guest, but he made no move to grab her, and slowly she began to relax. "He's a great cat," Blackheart said gently. "We had an interesting time waiting for you. What's his name?"

"Blackie."

"Very original. Except that he's not black—he's a dark gray."

"I know that, I have eyes."

"They're not functioning too well tonight. How much did you drink? Not that I'm meaning to criticize—far be it from me to pass moral judgments on other people," he said lightly. "I was just interested."

"Not enough to make me trust you," she snapped.

"Ah, but you're on the bed, aren't you? You must trust me a tiny bit. So why did you name your cat Blackie when he's gray?"

Yes, she was sitting on the bed, scarcely dressed. May as well be hanged for a sheep as a lamb. "I named him after you. I'd read about the infamous retired cat burglar in *San Francisco Nightlife* and thought it was a good name for an alley cat."

"I'm flattered. Come here, Francesca."

"You said you weren't going to make a pass." She eyed him doubtfully.

"And I'm not. I want to watch this movie, and I'd feel a lot more comfortable if you put your head on my shoulder and curled up, instead of glaring at me balefully. You'd feel more comfortable, too."

"No."

"Yes." He was stronger than she realized. One steel-like hand caught her by the wrist, dragging her off balance, and she fell against him. His other arm came around her, his hand catching the nape of her neck and holding her against the hollow of his shoulder. She struggled for a moment, then gave it up, the fight draining from her body. His hold loosened, and she relaxed against him. It really was comfortable, lying there next to him. His shoulder was surprisingly cozy, considering that it was composed of bone and muscle and not an ounce of soft fat. She sighed peacefully.

"That's not so bad, is it?" he murmured softly, one eye on the movie in front of them as his hand began threading through her loose bun of hair. A moment later it was free, a cloud around her sleepy face.

"Not bad," she murmured, snuggling closer. "Why did you retire, Blackheart?"

She could feel the grin that widened his face. "I thought you weren't sure that I did retire?"

"I'm not. I'm taking your word for it tonight. Why did you? Was it because you were caught? I wouldn't have thought your prison sentence was long enough to account for such a radical change of heart. It was only six months, wasn't it?"

"You know a lot more about me than I would have thought. I'm flattered." His voice rumbled pleasantly above her ear. "And I haven't had a change of heart."

"Then why did you quit? And why did you start in the first place?"

"And what's a nice boy like me doing in a place like this?" he paraphrased with a soft laugh. "It's a dirty job, but somebody's got to do it."

"You aren't going to tell me."

"I'll tell you, if you really want to know."

"I really want to know."

"I became a . . . how shall I phrase it—"

"A thief," Ferris supplied sleepily.

"That's a little crass, but I suppose it's accurate enough. I became a thief because it was the obvious thing to do. I was merely following the family tradition. My father was one of the most famous . . . thieves in the history of society burgling."

"I didn't know there was a history of society burgling. I can't even say it."

"My father was a member of polite society in London in the thirties and forties and even into the fifties. He was known everywhere, accepted everywhere, liked by everyone. By day he'd play cards and gamble and ride with his friends, at night he'd rob their wives of their jewelry."

"A charming friend," Ferris grumbled against his shoulder. He smelled positively delicious. Of warm flesh, and Scotch, and something else. She realized belatedly it was the dregs of Dixie Dinner. Blackie must have enticed him into feeding him. With a sigh, she burrowed closer.

"Oh, he wasn't too bad. No one was seriously injured by his pilfering. He knew his victims well enough to know who could afford to lose a diamond or two. I think he did it more for the excitement than the money. He made as much gambling, I think."

"What happened to your parents?"

"My mother died when I was twelve. Some complications after gall-bladder surgery. My father died four years later." His voice was even, his eyes trained on the television, but that strong, beautiful hand of his was stroking her thick dark hair with a steady, soothing beat.

"How did he die?" Ferris asked quietly.

"Occupational hazard. He fell one night. His partner was counting on him, and I took his place. He'd shown me a few things, but I mostly learned on the job." His calm, matter-of-fact voice allowed for no pity, and Ferris swallowed the sudden surge of sympathy. It wouldn't have been welcome.

"And what made you quit? You must have been at it a long time—ten years?"

"Closer to fifteen. And I didn't retire—it retired me. Same thing as my father. I fell."

She felt suddenly sick. "What are you guys, the Flying Wallendas? How many other members of your family died that way?"

"Just an uncle."

"Damn."

"And I didn't die. I just had a smashed leg. Unfortunately, my fall attracted a bit of attention. It was . . . several days before I managed to get help. By that time infection had set in, and . . ." he shrugged, the gesture bringing her body temporarily closer.

"Is that when you went to prison?"

"Yes." The short syllable was neutral, neither inviting nor discouraging further confidences, but Ferris persevered with brandy-tinged tenacity.

"And you can't rob places anymore?" she asked.

"It's difficult. I've had enough operations to make my knee comparable to that of a retired professional quarterback. Good enough, as long as I don't ask anything exceptional of it. No skiing, no ballet dancing and no cat burglary."

"Do you miss it?" she asked in a small voice.

"Sometimes. Not often. Not right now. There's no place I'd rather be than lying in bed with the virginal Francesca Berdahofski," he said lightly.

"Don't tease me," she said sleepily. He was still stroking her head, gentle, soothing strokes, and if he stopped she would die.

"I can't help it. You're so teasable." His other hand reached up to touch her face gently. "So now I've told you my deep, dark secrets. Your turn."

"I've already told you more than you need to know," she grumbled.

"You haven't told me how you managed to be the only twenty-eight—twenty-nine?—year-old virgin left in captivity."

"Twenty-nine. And maybe no one's captured me."

"Not for want of trying. What about Tommy Stanopoulos, for starters? Why didn't you go to bed with him?"

"I didn't want to."

"I don't believe you."

Ferris sighed. It was much more comfortable to put her hand on his shoulder, to snuggle closer against his warmth, to tell him what he seemed determined to know. "We were all set to," she said. "We'd been going steady a year, been necking and petting and getting pretty passionate. He was going away to the university and I was going to follow him the next year, and we decided to 'go all the way.' We waited till his parents were out of town for the weekend, we lied to my parents and I thought we were all prepared. But he wasn't."

"He wasn't?" Blackheart sounded perplexed, and his attention had shifted from the television screen with the low murmur of voices to her sleepy, troubled face.

"He didn't have any protection. He said we didn't need it, that I wasn't going to get pregnant the first time. I told him I didn't want to take chances, not with my family's track record, and he said, 'What's the big deal? We'll be married as soon as you graduate from high school, you'll be pregnant and have to drop out of college before the first year is over. I'll make more than enough to support you—you don't have to go to college.'"

"And did you then proceed to emasculate him as he deserved?" Blackheart questioned lightly.

"I should have. I told him I wouldn't sleep with him if he didn't use protection. He told me I didn't love him enough to trust him. I told him I guess I didn't. And that was that."

"So what's happened in the intervening years? You must know that there are ways for a woman to stop conception even more effectively than a man."

"Believe it or not, things just never came together at the right time. Whenever I felt like going to bed with a man it was a spur-of-the moment thing, and neither of us was prepared. By the time I had a chance to do something about it, the notion had passed. Until Phillip."

"And you haven't even slept with Phillip?" The hand had left her hair, was now gently stroking her shoulders, and she curled into him like a contented cat.

"Nope. I was all set to, but when he found out I was still a virgin, he decided we should wait till we were married. He figured if I'd waited that long I could wait a little bit longer and do it right. Phillip's very traditional at heart."

"Phillip's an idiot," Blackheart mumbled against her forehead. "So you're going to be married in white lace."

"You can come to the wedding," she murmured sleepily.

"I think I'll pass on that one. We're getting to the good part of the movie,

Francesca. Don't you want to see them lower the mute down through the window?"

"Nope. I've seen enough caper movies in the past week to last me a long time. I'm going to sleep. Wake me when you leave." She shut her eyes, nestling closer still, and one slender hand closed around his shoulder. A moment later she was sound asleep.

Blackheart looked down at the woman lying in his arms, the wonders of *Topkapi* forgotten. He'd kept away from her as long as he could, far longer than he wanted to. And now he really didn't know why.

Someday he'd tell her about Patience Hornsworth and the rat-infested cellar. Sometime he might even tell her what he had never told another living soul—that he'd begun to hate what he'd been doing and who and what he was.

But not now, not yet. For now she was going to have to go by her seldom-used instincts and trust him. And despite all evidence to the contrary, despite that wary, mutinous look that came over her usually serene face, he knew that she would trust him. She couldn't help herself.

He didn't bother to think about why it should matter. He didn't even bother to think about where this was leading. Silently, carefully he pulled her sleeping body closer against his, flicking off the remote control for the TV before putting his other arm around her. It was a moonlit night again, and he'd long ago given up fighting his regrets. He was trusting a woman who wasn't what she said she was, and he had the uneasy feeling that his distant crimes were once again going to catch up with him. His father must be spinning in his grave.

Patrick hadn't been sleeping well these last three days, but the comfort of the bed beneath him and the soft body in his arms were producing an erotic sort of lassitude. A wry grin lit his face. He'd promised her he wouldn't make a pass at her tonight.

The sooner he fell asleep the sooner tomorrow would come, and he'd made no promises about tomorrow. Shutting his eyes, he willed himself to sleep.

Chapter Eleven

FERRIS WAS AWARE of several things, all shifting and drifting in and out of her consciousness. It was another gray day—the early morning light filtered through the glass door and tried to pry her eyelids open. There was a heavy weight on her feet—Blackie, most likely. And another heavy weight across her breasts, which definitely couldn't be Blackie. And the mouth and tongue nibbling at her earlobe, nuzzling through her tangled hair had nothing to do with a cat. Or did it?

She opened her eyes, whipping her head around to stare at the man in bed with her. He just barely managed to miss getting knocked in the jaw by her forehead. "What are you doing here?" she asked in a shocked whisper. There was no need to raise her voice—he was more than close enough to hear her. She was lying curled up in his arms, her long bare ankles tangled with his, her breasts just touching his chest through the thin silk chemise. He was still wearing his shirt, and she felt his warm skin, his heart beating with surprising rapidity against hers as he stared quietly into her eyes.

"Waiting for you to wake up," he whispered back. He had just a fine covering of hair on his chest—not too much, not too little—and it aroused her sensitive skin. She found her own heart had started beating more rapidly, in time with his.

"Did you want to say good-bye?" she questioned breathlessly. It was such a big bed, why was she entwined so closely with him? Why didn't she want to move?

He shook his head. "I wanted to say hello," he said, his mouth so near that the soft breath tickled her skin. His lips reached hers before she could protest. Then protest was the last thing on her mind as his mouth caught hers, gently forcing her lips apart. Slowly, thoroughly, he began to kiss her, his tongue teasing past her teeth, exploring the soft, trembling contours of her willing mouth.

She made a quiet little surrendering sound back in her throat as his rough, dexterous hand slid up one smooth thigh, under the silky chemise, across her flat stomach and up to gently catch one full breast. It seemed to swell in his touch, and Ferris whimpered slightly against his mouth, trying to edge closer.

His mouth left hers, pausing long enough to nibble lightly on her lower lip before moving back to her earlobe, as his other hand caught her shoulder and turned her closer against his body. Her hands were trapped between their bodies, there was nothing she could do but spread them against the warm, enticing skin of his chest, threading her restless fingers through the fine, crinkly hair. He felt so good to her hands, so strong and warm and alive, and she wanted to feel all of him, wanted no barrier of faded jeans or silk chemises. His hand slid its relentless way underneath the light material, and then it was his strong, long fingers on her skin, the texture rough and arousing.

With a low moan she sought out his mouth herself, losing herself once more in the heady delicious thrust and parry of their tongues. Her hands slid lower, encountering the frustrating barrier of his jeans, and she had just reached for the zipper when his hand caught hers, holding her still against his arousal, his thumb and fingers like steel around her wrist, keeping her captive. His mouth moved away from hers, reluctantly, and his eyes were black as midnight as they looked down into her love-dazed ones.

"Are you sure you want this, Francesca?" he asked quietly, his voice slightly hoarse with controlled passion.

She looked up at him, at the passion-dark eyes, the tangled brown hair that was rumpled endearingly around his face, the mouth that was still damp from her kiss. He felt hard and strong against her captive hand, and she knew how much he wanted her. As much as she wanted him. Slowly she shook her head.

"I don't want this," she said coolly, calmly, a part of her shrieking in disbelief.

His hands released her, and she rolled away, pulling the skimpy chemise around her exposed body. Unfortunately the oversize bed wasn't made for dignified exits. She had no choice but to scramble across it, trampling on an outraged Blackie, who remained directly in her path, finally ending up at the doorway, rumpled, tousled, breathless and embarrassed.

Blackheart hadn't moved from the bed. He lay back, crossing his arms behind his head, and surveyed her with a calm she knew was completely false. She could see his chest rise and fall with the effort at controlling his breathing, and the state of his jeans hadn't changed appreciably since her escape.

"You're blushing," he drawled.

"You told me you wouldn't do that."

"Wouldn't do what?"

"Wouldn't try to make love to me," she said in a strangled voice.

"I said I wouldn't last night. I never made any promises about the morning."

"I trusted you."

"No, you didn't," he corrected her mildly. "You didn't trust me one bit. You were just tired and a little drunk and willing to play with fire. And I just proved to you how trustworthy I could be. I let you go."

"You didn't . . . you . . ." Her outrage suddenly deflated. "Yes, you did. Thank you, Blackheart."

His self-deprecating smile was only slightly mocking. "I could say my pleasure, but that wouldn't be entirely correct. I can't say I was happy to do it, either. I guess we'll have to settle for 'you're welcome.'" He continued to eye her from his position on the bed. "In return you might do me a small favor."

Ferris looked at him warily. "What?"

"Put some more clothes on. I could always change my mind," he murmured.

Ferris fled.

AND HE'D CALLED Merriam an idiot. What did that make him, calling a halt when she was lying in his arms, trembling, responsive, ready to be loved as she needed to be loved? If Merriam was an idiot, John Patrick Blackheart was the king of fools.

It didn't look as if he'd won any points for that magnificent bit of self-sacrifice. She'd looked at him out of those wonderful green eyes of hers like he was the devil incarnate, she wouldn't even stay in the same room with him, and her hands trembled when she handed him the worst cup of coffee he'd had in months. He'd used every ounce of his willpower not to tease her, when what he'd really wanted to do was say to hell with it and drag her back into the bedroom.

She would have gone with him. He knew from that slightly dazed expression on her face that she hadn't quite recovered from her near escape and wasn't sure if she wanted to. There'd been no questions about protection—for the first time in her life she'd forgotten all about it.

Well, he could wait. And that was what he was intending to do. But sooner or later he was going to have Miss Francesca Berdahofski exactly where he wanted her. In his arms, in his bed, in his life. And for now he was going to ignore the fear that he'd never want her to leave.

In the meantime, he had things to do. The San Francisco morning was cool and damp, and his leg ached slightly. Not enough to bring the almost forgotten limp back, but enough to slow him as he climbed the steep hill toward California Street. Francesca could wait until after the Puffin Ball. Could and should wait, until he could give her his undivided attention. She needed to be handled very carefully indeed. But he had no intention of waiting any longer than that.

There were things he had to check out. Something didn't feel right about this job, something was in the wind. He'd relied on his instincts during the past fifteen years, and they'd seldom failed him. Trace often scoffed at him, but Blackheart had seen the secret look of awe in his eyes. He'd laughed when Blackheart told him there was something funny about the Puffin Ball.

"You're getting spooked in your old age, man," Trace had said, clapping a heavy hand on Blackheart's shoulder. "This job is a piece of cake. Just a bunch of sex-starved ladies and their fancy party. There are no professionals in the city—we would have heard of them. And it would take a seasoned professional to handle something like the Von Emmerling emeralds. We have nothing to fear from amateurs. Not with your magic."

"Something smells funny about this," Blackheart had insisted. "I want you to be doubly observant."

Trace had looked hurt. "Don't you trust me to keep my eyes open?"

"Yeah, but I also know that pretty ladies have a habit of getting in your line of vision. I just want us to be extra careful."

Trace hadn't looked mollified. "You don't have to act so high and mighty. I've noticed you've been more than a little distracted on this job yourself. You should know better than to mess with Senator Merriam's lady. She's out of your league, old man."

"You were trying to mess with her pretty hard yourself, old man," Blackheart had replied mockingly.

"It's expected of me," Trace had said righteously, and Blackheart had let out a hoot of laughter.

"Well, for once, don't live up to people's expectations. Trust in my instincts. There's something going on."

"I always trust your instincts, Patrick. Even though they give me the creeps. I won't even blink Friday night."

"I knew I could count on you. Listen, don't mention this to Kate, okay? You know how she worries."

Trace had given him a funny look at that one, but agreed without question. Blackheart still wondered why he'd said it. Kate never worried; Kate was stern and unflappable. But she'd been more uneven in the past few months, and he didn't want to take any chances. He wouldn't even allow his mind to speculate how trusting someone who was as close to him as Kate would be taking chances. He felt enough like a traitor.

It was going to take some time today. He had to track down the man who'd installed the alarm system at Carleton House and have him tie in two more windows that had been considered impregnable. Blackheart had good cause to know they weren't.

And then he had another, more personal job to take care of. Miss Francesca Berdahofski could wait until after the Puffin Ball, but not long after it. Maybe an hour. And if he didn't want to be tossed aside like—what was the kid's name?—Tommy Popandopoulos or something like that, then he'd better be prepared. In more ways than one.

What had she called that expression that must be wreathing his face at the very thought? Rapturous. He had every intention of putting just such a look on her face as she lay underneath him, that mass of brown-black hair spread out around her.

Tomorrow night. The Puffin Ball was a fast job, worth a great deal of money and not an untidy amount of publicity and never had he wanted a job to end sooner. He had no choice but to put Francesca out of his mind for the time being, or a troop of Girl Scouts could march into the middle of the ball and carry off the emeralds under his nose. Business first. And then pleasure, he promised himself. Pulsing, pounding, delirious pleasure. For him, but most especially for her.

A wicked smile wreathed his face as he topped the hill and started down the other side. Most especially for her, he thought.

"ARE YOU SURE we ought to go through with this, Olivia?" Dale questioned with that well-bred whine that was one of his most irritating characteristics. "I mean, we're taking a pretty big chance, and—"

"Don't be tiresome, Dale. If you haven't got any guts, don't come bleating to me about it. We're taking no chance at all—I've looked at it from every possible angle, taken care of any possible loophole."

"What about our unwilling partner? Don't you think Blackheart . . . ?"

"Blackheart, Inc., will go down the tubes once they're implicated in the theft," Olivia said coolly. "No one is going to believe their protests of innocence. The police will know someone had to be paid off. They simply won't be able to find out who did the paying and who did the collecting."

"But what if—"

"Enough 'what ifs,' Dale! It's too late for cold feet. You wanted this as much as I did."

"No one wanted it as much as you did, Olivia," Dale said, with more force than he usually used with her. Her glare was enough to whip him back into servitude. "All right, Olivia. I won't come up with any more objections. Just remember when they're carting us off to jail that I told you so."

"Don't worry, darling. They'll know at once I was the mastermind. You couldn't think your way out of a paper sack. You'll just face accessory charges, and you can always tell them I brainwashed you."

"You are a cool bitch, Olivia," he said slowly.

"Yes," she said, "I am. Be thankful of that, or we'd be in real trouble right now, courtesy of your little habits."

He looked at her for a long moment. "I suppose you're right," he said finally, unconvinced.

"Of course I am. Now why don't you go downstairs and see what's keeping our confederate? I don't want cold feet to be catching."

"Yes, ma'am," Dale muttered under his breath. Olivia watched him go with a cool smile on her pink lips. She'd have to get rid of him sooner or later—he was too great a liability. It was a fortunate thing divorce was now allowed in politics—even the President had been married twice. There was no way she was going to spend the rest of her life carrying his dead weight.

She stretched her small hands, shaking them slightly to release the tension. Tomorrow night, and then it would be over, and she'd be so very much richer. And someone, she didn't really care who, would be in deep trouble. She smiled, quite pleased with herself, and lit another cigarette.

Chapter Twelve

THE APARTMENT was very quiet. For once Ferris hadn't gone through her usual binge-and-purge cycle of house-cleaning. She hadn't dropped her clothes all over the floor when she'd walked in early that afternoon, she hadn't shoved her empty ice-cream dish under the bed. She hadn't even had any ice cream. When she fed the demanding Blackie—she had to change his name!—his can of Savory Supper, she tossed the lid and the can into the almost empty wastebasket. Even her bed was made, with fresh sheets, and the dead panty hose and year-old magazines had been routed from under it. The rabbit warren of an apartment was close to spotless, and for a very good reason. Phillip was coming.

She could just imagine his fastidious horror if he ever looked under her bed. Not that he'd been anywhere near her bed. But assuming that she was going to marry him, and the discreet diamond on her left hand suggested that she was, and assuming they would sleep together, sooner or later he'd find out her deep dark secrets. She often wondered which would bother him more—her haphazard approach to housecleaning or her less-than-patrician background?

Of course, with Phillip's inherited money she wouldn't have to worry about housecleaning. Someone could follow her around and pick up the clothes as she dropped them, someone could whisk away the ice-cream dishes when she finished them, even bring them to her in the first place. It would be sheer, luxurious heaven. Why did the thought depress her?

If she had the energy after her grueling week, she could summon up worry about his reaction to her background. But she knew she'd be manufacturing problems. Phillip Merriam was no snob. He might be disappointed that she hadn't been frank with him, but even he would admit she had never told him an outright lie. As for her Italian-Polish background, Phillip was a suave enough politician to know that would aid rather than hinder him in garnering votes. Once she told him, he might very well want to move the wedding ahead a few months. Though he'd probably insist she change her name back.

Well, that wouldn't be too great a hardship. She'd chosen "Ferris" off the top of her head, and she had come to dislike the cool, distant sound of it. Recently "Francesca" had taken on a certain charm. It was probably only coincidental that it was Blackheart's soft, compelling voice wrapping around it that had made it suddenly appealing.

She'd had too much coffee and Diet Coke that day—the caffeine was giving her an uncustomary case of the jitters, and there was absolutely no need for it. Everything was in order, everything in place—all the committees had proved responsible. The Puffin Ball was set to begin in a few short hours, preceded by an elegant dinner, and there was nothing left for Ferris to do but enjoy it in the company of her fiancé. She simply had to avoid Blackheart's knowing eyes as she'd been avoiding his presence the last two days.

Everything was set for Phillip's arrival. The Brie was at the perfect stage of ripeness, the imported British wafers exactly the ones he liked. She had his favorite Scotch, the Dubonnet she'd affected early on in her transformation and had since grown to hate, and everything was in readiness.

Ferris controlled the temptation to take one last look at her reflection. There was no way she was going to improve on coolly calculated perfection. She was exactly what Senator Phillip Merriam expected to see, she was a work of art created by a master. Even if she was no longer so proud of her efforts, she could at least appreciate the results.

The dress was a slight departure from her usual boring good taste. When she went shopping, everything she tried on looked like something a republican would wear, and there was a limit to how far she would go in her quest for upper-class anonymity. Looking like a republican was beyond that limit. Her final choice was a deceptively simple white sheath, as demure as she cared to make it, which was very demure. It was made of a clingy, silky material, with cunning drawstrings that could raise the side slit from below the knee to halfway up her thigh, could move the neckline from somewhere near her waist up to the polite vicinity of her collarbone. She had opted for the most coverage available, piled her silky hair atop her head and put on strategic gold museum jewelry copies. An Egyptian collar from the Metropolitan Museum in New York, an Abyssinian slave bracelet from a small college museum in the Northwest and round gold-disk earrings from the Roman collection at the Palace of Fine Arts in San Francisco. She had deliberately not taken a raffle ticket for the emeralds. The last thing she wanted to do was parade around in priceless jewels in front of Blackheart's avaricious eyes. He might well find her irresistible, and then where would she be? In deep trouble.

Carefully, Ferris reclined on her camelback love seat, the closest thing to a sofa that would fit in her tiny apartment. Phillip was late, an almost unheard-of circumstance, and for a moment she considered sneaking into the kitchen and pouring herself a neat glass of his Scotch. Her nerves were on the screaming edge, and sitting around waiting didn't help matters.

Five minutes passed, with her longing for a drink and Blackie weaving his fat gray body around her crossed ankles. At one point he looked up, uttering a plaintive "mrrrow?"

"You couldn't be hungry again, you pig!" Ferris said. "You scarfed down all of the Savory Supper and got into the Brie besides. You're just lucky Phillip wasn't here. He barely tolerates you as it is, and if he knew you'd been munching on his precious cheese you'd be in big trouble." Blackie replied with another plaintive "mrrow," and Ferris rose to her feet.

"All right, I'll give you some more. I may not be back till very late, and God knows what you'll do to the apartment if I don't leave you enough food." She kept up the conversation as she followed Blackie's chubby form into the pocket-size kitchen. "But no more Brie. You'll have to make do with Seaside Surprise and be grateful. I don't—" Raising her head, she looked directly into John Patrick Blackheart's amused eyes.

"Merciful Mary in heaven!" Ferris said, falling back against the refrigerator. "You scared me half to death! You've got to stop sneaking up on me like that. And what—"

"—are you doing here?" he chanted in unison with her. "Really, Francesca, you're going to have to think of something more original to say every time I break in. It's getting redundant."

"Your breaking in is getting redundant. Don't you know there's a law against . . . against . . . ?"

"Breaking and entering is the legal term for it, remember?" he supplied politely. "Or B and E, as they call it in the trade. Who says I broke in? There's no sign of forced entry."

"You're too smart for that. I bet Blackie let you in when I wasn't looking."

"No, but I could always train him. He knew I was here long before you did."

"Damn it, Blackheart, you have to get out of here. Phillip's due any minute."

"Good. I haven't seen the senator in months, apart from talking to him on the phone about you."

"About me?" she squeaked, horrified.

"You remember," he said kindly. "He called and told me you'd take good care of me."

"God, Blackheart, you scared me!" she breathed, the panic never leaving her body. "You've got to get out of here," she said again. "I don't want Phillip finding you here."

"Why not?" He was leaning against the kitchen counter, in no mood to move, and his arms were crossed over his chest. A very elegant chest it was, in perfect evening dress, obviously tailored just for him. There was nothing prettier, Ferris thought with an absent sigh, than a gorgeous man in well-cut evening clothes. Unless it was a gorgeous man in nothing at all.

She shook herself, trying to regain a semblance of sanity in the face of incipient disaster. "Have pity on me, Blackheart. I don't want Phillip suspecting anything."

"What would he have to suspect?" Blackheart countered mildly, and the simple words made a tiny dent in her panic. "I mean, what have we done that's so awful? Shared a kiss or two?"

"Four," she corrected.

"I beg your pardon?"

"Four kisses," she elaborated, and then flushed in the face of his delighted grin.

"Bless your heart, Francesca, I didn't know you were counting."

"So I happen to have a photographic memory," she said defensively. "Anyway, how would you like it if someone kissed your fiancée once or twice, not to mention four times?"

"I wouldn't like it one tiny bit. But then, I wouldn't have left her in the first place with prowling wolves like me around."

"Alley cats," Ferris corrected him in a dulcet tone.

He grinned. "And I wouldn't have left her a virgin for so long."

"Come on, Blackheart." She grabbed his wrist and started dragging him toward the door, ignoring the little thrill that ran through her at the feel of his warm flesh against her fingers. "I really don't want Phillip to find you here. Be kind for once."

He stopped in the arch that separated the living room from the tiny dining alcove, and she couldn't budge him any farther. "I'm always kind, Francesca," he murmured, his voice a sinuous thread. "To you, at least. You just don't recognize it."

She gave a useless yank on his arm. "Please, Blackheart. You have to leave."

He was as still as a statue, his eyes alight with mischief. A moment later the wrist that had been so lifeless in her hand twisted around, capturing hers. Slowly, inexorably he drew her body toward him. She could have fought him, might have twisted away, but she didn't. She was mesmerized by those devilish eyes, that smiling mouth, and a wanting that all the sense in the world couldn't banish. When his mouth reached hers she met it hungrily.

The hand on her wrist pulled her arm around his lean waist, her other arm followed of its own accord, and suddenly she was clinging to him as if he were the only safety in the world, the only reality that existed. A reality that was promptly shattered by the intrusive shrill of the doorbell.

"Damn!" She tore herself out of his arms in sudden panic. "Get out, Blackheart. I don't care how you do it. You managed to get in here without using the front door, you can leave the same way. I don't want Phillip seeing you."

"Don't you think he'll notice?" Blackheart said lazily, not moving from his perch against the arched doorway.

"Notice what?" she demanded, harried, as the bell rang again.

"That you've just been thoroughly kissed. If I were him and found my fiancée looking like you look, with your cheeks flushed and your eyes shining and your hair coming down, I'd be very suspicious."

"Damn," she said again. "I'll get you for this, Blackheart. I swear I will.

At least wait on the terrace until we leave. He's late, we shouldn't be here long."

"Sorry. I told you I wanted to see the good senator. That's just what I intend to do." He moved then, striding past her horrified eyes, straight for the front door.

"No!" she gasped, diving for him in a vain effort to stop him. She may as well have been trying to tackle a quarterback. He merely proceeded to drag her the rest of the way, opening the door before she could do more than moan in despair.

Trace Walker smiled down at them with impartial benevolence. "Sure took you long enough, Patrick. Are you guys ready?"

If her cheeks had been flushed before, it was nothing compared to the scarlet mortification that washed over her then. Slowly she detached her stranglehold from Blackheart's neck, slowly she tried to right her dress and brush the tumbled hair away from her face.

"Hello, Trace," she managed serenely, and Blackheart burst out in unrepentant laughter. "What are you doing here?"

"Didn't Patrick tell you? The Senator was delayed in Santa Barbara—he'll meet you at the dinner. He asked Patrick and me to pick you up. Didn't you tell her, Patrick?" Trace's handsome face creased in confusion.

"I didn't get around to it," Blackheart replied innocently.

"You—you unspeakable piece of garbage," Ferris said in a low voice. "You miserable, slimy piece of crud. You—" His hand caught her wrist just as she was about to hit another human being for the first time in twenty years.

"I know a very good way of stopping your mouth, lady," he said lightly. "And I don't mind if I have an audience."

"You two got something going?" Trace inquired curiously. "Kate told me you did, but I thought that Ferris was engaged to the senator."

"We have nothing going," Ferris said icily. "Apart from dire enmity. I'm glad to know Blackheart, Inc., is so sure of themselves that they can leave the place they're supposed to be guarding with easy minds. You haven't bothered to wonder whether someone might not break in ahead of time, or any other mundane consideration, have you?"

"Not to worry, Ferris," Trace said jovially. "Patrick and I have got it all under control. The general security staff is watching things right now, Kate is sitting on the emeralds with three large men surrounding her, and the alarm systems are fully operational. Everything's fine. You ready?"

Blackheart was still holding on to her hand, but the iron grip had softened, the thumb absently stroking the inside of her wrist and sending melting little tremors up and down her spine. And she was standing there like a fool, reacting to it.

Quickly she snatched her hand out of his loose clasp. "I'll be ready in five minutes. I have to repair my makeup."

Blackheart grinned. "I guess you do. I'll feed the cat for you."

As long as Trace was such an interested observer, Ferris had to content herself with an answering glare. Without another word she disappeared into the bathroom, determined to stall as long as possible. She didn't care if she jeopardized the Von Emmerling emeralds, the Puffin Ball or her engagement. She needed time to compose herself before she had to face Phillip's trusting blue eyes. Especially when she knew the greatest betrayal wasn't Blackheart's, it was the gnawing longing in the pit of her stomach, the ache in her heart, the hunger in her loins. And she wasn't leaving that bathroom until she conquered it. At least temporarily.

Blackheart was right. She did look thoroughly kissed. Staring at her reflection in the mirror for a long moment, Ferris let out a deep, trembling sigh. "Damn his soul to hell," she whispered. "What am I going to do?"

"ARE YOU READY? Olivia, do you hear me?" Dale's querulous tones were definitely getting on her nerves. She would have to be circumspect in divorcing him. He had a vindictive streak—if she pushed him far enough he wouldn't mind destroying himself just to get at her.

"I hear you, Dale." She turned from the window, icy cool and elegant in a pale-blue silk dress that matched the wintry blue of her eyes. "I was just wondering how our friend was handling things."

"Oh, I don't think there's any problem. You have an innate talent for putting the fear of God into anyone. Things will be just as you planned."

"I do hope so," she said mildly as he draped a silver fox stole around her narrow shoulders. "Because not only would I be very displeased if something went wrong tonight, I would also have to bring the two of you down with me. And none of us would like that, would we?"

"No, Olivia."

His agreement was mumbled, but Olivia thought she could see a furtive flash of hate in his milky blue eyes. Good. Hate and anger kept you on your toes. As long as Dale was actively hostile, she didn't worry about him. It was when he grew affable that he became careless.

It was their third, unwilling partner who troubled her. The partner that was right now in place, eagle eyes trained on the Von Emmerling emeralds. Olivia had managed to drown all objections and doubts with her forceful personality, but from now on she had to rely on the residual force of her orders. There was no way she could be on hand, reminding her minions of what was expected of them.

She took a deep gulp of the damp, chilly fog that blanketed the city. *A good night for a jewel robbery,* she thought, a little cat's smile curving her lips. She could only wonder whether John Patrick Blackheart might agree.

Chapter Thirteen

FERRIS STOOD OFF to one side, half hidden by the heavy damask draperies that shut the fog-ridden night away from the gaiety of the crowded ballroom. The Puffin Ball was a smashing success, socially, artistically, and financially, and yet Ferris had never felt worse in her life.

The third winner of the Von Emmerling emeralds, a stocky brunette with the build of a fireplug and the voice of a sea gull was whirling around the dance floor in the arms of her equally unprepossessing husband. She'd chosen an unfortunate shade of chartreuse chiffon for her dress, succeeding in making the beautiful old emeralds look almost tacky in the candlelight. They'd fared better earlier. The first winner had been a slight, feathery blonde in pure white. Blue-blooded to her fingertips, she'd done the jewels proud for the two hours she'd worn them, giving them a stately elegance. As had the second winner, a fashionably blue-haired matriarch. And even if number three hadn't quite the style or grace, she more than made up for it in enthusiasm, Ferris thought wearily, leaning back into the drapes. Who was she to sit in judgment?

Damn, would she like to sit, though. From the moment she'd arrived she'd been on display, an ornament on Phillip's very urbane arm. She'd smiled till her jaw ached, her teeth felt windburned and her eyes were permanently crinkled. She'd shaken hands and chatted and danced and ate, and right now all she wanted to do was crawl under a blanket and hide. Her head hurt, her feet hurt, everything about her was a mass of pain. She would have given ten years off her life to go home right then, but she knew it was out of the question. Phillip had let her escape, reluctantly, when she insisted there was some important lady in need of her. That important lady had been herself, but Phillip didn't need to know that. He was still holding forth, this time on gun control, and part of her longed to stay and watch with real admiration as he told each listener exactly what he or she wanted to hear. But there was a limit to her endurance. She would have to be there until the last possible contributor to Phillip's campaign remained, she would have to stay until the Von Emmerling emeralds were safely stowed for the night.

If only the Honorable Miss Smythe-Davies had been up to the rigors of the Puffin Ball, a good many of Ferris's worries would have been over. Somehow she knew that she wouldn't have a moment's peace until the damned jewels were no longer even remotely her responsibility. And then there would be no reason ever to see John Patrick Blackheart again.

She looked down at her slender wrist. There was a bruise there, just above the bone, a smudge of darkness against the lightly tanned skin. Would he regret it if he saw it? She'd make sure he'd never have that chance.

Phillip had been waiting when they arrived, long arms outstretched, that smile that could charm old ladies into giving up their Social Security checks beaming down on her and her companions. Blackheart had relinquished her readily enough, almost too readily, his eyes black in the romantic candlelight as his mouth quirked up in wry amusement.

But there'd been no sign of amusement from then on. Whenever Phillip drew her into an admiring circle of men, Blackheart would be nearby, glaring at her. Every time one of Phillip's political cronies danced with her, and the times were far too numerous to count, Blackheart's expression darkened, and when Phillip finally drew her to the floor, executing turns and dips to the fatuous pleasure of almost everyone there but Olivia Summers, his face was nothing short of thunderous. Ferris had smiled, moving closer to her fiancé's stalwart form, each time she had caught sight of that unrestrained fury. Until she finally pushed him too far, and he'd cut in during the last one.

Phillip had relinquished her with a graceful smile and a hearty clap on Blackheart's back, not noticing that Ferris's smile was forced.

"You don't have to crush my wrist," she'd hissed at Blackheart when he'd swung her into the dance. The band was playing "I Can't Get Started," and the sound was slow and sad and sensuous. If Blackheart's tumble off the side of a building had hindered his career of thievery, it certainly didn't put a crimp in his dancing. He was smooth, graceful and more than able to concentrate on other matters as his body and hers did his bidding.

"Are you enjoying yourself, Miss Byrd?" he inquired acidly, the fingers biting into her wrist.

"Definitely, Mr. Blackheart." The more she strained against his imprisoning hand, the tighter the fingers held her.

"Do you think plastering yourself against the good senator sets a proper example for his constituents?"

"No one seemed to mind," she replied coolly, ignoring the memory of Olivia's pale anger. "I don't know what your problem is."

"Don't you?" His hand tightened for a moment, then loosened, and the grim look faded from his face. "No," he murmured, half to himself. "I won't do that."

"Won't do what?" Surreptitiously she flexed her aching wrist.

"Won't drag you closer and show you in specific, physical terms what my problem happens to be," he replied.

It took her a moment to understand his meaning. "You're a sick bastard."

"On the contrary, I'm a very healthy male, with healthy reactions, particularly to long-term frustrations. I've been in somewhat the same state since Wednesday morning."

"That's no one's fault but your own," she snapped.

"I wouldn't say that. You had something to do with it, willing or not," he continued in a musing voice. "Actually, I suppose if you'd been willing . . ."

"Could you please change the subject?" Ferris's voice was a little strangled.

"Certainly. If you'll move three centimeters closer to me. I'm not radioactive," he said gently. His thumb was absently stroking her abused wrist, the gentle caress sending shivers down her spine.

She looked up at him then, met his gaze directly. "As far as I'm concerned, you're even more dangerous."

His eyes were dark with a distant humor and something else, something she vainly hoped no one else would recognize. What in heaven's name would people think if they saw Senator Merriam's fiancée in the arms of an ex-cat burglar looking like that?

Of course, not that many people knew she was engaged, despite the discreet rock on her left hand. And not that many people would be able to decipher the mixed emotions in Blackheart's tawny eyes. But Ferris could, and it made her knees weak.

His temper, at least, had improved. "Do you want me to waltz you out onto the terrace for a little polite necking?" he murmured against her flushed temple.

"For one thing, Blackheart, we aren't waltzing," she said caustically. "For another, it's cold and damp and foggy out there, not at all conducive to necking, polite or otherwise. And finally, don't you think you might give at least a tiny portion of your attention to the Von Emmerling emeralds? After all, we're paying a rather exorbitant sum to have you protect them—I would think you'd like to earn your keep."

"Oh, but I am. As the only guest here under an assumed name, you're still my chief suspect. My assistants are watching the emeralds themselves."

"Don't be absurd, Blackheart. You know as well as I do I wouldn't steal those damned jewels. I didn't even take a raffle ticket."

"Maybe you still regret not taking the red shoes," he said. "Maybe you've been secretly acting out your aggressions, stealing here and there to make up for that one act of self-control," he continued, unmoved by her anger.

"I wish I'd never told you that," she said in a deceptively quiet tone of voice. "I should have known you'd use it against me."

"I wouldn't use it against you," he said softly, all the teasing gone from his eyes.

"You'd use anything to get your own way." She was horrified to feel sudden tears springing to her eyes.

There was no way he could miss them. "Francesca, love, I'm sorry," he said, stricken.

"Go watch your damned emeralds," she said, pulling out of his arms and moving with lowered head across the dance floor. She could feel curious eyes on her, but when she raised her head, the only face she saw was that of Olivia Summers, that cool-bitch smile on her perfectly shaped lips.

But if Blackheart had regretted his words, his actions the rest of the night didn't show it. To be sure, they kept their distance by unspoken mutual consent. But those dark eyes followed her, watching her when she least expected it, and she could no longer read their enigmatic expression.

And she watched him, from over Phillip's tall, broad shoulder, past Regina's stately coiffure, beyond the punch bowl and over the champagne. Every now and then his eyes would meet hers, sparks would shoot through her body, and she'd wonder how Phillip could miss her very strong physical reactions to his hand-picked security consultant.

Some of her tension must have penetrated, for at the end of the last dance he'd sent her upstairs. "You're wound up as tight as a spring, Ferris. Why don't you go and lie down for a few minutes? I can carry on without you. You've had a grueling week, I'm sure."

"So have you, traipsing all over the state," she replied conscientiously.

"Yes, darling, but I'm used to it," he assured her. "And I haven't got a tense bone in my body. I thrive on this sort of thing. I thought you did, too."

It would be useless to deny it. If she could say one thing for Phillip, it was that he was abnormally perceptive. "I usually do," she admitted. "I suppose it's been a little much for me tonight."

"Well, you go on upstairs and lie down for a bit. Try some deep breathing, all right?" He gave her his most winning smile. "You're as nervous as a cat."

Ferris couldn't help it, she winced at the simile. "All right, I will, Phillip." Reaching up on tiptoes, she kissed him on his smooth, scented, clean-shaven cheek. "I'll be back before too long."

"Don't hurry, darling. I can hold down the fort." With a smile, she turned to leave. And there was Blackheart again, that still, unreadable expression on his face. He'd seen her kiss Phillip, and Ferris told herself she was glad. She was only sorry she hadn't given him a more enthusiastic embrace, just to make certain Blackheart understood how things stood.

But the problem was, Blackheart probably understood far better than she did. "There you are, Phil," he said lightly, ignoring her. "Dale Summers was looking for you."

"Thanks, Patrick. See that my lady gets upstairs for a rest, would you? She's worn out on her feet and refuses to admit it."

"Be glad to," he said blandly. "Come on, Ferris." He held out his black-clad arm.

There was no way she could avoid it. Phillip was watching her, concern clouding those big blue eyes that were a major asset in his political career. She put her hand on Blackheart's arm, and she could feel the steel of clenched muscles beneath her light, touch. One strong, well-shaped hand covered hers with unnecessary force, and Phillip turned away.

Without a word he led her to the hallway, past a throng of merrymakers, both of them ignoring the curious glances cast their way. He stopped halfway up the wide, curving stairs, removing his warm, angry hand from hers, pulling his arm from her light grasp. "I think the senator's lady is more than capable of finding a bedroom on her own. You've made it clear you don't want my help."

She stared at him, a sudden, unwary delight filling her face. "You're jealous," she said, her voice soft with wonder.

His black expression didn't change. "That surprises you? I'd like to go back and rip Phillip's tongue out. If you marry him and spend the rest of your life as Mrs. Senator Ferris Byrd Merriam, you'll deserve it."

"How about ending my life as Mrs. President Ferris Byrd Merriam," she taunted. She shouldn't have, she knew it, but this unexpected fury was so flattering it went straight to her head. She wanted more of it, more proof that she mattered to him, no matter how dangerous it was seeking it.

"How about Mrs. Francesca Berdahofski Blackheart?"

That effectively wiped the smile off her face. "What?" she managed in a choked voice. "Are you serious?"

"That look of pained disbelief is hardly flattering," Blackheart drawled. "No, I wasn't serious. Never trust a cat burglar, Ferris Byrd. You've made your bed; you can lie in it." Without another word, he turned and left her on the stairs.

That was when her headache had started. For a brief moment she watched him go, wondering whether he really would rip Phillip's silver tongue out, whether there was any molecule of seriousness when he'd asked her to marry him. Of course there wasn't. She shook her head, trying to clear the mass of confusion, and continued up the stairs.

How did the man manage to move so silently, she wondered. It didn't seem to matter what he wore on his feet—he'd crept up on her in dress shoes, Nikes and Tony Lama boots. Could she ever learn to move about as silently?

The second floor was far too brightly lit and noisy. Practicing her quiet moves, she continued on up the broad staircase, passing only one or two curious guests. If she could only perfect it enough to sneak up on Blackheart and scare the shit out of him, just once, she'd die a happy woman. If you stepped just the right way on the ball of your foot, she discovered—

"Darling." A woman's voice sighed deeply, and she heard the rustle of clothing.

Ferris froze in place. The third-floor hallway was dimly lit, the open door to the bedroom was a pool of light on the floor. She had better than average eyesight, even in those less than perfect conditions, and she had no trouble at all recognizing Olivia Summers clasped in a fevered embrace. And the man holding her was distinctive enough. She'd know Trace Walker anywhere.

Never in her life had Ferris been so embarrassed and so fascinated. Cool, snotty Olivia wasn't just kissing Trace Walker, she was climbing all over him, her greedy hands pawing at him. He seemed to be enduring the attention with good humor, even if Ferris suspected his heart wasn't in it.

And then her hackles began to rise, as she recognized which bedroom the two of them had chosen for their tryst. The third-floor front bedroom was where the Von Emmerling emeralds were to be kept when they weren't on display or hanging around some lady's neck. And sure enough, that's exactly where they were, clasped around Olivia's skinny throat, the bracelet encircling the wrist that was traveling down toward Trace's lean buttocks. They looked prettier than Ferris remembered them, more delicate, and the emeralds shone more brightly.

Of course, it was probably a coincidence. Trace had been keeping the emeralds company, and Olivia had decided to keep Trace company, since Blackheart seemed to have no time for her. But Ferris couldn't stand around and let them use a fortune's worth of jewels as an erotic toy. She was going to have to interrupt them, no matter how embarrassing just such a move would be. And she'd better do it soon—Olivia's hands were getting positively indecent. Ferris caught the flash of the two-carat emerald ring before Olivia's hand slid down in Trace's front, and she could feel her face flushing. Damn them both, for putting her in such a position. It was just lucky that she'd come up here when she did.

She was about to clear her throat when she noticed the small dim figure by the far door. It was Kate Christiansen watching the embracing couple. She was wearing an unflattering floor-length dress of peach chiffon that made her short body look dumpy, and the expression on her face was a mixture of anger and such pain that it hurt Ferris to see it. She just stood there, her anguished eyes dark in her freckled face, too distraught to notice Ferris standing there like a voyeur.

Slowly, imperceptibly, Ferris backed away. Kate would interrupt them in another moment or two. Even if she wasn't sure she could trust one of Blackheart's associates, she knew that between the two of them the jewels would be safe. There was nothing to worry about. Olivia came from a family as old as the San Francisco hills, and the Summers fortune was equally legendary. She had no need to filch the Von Emmerling emeralds. As well suspect Regina Merriam of trying to run off with them.

By the time Ferris reached the stairs she could hear the voices from the bedroom, low, slightly embarrassed voices. There would be no problem.

THE TWO WOMEN watched Trace Walker leave the room, an embarrassed angle to his shoulders. She'd played it well, Olivia thought. Trace was so embarrassed at having been caught in such a compromising position that he'd put the responsibility of the emeralds low on his list of priorities. He hadn't liked the expression on Kate's face one tiny bit. As she'd suspected, there was something more there than poor little Kate recognized. Her grand passion might not be as unrequited as she supposed. But fortunately for Olivia, neither Kate nor Trace had any inkling of the other's feelings.

Kate was glaring at her, her lower lip thrust out unattractively, her eyes wide and angry. Really, the whole thing was laughable.

"Don't glare at me, Kate, darling," Olivia said easily, unfastening the clasp on the phony emeralds. "Have you got the real jewels?"

Chapter Fourteen

HER APARTMENT was still and silent as she let herself in. Phillip waited by her door, a pleased smile on his tired, handsome face. "You're dead on your feet," he observed kindly. "I won't come in."

She hadn't invited him in, but perversely she was annoyed. "I probably won't be able to sleep anyway."

"Sure you will. It's almost four in the morning. Just pour yourself a glass of Dubonnet and you'll be dead to the world," he assured her, and immediately Ferris was determined to stay awake till dawn. "I was glad to see that you and Patrick managed to get along," he added. "They did a great job, don't you think?"

"I suppose so. No one stole the emeralds, and that's the main thing." It had been with mixed emotions that she had watched the assembled staff of Blackheart, Inc., drive off with the beautiful gems safe in their possession. Now that it was all over, the Von Emmerling emeralds had suddenly taken on an added luster. She hadn't liked them much when she first saw them, but now that the responsibility was gone she found they were much prettier and more delicate than she'd first thought.

Blackheart must have lost his touch, though. He'd barely given them a cursory glance as he'd shoved the velvet cases into a briefcase that resembled something out of a James Bond movie. Ferris had little doubt that if some unauthorized person tried to open it, it would shoot poison darts at the very least. And he'd driven away from her, out of her life, without a backward glance.

"You'll have to admit that Patrick isn't so bad," Phillip persisted.

Ferris looked up at him then, suddenly curious. "He was no major problem. Why are you so concerned, Phillip?"

Phillip was a consummate politician. Even when he was avoiding a direct answer, he looked you straight in the eye. But this time he made no effort to avoid it. "Something my mother said," he replied lightly.

"She told you Blackheart and I were involved?" Ferris questioned, horrified that they had been so obvious, horrified that Regina Merriam would have said something to her son.

"Exactly the opposite. Apparently you two fight like cats and dogs. I've never known you not to get along with someone, no matter how offensive you find them. My mother was concerned, and so was I. You know how much Mother adores you. She's always considered you far too good for me.

She wants what's best for you—my interests come second."

"Don't be ridiculous, Phillip, your mother worships you."

He grinned, that engaging grin that had melted the hearts of women from eight months to eighty. "Of course she does. How could she help it? But that doesn't mean she'll sacrifice your happiness for my well-being. Think about it, Ferris."

"Think about what?" she said irritably. "I don't happen to get along with Patrick Blackheart. I don't approve of him—does that make it a federal crime?"

"You've got a bleeding heart, Ferris. You approve of ax murderers when they're properly repentant. There's something else, and—"

"Phillip, I think you're the one who's overtired," she interrupted ruthlessly. "You're making a mountain out of a molehill. If you want to talk about this, in depth, we can do so tomorrow when I've had more rest. All right?"

He gave her his charming, rueful smile. "I'd like that, darling, I really would. But I've got to be in Santa Cruz for the next three days, and then Sacramento, and then—"

"Never mind. I'll be coming back to work for you now that the Puffin Ball is finished." Something in his expression alerted her. "Won't I, Phillip?"

"Yes," he allowed. "Though perhaps not in the same capacity. But we can always—"

"Why not? I like being administrative assistant." Her voice was getting a little shrill, and she quickly toned it down.

"Of course you do," he said soothingly. "And I love having you there—there's no one I count on more. But Jack Reginald has a son in need of a job, and—"

"And Jack Reginald is making substantial contributions to your upcoming campaign," Ferris said lightly.

"You understand the political facts of life as well as anyone, Ferris. You scratch my back and I'll scratch yours, and that sort of thing."

"I understand completely," she said, her voice calm and accepting. "And you're right, I am dead tired. Why don't you give me a call this week when you have a chance, and we can work something out?"

"I'll call you Sunday at—"

"I won't be in Sunday," she broke in. "I have other plans."

"When will you be in, then?" he managed to look both hurt and forgiving at the same time. A talented man, was Phillip Merriam, she mused.

"I don't know. You'll just have to keep trying till you get me."

He stood there, still in the doorway, half in her apartment, half out, half in her life, half out, and Ferris fingered her diamond ring, considering her options. She'd never been a fool, and practicality told her not to make a move she might later regret. Even though deep in her heart of hearts she knew that move would have to be made, and soon, tonight was not the night. She left the ring in place. For now.

"Well," he said finally, his usual urbanity wiping out his temporary frustration. "Well. You get some sleep, then, darling. I'll somehow manage to squeeze a few days out toward the end of the week, or maybe early next week, and we'll go someplace. How does that sound?"

"Just fine."

"Do have a glass of Dubonnet. It will help you relax."

She looked up quite fearlessly into his clear blue eyes. "I," she said, "don't like Dubonnet."

"Well," he said. "Well. Good night, then." He still seemed uncharacteristically uncertain, and Ferris felt a moment's sympathy. Reaching up on her toes, she kissed that sweet-smelling, smooth-shaven cheek. And there was no way she could fool herself into thinking it wasn't good-bye.

"Good night, Phillip."

His footsteps clattered down the two flights of stairs. She stood there at the open door for a long moment, then shut it after the disappearing sound of his departure. She looked at the three locks for a moment, reached for them, then dropped her hand, shrugging. Nothing would keep Blackheart out if he wanted to get in. Not that he would, ever again. It had been a dangerous few days, and part of her had found it irresistibly attractive, playing with fire. But it was safely over now, and she could go back to living her life.

Blackie had no intention of spending the fogbound night in her apartment. She met his look of haughty demand with an affectionate scratch behind the ears, and then he was out on her terrace and gone a moment later. For a moment she considered leaving the door open a crack. It was cool—about fifty degrees outside—but the air was refreshing to her flushed cheeks. She could always huddle under a blanket for warmth.

She kicked off her heels and let her bare feet sink into the carpet. Phillip was right; Phillip was always right. What was she going to do without him telling her what she needed? She did need her bed, and she needed a drink to take the edge off the nervous energy that was still sparking through her. Whenever she closed her eyes she could see Blackheart's eyes, watching her, following her, wanting her? Damn, but he gave up easily.

She must be more tired than she thought, to have regretted his sudden lack of interest. She trailed out into the kitchen, poured herself a small glass of Drambuie and wandered back into the darkened living room. Without bothering to turn on the lights, she curled up on the sofa. Like a fool she'd left the Brie out when she'd taken off with Trace and Blackheart hours earlier, and Blackie had made a hearty meal of most of it. He'd even been piggy enough to sample a few crackers, but obviously found them less than entrancing.

Reaching forward, Ferris took a non-felined cracker and bit into it, following it with a sip of the sweet, rich Drambuie. A trip to her sister Cecilia's might be a good idea. Cecilia could be counted on for her good sense, her warmth and her marvelous ability to give a person space. A week

spent at her ramshackle farmhouse, surrounded by half a dozen nieces and
nephews in all shapes and sizes, with the soothing example of Cecilia's and
Joe's love for each other and their numerous offspring, and she should be
able to view her life with a better sense of reality.

The sound of the buzzer startled her out of her pleasant reverie. Leaning
back she stared at her blank white door for a long moment. Of course it could
be Phillip, come back to have his wicked way with her. He'd looked more
than faintly disgruntled when he'd left, maybe he thought it was time to show
her who was boss. This time she would give him his ring.

Or maybe it was the police, come to tell her that Blackheart, Inc., had
never showed up at the Mark Hopkins suite of the Honorable Miss
Smythe-Davies and was now wanted for grand larceny.

Or maybe it was Blackheart himself, come to tell her he loved her and renew that whimsical offer of marriage. No, that was the one person it wouldn't
be. He wouldn't bother to ring the bell, he'd just come right in.

The bell rang again, interrupting her lazy thoughts. Whoever it was, she
wasn't about to get up from her comfortable perch on the love seat. If she
could help it, she wasn't going to stand on her feet for twenty-four hours. She
could crawl into her bed.

One more ring. She considered it, then shrugged. If it was a rapist—ax
murderer, he would doubtless find a way to get in anyway. Right now she
really didn't give a damn. "Come in," she called in a throaty voice. "It's
open." And she took another sip of her Drambuie.

There was a long pause on the other side of the door, and then it opened.
And Blackheart stood there, a package in one hand, a furious expression on
his face.

IT HAD BEEN A struggle for him, all night long. Blackheart wasn't used to
being consumed by jealousy, he wasn't used to giving a damn. He wasn't so
egocentric that he had to have every woman who didn't want him. When he
was turned down, as every man was now and then, he usually shrugged his
shoulders and looked further. But the more Francesca Berdahofski dodged,
feinted, refused, insulted, fought, and struggled, the more determined he
became.

He still couldn't figure out why he'd said that to her on the wide, busy
staircase. Just to see the shock widen her eyes? Except that he'd been even
more shocked. He'd never proposed to a woman in his life, never even been
tempted. Yet the moment the words were out of his mouth, he hadn't wanted
to recall them. In fact, he'd wanted to throw the troublesome wench over his
shoulder like something out of an Errol Flynn movie and carry her out of that
house, and be damned to her charming senator and her idiotic pretensions.

Phillip Merriam hadn't made things any easier. He'd been so damned decent, so revoltingly good-fellowship that Blackheart really had been tempted
to rip out his tongue. If Blackheart was anywhere near the decent human

being he tried to be, he would have then and there renounced his designs on Francesca Berdahofski's luscious body. But decency was in short supply nowadays. He could keep his hands off the Von Emmerling emeralds, but he couldn't keep his hands off Francesca.

He'd left Kate and Trace at the Mark Hopkins. Neither of them was looking particularly happy, but he racked that up to their tangled relationship. If he were the meddling kind, he'd drop a hint in Trace's inattentive ear. But then, maybe Trace knew, and figured that ignoring it was the kindest way to deal with Kate's languishing glances. Maybe.

He'd swung by his apartment, changing out of that damned monkey suit. He hated full dress nowadays. For so long it had been his working costume. He couldn't put on a tuxedo without remembering other nights, long ago, and his hands would start sweating.

He still hadn't decided how big a fool he was being. He'd probably get to Francesca's ridiculous little apartment and find Phillip Merriam in that over-size bed. And then what would he do? Slink away into the fog like a beaten dog? Or maybe rip out Phillip's tongue.

Tonight wasn't a night for a touch of B and E, just on the off chance that the good senator had finally chosen to initiate his virgin bride. He took the two flights of steps slowly, silently, unaccountably nervous. Would she be asleep already? Would she glare at him out of those green eyes? Was he being ridiculously sentimental? Maybe he should turn around, give it a few days.

Damn, he was acting like an adolescent boy on his first date. His hands were sweating for sure now, and shaking just a tiny bit as he reached for the bell. There was no way he could wait any longer. Push had come to shove, and he wasn't going to sleep until he knew that she was irrevocably in love with the good senator. Not that he could blame her. Any woman with good sense would be. The man was handsome, rich, charming, friendly, and possessed of a great mother. What did a man with a past like John Patrick Blackheart have to offer in comparison? As he rang the bell again, the box beneath his arm suddenly felt very heavy. Where the hell was she?

BLACKHEART HAD changed his clothes, Ferris noticed. He was wearing jeans again, and his boots, and the black, body-hugging turtleneck beneath a corduroy jacket. She had never liked turtleneck shirts on men, but on Blackheart the effect was absolutely demoralizing. She wondered what he was angry about now.

"Why didn't you lock your door?" he demanded crossly, shutting the heavy door behind him and snapping each lock, including the chain. "Don't you realize there are dangerous criminals out there, waiting to prey on people like you?"

"It didn't seem worth the trouble. In the past four years the only person who's broken into the place has been you. And I knew those locks wouldn't keep you out."

"Certainly not these flimsy ones," he scoffed. "A stoned-out junkie with a credit card could get through those locks."

"Why would a stoned-out junkie have a credit card?" Ferris inquired prosaically.

"That's beside the point. Where's the good senator?" He moved toward her then, with his usual feline grace.

"Not here. What do you want, Blackheart? I thought we were finished with our dealings. Did the emeralds get safely back to Miss Smythe-Davies?"

"I wouldn't be here if they didn't."

"No, you wouldn't," she mused. "What's in the box?"

Blackheart pulled it out from under his arm, looking at it as if he'd never seen it before. "A present for you."

"From whom?"

"From me, of course. Don't just recline there like Cleopatra waiting for an asp," he snapped. He tossed the box to her, and she caught it expertly. "Open it."

She held it in her hand, weighing it, and her green eyes were extremely wary. "What is it? A time bomb? I don't hear any ticking."

"I sent the time bomb to the senator," he said. "May I have a drink? It's been a long night."

"Help yourself." She still didn't move, just stared down at the rectangular box. "My feet hurt too much to get up."

A moment later he was back, a glass of whisky in one hand, and he tossed his jacket across a chair before sitting down beside her, at the opposite end of the love seat. She had to pull her feet up, and she eyed him with a mixture of suspicion and wariness. If she didn't know better she'd say he was nervous. Maybe it *was* a time bomb. Or a rattlesnake. She shook the box again, but only a quiet thud rewarded her straining ears.

"It won't bite, Francesca," he said quietly. "Consider it a farewell present. Open it."

"You going somewhere?" she inquired in a desultory voice as she pulled at the wrappings.

"I hadn't planned to. What about you? Have you and the good senator set a date yet?" He took a sip of his drink, and his hand shook slightly. He was nervous, Ferris thought with amazement.

The brown paper came off, and the box underneath it read Ramon's. She looked up at him. "Ramon's what?" she queried lightly, mystified.

"Open it," he said again.

It was a pair of red shoes. The most beautiful red shoes she'd ever seen, made of shiny, metallic crimson, with high stacked heels, diamond buckles and no toes. There were little metal taps on the heel and toe, and she turned to look at Blackheart, her face very still.

He cleared his throat. "The taps are for when you dance. You're supposed to click them against the floor, and—"

"I know what the taps are for." Her voice was very quiet in the darkened room. "Why?"

He didn't pretend to misunderstand. "I thought you ought to have something to remind you of Francesca Berdahofski when you're Mrs. Senator Merriam."

The shoes lay in her lap, and she stared down at them. She was used to tears. She cried when she was frightened, she cried when she was unhappy. But she couldn't understand why she felt like crying right then, why the tears were stinging her eyelids, burning the back of her throat, taking control of her body so that she sat there and shook, imperceptibly, as Blackheart watched her out of distant eyes.

She felt him rise from the love seat, saw the strong, beautiful hand place the empty whiskey glass on the coffee table in front of her. "Good-bye, Ferris," he said gently, leaning over to kiss her cheek. "Have a good life."

His lips brushed her cheek gently, and he could taste the dampness on his lips. He drew back, startled, as she turned her tear-streaked face up to him. "Don't call me Ferris," she said with great, hiccupping sobs. "I hate that damned name."

"Francesca . . ." She could feel his hand on her shoulder, the fingers strong and warm on her bare skin.

She raised her head. "And don't you dare leave me," she added, her voice raw with tears. "Don't you dare."

It was too dark in the room to see his face through her blur of tears, but his voice was clear, with a thread of warm laughter running through it. "Oh, love, I wouldn't think of it." And he drew her weeping body off the couch.

Chapter Fifteen

SHE TUMBLED INTO his arms, the tears coming faster and more freely. She could feel the tender laughter shake his strong body as he held her there, the two of them in a tangle on the floor, trapped between the love seat and the coffee table. Gentle hands held her, cradled her against that smooth chest, as she wept furiously.

It was a very long time before the storm of tears abated. One long finger reached up and brushed her tears away, and when they had finally slowed he shifted to a more comfortable position, holding her shivering body in his arms as he kicked the table away from them and leaned back against the sofa.

"Such a great many tears," he whispered against her cloud of hair. "Did the good senator jilt you?"

She managed a watery chuckle. "Pig," she said comfortably. "I'm about to jilt the good senator. How do you do this to me, Blackheart?"

"Well, first I get you off balance, then I pull you into my arms, and then—" his mouth feathered hers "—I kiss you. Not too hard—" he did it again, lingering a moment "—just enough to distract you. Then I move my hand, like this " His strong hand moved up to cup her chin, holding it gently in place as he kissed her again, and this time, when his soft, tempting lips left hers, she emitted a tiny moan, her tears forgotten. "And then, when I think you're ready for it, I kiss you again. A little longer, a little deeper." His mouth dropped once more onto hers, nibbling, tantalizing, the gentle pressure of his fingers on her jaw opening her mouth beneath his.

Slowly, delicately, his tongue slid into her mouth, gently exploring the secrets of the soft interior, and for the moment she lay quiescent against him, glorying in the feel of him. With the gentle prompting of his tongue she began to kiss him back, sliding her bare arms around his neck and meeting him thrust for thrust, the glorious hot wetness of their mouths causing tremors of desire to twist and turn through her body.

She could feel his hand fumbling in front of her, and a moment later the neckline plunged to its lowest level, the silver cord loosely entwined in Blackheart's clever fingers. Reluctantly he pulled his mouth away from hers. "There," he said, his voice rich with satisfaction. "I've been wanting to do that since I first saw you tonight. Covering up all that beautiful flesh is a crime against nature." Leaning down, his hot, wet mouth traced random, teasing patterns along the tops of her almost exposed breasts as his hands cupped their lush fullness.

Ferris moaned, deep in the back of her throat, and arched against his hand and mouth. The silky covering was frustration beyond bearing, but she didn't know how to tell him.

There was no need. Another gentle tug of the silken cord, and the dress tumbled to her waist. His warm, damp mouth followed, catching one hardened peak with practiced care as his hand tended the other. His tongue swirled, teased, enticed, and she could feel a knot of wanting so strong that hurt twisted deep inside her, between her legs. She could feel him beneath her soft hips, hard and pulsing against her tender, silk-covered flesh, and the knot twisted again, so that she cried out with the pain of it.

She wanted him with a longing she'd never felt before. She wanted his warm bare skin beneath her fingers, smooth and hot and hard beneath her mouth, she wanted him above her, beneath her, around her and in her, she wanted to melt into the golden wonder of his body and never escape. She wanted him and she didn't know what to do.

Slowly, reluctantly, his mouth moved from her breast, leaving a warm wet path across her exposed skin as he reached for her mouth again. This time she was more than ready for him, kissing him with all the passion and aching love that had been locked away for too long.

When he finally broke away he was as breathless as she was, and his heartbeat thudded against her hand. His eyes were staring down into hers with dreamy desire, a desire that matched hers, a desire she could no longer control.

"Will you go to bed with me, Francesca?" he asked, the words slow and quiet and very distinct.

She wanted to sink against him with a helpless sigh, she wanted to fill his mouth with hers so that there'd be no more room for words. But she owed him more than that. "Yes, Blackheart. Please. Take me to bed and show me what it can be like."

He was very strong indeed. He lifted her effortlessly in his arms, rising from their cramped position on the floor with fluid grace. He moved through the darkened, twisting apartment with the eyes of a cat, with never a misstep. The first gray light of dawn was spreading over the city as he drew her down on the bed, and his hands were gentle as he settled her among the tumbled pillows.

Slowly, deftly, his hands withdrew down the length of her body, bringing the silky gown with him. He tossed it on the floor with a disregard worthy of Ferris at her most slothful, and stood there at the foot of the bed, watching her out of warm, wanting eyes.

She could feel the intensity of his gaze washing over her, her long legs, the skimpy swathe of silken panties across her hips, the smooth torso with its gently curved stomach and her full, aching breasts.

He stripped the turtleneck over his head with one swift move, kicking off his boots as he did so. She looked away as he reached for his belt buckle, and the sound of his soft laughter mingled with the rasp of the zipper, the rough slide of denim against flesh.

"Such a chicken," he chided, and in the morning twilight she dared a furtive peek at him. "Haven't you ever seen *Playgirl?*" He slid into bed with her, dropping his jeans within easy reach beside the bed.

With sudden nervousness she nodded, keeping her eyes firmly fastened to his face and nowhere lower.

"Well, I'm just like them," he said, and his hands began a warm, reassuring stroking along her bare arm.

"There seems to be a lot more of you," she said gruffly.

Leaning over, he kissed her gently on the mouth. "Nothing more than you can handle, I promise you."

"Are you sure?" Her voice was plainly doubtful, and she cast a nervous, scuttling glance downward before returning to his face.

Slowly, carefully, so as not to frighten her, his hand slid down her arm until he reached her wrist. He brought her hand to his mouth, kissing each trembling finger, one by one, letting his tongue gently caress her palm. And then he placed her open, relaxed hand on his chest, letting her become accustomed to the feel of his flesh against her, the muscle and hardness. Slowly he moved her hand downward, sensitive to her slightest hesitation. Her eyes met his, mesmerized, as he brought her hand down to meet his swollen cock.

The quick intake of breath was his own, and when he opened his eyes again she was smiling at him. "There," he breathed. "That's not so bad, is it?"

She shook her head. He released her wrist, but her hand stayed where it was, the fingers cool and curious on his fevered skin. Slowly she encircled him, tugging gently, and he moaned softly.

She pulled away, suddenly skittish. "Did I hurt you?"

With a lazy smile he shook his head, recapturing her curious hand. "It feels very good," he whispered against her lips. "Too good." And he moved his hands to her waiting body, encircling her waist with his long deft fingers. They traced a path across her gently rounded stomach, slid inside the skimpy bikini panties and drew them downward over her unresisting legs.

"Oh, love," he breathed, "you are so very beautiful." Gently, carefully he nuzzled her full breasts as his hands moved back up her legs, sliding inexorably toward their ultimate goal.

He found her then, one large, strong hand reaching the damp, heated core of her, and she bit back a cry of part frustration, part joy, part unadulterated panic. Her legs instinctively clamped together, and her hands left the delights of his body to ward him off.

He was prepared for the panic. One hand caught her wrists in a gentle but unbreakable grip, and he threw a strongly muscled leg over hers, pulling them apart. She whimpered, struggling for a moment, and then she saw the stark whiteness of the scar along the length of his leg. There were two of them, running parallel from mid-calf to mid-thigh. And suddenly the fight left her. This was Blackheart, her nemesis, a man who had somehow managed to get closer to her than any human being outside her family ever had. And he was about to get even closer.

"Let go of my hands," she whispered. He must have felt the change, felt the tension leave her. He released her wrists, and she twined her arms around his waist, pulling herself up close to him, pressing her breasts against the smooth planes of his chest, pressing her trembling hips against that frightening, enticing arousal, pressing her mouth hungrily against his, giving and receiving a kiss that was a release in itself, and this time when his hand slid down over the gentle curve of her hip she turned for him, opening her legs at his gentle urging.

She hadn't known it could be so sweet. His hands were clever, so clever, and she could feel that burning need within her escalate out of control, until she knew she'd explode if she had to wait any longer. She touched him, and he was as damp as she was. She looked up through a haze of desire, puzzled, and his warm laugh shook against her swollen breasts.

"It's just me, wanting you," he said softly, his lips brushing hers, and she smiled against his mouth.

"Me too," she whispered. "Now, Blackheart. Please." Her voice was plaintive, polite, and he kissed her again.

"In a moment." Once more his hand reached down, the gentle, insinuating strokes preparing her for a more overwhelming invasion. She arched against his hand, her eyes closed, her senses slipping away.

And then his body covered her, and she could feel him against her, hard and strong and needful. She wasn't expecting the pain, the sharp burning of stubbornly resisting flesh. Her quiet moan turned into a whimper as he pressed against her, and she could feel his hands on her hips, holding her still for his steady invasion. When he came to rest, deep inside her, he was panting, beads of sweat sparkling against the dark planes of his face, and his tawny brown eyes were sorrow-filled.

"I didn't want to hurt you," he whispered, and she could feel the tension in his body, the rigid control in his muscles as he held himself above her.

Already the pain had begun to recede, in its place a wonderful lassitude that overlay that still-burning need that she didn't quite understand. She smiled up at him, love and longing all mixed up in a dazed, dreamy expression. "It's okay," she murmured. "It's more than okay. It's . . . very . . . nice." The words drifted in a gasp of pleasure as he began to move, as his iron control began to melt within the heat of her body. The hands that held her hips slid down and wrapped her legs around him, and his mouth caught hers in a searing kiss.

And she was lost, lost in the tumble of flesh, pulsing heat and aching want that somehow coalesced through the shifting, pounding rhythms of his body and hers. She was there, floating, dreaming, awash in a current of slumbering sensual wanderings, when suddenly it peaked, and she was gone, exploding into some starry universe with only Blackheart for safety.

In the distance she felt him collapse against her, felt the shudders rack his body, heard the distant echo of his voice. What had he said to her, when she was consumed in that fiery tumult? She could no longer hear the distant echo of the words.

But the vast sense of well-being had washed over her body and now enveloped her in a cocoon that was too strong to be denied. Her low wail of despair when he gently extricated himself from her embrace was greeted with a low, loving laugh.

"I'll be right back, love," he whispered. She was too sleepy and too peaceful to open her eyes, to ask him where he was going. She heard the water running in the bathroom, and then he was back beside her, traversing the huge bed with far more grace than she usually managed.

"What're you doing?" she murmured sleepily.

"Administering first aid." A cool, wet cloth was placed between her legs, and then he drew her into the circle of his arms, her head resting naturally against his shoulder. "Poor angel," he murmured. "Are you feeling battered?"

"Gloriously abused," she murmured sleepily against his smooth skin. "Are you going to make a habit of this?" The moment the sleepy words were out of her mouth she could have bit her tongue. She had been determined not to make demands her body and soul and heart craved. But it was hard to be strong and independent when you were lying in your lover's arms.

If Blackheart felt her withdrawal, he didn't comment on it. "As often as I can. Would you fancy a pair of green shoes next?"

She should have been furious. Instead she giggled. His strong hand reached up and brushed the tumbled hair away from her flushed, sleepy face. "I like to hear you laugh. You should do it more often." He kissed her nose. "Do you have any regrets?"

"Fishing for compliments, Blackheart?"

"Just curious."

"You're asking me if I should have surrendered my virginity on my wedding night to a rich, handsome man who happens to love me, rather than lose it to a sneak thief who's offered me nothing." She said it baldly.

"Don't forget the shoes," he said lightly, but she could feel the tension in his arms. "Answer me, Francesca. Are you sorry you didn't give the good senator his pound of flesh?"

She smiled against his sweat-damp skin. How unlike Blackheart to need reassurance. She never would have thought he'd suffer from a guilty conscience. "No."

"No?" he echoed.

"No, I don't regret it. No, I don't wish I'd waited for Phillip. I'm content. Blissfully, gloriously content." She snuggled closer and felt the tension leave his body as his arm drew her even closer.

They were silent for a while, and Ferris was almost asleep when his warm, sweet voice broke through her lethargy. "You forgot to ask."

"Forgot to ask what?" she murmured.

"You don't want to end up like your brothers and sisters, do you? Or did you do something about it?"

"No." Ferris was suddenly wide awake, pulling her protesting body out of his arms in sudden horror. "Oh, God, no! I forgot all about it."

Blackheart laughed, a heartless laugh. "That must be a first for you."

"This isn't a laughing matter, Blackheart. It's just the wrong time of month, and I—"

"Hush, love." He was still laughing, and his hands were gentle as he pulled her back to him. "There's nothing to worry about. I took care of it."

"You did? Why didn't I notice?" She nestled back against him, still doubtful.

"You were, uh, otherwise occupied. Don't worry, sweetheart—next time I'll let you help me."

"Are you sure . . . ?"

"I'm sure, love." Reaching down, he rummaged through the jeans he'd dropped beside the bed, and a moment later half a dozen silver packets rained down on her. "Satisfied?"

"Silly question," she murmured, her hand drifting lazily downward across his stomach. She watched with interest as the muscles contracted. "Blackheart?"

"Mmmmh?"

"Thank you."

He looked down at her, a lazy smile lighting his face. "My pleasure, love. My pleasure."

SHE DIDN'T WANT to hear the pounding. She felt too good, lying curled up against Blackheart's warm skin, his arm possessive around her sleeping body. She didn't know when they'd gone to sleep the final time—there wasn't a clock in sight and she hadn't really cared. Her body ached in a thousand places, she ought to get up and have a long soak in the tub, but she had no intention of moving until she absolutely had to. The last thing she wanted was for reality to intrude.

But the damned pounding continued, and she felt Blackheart stir beside her. "Who's that?" he whispered against her ear, his tongue making tiny, darting forays that were stirring fires better left banked, given her physical condition.

"Nobody I want to see," she replied, moving closer and pressing up against him. "They can't know we're here. Let's just pretend we went to Australia."

Blackheart looked disturbed and overwhelmingly young in the late morning light. His long brown hair was rumpled around his sleepy face, and the white quilt they'd thrown over them sometime during the night made his tanned skin stand out in golden contrast.

But at that moment the pounding ceased, and Ferris breathed a sigh of relief. "It was the landlord, wanting to know if I had a man in here," she said, pushing him back against the sheets.

"And do you?" he questioned mischievously.

She slid her hand down across the flat plane of his stomach to brush against him tantalizingly. "I guess I do," she admitted with an air of wonder. "That's quite a surprise." She moved her hand back up, across the surface of his chest. "You're too skinny," she observed. "Very strong, but too skinny."

"I know the cause of that," he replied, nibbling on her exposed arm. "Not enough cannoli."

"Blackheart," she said, filled with an overwhelming emotion that felt uncomfortably close to love. "I—"

The pounding began again, louder than before, and Blackheart jumped, swearing, and pulled away from her. "I'm going to see who the hell it is," he said, grabbing his pants and crawling back down the bed. "And then I'll give you the attention you deserve."

"Blackheart, no!" she wailed, jumping up and heading after him. "You can't answer my door looking like that." She grabbed a robe and yanked it on, reaching the living room just as he was opening the last lock. His jeans were zipped but unbuttoned, his bare chest had a few artistic scratches that she hadn't realized she'd contributed, and there was little doubt as to what the two of them had been doing. "What if it's somebody?" she hissed.

The look he gave her would have quelled a sterner soul. "I expect it is," he said calmly, unhooking the chain and flinging the door open. Ferris held her breath, expecting Phillip, expecting Regina, expecting God knew who. But not expecting the small, dapper man who stood there, temper darkening an already overtanned face.

"Rupert," Blackheart said numbly, pulling the door open to let him storm in. "What's wrong?"

"What's wrong?" the angry man demanded. "What's wrong, you ask me? What the hell isn't wrong? You had to pick last night of all nights to do a disappearing act. Let me tell you, kid, your timing couldn't be better. Couldn't you have kept your pants on until the damned job was finished?"

Ferris flinched, looking anxiously from Blackheart's suddenly still face to the angry man in front of her. "Since no one's making introductions," she said with a last attempt at calm, "would you mind telling me who you are?"

"I'm Rupert Munz," he snapped. "And I'm this idiot's lawyer."

"Lawyer?" she echoed, her voice a little rusty. "Why were you looking for Blackheart?"

"Because, Ms. Byrd, his partner was arrested last night for grand larceny. And the San Francisco police department are greatly interested in Patrick Blackheart's whereabouts."

"Grand larceny?" Ferris echoed, a horrid sense of déjà vu washing over her.

Blackheart had a grim expression on his face. "The Von Emmerling emeralds."

"There's nothing wrong with your thought processes," Rupert snapped. "And at least you had a good alibi. She'll testify?" A jerk of his head indicated Ferris, and Blackheart's eyes followed meditatively. She knew what her face looked like, mistrust and condemnation wiping out the last trace of warmth. He'd used her, and she hated him for it.

She could tell by the darkening of his face that he read her reactions clearly. Turning back to Rupert, he shrugged. "I don't know. Do you think it will come to that?"

Rupert frowned. "Who can say? They had a very nasty look on their faces when they questioned me about you. You may be about to have your first experience with the American penal system."

"No," he said sharply. "I told myself when I got out of prison in England that I'd never go back; I'll be damned if I let them pick me up when I haven't been doing a thing."

"I don't know if you'll have any say in the matter. Not if you want to help Trace," Rupert said heavily. "You can disappear for a while and leave Trace holding the bag, or . . ." He let the sentence trail off.

"Trace is as innocent as a lamb—he doesn't belong in jail, and you know it as well as I do. Has bail been set?" Blackheart snapped.

"Not yet. I was on my way back there when I thought I'd check here. Kate said you might be here. She's pretty upset, Patrick."

"I imagine she is." He was still staring at Ferris's shuttered face. "What do you want me to do?"

"Stay put. I'll check on what sort of evidence they have—they probably won't arrest you without something to go by. Unless they're so happy to finally be able to pin something on you that they don't bother with such technicalities. You don't need to worry—if they do, I'll slap a false arrest charge on them so fast their heads will spin."

"I don't know if that's reassuring," Blackheart said, his eyes grim.

"Don't worry about it. I'll see if I can get them to drop the charges before they actually arrest you. But keep out of sight. Let her answer the phone, the door, whatever."

She could feel those tawny brown eyes on her averted face. "I'm not sure if Ferris is willing to be Bonnie to my Clyde," he drawled. "I'll be in touch, Rupert."

Rupert opened his mouth to protest, then shut it again. "Don't let him answer the door," he ordered Ferris sharply. "Not if you don't want to see him in jail."

There was dead silence in the apartment when the door closed behind Rupert's dapper figure. Ferris kept her face averted, the old terry-cloth robe pulled tightly around her as she turned to head down the two narrow stairs to the kitchen. Her sense of betrayal was so strong that it tore at her body, engulfing her in pain that left her numb and shaken. Blackheart didn't move, but she could feel his eyes intent on her narrow back.

"Rupert was making too many assumptions," he said finally.

Somewhere she found a rusty semblance of her voice. "What was that?"

"That you don't want to see me in jail. I get the feeling you'd be very happy to see me locked up right now, with the key thrown away."

She couldn't even trust herself to look at him, much less deny his gentle accusation. "Would you make me a cup of coffee before I go?" he said suddenly.

She had no choice but to turn at that, and the look on her face was cold and angry. "You're going to abandon Trace after all," she accused him. "You're going to run off and leave him bearing the blame."

She had never seen such a look on any man's face. It was as cold and still as death, and she stumbled backward against the kitchen door in sudden panic.

An unpleasant smile curved his mouth. "I won't hit you, Ferris," he drawled. "Much as you deserve it. And you can believe what you want to believe. I'm not going to sit around and wait for the police to find me, and I'm not going to give you the chance to turn me in. I'm going out to find out who did take the emeralds, and when I find them I'm going to shove them down your throat." He brushed past her on the way to the bedroom, and she controlled the urge to flinch away. Just as she controlled the urge to fling her arms around his sleek, muscled body and beg him to tell her he was innocent.

She was still standing there when he emerged, black turtleneck pulled over his tousled head, boots on his feet, his jacket slung over his shoulder. "No coffee?" he drawled. "Nothing to send the weary felon on his way? Not even a good-bye kiss or a simple question? Such as, did you do it, Blackheart? Not that I'd find that element of doubt reassuring, but it would be a hell of a lot better than instant condemnation."

"Did you, Blackheart?"

He stared at her for a long moment. "Damn you," he said succinctly.

The buzz of the doorbell shattered the tension. The two combatants stood there in the narrow hallway, motionless, condemning eyes watching the other. Ferris couldn't move, couldn't breathe, could only watch him with sudden desperation shattering her heart.

The bell buzzed again, impatiently, followed by a steady pounding. A wry smile lit Blackheart's bleak face. "It would appear the police have found me."

She ran a nervous tongue over suddenly dry lips. They felt bruised to the touch, bruised from Blackheart's mouth. "It might be someone else."

"Who else would be so vehement?" Blackheart murmured. "Don't answer the door, Francesca."

His use of her real name almost convinced her. "They know we're here," she whispered.

"They probably don't have a search warrant. Just give me enough time to climb out over the terrace. Come on, lady, don't be such a damned prude. Let me go. I don't want to end up in jail for something stupid like this. It's a matter of honor."

"Honor?" she echoed, her voice rich with bitter accusation. "You call it honorable to let your best friend take the blame for your robbery?"

He froze, and the last bit of emotion died from his eyes, leaving them cold and brown as winter leaves. "Answer the damned door, lady," he said savagely.

"I didn't say I wouldn't—"

"Answer the damned door. Or I will."

She couldn't move. She could only stand there under the force of his rage and inexplicable pain and wonder if she had made the very worst mistake of her life.

"Then I will." He moved past her, careful not to touch her body, and the locks melted beneath his practiced touch.

And still she stood there, as she heard the words drift past her. "You have the right to remain silent. If you give up that right . . ." And when she was finally alone again in her small apartment, when Blackheart had been marched away, those awful handcuffs on his beautiful wrists, when he'd gone without a backward glance, she'd stumbled back into her bedroom and fallen on the tumbled sheets, her heart and her eyes burning with pain and disillusionment and a doubt so horrifying that she pushed it resolutely away.

Chapter Sixteen

"REALLY, DEAR, I couldn't be more distressed," Regina Merriam murmured. "I can't imagine how such a thing could have happened. I've known Trace Walker for years now, and he's incapable of dishonesty."

"You can't say that about Blackheart," Ferris said in what she hoped was a desultory voice. They were having tea in a small coffee shop in the Mark Hopkins after doing their best to placate a semi-hysterical Miss Smythe-Davies, and Ferris wished they'd opted for the bar instead. In the three days since the robbery and the arrests, all hell had broken loose, for the Committee for Saving the Bay, for Senator Merriam and his staff—which included Ferris, in her own nebulous position, and his worried mother—and most particularly Blackheart, Inc. In the two years since Blackheart, Inc., had become society's darling there hadn't been a whisper of scandal about them. That halcyon reputation had come to an abrupt end.

"I wouldn't say that," Regina replied. "Despite his earlier manner of earning a living, I'd trust Patrick with my life."

"Yes, but would you trust him with your jewels?" Ferris countered. It was only through constant vigilance that she had kept her inexplicable feelings of guilt at bay, and if Regina had noticed her unusual hardheartedness, she tactfully ignored it.

"Absolutely. And if you thought about it, so would you. If he had taken the jewels, he certainly wouldn't have hung around waiting to get arrested. If he were the kind of man the police and you seem to think he is, he would have taken off the moment the theft was discovered and let poor Trace rot in jail all alone."

"I don't imagine Blackheart chose to get arrested," Ferris murmured cynically.

"Let me assure you, that if Blackheart had wanted to avoid getting arrested he would have. And even the police found they had nothing to hold him on. I think they just arrested him because they'd always wanted to. They just took the least little excuse they could find—"

"The disappearance of a fortune in emeralds is not a little excuse," Ferris said sternly.

"No, I suppose not. But I know in my heart of hearts that Blackheart didn't have a thing to do with it. And so would you if you were any judge of character. I just thank God he didn't have to spend the night in jail." Her patrician cheekbones were pink with indignation, and Ferris leaned forward to pat her hand.

"Sorry, Regina. I'm afraid when it comes to Blackheart I'm no judge of character at all." She sighed, taking a sip of her too-cool Hu Kwa. "Have you heard from Phillip recently?"

"Last night. He's distressed, of course, but handling it with his usual aplomb. He told me to tell you he'd be in touch next Sunday. He thought it would be best if he kept out of the Bay Area for the next week or so. That way he won't have to answer any impertinent questions."

Ferris smiled wearily. "But he's so good at dealing with impertinent questions."

"Better than Blackheart, certainly. I gather he punched a reporter from the *Chronicle*. Very unwise of him," Regina mused.

"Why did he do that? I'd missed that installment in this ridiculous soap opera."

"I gather the man was brash enough to ask Blackheart where he was the night of the robbery. Apparently he wasn't arrested till the next afternoon, and various people are wondering if he was off stashing the jewels someplace and leaving Trace to take the blame. They haven't turned up, you know."

"They will," Ferris said, with more wishful thinking than any grasp of the situation. She could remember the look on Blackheart's face when she'd suggested that he was going to abandon Trace, and knew with sudden clarity that when Blackheart had taken a swing at the reporter he'd been seeing her accusing face. She swallowed. "And then I'm sure it will become clear that Trace had nothing to do with it."

"And Blackheart, too," Regina said sharply. "I certainly hope so. In the meantime—"

"I was hoping I'd find you two ladies here," Olivia Summers's cool, arch tones broke into their conversation, and it was all Ferris could do to control the glare she wanted to direct in the tall blonde's direction. "Miss Smythe-Davies didn't seem any happier to see me than she was to see you. I thought I'd help placate her, but I didn't seem to get any further than you did."

Regina gave her a distant, welcoming smile. "Join us, won't you, Olivia? I expect Miss Smythe-Davies's shattered nerves are beyond mending. I'm afraid we were less than a success. It was sweet of you to try your luck."

"Forgive my frankness, Regina, but are you sure you picked the right committee member to accompany you?" Olivia slid into the seat with her customary smooth grace. "Not that you wouldn't be welcome, but given the circumstances I would have thought Miss Byrd would have been a less than wise choice."

Regina didn't even try to hide the amazement that washed over her beautiful, lined face. "What in the world are you talking about, Olivia? What circumstances?"

"Didn't you know?" Olivia managed an expression of embarrassed concern that was just a shade too perfect. "I realize the details of Patrick's arrest didn't make the papers, but I assumed since you were so intimately involved . . . I'm sorry, I've been indiscreet. Forget I said anything."

"I think I should," Regina snapped. "You know I don't care for malicious gossip, Olivia, particularly about my friends." Tossing the linen napkin down, she rose to her regal height, and even Olivia managed to look paltry. "I have things to do. Are you coming, Ferris?"

Ferris's wary green eyes went from Regina's disapproving expression to Olivia's sly smile. "I think I'll share a cup of tea with Olivia. Call me, Regina?"

"Certainly, dear." She kissed Ferris warmly on her cheek. The look she gave Olivia would have withered a less self-centered person. "And you, young lady, watch your tongue."

"She's a dear soul," Olivia said with a bite of acid as they watched Regina thread her way gracefully through the closely set tables. "It's a shame she has to be disillusioned."

"Does she?" Ferris sat very still, waiting for Olivia to strike.

"But of course. Even if she won't listen to me, someone, at some time, will tell her."

"Tell her what?"

"Tell her about Francesca Berdahofski," Olivia murmured. "Tell her where Blackheart spent the night when he was trying to establish an alibi and where he was arrested the next day, and then I doubt her fondness will extend enough to cover those particular transgressions. She's a sweet old lady, but I don't expect she'll enjoy being lied to. It has the tendency to make people feel like fools when they've been tricked. Most unwise of you, Miss Berdahofski." Her pink mouth curved in a pleased smile. "Tell me, does Phillip have any idea? I wouldn't think so, but the man has surprising depth. I would be surprised if he'd overlook the night of the Puffin Ball, however. I still can't imagine what Blackheart was doing there and not Phillip. Or were they both enjoying your rather earthy charms?"

That had pushed it too far. Up till then Ferris had sat there, misery and guilt washing over her. But belated pride made her snap her head up, and the look in her green eyes daunted even Olivia for a moment. A few little pieces of the puzzle had begun to fall into place. The unexpected arrival at Carleton House last Sunday. A tryst with more witnesses than she had expected. The Von Emmerling emeralds clasped around her skinny neck. Ferris smiled, a dangerous smile indeed.

"Nothing for me," Olivia told the waiter who'd just made his appearance. "I'm leaving." She rose, stretching gracefully, but Ferris wasn't fooled. Every muscle in her slender body was tense. "You might remember not to trust every ex-felon who tumbles you into bed, Francesca. I never got my recreational sex confused with real life. As good as Blackheart is in bed, security is better. And you've just lost both."

Ferris gave her more than enough time to leave. She sat there, sipping at her cold tea, thinking with careful deliberation. She had jumped to too many conclusions in the last three days—she should have enough sense not to jump again.

To be sure, only Blackheart had known her real name. He was beyond anger when they'd arrested him three short days ago. Would he have hit upon Olivia as the perfect revenge? But for all her doubts, Ferris had never suspected Blackheart of being vengeful. No, Olivia must have found out some other way.

Nothing would keep that mouth of hers quiet. But why did Olivia care, one way or the other? Who and what Ferris Byrd was and what she'd done seemed of little importance right now, compared to the burning question that had left her with little sleep and no appetite. If it hadn't been Blackheart, who had taken the emeralds?

She got only that damned recorded message when she called Blackheart, Inc. And when she called the only K. Christiansen in the phone book, she got no answer. That left her one place to check.

Blackheart's apartment was within walking distance, a pretty classy neighborhood for a retired cat burglar. If she called him, he might very well hang up; if she showed up, he could only slam the door in her face. But she couldn't wait any longer. More and more pieces of the puzzle were falling together. The only other person who knew about Francesca Berdahofski was Kate Christiansen. And Ferris needed to talk with Blackheart, to find out if her sudden, overwhelming suspicion was only wishful thinking.

It was a small narrow building on one of the cross streets. The disreputable Volvo, complete with a new passenger side window, was parked way down the street, and Ferris felt a sudden tightening in the pit of her stomach. Not an hour had passed in the last seventy-two without her remembering, her body feeling once again the silken slide of flesh within flesh, and her skin began to tingle.

Damn it, she wasn't going there to get tumbled into bed again, she reminded herself angrily. They were past that now—too much distrust had shattered what had always been too fragile a relationship. But she had to know whether she was manufacturing a scapegoat because she couldn't stand the thought of being used by him, or whether there was any chance that what she had begun to suspect was true.

The elevator was small and silent as it carried her up to the fifth floor, and it moved much too swiftly. She hadn't had time to get her composure in order before it spilled her out in the miniscule hallway. She stood there in front of 5B, hesitating, wondering if she shouldn't turn around and leave, when the damned door opened and Blackheart came out.

He didn't see her at first. When he did, his reaction wasn't promising. His eyes were shadowed, he looked as if he hadn't slept in days and his mouth was grim. He was wearing faded jeans, and she wondered briefly if they were the same pair that had resided by her bed so recently. The look he gave her was wary, unwelcoming, and she couldn't blame him.

"What are you doing here?" he demanded roughly. He hadn't closed the apartment door behind him yet, and Ferris thought she could see movement behind him. It looked like a woman.

Pain sliced through her like a knife. "Absolutely nothing," she mumbled, turning back and punching the elevator button. But the hall was too small for her to escape, the elevator had already stopped on the second floor and Blackheart just stood there looking at her.

"You must have had some reason for coming," he said coldly. "Did you want to see what hideous mark five hours of American prison left on my recalcitrant soul?"

"It doesn't matter now," she muttered, pushing the button again.

His hand closed over hers, pulling it away from the wall, and it was all she could do to control the little rush that went through her skin at his touch, no matter how impersonal it was. "Leave it alone," he said. "The elevator will come when it's ready. Have you come to apologize? Because if you have, you'd better save it. I'm not ready to accept it, so it would just be a waste of time."

"I didn't come to apologize," she shot back.

"All right, then what did you come for?"

She hesitated, trying to peer past him into the apartment. It couldn't be Olivia—not that fast. "Nothing important. Forget it."

"Don't be a pain, Francesca," he grumbled. "I'm going out for beer and sandwiches. Go on in and hold Kate's hand for me till I get back. She needs someone to talk to."

Kate, Ferris thought, relief washing over her, followed swiftly by determination. "All right."

"And when I get back, you can tell me what made a saintly character like you enter this den of thieves."

"I may not be here when you get back," she temporized, not liking the command in his hostile voice.

"You'd better be. Or I'll find you. And in case you don't remember, locked doors don't keep me out." The elevator finally chose that moment to arrive, and Ferris considered shoving him out of the way and bolting for it. But he was stronger than she was, and probably faster, and it would be an embarrassing waste of time. "I'll be here," she muttered gracelessly. And with a short nod he left her.

"Oh, no, just what I needed!" Kate greeted her from her curled-up position on the sofa. "What made Patrick think you could be of any help?"

Ferris paused just inside the doorway, surveying the room and its inhabitant with real curiosity. If she'd had to imagine how Blackheart lived, she never would have guessed with any degree of acumen. It was uncomfortably like her own apartment, from the haphazard piles of books and magazines to the rich, deep colors of the Oriental rugs on the hardwood floors. His furniture was bigger, and seemed a great deal more comfortable, and the paintings on his walls were modem and original, not copies of old French masters. But the room was surprisingly welcoming, warm and comfortable and aesthetically pleasing. Despite the lump of angry female flesh smack dab in the middle of it.

Kate had commandeered the blue sofa. She had a thousand used tissues scattered around her, a half full box in her lap, a cup of coffee with a cigarette floating in it on the table beside her and red swollen eyes above her belligerent pout. The look she gave Ferris was more than baleful, it was positively filled with hate. It was such an overreaction, as a matter of fact, that Ferris wondered if that was fear beneath the petulance. Or was she still just looking for what she wanted to see?

Kate's unprepossessing greeting didn't augur well for the time Blackheart was gone, but then, Ferris didn't particularly care about Kate's comfort, or her own for that matter. What she cared for was the truth.

Closing the door behind her, she advanced into the room. "I don't imagine he thought I'd be much good at all. He doesn't have much use for me right now."

Kate laughed—a coarse, humiliating laugh—as she dabbed at her reddened nose. "Oh, he has a use for you, all right. But I don't think it's what you have in mind, Miss Prissy Pants. Women like you make me sick. All your gold jewelry and your designer suits and you think that makes you better than the rest of us."

Yes, it was definitely fear lurking in the back of those red-rimmed eyes. Ferris sat down in the rocking chair opposite Kate, crossing her slender ankles and leaning back. "You know as well as I do that I wasn't born to gold jewelry and designer suits. You needn't have such a chip on your shoulder."

"What do you mean?" Kate was definitely edgy now, and the tissues lay forgotten in her lap.

"Blackheart had you check me out before he took the case. You must have been the one to tell Olivia Summers about my background," Ferris said easily, wishing she smoked—it would help her nervous edginess if she could toy with a cigarette. "I don't understand why you told her where Blackheart spent the night, though."

"I don't know what you're talking about. I don't even know Olivia Summers," she said staunchly.

"Certainly you do. You were watching her wrap her skinny little body around Trace Walker just three nights ago."

"What?" Kate looked ghastly, her face papery white around her red-rimmed eyes.

"You didn't notice that I was there, too. You weren't surprised at the little scene you interrupted, but you weren't unmoved, either. I saw your expression, Kate. You were mad as hell."

"I still don't know what you're talking about." Kate's voice was hoarse with pain and fear.

"What I don't understand is why, if you hate her so much, did you help her steal the emeralds?" Ferris said. A movement beyond the sofa drew her attention, and she saw that Blackheart, with his customary silence, had returned.

Kate must have felt his presence, for she swiveled around on the sofa, tears falling afresh.

Here it comes, Ferris thought. *Now he's going to kick me out for sure.*

Blackheart moved forward, taking Kate's plump hand in his, and his tawny eyes were dark with sadness. "Yes, Kate. Why did you help her?"

She fought it for a moment. "You can't believe what that stupid lying woman says. She's the one who turned you in to the police, remember? She's just jealous, trying to distract you so you won't think—"

"Why, Kate?" he repeated calmly, and her last bit of self-control vanished. She burst into loud, ugly sobs, her face crumpled in pain and shame. Ferris sat very still, wishing she were any place but right there as Blackheart moved around the sofa to take Kate in his arms. She was embarrassed, and she was stupidly, painfully jealous. Ferris wanted Blackheart's arms around *her*, she wanted to weep against the white cotton shirt and feel his soothing hands sweep down her back. Maybe he had some cigarettes lying around.

For a moment, Blackheart's eyes met hers over the weeping figure. She couldn't read their expression: She could only tell that it wasn't condemnation or dismissal. He seemed to want her there, though she couldn't imagine why. So she stayed.

"I was going to tell you," Kate snuffled noisily. "I never thought Trace would be blamed, or you either. She told me no one was even going to catch on. The copies were so good that it was impossible for anyone to tell."

"They were good," Blackheart said. "Too good. They're much prettier than the real Von Emmerlings—I know from experience." He was capable of a wry smile in the midst of all this drama.

"If only she hadn't come . . ."

"I knew, Kate. I always knew. I just didn't know how you managed it, and I still don't know why. Was she blackmailing you?"

Kate shook her head miserably. "There were a hundred reasons. One was the money. She was offering a lot, and I needed it. Another was blackmail. I—I did something I shouldn't have . . . a few years back. She was going to make sure certain people found out about it."

"How did she know?"

Kate's flush turned her already red face an ugly mottled shade. "She was involved, too. She helped me out at the time—lent me some money when I needed it. When she first asked me to help her, she said it was for old times' sake."

"And when that didn't work she threatened you," he murmured. "And by that time you were so mad at Trace you didn't care who you hurt."

"I cared. But that big moose can't see two feet in front of his nose. I would have died for him."

"You don't have to die for him. You just have to come down to the police station and tell them the truth. How Olivia got in touch with you, how it was planned, exactly what you did."

Kate was shaking her head. "It won't do any good. She's got an airtight alibi. And no one's going to believe me anyway. The moment I start making accusations, some very nasty photographs get sent to the newspapers. You see, I was in some—home movies, you might call them. With a few influential businessmen and politicians, and we weren't exactly fully dressed, if you know what I mean. And you can take that look off your face, lady," she snarled at Ferris. "Senator Merriam wasn't one of them."

"I'm sorry," Ferris stammered. "I didn't mean to be disapproving."

"Hell, you can disapprove all you want," Kate said wearily. "I was young, just dropped out of college, and I was into some things that I should have been smart enough to leave alone. And now it's too late. The *Chronicle* wouldn't print the pictures, but plenty of others would sure the hell jump on it. And anything I said to implicate a blue blood like Olivia would be laughed at. I don't even know how she was involved. I just know that she seemed to know everything that went on."

"So you won't testify?" Blackheart asked, no surprise or shock clouding his expression.

"If it will help you and Trace, I will. But Olivia covered her tracks too well. The only way for her to be caught is with the stuff right on her."

"And is it? Does she have the stuff in her apartment?"

Kate shook her head. "I don't know, Patrick. She didn't tell me or Dale a thing."

"Dale was in on it with her?" Ferris couldn't keep still a moment longer. "But why?"

Kate cast her a withering glance. "Gambling debts. And he does everything Olivia tells him."

"How did you do it, Kate?" Blackheart questioned, handing her a tissue as she snuffled noisily.

"It was easy enough. You trusted me." She dissolved into fresh wails. "Olivia got the copies made, and I carried them in a little bag sewed inside my dress. Olivia had the dress made for me. I looked like a stuffed cabbage in it."

Blackheart's mouth twisted up in a reluctant grin. "It wasn't the most flattering dress."

"I hated it. Olivia must have gotten it on purpose. That's the kind of person she is."

"So you were the courier? When was the switch made?"

"Just after the last raffle winner."

"But what did Trace have to do with it?" Ferris couldn't help but ask.

"Why did she throw herself at him like that? He didn't need to be distracted—he trusted you to look after the jewels."

Kate flinched at the memory of that betrayed trust. "That was just the icing on the cake. I told you Olivia was that kind of person. She knew that I—I cared about him, and she decided to amuse herself by showing me just how out of reach he really was. Well, she showed me." She blew her nose heartily into the tissue.

Blackheart leaned back wearily against the sofa, stretching his legs out in front of him and shutting his eyes. "That answers most of my questions," he murmured. "But it doesn't answer the most important one. What has she done with them?"

"Does it matter that much?" Ferris ventured.

The look he gave her held withering disdain, and she realized with despair that now she had proof that he'd done nothing, that her accusations had been groundless. And he despised her all the more. "Of course it matters," he said patiently. "They can't arrest Olivia without some proof. At this point it's only Kate's word against hers, and Olivia McKinley Summers's word holds a great deal more clout. We need proof. And it's a waste of time to go to the police without it. They'll just assume I'm trying to foist the blame on someone else. They dropped the charges against me very reluctantly."

"But what can you do?" Ferris questioned anxiously.

His smile was mocking. "Not what can *I* do, Francesca, my trusting one. What can *we* do? And the answer is absurdly obvious and quite, quite simple."

Ferris knew a sudden sinking sensation. "All right, I'll bite. What are *we* going to do?"

He smiled seraphically. "We're going to break into Olivia Summers's apartment."

Chapter Seventeen

"YOU HAVE TO be out of your mind," Ferris snapped.

"Not in the slightest." Blackheart was placidly grinding coffee beans in the warmly lit kitchen of his apartment. It was much larger than her kitchen—there was even room for a butcher-block table and several stools in the middle of it. She had been hard put to control the sigh of covetousness that had filled her when she first saw it. The gleaming copper pots and pans had just enough discoloration to prove they were there for hard use, not decoration. The butcher-block countertop was scarred and pitted from a thousand knife strokes, the food processor was artistically battered, and the electric coffee grinder was buzzing its overworked heart out. If she had a kitchen like this, she just might give up her allegiance to frozen dinners.

"You can't seriously expect me to help you rob Olivia Summers's apartment. For heaven's sake, it's a twentieth-floor penthouse!"

"The very best kind," he said sagely, dropping the pulverized coffee into a filter. "High enough to be out of sight, not too high. We've gone over this already, Ferris. And you're coming with me."

He was still very angry with her, she could tell. Despite his calm tone of voice, his use of that hated name tipped her off. And if he weren't mad, he wouldn't be trying to punish her by dragging her into life of crime. "But why?" she wailed.

Blackheart sighed. "Reason number one—it's your reputation and future that's on the line as well as mine. Number two—if I do it alone, what's to stop me from running off with the emeralds and never being seen again? Number three—with my bad knee I don't know if I can do it without help. And number four—you're the one who accused me of it. You can damn well find out for yourself whether your charming lack of trust was justified." He poured the hot water over the grounds, his face bland, his voice easy.

"What did you expect from me, Blackheart?" she said, suppressing her justifiable guilt. "The circumstances were pretty damning."

"Sure they were. I don't know why I would have thought the night we'd spent together might have earned some vague sort of loyalty, not to mention commitment. But what I really don't understand is why you've suddenly chosen to believe that I'm innocent. Kate could be wrong, you know." Together they watched the water level descend in the coffee filter. "I wouldn't be surprised if you suddenly decided that I was in on it with Olivia, the mastermind behind it all. You could ignore the fact that if I were interested there were a lot bigger scores available in the last two years. Not that the Von Emmerling emeralds aren't worth a substantial amount, but I could have done better." He poured her a cup of coffee, black and dark and rich, and she looked at it distrustfully.

"I don't think I ought to have any," she demurred. "I've had too much caffeine as it is."

Blackheart smiled that wry smile that was now completely devoid of tenderness. "Haven't you seen the ads on TV? This is decaffeinated. Just what us artistic types need before a big job."

"Blackheart, you can't blame me," she said suddenly, ignoring the innocuous topic of conversation. "It looked like a setup. I couldn't hide you from the police, it would have been aiding . . ."

Blackheart walked out of the kitchen, and her words trailed off. Well, he'd told her he wasn't ready for an apology, and she still wasn't completely convinced he deserved one.

Looking down at her inky cup of coffee, she sighed. She didn't need any more sugar—she was too wired as it was. She wondered if she could fling herself at Blackheart's feet, beg him to let her cry off? It wouldn't do any good, and she would be damned if she'd tell him. . . .

But why did it have to be twenty floors up? Why couldn't Olivia be sensible and have a basement apartment? Only Blackie knew of her weakness, it was only for Blackie's sake that she'd venture out on her unused, windy second-floor terrace. It wasn't paralyzing acrophobia; if she had to, she could tolerate high places. She just didn't like them much. Her family's trip to the Grand Canyon when she was fifteen had been torment, she'd never even taken a close look at the Coit Tower, and the only way she managed the steep hills of San Francisco was to drive as fast as she possibly could, and yet now Blackheart expected her to traverse twenty-story buildings without a qualm.

Well, she wasn't going to tell him. She'd be more likely to get mocking disbelief than compassion, and nothing would make him let her off. It was his revenge, and if he was innocent, then he had every right to it.

And if she didn't go, if she somehow managed to cry off, then what? Then she would never be certain of him. There'd always be room for doubt, and she'd never know if she was the lowest slime bug in creation or a painfully good judge of character. And that uncertainty wasn't something she could live with.

The living room was in shadows when she finally trailed in after Blackheart. He was sitting on the sofa in the twilight, his feet up on the coffee table, hands clasped loosely around the mug of coffee, eyes trained on the skyline. He didn't move when she came in the room, didn't turn. Kate had left hours ago, with stern instructions to stay in her apartment and not answer the telephone or the door unless it was on Blackheart's prearranged signal. The solitude of the apartment pressed down on Ferris, and she idly wondered what Blackheart would do if she gave in to her irrational temptations and leaped on him. He probably would have dumped her on the floor.

Sighing, she took a chair opposite him. "When are we going to do this?"

"Nine-thirty."

"Nine-thirty!" she shrieked. "That's four hours from now."

"Three hours and forty-five minutes," he corrected. "And that's when Olivia and her husband should be well settled in at Regina Merriam's. If we leave earlier they might decide to be late, or even worse, not go at all. If we go later they may decide to come home early. Regina's going to do her best to keep them, but there's nothing she can do, short of force, if they make up their minds. She's a redoubtable lady, but I can't see her barring the door."

"Regina's in on this?" Ferris couldn't control her astonishment.

Even in the gathering darkness she could see the flash of teeth as he smiled his ironic smile. "Regina trusts her own judgment, and she trusts me."

"Was this her idea or yours?"

"Oh, mine. She just offered her assistance."

"And does she know I'm going to be part of this?" Blackheart turned his head to look at her then, and she wished she could read his expression in the gathering darkness. "Don't worry, Ferris. Your secret is safe with me. None of the Merriams have the faintest idea that you ever had doubts about my perniciousness. I imagine if all goes well no one will believe what Olivia has to say about my whereabouts the night of the ball. And once the police are convinced of my innocence, I imagine they'd have no reason to tell anyone where I was when they arrested me. Rupert had a damned hard time keeping it out of the papers as it was, but we've been fortunate so far. If you're cool-headed and lucky, you should be able to carry it off and have your white wedding after all."

"Don't, Blackheart." Her voice was very still in the dark room. A long silence ensued. Despite her tightly strung nerves, the sleepless nights were beginning to take their toll. In the dark, silent living room she found her eyelids drifting closed, and the half-empty mug of coffee tilted in her hand.

"Come here," he said suddenly, and despite the softness of his voice she jumped, spilling coffee on her camel-colored skirt.

"Why?"

"Because we have hours before we have to leave. You need to sleep. You may as well curl up in the corner of the couch."

"Why don't I just go home and take a nap?"

"Because I don't trust you to come back," he said simply.

There was no way she could argue with that. "What about the bedroom?"

"I keep that for sex," he drawled. "Come here, Francesca. I promise you, you're entirely safe."

She should have been offended by that snotty tone of voice, but at least he'd called her Francesca. It could have been a slip of the tongue, but for some reason Ferris felt cheered. Without a word she set down the mug of coffee and moved over to the sofa.

He was right, there was more than enough room for her to curl up without touching his body on the far end. "What are you going to do?" she asked sleepily, trying to make herself comfortable.

"What I usually do before a job. Empty my mind of everything."

Ferris couldn't control a sleepy laugh. "I guess meditation has a thousand uses."

"It does," he agreed softly. "You're at the wrong end of the couch."

She lay very still, her nerves atingle. "I thought the bedroom was for sex."

An iron hand closed around her wrist and she was hauled upright and over to his side of the sofa. A moment later she was curled up by his side, her head resting against his shoulder, his arm around her. "It is. Go to sleep, Francesca."

A thousand protests sprang to mind, but she uttered not a one. He smelled of coffee and Kate's cigarettes and Blackheart, and she hadn't realized how much she missed him, how much she missed the feel of his body against hers. She wanted to turn her face against the smooth cotton of his shirt, put her arms around his waist and tell him how sorry she was. But he was right—it was too soon. He wasn't ready to forgive her, not yet. But the feel of his arm around her body, holding her comfortably against him, told her that he was getting there. With a sigh she closed her eyes.

FERRIS HAD BEEN half hoping that she'd awake to find herself stretched out along the wide couch, safe in his arms. When she awoke she was alone in the darkness, the light from the bedroom a small pool of brightness in the inky room. She lay there for a moment, hoping she could pretend to be asleep, hoping against hope he'd go without her. Without any warning her heart had begun a steady, violent thudding, and her palms felt cold and damp.

Blackheart's shadow blocked the light, and then he moved across the room. She lay there absorbing his approach. As usual she couldn't hear him, and once he was out of the lamplight she couldn't even see his silhouette. But she could feel him, feel the displaced air as his body moved closer. Maybe he'd lean down and kiss her. Maybe brush the hair away from her sleeping face. Maybe even—

The pile of clothes hit her with a whoosh. He must have dropped them from quite a distance, and the force of their landing made her sit up with a startled squeal. "Damn you, Blackheart!" she snapped. "Haven't you heard about waking people up gently?"

"I don't have the time," he drawled, leaning over to turn on the light. "Besides, you were awake."

Ferris didn't bother to argue with him—Blackheart always knew too much. She looked up at him, silently impressed. He was dressed for work; that much was obvious. The faded jeans had been traded for soft black denims, the black turtleneck covered him from wrist to chin, even his running shoes were black. A pair of thin black gloves was tucked into his hip pocket, and a black watch cap balanced the other side.

"You look very effective," she said, and her voice was slightly strangled. He also looked devastatingly attractive, and that thought didn't help her inner turmoil.

"Put those on." He nodded toward the clothes. "They're the same sort of thing. I can't see you climbing over rooftops in a business suit."

The very thought made her stomach lurch, but she managed a brave smile. "No, I suppose not. Whose clothes are they?"

"Mine," he said without batting an eye. "You'll have to roll up the pants, but they should fit well enough." He cocked his head to one side. "They may be a little tight in the hips."

"Pig," she said, too nervous to be as insulted as she should be. "What do I do for shoes?"

"That may prove a problem." He gave her high-heeled sandals a disapproving glance. "I'll check and see if I have anything that will do. We may have to stop on our way over to Olivia's. I think black ballet slippers would be the best."

"Won't I look funny walking around in ballet slippers?" she questioned caustically.

"This is San Francisco, remember? Everybody looks funny. Hurry up. Are you hungry?"

The very thought of food made her knotted stomach twist, but her panicky brain reminded her that food would take time. "I'm famished," she said brightly.

"Too bad. I never eat before a job."

Ferris looked up at him, a sudden, furious suspicion entering her mind. "You're looking forward to this, aren't you?" she demanded. "You're excited, you're glad to be breaking into a twenty-story building."

He smiled at her with more benevolence than he'd shown in the three days since the emeralds were stolen and he'd been arrested. "Damn straight. Wanna make something of it?"

As the sinking feeling filled her heart, she realized there was nothing she could say. "No."

"Then change your clothes and let's get going."

Heartless, the man was *completely heartless,* she thought, struggling into the clothes in the small confines of his apartment-size bathroom. And damn his soul, the soft, faded black denims *were* tight in the hips. Sucking in her stomach, she pulled the zipper up, then turned to admire the back view in the mirror. Even if they were tight, they looked very enticing. Maybe she'd do her best to precede Blackheart up a ladder. Oh, dear God, what was she thinking?

Blackheart was waiting impatiently by the door when she finally emerged, and his expression was critical, not admiring. "You'll need to tie your hair back," he said, his eyes running over her body with a professional eye. "Maybe we ought to cut off those pants, rather than roll them up."

"Don't you think you might need them again?" she said sweetly.

Blackheart didn't rise to the bait. "If I do, I could afford to buy new ones. B and E is a lot more lucrative than security work. Come on, we're running late." He tossed her a wool hat and a pair of thin kid gloves. "Keep those stowed until we get up on the first roof."

"First roof?" Her voice came out in a tiny squeak, and his smile was chilling.

"I've been thinking about it. There are two ways we can get in. One way is from the bottom, but the security in Olivia's building is very tight. Our alternative is to go from the top. There's a building on the corner that's fairly accessible, and the rooftop route is straightforward enough. No peaks, at least. We'll scout around a bit before we actually do it."

"Don't you want to try starting from the bottom?" she said wistfully. "It sounds a lot more direct."

"And a lot more dangerous. Five hours in jail is just about my limit. Much as it would please me to drag you along with me, I think I could do without another arrest." He peered at her, and his sadistic smile widened. "You aren't afraid of heights, are you, Francesca?"

She managed a creditable shrug. "Of course not."

"That's good," he murmured. "Because if you were, you wouldn't like to-night at all. Not one tiny bit." And his smile was nothing short of sinister.

"Don't try to scare me, Blackheart. I'm tough enough to take anything you have to dish out and more," she snapped, her backbone stiffening. "What do I wear on my feet?"

"I found these in the back of my closet. They should do." He tossed her a pair of dark-brown flats, a size too small for her size-eight feet.

"Whose are they?" she queried, then cursed herself for opening her mouth.

Blackheart smiled. "Let's just say they came from the bedroom. Are you ready?"

He wasn't going to goad her. "Ready."

"Well, I'm not." He'd been standing a few feet away, watching her. Before she could realize his intent, he'd crossed those few feet and pulled her into his arms, his mouth coming down on hers with a fierce hunger that washed everything away, her panic, her doubts, her guilt.

Twining her arms up around his neck, she opened her mouth for his tongue, lost in the sudden swirl of wanting that washed over her. He'd caught her hips in his firm, strong hands, pressing her up tightly against him, and she whimpered softly as his tongue met hers, seeking a response that was there for the taking. His hands slid up her black-clad sides, around in front to cup her breasts, and his fingers were enticingly rough and arousing. She pressed herself against those hands of his, her own traveling up his strong, narrow back, the feel of the soft cotton turtleneck frustrating when she wanted silken skin. His blatant arousal ground against her, and for one brief, mad moment she considered tripping him up and jumping on him. Anything to avoid heights, she told herself righteously, pressing closer to his enticing body.

His hands left her breasts, caught her arms and drew her away from him, slowly, deliberately, being very careful not to hurt her. His breathing was labored, his eyes glistening in the darkness, and she could hear the rapid thudding of his heart in counterpoint to hers. "Now I'm ready," he said finally, dropping her wrists and turning away. "Let's go."

Chapter Eighteen

IT WAS A COOL, damp night, with a low-hanging mist that just might obscure the deadly drops between buildings, Ferris thought hopefully. It might also obscure her footing, but she was resigned to that. She was going to end up smashed on the sidewalks—she'd prefer not to have to see anything as she fell.

Blackheart was right, as always. Nobody gave them a second look as they strode arm in arm, two black-clad cat burglars out for a stroll, she thought bitterly. She kept casting nervous glances up at the jagged roofline that looked like sharks' teeth, with Blackheart constantly pulling her attention back to the earth where she'd so much rather stay, please God.

"Where are we going now?" she whispered angrily as they strolled past Olivia's building for the second time. It was a stately, post-earthquake building on Nob Hill, heavily doormanned, as Blackheart had warned her. She cast the uniformed guard a longing look. Maybe she could entice him into a back alley while Blackheart slipped upstairs alone. Without her archaic virginity to protect, she'd choose additional dishonor before death any day.

But Blackheart had dragged her past the building without allowing her more than a wistful glance. "Forget it," he'd ground out in her ear. "I've already checked everything. The only way we could get into that place is with a Sherman tank or the Pope by our side—and even then they might still want IDs. And I'm afraid anyone connected with Blackheart, Inc., is strictly persona non grata around here."

"But maybe I could distract him."

His laugh was heartlessly derisive. "You're starting to see yourself as a Mata Hari after one night of passion? If you managed to get past him, there'd still be the elevator operator. This is a full-service apartment building."

"Oh."

"Oh," he echoed cynically. They plowed onward, Ferris's hand numb on his arm. "We're here," he said finally, and her heart plummeted to the too-tight shoes.

It was a small building, a little seedier than its sisters on the neat upper-class street, its facade smog and pollution-stained. "What is it?"

"A hotel. Look sultry." He began to steer her in through a tawdry lobby, and the woman behind the desk looked up with absolutely no expression on her tough, tired face. Her hair was an improbable shade of blond, her eyes were dead, and the stub of a cigarette hung from a coral-lipsticked mouth.

Ferris stared at her for a moment, wondering how she managed to smoke so far down without burning those overripe lips of hers.

"We'd like a room," Blackheart announced, still maintaining a tight grip on Ferris's arm.

"So what else is new?" the woman returned, shoving the register at them. "Mr. and Mrs. Smith, I presume?"

Still clamping the defiant Ferris to his side, Blackheart signed in a dark, sprawling script. The desk clerk turned it back, peered at it, then glanced up at the two of them suspiciously. "Berdahofski?" she queried. "Mr. and Mrs.," Blackheart said sweetly.

"Any luggage?" She dropped her cigarette butt in the Styrofoam cup of congealed coffee by her side. She didn't bother to look or wait for an answer. "No loud noises, no screaming, no breaking the furniture. Twenty bucks."

"We'll be discreet," Blackheart assured her, dropping thirty on the desk. She pocketed it without looking up, tossed them a key and jerked her head in the direction of the elevators.

"She didn't tell us the checkout time," was all Ferris could find to say as they traveled upward in a creaking elevator that had served as a urinal in the not-distant past.

"That's because she doesn't expect us to stay more than an hour or two," Blackheart said patiently, finally freeing her arm from that iron grip.

Ferris's eyes opened wide. "Why?"

"This place caters to the hot-sheet trade, darling. They get quite a turnover, if you'll pardon the expression." The elevator doors creaked open, and Ferris wrinkled her nose.

"How could such a sordid place be so close to Olivia's?" she demanded. "Isn't there such a thing as zoning?"

"They don't zone places like this. And the neighborhood's on the up-swing. I'm sure this place hasn't got much time left." He slid the key into the fifth door down from the elevator, opening it with a flourish. "After you, *madame.*"

Ferris cast him a worried look. "You don't seriously expect me to—to—"

He shoved her inside, switching on the light and closing the door behind them. "No, I don't seriously expect you to—to—" he mocked. "I can think of pleasanter places and better times. This is hardly my idea of romance." He gave the sagging bed with its rose chenille bedspread a withering glance. "Make yourself comfortable, Mrs. Berdahofski."

"But why? I thought Olivia would have been gone for hours now. We don't want to run into them coming home." She plopped herself down on the bed, alternating relief and panic washing over her. On the one hand, she was in no hurry to end her life in a fall from a San Francisco rooftop. On the other, the longer she put it off, the harder it was going to be. She didn't want Blackheart to have to drag her, kicking and screaming, up there. She had no doubt at all that he would.

"I don't want to run into her, either. But the desk clerk was watching the elevator when we went up—she'll probably keep an eye on it for a while. I wouldn't put it past her to head up this way. I want to allay her suspicions."

"She wasn't suspicious," Ferris protested, bouncing slightly on the loose springs. "She didn't give us more than a second look."

"She wouldn't have done that if you hadn't been giving her that helpless white-slave routine. If I hadn't kept a grip on you, you probably would have bolted. And if I were you I wouldn't sit on that bed—you never know what might be crawling around."

She was off it in a flash, casting a dubious glance back. "How long do we have to wait?"

Blackheart smiled, that sinister, heartless smile. "It's time. Come on, chicken. We're going a-thieving."

Even through her panic Ferris had to admire him. He picked the lock to the roof with practiced ease, using a small collection of tools that resembled a manicurist's weapons. No one would have been faster with a key, and for a moment she wondered whether she could get him to teach her. Then she abandoned the idea as tactless. Besides, when would she have cause to break into a place? But still she paid close attention—anything to keep her mind off what was awaiting her.

The breeze was stronger up on the roof, but the reality of it was far less threatening than her imagination. The adjoining building was gloriously flush with the hotel, and a mere two feet higher.

"Put your hat and gloves on," Blackheart instructed, doing the same himself. He looked different like that, she thought as she hastily complied. He looked like a cat, lean and lithe and dangerous, with his eyes aglow and his nerves tightly strung.

"You sound like my mother on Sunday morning," she grumbled. The gloves were too small, the hat too big, with an unfortunate tendency to slip down over her eyes. She smiled up at him brightly. "I'm ready."

He paused, looking down at her with a wry smile. "Okay, Poncho," he said, pushing the hat back off her forehead. "Remember to do everything I say, without hesitation, backtalk or panic. Look ahead, look up, but never look down. You got that?"

She didn't like the sound of that, but she nodded. "Good girl," he said, kissing her on the forehead with unexpected warmth. "Let's get going."

Ferris scampered after him, up onto the adjoining building, her feet silent and just a tiny bit slippery on the tarred roof. *This isn't so bad,* she told herself with a hint of pleading to the patron saint of cat burglars. *I'll be fine.*

In the misty darkness the huddled shapes of the heating vents made eerie obstacles, but she kept her eyes trained on Blackheart's narrow back, unconsciously imitating his catlike grace. He was waiting for her at the far end, and this time the neighboring building was a good two stories higher. He was standing by a rusty wrought-iron ladder.

"You first," he offered kindly.

"Very convenient of them to have left a ladder," she grumbled, glad now for the tight gloves. They gave her better purchase than her cold, wet palms.

"Most buildings have them. Didn't you ever watch cop shows?" She had paused three rungs up, and he put his hands beneath her black-denimed rear and shoved. The sound of his voice was blessedly distracting. "They're always chasing around on roofs, and there are always convenient ladders."

"And if there aren't?" Her voice quavered slightly as she neared the top. She nearly collapsed on the next roof in relief, but with a superhuman effort she maintained her balance. Not dead yet.

"Then we're in trouble," he said with callous cheer, dropping down on the roof beside her, making no noise at all. "You're doing okay, partner. Ever thought of taking up mountain-climbing?"

"No," she snapped. "How many more buildings to go?"

"Only three," he said, with genuine sadness, the swine. "And we're just beginning to get the feel of it. I hope it's not all as tame as this. You won't get any proper taste of it."

"I don't want a proper taste of it," she said through clenched teeth. "I want to get the damned job over with and get home."

"You have no soul, Francesca," he murmured, peering past her through the murky darkness. The tangle of antennas stretched against the cloudy night sky like bare tree limbs, and a look of inhuman delight lit his face. "Ah, now that's more of a challenge."

"Wh-what is?"

"No ladder."

She swallowed the yelp of panic. "How are we going to get up?"

"Leave it to me."

She only wished she could. She only wished she dared turn around and head back down, back to street level to disappear into the fog and never be seen again. South Dakota could be very pretty in February. If you liked the Arctic.

She'd thought those clothes of his fit like a second skin, but somewhere beneath them he'd managed to hide a thin coil of rope. Sudden dizziness assailed her, and she sat down abruptly on the rooftop, taking deep, covert breaths as she watched Blackheart size up the wall.

He looked back at her for a moment. "Sitting down on the job, Francesca?" he inquired.

"Just for a moment. I figure I may as well relax while I wait," she said with deceiving calm.

Except that when had she ever deceived Blackheart? Maybe now, when he was distracted. She could only hope so. Her heart was thudding so loudly that surely he could hear if he weren't so busy trying to figure out how to kill them both. She wouldn't look any closer, she wouldn't. But she had to.

Slowly she rose, edging toward the next building. Her quiet little moan was swallowed up in the night air. There was a good two feet between the two buildings. Enough for her body to bounce down, ending wedged in some narrow alleyway.

Blackheart had taken a small cylinder from his pocket and was unfolding it into something that resembled a cross between an umbrella and an anchor. From somewhere in the murky mists of memory Ferris recognized it as a grappling hook, the kind used by mountain climbers. She watched him attach it to the end of the thin rope with practiced ease. He tossed it expertly, and it caught on the next building, some twelve feet higher than their current uneasy level.

"You want to go first?" he offered courteously, yanking on the rope a few times to ensure that it was sound.

"No, thank you," she said, choking. "After you."

He went up easily enough, though she could see that he was favoring his right leg. What would happen if he fell, she wondered. He'd done so once, and his father had died from a fall. Would it be better or worse if it was his body smashed against the pavement and not hers? She really didn't know.

"Come on, chicken heart," he called softly from the roof above her. "Time's a-wasting."

I can't do it, she thought suddenly. *I simply can't do it.* Taking a few steps back, she shook her head. Blackheart was up there, waiting patiently. "Come on, Francesca," he said softly, and his voice was a siren's lure. "I can't leave you alone on the roof. Either come with me or I'll have to take you back, and it will all be for nothing."

Good, she thought, still not saying a word. She no longer cared about Trace Walker, the emeralds or anybody's reputation. But Blackheart was looking down at her, and through the misty darkness she could see those calm, laughing eyes, daring her to come up. And she knew that if she turned and left she'd never see him again.

Some things were worth dying for, she thought dazedly, grabbing the rope. Was Blackheart one of them? Was the truth one of them? Would she ever find out?

"That's right, love," he crooned down at her, his voice soothing. "Just don't look down. The rope's more than strong enough to hold you—I'm up here to catch you when you get in reach." He kept up the calming, gentle litany as she climbed, hand over hand, her feet bouncing off the opposite brick wall. Her face felt chilled, and she realized that tears were pouring down unbidden, tears of pure, simple terror. She couldn't take her hands off the rope to wipe them away, and it would have done no good. They just kept coming, silent, copious, slipping down her face as she moved up the rope.

His hand on her wrist was like a vice, biting, blessedly painful, as he hauled her up the rest of the way. She kept herself stiff, not falling into his arms as she longed to do. If she did, she would start to howl and scream and he'd never get her to move another foot.

"Is this it?" she inquired, her voice calm, her face wet with the tears.

"One more," Blackheart said. "We'll have to jump." She thought she'd reached the apex of terror, but she had been mistaken. She looked at him with shock and disbelief, but he just shrugged his shoulders. "Don't think about it," he advised. "Do it before you have time to be frightened." He hadn't released her wrist, and she felt herself being dragged to the opposite end of the roof.

There was a yawning abyss between the two buildings. A vast chasm of perhaps thirty inches. She couldn't do it—she'd reached her limit. If that same space was flat on the sidewalk she would have made it with feet to spare. But if she tried to jump those thirty inches, twenty stories above the street, she would die. It was just that simple.

Blackheart jumped first, making it look ridiculously easy—a child's hop-scotch game. He stood on the other side, waiting for her. "Come on, Francesca," he said. "Prove that you love me."

"But I don't," she said, and knew it was a lie.

He smiled, unfazed. "Then prove that you don't. Jump. For once in your life, trust me."

It was rotten and unfair of him, and it left her no choice whatsoever. She knew if she hesitated one more moment she'd never move in the next five hundred years. She leaped, not preparing herself, and her shins hit the edge of the opposite building as she began to tumble downward.

Of course Blackheart caught her. How could she ever have had any doubts about it? One moment she was sliding down the outside of a building toward certain death, in the next his hands had clamped around her wrists and she had been hauled onto the roof before her knees had even made contact with the building. They tumbled onto the rough surface, his arms locked so tightly around her that she couldn't breathe. She didn't think she wanted to, anyway, and she hugged him back, closing her eyes and willing the dizziness to fade.

"Damn you," he muttered in her ear. "Damn, damn, damn you. I ought to wring your neck. Why the hell didn't you tell me you were scared of heights?" There was no way she could answer, first because the arms crushing her didn't give her enough breath to do so, then because his mouth had come down over hers, stopping any effort at speech.

She considered protesting for a brief moment, then decided against it. She'd really rather be kissing him than breathing anyway. Especially since he had just ensured that she would be breathing in the near future, she could give up a few moments of air in a good cause. And his mouth was so very wonderful. There was a faint, windy sort of humming in her ears, and little blue and pink stars in front of her eyes, and she wondered if she was going to come just from being kissed, and then realized that no, she was more likely simply going to pass out from lack of oxygen, when he released her. The return of her breathing almost made up for the absence of his mouth. Almost, but not quite. She lunged back for him, but he held her at arm's length.

"None of that, wench," he cautioned sternly. "We have work to do."

"Oh, no, Blackheart," she wailed. "No more rooftops."

"No more rooftops. Everything is downhill from now on. We're on Olivia's building. See those trees down there? That's her terrace."

The tops of the trees looked bizarre twenty stories up, but Ferris took his word gratefully. "How do we get there?"

By this time she was past fear. Very slowly, very carefully he lowered her down the eight feet to Olivia's flagstone terrace, very carefully he leaped after her, landing lightly on his cat's feet.

"Blackheart, there's a light on in the apartment," she hissed, ducking behind a potted Douglas fir.

He caught her arm and dragged her back out. "Do you think Olivia worries about the electric company? It is—" he peered at his watch in the darkness "—ten forty-five. I don't expect them back before eleven at the earliest."

"Blackheart!" she moaned.

"More likely midnight. Regina promised she'd stall them. Come along, darling. You'll reach street level by the service elevator."

It sounded too good to be true. "Do you mean it, Blackheart?" she breathed as he busied himself with the terrace door. He was using an American Express card, and the door opened immediately and soundlessly.

"How did you do that?"

He grinned. "I never leave home without it. And yes, you'll leave by the elevator, or at worst twenty flights of stairs wouldn't be so bad, would it?"

"It would be sheer heaven. But what about the people in the lobby?"

"It's a lot easier going out than in," he explained patiently as he stepped through the sliding glass door, beckoning her to follow. "Even so, we'll probably leave through the basement. It should be deserted this time of night."

The apartment was still and silent, the bright lights lending a false sense of security to the whole operation. "You take the bedroom," he ordered. "I'll start in here. Use your gloves, and don't disturb anything. We just want to make sure the emeralds are here, we don't want to take them."

Ferris nodded obediently, heading into the bedroom and shuddering at the strong reek of Olivia's perfume. Shalimar. Wouldn't you just know it? The room was spotlessly, compulsively neat, even the makeup and perfumes on the glass-topped dressing table in alphabetical order. The clothes in the closets and drawers were arranged by color and season, each shoe had its mate, and though the jewelry looked very valuable to Ferris's untrained eye, there wasn't an emerald among them.

Nothing between the mattress and the box spring, nothing under the bed, not even dust or a missing paperback novel. The woman was definitely sick, Ferris decided righteously.

The bathroom was an equal washout. Nothing secreted in the back of the toilet, hidden among the color-coordinated towels, concealed in the extra roll of toilet paper. There was one advantage to the demented neatness, Ferris conceded. It made searching surprisingly easy.

"Any luck?" Blackheart appeared in the doorway, and Ferris told herself she could see the pleasure and excitement jumping in his veins.

"Nothing. Except I can't open that door." She gestured toward the locked door hidden beneath a row of curtains.

He gave it a critical look. "Piece of cake. Does Olivia have anything as mundane as a nail cleaner?"

"Olivia's nails don't get dirty," she said dourly. "Will this do?" It was a narrow emery board, and he nodded his approval.

"Go to it, kid."

"Don't be ridiculous, Blackheart. We don't have time for games."

"This is a learning experience. You can do it, Francesca. And we're staying right here until you try," he said blandly, leaning against the doorway.

And she'd thought she was over being scared for the night. Gracing him with an obscenity she seldom used, she set to work, jabbing at the keyhole in a fine temper.

"Don't be so rough," Blackheart advised. "You have to coax a lock to open, tease it open. Treat it like a lover, talk to it."

"Go to hell, Blackheart!"

"Of course, since that happens to be the way you talk to your lovers, it might be better if—"

"Oh, my God, I did it," Ferris breathed, sitting back on her heels in amazement as the knob turned with a well-oiled click.

Blackheart strode past her, giving her an approving pat on her capped hair. "Of course you did. I knew you had the makings of a felon in that heart of yours." He stepped inside the room and stopped dead still, blocking her entrance. "Well, well, well."

"What is it?" She pushed past him, curiosity getting the better of her.

"I think I've discovered how Olivia knew what Kate had become involved in. And how she's been making money for the last few years."

Ferris looked around, her forehead wrinkled. "It just looks like a lot of electronic equipment."

"Exactly. DVD recorders, a video camera, a small pile of DVDs. I think Olivia and Dale have been involved in experimental filmmaking for very high profits."

"What makes you think they haven't just been bootlegging movies? Isn't there a big profit in that, too?" she questioned curiously, roaming around the small, dark room, trailing a gloved hand over the shiny equipment.

"Not as big as the profit in blackmail," Blackheart drawled. "I wouldn't have thought Olivia would be so enterprising. Though she always was a little kinky."

"What do you mean, kinky?" Ferris demanded, her interest in the machines vanishing.

Blackheart smiled seraphically. "Never you mind, Miss Innocence. Let's just say that Olivia's not particularly my cup of tea. Why don't you go ahead and check her drawers one last time? I'll give this place a quick once-over and see if I can come up with anything."

"You think they might be in here?"

"They might," Blackheart said. "They might be anywhere. And we're running out of time as it is. Hurry up, Francesca. The sooner we get out of here, the better."

Ferris left readily enough as he pushed her out the door. The small silver clock by the spotless king-size bed said five past eleven, and once more Ferris was struck with the difference between this compulsive neatness and the squalid mind that conceived of blackmail as a way to make a living. Poor Kate, enmeshed in Olivia's schemes. And poor Trace, set up like a clay pigeon. And poor Blackheart, and poor Ferris, more unwilling pawns. Damn her soul to hell.

She found them by accident. All her mental energy was spent on her fury with Olivia, and her search was desultory, mindless, instinctive. She hadn't bothered to check the wastepaper basket the first time around—the idea had been too absurd. But this time she was going by instinct, not ideas, and the solid weight of the supposedly empty tissue box tipped her off.

She was kneeling on the floor on the far side of the bed, the box held loosely. With shaking hands she opened it, and the Von Emmerling emeralds tumbled into her lap.

She stared at them for a long, speculative moment. They looked garish, ornate, and tacky in the electric light, and sudden doubt assailed her. She didn't even look up when Blackheart reentered the room, carefully locking the door behind him.

"Nothing in there," he said. "Not even any video. She must have them stored someplace else. Though from the dust on the machines I don't think she's been using them for quite a while. Maybe she decided theft was more lucrative than blackmail. I expect it's safer."

"I think I found them," Ferris said quietly.

"What?" She had his full attention now, and he materialized by her side immediately, squatting down next to her. "You've got 'em, all right," he said, a rich note of satisfaction in his voice as he looked at them. Reaching forward, his long slender hands lifted them, holding them up against the light, tender as a lover stroking satin flesh.

And what was she doing, being jealous of a few rocks, she wondered, miserably aware that that was exactly what she was feeling. "How do you know they're the real ones? Didn't Olivia have copies made?"

"The police have the copies," he said absently, never taking his tawny gaze from the jewels. "Don't you remember, we tried to pawn them off on Miss Smythe-Davies? No, these are the real things. You can tell by the shimmer of blue light in the heart of the big emerald." He held it out for her admiration, but like any jealous woman, she only gave it a cursory glance, controlling an urge to sniff contemptuously. "What makes you think they might be fake?"

"They look so . . . so tacky," she said finally. "I remembered them being a lot prettier."

"Jewelry usually looks prettier by candlelight, particularly those that were designed when that was the main form of light. But that's your proof right there. The Von Emmerling emeralds are famous for being vulgar. The fakes were much prettier. If I'd had my mind on my business and not on—something else the night of the Puffin Ball, I would have noticed immediately when the substitution was made."

"What did you have your mind on, Blackheart?" she asked quietly.

"Sex," he said bluntly. "Put them back, Francesca. We found out what we came for. The sooner we get out of here the better."

"Shouldn't we just take them?" She was wrapping them reluctantly and shoving them back in their box. "I mean, they may find out we've been here. Wouldn't it be safer if we took them to the police ourselves?"

"And you think they'd take the word of Patrick Blackheart against the likes of Olivia Summers?" he scoffed. "They were overjoyed to have finally managed to arrest me—it just about broke their hearts to let me go. Even if they couldn't make any charges stick, they still knew exactly what I was doing for the last fifteen years of my life, and most people figure six months at a minimum-security British prison wasn't punishment enough. They'd love to get something new on me. If I showed up at the police station with the Von Emmerling emeralds and some cock-and-bull story about the Summerses, I don't expect they'd waste too much time listening." He shook his head, rising to his full height. "No, we'll leave them right where we found them.

Olivia's foolish enough to think she's home free. Tomorrow morning Kate and I will make a visit to our local police station in the company of Rupert and set our case before their impartial judicial eye."

"And then they'll believe you?"

"Of course not. They won't believe me until they get a search warrant and find the jewels themselves, and even then they might not be certain. Come along, darling. This isn't the place for postmortems. That's the second rule of thievery, right up there after don't look down. It's don't stop to count the loot while you're still at the scene of the crime."

"Yes, sir." She stuffed the box back in the trash. "How are we getting out?"

"Service entrance just off the kitchen." He headed for the door, and Ferris paused for a moment. Had the bedside light been on or off? She couldn't recall, but what was more important, would Olivia remember? She was about to call after Patrick, but he was already gone.

Well, she'd just have to chance it. Flicking it off, she sped across the thick wall-to-wall carpet in search of the kitchen. Blackheart was standing in the open door, looking impatient.

"Off with the hat and gloves, Francesca," he ordered. "You don't want to advertise what we've been doing."

Sudden guilt assailed her at the memory of that bedside lamp. "Blackheart, I don't remember—"

His hand suddenly covered her mouth as he pulled her back against him. The only sound was his heavy breathing. And the rattle of the lock being turned on the front door of the apartment.

Chapter Nineteen

THEY WERE HALFWAY down the twenty flights of stairs when reaction began to set in. One moment she was racing after him, the too-tight flats flying down the narrow metal steps, the next she was clinging to the railing as a sudden wave of dizziness assailed her.

He was half a flight ahead of her when he realized she was no longer following him. In a flash he was back beside her, gently prying her clutching hands from the railing and rubbing an elbow over the section of metal to wipe out her fingerprints.

"You go on ahead," she said in a choked voice. "I just need a minute." She tried to break free of his grip, but he held fast.

"Francesca, love, we can't hang around the scene of the crime. That's rule number three, darling. Rule number four is don't touch anything once you take your gloves off."

Her knees were trembling so much she doubted she could stand much longer, and there was a shocked look to her face and eyes. "I'll be along in a moment, Blackheart," she pleaded.

"Rule number five, and most important. Do as the senior partner says, without question. Come on, my fledgling felon. We're getting out of here."

"Blackheart, I can't," she whispered, sinking down to sit on the narrow steps.

Her rear hadn't even made contact before she was hauled up again, his fingers digging painfully into her arms as he gave her a hard, teeth-rattling shake. "The next step is a slap, Francesca," he informed her coldly. "Do you want that?"

The shocked expression was leaving her face, her cheeks were filling with color and her eyes with fury. "Don't you dare!"

"Then stop whining and come on," he snapped, dragging her on down the steps. She stumbled after him, gritting her teeth and concentrating on the cold anger that was filling her.

Five minutes later, when they ended up in a deserted alleyway that looked as if it belonged more to the Bontemps Hotel than to Olivia's classy condo, that anger was still rampant. Blackheart finally released his grip on her hand, leaning back against a brick wall and taking in slow, deep breaths of the foggy night air.

For a brief moment Ferris considered flinging herself down and kissing the blessed ground. She contented herself with a surreptitious caress with her foot, while she continued to glare at Blackheart's shadowy figure.

"Don't give me that look, Francesca," he drawled out of the darkness. "You know as well as I do that you couldn't afford to stop on the stairs like that. If I hadn't dragged you you'd still be there, just waiting for someone to find you."

The fact that he was probably right didn't help her nerve-induced temper. "I was just wondering, Blackheart. We had no trouble leaving by the basement, ending up in this deserted alleyway. Why didn't we go in this way? And don't tell me the service door is locked—I've seen the way you deal with locks. They melt beneath your fingertips."

Blackheart shrugged. "What can I say? There's not much challenge in unlocking a service door and climbing twenty flights of stairs. Besides, there's usually an alarm system wired into those service entrances, and I'm not familiar enough with American current to dismantle it."

Ferris held herself very still, outrage coursing through her veins. "Was there an alarm system?"

"No."

"Then we could have gone up that way?" Her voice was low and dangerous in the aftermath of her fright.

"Yes."

There was nothing she could say in the face of that bald confession—rage left her momentarily speechless. That was one she owed him—and by now they were almost even.

"What about the hotel?" she asked finally, her voice a semblance of normalcy. "Aren't they going to wonder when we don't return the key?"

"Nobody wonders about anything at places like that," he replied, taking another deep breath of the cool night air. "I left the key on the dresser—someone will find it and figure we had a fight before we did it."

"Maybe I should have messed up the bed?"

"A made bed would get more attention than an unmade one, but no one's going to give a damn. Trust me—the Bontemps Hotel is the least of our worries."

"And what's the greatest of our worries?" she asked after a moment. Some of the rage had left her, some of the panic, but her blood still sang with nervous energy.

"First, getting back to the apartment without being seen. Second, getting the police to issue a search warrant. And third, making sure the Summerses are caught red-handed."

"Do we have to worry?" she asked in a very small voice, and through the misty darkness she could see his wry smile, like the Cheshire cat.

"We always have to worry. Come along, my intrepid mountain-climber. Let's get the first worry out of the way. Hold on to my arm, look up at me as if you adored me, and we'll go for a stroll."

"I don't know if I'm that good an actress," she bit back, taking his arm in her slender hands. The muscles were taut and iron-hard beneath her hands, telling her he was far from relaxed, despite that drawling tone of voice.

"You can manage, I'm sure," he returned, moving out of the shadows with her clinging to his side. His hand reached up and covered hers, and the touch of his skin was comforting. He probably did it just for that reason, Ferris thought, knowing she should pull away, knowing that was the last thing she wanted to do. He must be right—it would look more believable if she snuggled up against him as they walked.

It was a long walk. Blackheart made no move to get a taxi and Ferris made no move to request one as they made their circuitous way back to Blackheart's apartment. The long, leisurely walk, up and down the hills, skirting Chinatown, started to soothe her shattered nerves. They stopped once, and Blackheart bought her a Double Rainbow coffee ice-cream cone; later he bought her a bag of coconut-and-macadamia-nut cookies and then proceeded to eat most of them. The night was getting cooler, the fog was fitful, but Blackheart's body next to hers was a furnace. She wanted to curl up next to it, to luxuriate in its animal heat, to get as close as one human being could possibly get to another. It was getting harder to remember this was an act to fool passersby into thinking they were just a couple in love, out for a walk on a foggy winter's evening. As she looked down at the strong arm she was holding, she found herself wishing she still believed in fairy tales.

Blackheart's street was deserted. The Volvo was still parked down the street from his entrance, the streetlights provided pools of light to keep muggers and their ilk at bay. With a start Ferris realized that she and Blackheart qualified as "their ilk." They had broken into someone's apartment that night, and even if their motives had been pure and their victims evil, even if they hadn't taken a thing, they were still technically criminals.

That knowledge appeared to affect Blackheart in the strangest way. He seemed positively lighthearted as they climbed the front steps of his apartment building, and if the arm beneath her hand was still iron-hard with nervous tension, his spirits were soaring.

When they reached the front door of the building, she quickly detached herself. "I'll see you tomorrow," she murmured. "It's late."

Blackheart smiled then, that ironical, laughing smile that always made her feel like a fool. "Don't be an idiot, Francesca. You don't want to wander around town in my clothes. Besides, you've been limping for the last three blocks. Come in and change and I'll call you a taxi."

If that wasn't what she wanted to hear, she would have gone to the stake rather than admit it. But her feet did hurt, and the sooner she retrieved all her possessions from his cool, airy apartment the sooner she could get him out of her life, where he belonged.

She'd thought the elevator was small when she rode up alone. With Blackheart's warm, black-clad figure sharing the space with her, it was practically a coffin. Or a bed. Her nerves were still jumping, the blood pumping through her veins, and her hands were trembling slightly. But she could be just as cool as Blackheart, she told herself as he unlocked the three professional-looking locks on his door.

"Your locks look a great deal more solid than mine," she said, striving for a calm she was far from feeling. With a sudden sinking feeling she knew she'd have to change and get out of there fast, before she threw herself at his feet.

"They slow me down more than most when I've forgotten my keys," he replied, almost absently, as he swung the door open and gestured for her to precede him. "Those pieces of tinfoil on your door wouldn't stop an eight-year-old."

"I'll get them replaced." He hadn't bothered to turn on the light, and as he closed the door behind them they were plunged into a thick, velvet darkness.

"Do that," he murmured, and she could feel his soft breath on the back of her neck, his long fingers in her hair, deftly releasing it from the hairpins. She stood motionless beneath his touch, afraid to say a word and break the sudden spell that had come over her. The hair tumbled down onto her shoulders and his hands ran through it, caressing it with a feather-light touch. And then suddenly she was trembling all over again, her knees weak, her heart pounding, her breath rapid in the thick darkness.

"Will they keep you out?" She struggled for a last brief moment. He was only touching her hair, and that so gently she might almost be imagining it. If she were abrasive enough he might move away, turn on the light, and watch her go with that enigmatic expression in his dark eyes.

The hands lifted her hair up, and his hot, wet mouth touched the vulnerable nape of her neck in a slow, lingering kiss that melted the last hope she had of escape. "Nothing will keep me out," he whispered against her sweetly scented skin.

The small, lost wail that came from her mouth could have been despair, could have been surrender, could have been protest, could have been all three. "Don't, Blackheart," she murmured brokenly. "Please, don't."

His hands caught her shoulders and turned her around to face him, and she could feel the tension running through him. Her own tension matched it. "Why not, Francesca? Give me one good reason to leave you alone and I will."

"Phillip . . ."

He shook his head. "That's not a good reason. Try again."

"We don't have anything in common."

"No good, either. We have a great deal in common, and well you know it. You're a born cat burglar. If I'd met you five years ago, there would have been no stopping us."

"Don't be ridiculous, Blackheart." Her words were brisk, her tone breathless as his hands gently brushed the hair away from her face. She couldn't help herself, she turned her face into that hand and kissed his palm.

"Give me another reason, Francesca," he said, his voice low and husky and unbearably seductive. "Just one."

She was struggling hard; her Catholic mother would be proud of her. "I don't trust you," she said. "Do you want to go to bed with a woman who doesn't trust you?"

"No," he said, his hands cupping her face and holding it still. "But I saw you jump tonight, Francesca. You couldn't have done it if you didn't trust me." His lips feathered hers, lightly, tantalizingly, and she found herself reaching for more. "Could you, Francesca?"

"No," she murmured against his mouth. "Yes." She no longer knew what she was saying, but she liked the sound of the latter. "Yes," she said again, kissing him. "Yes, yes, yes."

She was glad the lights were out, glad she wouldn't have to see the look of cynical triumph that must be on his face. It was all an act, a sophisticated, manipulative act to get one more notch on his list of bedmates. So why were his hands shaking as he pulled the close-fitting turtleneck jersey over her head and tossed it in the corner? Why was his heart pounding as fast as hers, his lips traveling over her face as if he wanted to memorize her features with his mouth? And why was the tightly strung tension in his body transmuting into a pure sexual tension that trapped her within its threads?

Somehow she had gotten pressed up against the wall, the grainy texture of the plaster cool and rough against her bare back. He'd unfastened her bra and disposed of it, and his mouth traveled down her collarbone, his tongue slipping over her satin skin, enticing, arousing, worshipping, as his hands caught the zipper of her black denim pants and drew it downward. His hands pulled the jeans off her hips, sliding them down her long, trembling legs, and she was grateful for the support of the wall behind her. She stepped out of the crumpled jeans, and it wasn't until his hands reached her hips again that she realized he'd taken her panties with him, and she was naked.

His hands cradled her hips, the long fingers easily encircling their ripe contours, as his mouth moved slowly, sensuously across her bare stomach. She felt like a pagan goddess with Blackheart kneeling in front of her, slowly worshipping her body with his mouth and fingers. She felt decadent and sinful and gloriously alive, and when his mouth sank lower to the tangled heat of her, her heart and soul emptied in a rush of pleasure so heady that she had to brace herself against his strong shoulders or lose her balance.

This was new to her, and unbearable, sweetly glorious. Her body trembled against his mouth, and the world began to slip away, bit by bit, until it finally shattered in a tumbled rush, and her body convulsed in a white-hot heat of love.

She was falling, falling, and she cried out. But he was there, warm and solid and loving, catching her against his hard body, and she hid her face against his shoulder, frightened of her sudden vulnerability.

He held her until the trembling ceased, held her until she somehow

found the courage to lift her head and look at him, half fearfully. There was
no trace of cynical triumph in the shadowy darkness of his face, no cool
calculation. There was nothing but love and desire in those eyes of his, a love
and desire that mirrored her own.

A moment later she was swung up high, and he was carrying her through
the darkened apartment with the sureness of a cat. He laid her down on the
bed, stripping off his clothes with thoughtless grace before stretching out
beside her. She felt lazy, sensual and well loved, but the sight of his strong,
slim, absolutely beautiful body sent the slow-burning embers of desire
glowing into a brighter flame. With a shy sort of boldness she reached out for
him, relearning the planes and hollows of his body with a wondering delight.
In the darkness there were no rules, no pride, no ego and no fear. No safety,
either, but the most elemental trust. He needed her on every level that existed, and that need was her delight.

He moved to cover her, lean and strong and powerful, and she reached
up, wrapping her arms around him, drawing him into her heart, into her life,
into her body. Her sigh of pure pleasure met his, and then his mouth covered
hers as he suddenly turned deliciously, playfully rough, arousing her to a fever
pitch that left no room for anything but the heated, pulsing, shattering
intensity that swept between them like wildfire.

Their love was fast and furious, a celebration and a culmination of the
tension and danger they had shared, washed clean by love and sweat. She was
reaching, reaching for a summit that was somehow beyond her, and he was
there with her, holding her, helping her as they reached it, and together they
fell. He collapsed against her, and for the first time that night she felt the
tension drain from his body.

Ferris wanted to cling to him forever, wanted to keep her arms and legs
wrapped around him, holding him tight against her. But he began to stir,
restlessly, and she knew she had no choice but to let him go.

He rolled away from her, leaving her alone in the darkness. A moment
later he was lying back against the sheets, and his breathing was still uneven.
Ferris realized suddenly that he hadn't said a word since he'd begun to make
love to her. It had all been silent and intense, and she had the sudden, age-old
need for reassurance.

Blackheart wasn't the man to give it. They lay together in the darkness for
a long time, not touching, and then Blackheart reached out and turned on the
bedside light. Ferris blinked at the sudden brightness. When she could focus,
she wished she'd kept her eyes shut. On Blackheart's face was the cynical
expression she'd dreaded.

He yawned, stretching, and gave her a distant, cool smile. "There's
nothing better than a little quick sex after a job," he drawled. "The perfect
way to wind down, don't you think?"

She stared at him for a long moment as a tiny part of her heart started to
wither and die. And then her head snapped up, her backbone stiffened and

she pulled herself into a sitting position, doing her level best to ignore her nudity.

"Cut it the hell out, Blackheart," she shot back, determinedly unmoved. "You don't fool me with that crap."

If she expected to shock him she was disappointed. Blackheart was unshockable. But that cold look vanished from his eyes, and the smile warmed up several degrees. "What crap?" he inquired pleasantly. His nudity was a lot harder to ignore than her own, but gamely she persevered.

"Don't try to pretend you took me to bed to wind down," she said severely. "That's hogwash, and you know it."

His smile broadened. "Then why don't you tell me why I did take you to bed? Not that I approve of that terminology. Whether you like it or not, it was mutual."

"Did you hear any complaints?" Ferris said dangerously.

"No. So why did we have sex?" He crossed his arms behind his head, prepared to be entertained, and for a moment she contemplated mayhem. It had been a long time since she'd hit anybody, but now might be the time to start.

Well, maybe she deserved it, she thought forlornly. But she wasn't going to give up without a fight. "We didn't have sex, Blackheart," she said flatly. "We made love. There's a difference."

"And that difference is very clear to one of your great experience?"

She sat there, looking at him out of frustrated eyes for a long moment. "Blackheart," she said wearily, "I'm in love with you. You know it—you've probably known longer than I have. So stop playing these stupid games."

Blackheart just watched her, and she couldn't read the expression in his eyes. "And what does this mythical love entail?" he said finally, in a bored voice. But Ferris knew he was far from bored.

"For God's sake, Blackheart, give me a break! I've given you my virginity after fighting off scores of determined men, I've turned to a life of crime for your sake, and I've leaped tall buildings in a single bound. What more do you want?" she demanded, desperate.

He grinned at her, and sudden relief washed over her. It was going to be all right. It might take some time, but it was going to be all right. "So you love me, do you?"

"Yes."

"What about the good senator?"

"The good senator will have to look elsewhere for a suitable . . . senatress," she said finally.

He still watched her out of those distant eyes. "Scores of men, eh?"

"Hundreds," she replied.

He cocked his head, as if weighing her. "All right, wench. If you love me, come here and prove it."

She sat very still. After all, there were limits. "You come here," she said sternly.

And he did.

Chapter Twenty

FERRIS LIKED SHEETS. She'd never noticed before, not really. To be sure, she'd bought pretty sets for her own bed, dribbled chocolate and ice cream and even spaghetti sauce on them on occasion. But she'd never noticed their erotic potential.

Mind you, having Blackheart's sleeping body between them, pressed up against hers, helped. He had particularly nice sheets, she thought dreamily. Navy blue, with white piping. It made his skin look gloriously golden, and she wanted to touch the rumpled brown hair against the pillow.

He'd look nice in charcoal-gray sheets, she mused, snuggling closer with the subconscious hope of waking him. Or maybe beige. He'd even looked glorious against the tiny blue-and-white flowers that had decorated her bed.

If she had a lover, she thought lazily, or a husband, she wouldn't waste money on sexy nightclothes that would end up on the floor before long. She'd buy sheets. All colors and patterns, deep rose and black and purple and yellow. Flowers and stripes and solids, cottons and satins and flannels. The very image made her giddy with anticipation.

Was she going to have a husband or lover? Blackheart looked angelic when he slept, but he'd given her no clue last night. She'd presented him with her heart and soul, and he'd accepted them willingly enough. But he hadn't offered anything in return. Not yet. Would he?

It was too early to wake up. Dawn was just creeping over the rooftops, the sun fighting its way through another gray, misty day. It hadn't been that long ago when Blackheart had fallen asleep. If she was going to be worth anything, she'd better try to sleep herself. She and Blackheart had a long way to go. She'd need all her wits and her energy to get there.

He was so warm under the cool blue sheet. Turning over, she pressed up against him. One arm came around her waist, pulling her back against him. "Love," he murmured in her ear. She tensed, waiting for something else. But the rhythm of his breathing told her he was sound asleep, and his murmured word could have meant nothing. Or something too important to bear. Ferris sighed, closing her eyes against the brightening sunlight, and drifted off.

FOUR HOURS LATER he looked down at her, sleeping so peacefully in the center of the dark blue sheets. She looked good there, with her thick mane of hair spread out around her. She looked like she belonged.

And he belonged there in bed with her. The last thing he felt like doing right now was trying to convince a stubborn SFPD that Olivia Summers was the jewel thief, not him. And despite what he'd said last night, he wasn't any too certain he was going to be able to do it, even with the jewels in place.

The last thing he felt like doing was returning to the precinct that had held him with such unrestrained glee a few short days ago. If it were up to him, he'd never set foot inside a police station again.

The last few days had brought home the hard-learned lesson of his life. Never again could he stand the suffocating, demoralizing, slow death of prison. He'd flirted with the idea that he could go back to the rooftops any time he wanted, as long as his leg could support him. Last night had proved beyond the shadow of a doubt that he could scramble over all the rooftops he wanted. The magic touch was still there, and his body still did his bidding.

But his luck was gone, and his options with it. He'd lost his innocence as surely as the woman in his bed had lost hers, and things would never be the same and it was past time for him to face up to things.

When he looked at his life devoid of any illusions it was more than clear to him that he no longer wanted to make his living from other people's possessions, and hadn't for a long, long time. The fall and the shattered knee had been an excuse, a welcome one. The prison sentence had done more harm than good—he'd stubbornly refused to let someone else make that decision for him. But if it hadn't been the fall, it would have been something else, sooner or later. John Patrick Blackheart had been more than ready to settle down, and last night was his last fling.

How would Ferris-Francesca react when he told her? And he'd have to tell her, sooner or later. Though he hated like hell to give her that trust when she was still withholding hers. If it hadn't been for her sudden excess of morality, he could have gone through life with only that one arrest marring his career. But then he might have gone through his life never having faced the welcome end to his inherited profession. In the last few days he'd finally faced who and what he was, and who and what he wanted. And the woman in his bed was part and parcel of that wanting.

Kate was meeting him downtown. Trace would be with her, she'd said, and Blackheart's interest had been piqued. Had she already told him? How would he react to Kate's treachery? Knowing Trace, he'd be surprised if the big moose was anything less than sympathetic. Trace never blamed anybody for anything, just accepted people, warts and all. Pray God things went as they should, and he wouldn't have to pay for his trusting nature.

And once that was settled, then maybe he could figure out what he was going to do with Francesca-Ferris Berdahofski-Byrd. He didn't for one moment believe that she loved him. Her religion and her working-class up-bringing had taught her that you have to love the man you sleep with. He had given in to overwhelming temptation, seduced her and *voila*, true love! It would take care and time to elicit the real thing from her.

But that was exactly what he intended to do, once he got Olivia Summers sorted out. Because even if he didn't trust Ferris's protestations of true love, he knew exactly what he was feeling. For the first time in his life, in thirty-six misspent, fairly promiscuous years, he had fallen in love. And he wasn't about to give up without a fight.

Neither was she. The memory of her drawling, cutting temper last night still made him grin. He thought he was going to keep her at arm's length, maybe teach her a lesson or two. She should know what it felt like, to make soul-shattering love and then have your partner look at you with complete distrust. It still smarted, even though part of him couldn't blame her. Things had looked suspicious. But damn it, she should have trusted him.

Well, she trusted him now. Now that she'd seen the proof with her own eyes, heard it from Kate. And she'd trusted him enough to follow him up on that roof when she was petrified of heights. If he'd had any idea, he wouldn't have made her go.

But she'd gone, without a word, and he loved her for it. And he loved her for her messy apartment, her temper and her lopsided morality. He could go on, making a list of all the things he loved about her. But now wasn't the time. He could save that for some night when he was alone and couldn't sleep for wanting her. That time would come sooner than he wanted. Francesca Berdahofski wasn't going to give up being Mrs. Senator Phillip Merriam without a struggle, no matter what she said in the heat of passion. He'd just have to take every unfair advantage he could think of, to make sure she ended up with him and not in Washington. It was all for her own good, he thought righteously.

She needed her sleep, but he couldn't resist. Leaning down, he kissed her on the soft curve of her jaw, trailing his mouth up to her high cheekbone, glancing off her brow and ending on one closed eyelid. The eyelid fluttered open, and she smiled up at him, shyly, sleepily, and he almost jumped back on top of her.

"I'll be back," he said, trying to keep a disinterested tone in his voice. "I'm not sure when."

"I'll be here." She frowned sleepily. "If that's all right?"

"You stay. If you're gone I'll find you." It came out sounding almost like a threat, and he could have cursed himself. Ferris didn't seem to mind in the slightest. Smiling, she closed her eyes and fell back asleep.

If you're gone I'll find you, he echoed to himself grimly. Fine. Real cool, Blackheart. That's just the way to keep a distance from her. Next you'll be proposing again, and then where will you be? Up a creek without a paddle. And without Francesca. Damn.

It was all he could do to keep himself from slamming the door behind him. He closed it very silently, turning the three locks. He'd have to do something about her apartment. He didn't want anyone else breaking in there. It was his domain, and she was his woman. It might take some time, but sooner or later she'd come to terms with that. Please God it was sooner, or he still might have to rip out Phillip Merriam's tongue.

IT WAS PAST NOON when she finally decided to wake up. Each time she opened her eyes earlier she'd reached out for Blackheart and he hadn't been there. She could think of no reason for getting up without him, though she probably would have been even more loath if he'd been with her. But high noon was getting just too decadent to be believed, and her stomach was putting up a noisy protest.

"Damn," she said out loud to the silent apartment, throwing back the cool blue sheets and staring around her. Her stomach replied with a grumble, and she moaned. Every muscle in her body ached, both from the unexpected romp over San Francisco's rooftops and the romp that followed. She needed a hot bath and a huge amount of food, not necessarily in that order. And then she needed Blackheart.

There was a pot of coffee keeping warm on a hot tray, half a loaf of moldy bread in the bread box, and a six-pack of Beck's dark in the fridge. And not even a cannoli in sight, she thought with a groan, sagging against the open refrigerator door. The hell with the long hot bath—a shower would have to suffice. And then she'd be bold enough to go out and buy enough food to feed them both, and to hell with him if he thought she was being encroaching. She was, and he'd have to put up with it. After all, he'd started it.

The shower went a long way toward making her feel more human; two aspirins helped, and a cup of rich, strong coffee almost completed the job. All she needed was food in her stomach and she'd feel like a new woman.

The light wool suit and high heels felt tight and restricting after the freedom of Blackheart's black denims, and for a moment she considered raiding his closet for something more comfortable. Then she dismissed the idea. The last thing she wanted to be caught doing was rummaging through his apartment. She'd just managed to convince him that she did trust him—and she didn't want to risk blowing that fragile belief.

He'd left an extra set of keys on the hall table. Tossing them in her leather purse, she let herself out of the silent apartment and headed for the nearest food store.

It took her longer than she expected. The first place she stopped had fresh croissants and Ben and Jerry's ice cream, a good enough beginning for the day, but as she was leaving she developed a sudden craving for cannoli. They weren't to be found for seven blocks, and by that time several other delicious ideas had come to mind. It was one of those rare, brilliantly clear days that San Francisco so seldom got, with a chilly little breeze that made her glad for the wool suit, if not for the tottery high heels. By the time she was back on Blackheart's street her arms were aching, her ankles were tired and her stomach was knotted. So preoccupied was she in getting back to the apartment that she almost didn't notice the small dark Porsche parked illegally by the curb. It was a pretty car, oddly familiar. But even more familiar was the slender figure strolling casually down Blackheart's front steps.

Even half a block away Ferris could recognize Olivia Summers's greyhound elegance. Ducking quickly behind a large American car, she watched with dawning horror as Olivia made her way back to the Porsche, sliding into the front seat with a pleased expression hanging about her pale lips. Every blond hair was in place, and her patrician blue eyes were glistening with triumph. Triumph that didn't allow her to notice Ferris's watching figure as she drove off down the street, gunning the motor.

Ferris ran the rest of the block to Blackheart's apartment. The elevator was in use, and after slamming her hand against the buttons and cursing, she dashed to the back of the hall and ran up the five flights of stairs, pausing only long enough to yank off her obstructive shoes.

Blackheart's door looked the same—no sign of forced entry. But what the hell did she expect? Olivia Summers carrying a crowbar beneath that elegant suit she was wearing? With shaking hands Ferris fiddled with the three locks. They all turned beneath the key, and Ferris's blood ran cold. She'd only locked two of them.

The apartment looked exactly as she'd left it, silent and deserted, the lingering smell of the warming coffee lending a false air of coziness to the place. And with a sudden, horrifying clarity Ferris remembered. The light beside Olivia's bed *had* been on when they'd broken in. And she had been stupid enough to turn it off when they left.

It was a small enough thing, but anyone with Olivia's compulsiveness would notice it. And know that someone had been in the apartment.

What had she done? Why had she sneaked into Blackheart's apartment when no one was there? There could only be one reason. To find some way of incriminating him, rather than herself. Olivia could feel the noose tightening around her, and she needed another scapegoat. Trace and Kate weren't enough. Blackheart was a big enough prize to divert attention from the Summerses permanently. And this time, when the police came after him, they'd hold him a great deal longer than five hours.

Ferris quickly, methodically, began to tear the apartment apart. Somewhere was something incriminating enough to send Blackheart to prison for a very long time. It might be something as easily overlooked as a receipt for copying the jewels. If forgers gave receipts. Or it might be the Von Emmerling emeralds themselves.

Nothing but clothes in his drawers and closets. Nothing but papers in his desk. She tried to take the time to see whether anything was incriminating, but panic was beating down around her like bat's wings and she couldn't concentrate. Nothing under the couch, unlike her own apartment, nothing under the bed or between the mattress and spring. To her horror she found a handgun, complete with ammunition, in his desk, and she slammed the drawer shut on it with absolute terror.

No, you can't do that, she told herself sternly. Olivia might have planted a murder weapon. Not that anyone's been shot, much less murdered. But you have to check.

She opened the drawer again, staring down at the ugly black thing with a shudder of distaste. Slowly, reluctantly, she picked up the cold gray metal and brought it to her nose, sniffing for the smell of gunpowder. It smelled of metal and oil, and if it had been fired recently there was no way she could tell. With a shudder, she dropped the gun back in the drawer, slamming it shut.

She was mumbling under her breath as she upended sofa cushions and dropped them back haphazardly. "Where is it? Where the hell is it?" Inspiration struck, and she dived for the ice bucket. Nothing in it but three inches of cold water.

"The kitchen," she murmured under her breath. "Check the kitchen. Lots of drawers. Maybe in the freezer."

The first drawer spilled onto the floor as she yanked it out, and she re-filled it with shaking hands. Cabinets, drawers, refrigerator, oven—all were empty of anything remotely suspicious. The bags of recently purchased groceries were in a pile on the floor, the croissants and cannoli probably crushed, the ice cream melting. The coffee had heated down to a thin layer of sludge in the bottom of the pot, and she reached over and turned it off, her mind still intent upon her search. There was a two-pound bag of coffee beans out on the counter. How odd that a coffee snob like Blackheart hadn't put the beans back in the air-tight container with the other two-pound package. And why did he have two packages, when beans were better fresh roasted? He certainly didn't stock up on anything else.

The other bag was half full. With shaking hands she reached for the new one. Did it feel heavier, was there anything bulkier than coffee beans in it? She upended it on the counter, and the small dark beans scattered over the butcher-block surface, raining over the floor like marbles. But it wasn't two pounds of beans. In the midst of the pile lay a plastic-wrapped package of tawdry silver and green. The Von Emmerling emeralds.

Damn her, Ferris thought savagely. *Damn her soul to hell.* Her fingers were trembling so badly she had trouble dialing the phone. Which precinct, damn it, which precinct? She got lucky on her third try. Patrick Blackheart was there, all right, but he was in conference. Would she care to leave a message?

What the hell kind of message could she leave, she thought savagely after she'd hung up. The stolen jewels are in your apartment, but don't tell anyone. Damn and double damn.

They'd arrive at Olivia's, search warrant in hand, and would find exactly nothing. And it wouldn't take much effort on Olivia's part to put the shoe on the other foot. Even if Ferris re-hid the emeralds, what in heaven's name was she going to do with them? And how would anyone ever prove that Olivia had masterminded this whole plot?

She had no choice. And no time to hesitate, to panic, to have second thoughts. Her course was clear, and she had to take it.

"Darling, what's wrong?" Regina responded to her breathless phone call.

"You sound in an absolute panic."

"Regina, can you do me a huge favor? Can you somehow get Dale and Olivia to come over to your house? Right now? You could tell them they left something—"

"They're not home, Ferris," Regina broke in.

"They're not?"

"Blackheart called me from the police station a while ago to tell me they were being brought in for questioning. I don't like Olivia Summers, but I still can't believe—"

"Good-bye, Regina." Ferris slammed down the phone. So it had already started to happen. Would the police search their place while they were at the station? Or would they question them first? She'd have to count on it being the latter. Damn, why didn't she know more about criminal law? If Olivia had the right to be present when her apartment was searched, she'd doubtless insist on it. Ferris didn't fancy being caught red-handed by some of San Francisco's finest.

She wasted precious minutes changing back into Blackheart's burgling clothes. She found an old zippered sweatshirt hanging on the back of the bathroom door. The pocket was large enough to hold the bulky packet of emeralds. In the other she slipped Blackheart's lockpicks and trusty American Express card. Pray God she remembered enough from last night to retrace his steps.

It was with a sinking sense of horror that she realized she'd have to traverse those rooftops once more. Blackheart could have made short work of the service door to the basement of Olivia's building, but Ferris was still a rank amateur. It would take all her concentration and a fair amount of luck to get through the simple locks of the night before. She had no choice but to take the high road. And to hope that she made it in time.

Chapter Twenty-one

"YOU, AGAIN?" IT was a different cigarette dangling from the desk clerk's lips, a different shade of fuchsia on those lips, and her unlikely blond hair was up in curlers. But those same hard eyes flitted over Ferris's figure briefly, then went back to the magazine she was reading. *Cosmopolitan*, Ferris noticed. One hand with red chipped nails pushed the register at her. "Twenty bucks," she said flatly.

She hadn't signed her name Berdahofski in years. For a moment she hesitated, then wrote in bold, black letters. She pulled a twenty out of her wallet and dropped it on the desk. The woman just looked at her, and belatedly Ferris remembered. Another ten floated to settle on top of the twenty, and the woman took it, tossing a key back at her. "He meeting you up there?" she queried in a bored voice.

"Uh . . . er . . . yes," she finally managed.

"That'll be another five," the blonde said flatly.

"Another five?"

"For the inconvenience. Not to mention the security problems," she said with a straight face. Another five followed, and the woman nodded. "I gave you the same room, seeing as how you didn't bother to use it last night. This time, sweetie, wait till after to have your fight. And next time bring me back the key," she called after her, as Ferris scurried toward the elevator.

She didn't even bother to open the hotel room door. Getting off on the ninth floor, she headed up the stairway to the roof, the emeralds weighing heavy in her pocket. She felt like she was playing Dungeons and Dragons. Her first obstacle loomed ahead—the locked roof door.

It seemed to take hours. Her hands were slippery with sweat, but she didn't want to bother with the gloves just yet. She concentrated fiercely, poking with the little tools, sweat pouring off her forehead. She broke one, snapping the end off, and she cursed. Just one more try, she kept telling herself grimly as the stubborn lock held. One more, and then I'll give up. One more try.

She almost missed it when it finally worked. The tiny click was almost too good to be true. Reaching up, she turned the greasy knob. It opened with the lightest of touches.

That gave her enough confidence to carry her across the first two roofs. It was better in the daylight, with the blue sky overhead. It gave her something to concentrate on, rather than the inky blackness of certain death below. The ladder between the second and the third building looked more rickety in the daylight, but she reminded herself that it had held both of them last night. It could hold just her slight, shaking weight with no trouble.

It took her three tries to get the grappling hook safely attached to the fourth roof. Each time she yanked it to test its purchase it would clang back at her. When it finally held, she almost wished it hadn't. She had no choice but to go ahead, and the longer she hesitated the worse it would be. She pulled on her gloves, knowing that her sweat-slick hands could easily slide right down that thin nylon rope.

"Hail Mary, full of grace," she muttered under her breath, and swung out between the two buildings.

It was over in a minute. She was lying flat on her stomach on the pebbled roof, the sun-heated asphalt hot beneath her face. The worst was yet to come, and she had to force herself up to face it. But not yet. She needed a brief silent moment to regroup her scattered bravery. Just to the count of sixty, and then she'd move on.

It had looked like the Grand Canyon last night when they'd made their final jump to Olivia's building. This afternoon it was more like the Pacific Ocean. There was no way she was going to make it without Blackheart there to catch her. She was going to tumble down between the buildings, bouncing off the sides and ending in an ignominious, very dead heap on the sidewalk.

If there was any justice in the world, Olivia would be beneath her when she fell. And she'd taken too long as it was—she couldn't stand there and stare at the great chasm waiting to swallow her up. This time she'd take a running leap, and if she didn't make it . . .

Well, she would make it. She wasn't going to die a tragic death and leave Blackheart to chase after bored socialites. He needed taking in hand, and she was the one to do it. She moved backward, slowly, carefully, until she was a good ten feet from the edge of the roof. And then, before she could think about it anymore, she ran and leaped.

"Ooooh, damn!" she cursed in a muffled shriek, as her knee hit the pebbled roof and she sprawled in a graceless belly flop that knocked the wind out of her. She lay there like a beached whale, struggling for breath, hugging the rooftop like a crazed creature.

Her breath came back in a sickening whoosh. Her knee felt smashed in a hundred places, her gloves tore and her palms were scraped by the rough roof, but she had made it. This time she did kiss the roof, her fingers caressing its rough surface. She'd made it.

Jumping down onto the Summerses' terrace was a piece of cake compared to everything else. Her knee almost gave way as she landed, but she caught on to a wrought-iron chair that held her upright. No sign of life beyond the sliding glass window. No men in blue staring back out at her.

Reaching around in her back pocket, she panicked once again as she came up empty. She didn't find the card until she checked her front pocket for the third time, and by then her nerves were screaming once more. She'd taken Blackheart's American Express card for luck. Her hands were shaking again as she jammed the thin plastic between the two doors. It had looked so easy when Blackheart did it. One little push, and the door had slid open. Why couldn't it be as easy for her?

She jammed again, and the card made an ominous cracking noise. Ferris was mumbling and moaning under her breath, prayers and curses tumbling forth. What had Blackheart told her last night? So many things, and right now they were all jumbled in her panicked brain. *Caress it open,* he'd said. *Treat the lock like a lover. Tease and soothe it.*

She pulled the card out, swearing at the splintered end. Reversing it, she gently slipped the undamaged end between the two doors, using the lightest possible touch. Like a lover, she thought with a rueful grin, Blackheart's smiling eyes dancing in her mind. The door clicked open.

The apartment was still and silent, blessedly so. Ferris took a deep breath before stepping inside, her feet silent on the thick wool carpet. She had made it, in time. Reaching into the sweatshirt pocket, she drew out the plastic-wrapped emeralds and headed for the bedroom.

The door was open, the video equipment and cameras and stacks of videos gone, she noticed with sudden surprise. A desk had been moved in place, with a typewriter and a pile of correspondence, everything bright and businesslike. *All clean and nice and normal,* she thought with a twisted smile. Olivia certainly knew they were coming.

The empty wastebasket was her next shock, and it stopped her for a moment. Of course the tissue box would be gone, along with the trash. And she couldn't very well just dump the plastic bag in there without any covering. It took her a moment to realize it didn't have to be where Olivia had originally left it. Anywhere reasonable would do the trick. The police would be politely thorough if . . . when . . . Blackheart prevailed on them to get a search warrant. Olivia would be unlikely to raise more than a token objection, being blissfully secure that the jewels were residing among her nemesis's coffee beans. It would be interesting to see how she planned to turn the tables. Of course she wouldn't get the chance.

Underneath Olivia's silky lingerie would be the best bet. With her fastidious tastes, she wouldn't like strange men pawing through her panties, and she'd dislike even more the thought of someone planting the loot there. Did she know her secret room had been breached last night? Maybe she hoped they'd come across the jewels before they found her lucrative sideline.

She would have given anything to be a fly on the wall when they found the jewels. But that was far too risky, just as standing around dithering was. With exquisite care Ferris slipped the bulky jewels beneath the pastel silk lingerie, careful not to disturb the neat piles. This time she had to leave no sign that she'd been there. It had been her own stupid fault that Olivia knew they'd broken in the night before. If she'd just remembered about the damned light none of this would have been necessary.

Her knee and shin were beginning to throb. The sooner she was out of there, the better. It was going to take some time getting down those twenty flights of stairs. And this time she was going to stop and rest if she needed to. Her leg was stiffening up, and there was no longer any need to push it. She'd make her way slowly, carefully down those narrow metal stairs, maybe get a taxi and head out toward Oakland, just in case anyone happened to be watching. In another hour or two she could end up back at Blackheart's and receive the praise and love due her. With a weary sigh, she let the kitchen door shut quietly behind her and headed down the first flight of deserted stairs.

"DID YOU SEE THE expression on her face?" Rupert demanded for the third time. "I thought she was going to have a fit."

"Very satisfying," Blackheart drawled in agreement as they climbed the front steps to his apartment an hour and a half later. "What I can't figure out is why she looked so damned surprised. And why she'd moved them from her first hiding place. Hiding the emeralds under her underwear seemed just a bit too obvious for someone like Olivia."

"Her husband certainly thought so," Rupert chortled. "It was just like 'Perry Mason.' The accomplice takes one look and starts ratting on the other. The police couldn't even keep up with him to take notes. I love it, just love it."

"There's still something that doesn't seem quite right about it," Blackheart murmured, punching, the elevator button. "I can't get rid of the feeling that something more was going on. Why did Olivia look so surprised, when she'd been so smug beforehand? And why was that room cleared out, if she wasn't expecting the place to be searched?"

"The less you tell me, the better," Rupert warned him. "I don't want to know what you were doing last night."

"Rupert, you're my lawyer," Blackheart drawled, gesturing for the shorter man to precede him into the tiny elevator. "You're allowed to hear privileged information."

"Well, I don't want to. I'm too cheered by how things worked out. Stop raining on my parade, will ya? For once just appreciate that everything worked out and stop trying to find problems. Jeez, you're such a downer, Patrick."

"Sorry," Blackheart murmured, unmoved. "I can't help it." He began unlocking the three locks. If only there was some way he could rid himself of that nagging feeling that something had gone wrong. Over the years he'd learned to rely on an almost mystical instinct, and that instinct was clanging loudly inside him, and had been for hours now. He'd been almost as surprised as Olivia when the jewels turned up. He'd taken one look at that smugly opened inner door and been prepared for the worst.

The apartment was dark and silent when he opened the last lock, and his feeling of foreboding increased. She'd said she'd be there, waiting for him. It was getting darker—she must have been gone for some time. Where the hell had she gone?

Without betraying his uneasiness, he flicked on the light. "I don't know where Ferris is, but I imagine she'll be back in a while. Do you want to meet us for dinner? I imagine love's young dream will want to be alone."

Rupert laughed. "Kate and Trace were pretty funny, weren't they? He seemed almost glad she'd helped with the robbery. I've never seen so many meaningful glances in my life."

Blackheart shrugged. "They're in love. Trace is the most tolerant man I know—he doesn't give a damn what she did, he only cares about what she's feeling now. I guess he was so busy being her buddy that he didn't realize he was in love with her. And of course, given her earlier standoffishness, he didn't think he had a chance with her. You can tell it's the real thing—the two of them look absolutely ridiculous together."

Rupert snorted. "Ain't love grand?"

Blackheart grinned. A month ago, ten days ago, he would have echoed Rupert's cynicism. But that was before Francesca Berdahofski had argued her way into his life. "Yes, it is," he drawled. And then stopped short, as that instinct began clanging loudly inside his head.

"Something wrong, Patrick?" Rupert was quick to pick up the sudden tension.

"The apartment's been searched."

"Oh, surely not. It's a little messier than usual, but no one's trashed the place."

"No one had to," he said grimly, taking in the cushions still askew, the desk drawers left haphazardly open. "She had plenty of time to go through it—she didn't need to dump everything on the floor."

"She? Surely you don't think Ferris . . . ?"

Blackheart turned a bleak face to his lawyer and friend. "Of course it was her. I left her here, with a set of keys. Anyone else would have had to break in."

"Think about it, man. Why would she do such a thing? What could she expect to find? She knew the emeralds were at Olivia's. Maybe she was just curious. Women are like that sometimes."

"Simple curiosity wouldn't involve a thorough search like this. And she wouldn't have been so clumsy. I think maybe she wanted to see if I was involved after all. Maybe see if I had some jewels left over from before. Maybe she didn't think it was before, maybe she thought I was still working even if I didn't do the Von Emmerling job. Damn her." His voice was furious.

Rupert stared at him for a long moment. "Listen, Patrick, give her a chance to explain. There may be a perfectly logical reason for this."

"There is. She didn't trust me," he said bitterly, flinging his tired body onto the sofa. "Get me a drink, will you, Rupert? Something strong. And get something for yourself."

Rupert paused, looking at his friend. "Okay," he said finally. "But think about it before you start making accusations. You want me to stay in the kitchen?" They could both hear the fumbling with the unfamiliar locks.

"I don't give a damn," Blackheart said. "Do what you want."

"See you in a while," Rupert said hastily, vanishing into the kitchen as Ferris finally opened the door.

She looked tired, Blackheart thought, feeling not an ounce of pity. She dumped his keys on the hall table and looked up, and the exhaustion on her face vanished, replaced by a look of intense joy as she moved toward him, limping slightly.

"Blackheart, you're back," she cried happily. "What happened? Did . . ." her voice trailed off, and the joyful look on her face disappeared, leaving a wary expression in its place. He just sat there on the sofa, looking up at her with a cold, bleak expression. "Didn't they arrest Olivia?" she asked.

"They did. Caught red-handed, and Dale started blabbing and nothing could stop him. There'll be no problem. The charges against Trace and me were dropped, and Rupert says Kate will probably get off with a suspended sentence." His voice was clipped and dry.

"Then what's the problem?" Ferris demanded, relief warring with the wariness. "Everything's wonderful. Blackheart, I have to tell you what I did. I—"

"You don't have to tell me," he interrupted in a savage voice. "It's more than clear."

She had started toward him, but the cold words stopped her. "What is it you think I did, Blackheart?" If he'd bothered to look at her, he would have recognized the pain and surprise that washed over her face. But he kept his eyes on the skyline.

"You searched my apartment. Couldn't quite trust me, could you? Despite all those pretty words, when it came right down to it you had to make absolutely certain that I wasn't still a felon. Didn't you?"

"Didn't I what?" she asked very calmly.

"Didn't you search my apartment?"

"Yes," she said.

"And did you find what you were looking for?"

"Yes," she said again. She stood there for a long moment, not moving. "Good-bye, Blackheart."

He didn't turn his head until he heard the door shut quietly behind her. And then he began to swear, steadily, obscenely.

Rupert appeared from the kitchen, two dark drinks in his hand. "You got rid of her, I see. Didn't listen to my advice, did you?"

"When I want your advice I'll ask for it and pay for it," Blackheart snapped.

"I do think I ought to mention something to you," Rupert said casually, handing him the drink and sitting down opposite him. "Your kitchen is a mess. She was in a bigger hurry when she got to it."

"So?"

"So, there are coffee beans all over the counter and the floor, and the bag that held them is ripped apart."

Blackheart just looked at him. "This is supposed to be edifying? Maybe she didn't like my kind of coffee."

"It wasn't your kind of coffee, Patrick. You drink Sumatran coffee exclusively. This was a bag of Colombian beans."

He'd finally gotten Blackheart's interest. "I don't like Colombian coffee."

"Exactly."

"And what does your analytical mind tell you, Rupert?" Blackheart was genuinely curious.

"Oh, I wouldn't jump to any conclusions, unlike you who thinks he knows everything. But I will mention that the police noted one curious thing about the emeralds. There was a coffee bean wrapped up in the plastic wrap."

Dead silence filled the room as Blackheart looked at his friend in horrified comprehension. "I'm an idiot!" He slammed his drink down and was at the door two seconds later. There was no sign of her—she was long gone. He turned to look for his keys, and swore again. Sitting there on the hall table were his butchered lock picks and a shredded American Express card. And a key to the Bontemps Hotel.

Chapter Twenty-two

BLACKIE GREETED her at the door when she let herself in. The apartment had that faintly stale, musty odor places get when they've been closed up for a while. It hadn't been that long since she'd been home, she thought wearily. Only a lifetime ago.

Seaside Surprise wasn't compensation enough for her outraged gray tomcat. The look of contempt in his yellow eyes was unnervingly like Blackheart's, and Ferris hastily rummaged for a tin of people tuna. Blackie gave her a look that said, Don't even try.

"Well, what do you want?" she demanded, harassed. He raised his tail with supercilious grace and she gave in, reaching for the leftover bit of Brie. She wouldn't be entertaining Phillip again, anyway, so there would be no one to begrudge its absence.

Very carefully she stripped off the black denims, dropping them in the middle of the kitchen floor. Her fall had scraped layers of skin off her shin and knee, and the blood had crusted over, sticking to the denim. She moaned softly as she pulled the cloth away, and Blackie looked up from the cheese for a moment, offering a questioning "mrrrow?"

"It's nothing, kid," she murmured, peeling the turtleneck over her head and dropping it on top of the discarded jeans. "Just a battle scar." Clad in her underwear, she limped into the bathroom. For the time being she wasn't going to think about Blackheart, wasn't going to tear her heart out over him. She was going to sink into a hot, soothing bath and soak all the aches and pains out of her bones, then she was going to eat everything she could find in the house, short of Seaside Surprise. And then maybe she'd feel like thinking about Patrick Blackheart.

SHE WAS IN THE kitchen when the doorbell rang. She was clad in a pair of powder-blue ladies' boxer briefs and matching tank top, and for a moment she considered ignoring the summons. If it was Blackheart he could find his own way in there, and she didn't know whether she felt up to facing anyone else. Especially if her afternoon's activities weren't as discreet as she had hoped, and someone had seen her clambering over the rooftops.

The bell rang again, and she reached for her old terry-cloth bathrobe, padding to the front door on bare feet. Peering out the tiny peephole, all she could see was a huge basket of red roses.

"It's me," a tinny voice said. "Mrs. Melton from next door. These were delivered for you earlier today and I took them in."

She controlled the immediate pang of disappointment, hastily opening the door to let the little woman in. "You were out," Mrs. Melton continued, eying Ferris's bathrobe as if she knew full well what lay underneath and disapproved of it heartily. "I told them they could leave them with me, but they ought to be watered."

"Who are they from?" The question was desultory. If they arrived this afternoon they couldn't be from Blackheart, complete with a heartfelt apology.

Mrs. Melton drew herself up to her full height of four feet eleven inches, bristling with outrage. "I haven't the faintest idea, Ms. Byrd. I wouldn't think of looking. I'm not a nosy neighbor."

Mrs. Melton was an extremely nosy neighbor, but Ferris let that pass. She was rummaging through the roses, looking for a card, when her neighbor spoke again.

"It's in the back," she said, and blushed. "I didn't read it, I just happened to notice it was there."

Ferris gave her her nicest smile. An overwhelming curiosity about one's fellow man surely wasn't the worst trait in the world to possess. The card wasn't sealed, and there was a smudgy fingerprint on it.

The roses had to be from Phillip. But the card was a definite surprise.

"I understand," it read. "Love, always. Phillip." What did he understand? Mrs. Melton was craning her neck, trying to read the card, but Ferris tucked it back in the envelope. "Do I owe you any money?" she inquired tranquilly.

"What for?" She was still looking forlornly at the card.

"Did you give the messenger a tip?"

Mrs. Melton sniffed. "Of course not. He's paid for delivering things, isn't he?"

Ferris controlled the smile that threatened her. "Of course. Thank you again, Mrs. Melton."

There was nothing the woman could do but leave. Ferris watched her go, refastening the ineffectual locks with an abstracted air. Phillip understood, did he? The note sounded like a farewell. A farewell that was long overdue, but she had expected it was going to be more of an ordeal.

Well, maybe things were improving. She'd send Phillip back his ring, and perhaps that would be the end of it. She only hoped she could remain friends with Regina. She'd always liked Phillip's mother a tiny bit more than Phillip himself. It would grieve her more than she liked to admit to lose that relationship.

Phillip's ring was nowhere to be seen. She searched over every available surface, under the bed, in the drawers, in her pockets. *Don't panic,* she told herself. *It'll turn up. You never lose anything for good. When did you last see it?*

The memory wasn't reassuring. She didn't remember seeing it since the night of the Puffin Ball. Had Olivia somehow managed to get her slender, patrician fingers on that, too?

It was late, after midnight, when she gave up and finally headed for bed. She'd been avoiding that room like the plague. It was ridiculous—she'd lived in the apartment for three years, and after one night it had taken on all sorts of unshakable memories.

There was no way she could summon up a great deal of self-pity, she thought with determined fairness. She'd condemned Blackheart without a hearing the moment the theft was discovered. It served her right to have the same lack of trust thrown back in her face.

The red shoes were sitting on top of her dresser. She slipped them on her feet, giving her reflection a wry grin. Powder-blue jockey shorts and red high heels. Too bad Blackheart wasn't here to enjoy it. Flopping down on the bed, she grabbed a pillow and tucked it underneath her as she flicked on the TV. And flicked it right off again. Channel 12 was still running its series of caper movies, and the last thing she was going to do was lie on her big empty bed and watch *To Catch a Thief.*

She lay there, staring at the sheets for a long moment. They were new, a deep wine color. Blackheart would look beautiful on them.

Damn, there was no way she was going to get him out of her mind. She may as well watch the movie—his memory was going to drift in and out like the Ghost of Christmas Past as it was.

And damn Blackheart. Cary Grant he wasn't, but there was still no way she could lie there and watch and not be inundated with the memory of Blackheart. The sound and smell and feel of his supple flesh, the memory of his laughing eyes and mocking, arousing mouth.

She was lying at the opposite end of the bed, the shiny red shoes on one of the pillows, her head at the foot, watching the television set intently. Hugging the pillow as Cary Grant sank onto the couch with Grace Kelly and the fireworks flashed overhead. She moaned miserably into the sheets. Maybe ice cream would help her forget her sorrows.

"Where did the flowers come from?"

She kept very still, her fingers still clutching the pillow beneath her. Maybe that low, warm voice was a figment of her imagination. Maybe she'd died and gone to heaven. Slowly she lifted her head, to look straight into Blackheart's dark, rueful eyes.

"From Phillip," she replied breathlessly.

"Did he have anything interesting to say?" Blackheart was determinedly casual. Blackie was reposing in his arms, and one long-fingered hand was stroking the furry gray head.

"I guess he was saying good-bye." She tried to summon a tentative smile. "He beat me to the punch. You can get rid of them, if you want." She held her breath, waiting for his response.

"I already did." Blackie jumped out of his arms then, stalking back toward the living room without a backward glance.

"I'm going to have to find Phillip's engagement ring to send back to him," she said, still not able to gauge Patrick's mood. "I looked everywhere for it, but I couldn't find it."

"Are you accusing me of stealing it?" he asked, and she flinched.

"No, of course not. I wouldn't think—"

"Because I did," he continued smoothly.

"—of accusing you of . . . You did?"

His smile was entrancing. "Guilty. I couldn't resist. It was just sitting there, abandoned, and my palms started itching."

She stared, at him for a long moment. "What did you do with it?"

"Sent it to Phillip. I neglected to mention that it came from me and not you. I didn't think it mattered," he said gently.

"Why did you take it?"

He shrugged. "I guess I can't resist. Every now and then something comes along and all my good intentions go out the window. I really need someone to keep me in line."

"What sort of someone?"

"Well, I'd prefer another cat burglar. Someone who could climb over rooftops with me if the need arose. Someone who could even do it by herself if she had to."

Ferris held her breath. "Wouldn't that be encouraging you?"

"Oh, I don't think so. She could make sure I only broke into places that I had to. Maybe she should be afraid of heights. That way she won't be into doing it at the drop of a hat."

"Sounds logical," she said softly. "Does she need anything else?"

"An American Express card. Mine got mysteriously shredded. I don't know how I'm going to explain it to the company. Not to mention getting certain slightly illegal tools replaced. I suffered a lot of losses today."

"Did you?"

He nodded, moving into the room with his usual catlike grace. "I lost my secretary to my assistant. It looks like they're going to make a match of it."

Ferris grinned. "That's wonderful."

"And my tools of the trade suffered considerable damage," he continued. "I've probably earned the displeasure of Regina Merriam, not to mention half of San Francisco society, for my part in Olivia and Dale Summers's fall from grace."

"I think you're more likely to win appreciation for that one."

"Maybe." He shrugged again, and Ferris suddenly realized that cool, sophisticated Patrick Blackheart, cat burglar extraordinaire, was nervous. Nervous as a cat. "Most people knew about their gambling debts, so I don't think it came as too great a surprise."

"What else did you lose today?"

"The respect of my lawyer, for jumping to conclusions. And I may have lost the woman I love. I'm sorry, Francesca."

Slowly she closed her eyes as relief washed over her. When she opened them, he was staring down at her intently, and she smiled, a tremulous, loving smile. "You haven't lost her," she said. "You haven't even discouraged her a little."

He still didn't cross the last few feet of space. "Trust is a funny thing," he said meditatively. "It's a gift that's given, it's something you earn, and yet it's so damned fragile. And without trust, love isn't worth a damn."

Ferris pulled herself into a sitting position, looking at him intently. "Blackheart," she said steadily, "there's trust and there's trust. I trust you with my heart and my soul and my life. If I find that I can't trust you with other women's jewels, I'm just going to have to accept the fact that I'll be spending a lot of time returning them when you're not looking. At least I'm not without experience."

Those beautiful hands of his caught her bare shoulders, and he was drawing her slowly up to him, almost into his arms, when a startled look came into his eyes. "What the hell are you wearing, woman? You have the strangest taste in nightclothes."

"You can always take them off me," she murmured, moving the rest of the way. His mouth met hers in an open, searing kiss that weakened her already abused leg. She sank against him, and slowly he lowered her to the bed, following her down. His hands were eager, hurried, but oh, so gentle as they stripped the ridiculous clothes away from her body. Slowly, carefully he loved her, his body tuned to her every need, anticipating them and satisfying them with an almost mystical cleverness that left her reaching, longing, aching, and then blissfully sated.

She lay in his arms, cradled against his warm body. He did look beautiful against the wine-colored sheets, his skin warm and firm and faintly damp with sweat.

"I suppose it's only fair to tell you," he murmured against her cloud of hair.

"Tell me what?"

"That I've decided I don't need to replace my tools of the trade."

She lay very still against him, holding her breath. "Why not?"

"I think I've broken into enough places in my misspent life," he drawled. "I held on to the lockpicks just in case I wanted to go back to the life. I've realized in the last few days that I never want to go back. My fall and the prison term were only an excuse to put a stop to it."

"Won't you miss the excitement?" She had to ask. She could feel the smile that creased his face as it rested against her temple.

"Not with you around." His lips brushed her damp forehead. "I don't suppose there's any chance of your making a similar sacrifice?"

"Hell, no," she replied lazily. "I intend to keep on breaking into places."

"I wasn't talking about B and E," he said with mock severity. "I was wondering when you felt like facing Francesca Berdahofski."

She bit him, lightly, on the smooth skin of his bony shoulder. "I did, Blackheart. Days ago. If you'd stopped to buzz my apartment, you would have noticed the new name on the mailbox. Ferris Byrd bit the dust the night of the Puffin Ball."

"I'm glad. I have my reputation to consider, after all. I wouldn't want it known that I was consorting with someone living a double life."

She bit him again, a little harder, her mouth nibbling at his warm, enticing skin, and he growled an approving response.

"There's one major problem with all this," he said as his hand reached up to stroke her neck.

"What's that?" She wasn't going to fall for one of his teasing ploys this time. There were no major problems that would stop her.

"If you marry me and change your name, you won't be able to call me Blackheart in that deliciously scathing voice of yours. Not when you share the same name."

She grinned up at him. "Of course I can. You don't think I'd settle for anything as tame as Patrick, do you? You have a wicked, black heart, and your name suits you better than anything your parents might have saddled you with."

"I thought so, too," he said complacently.

"What do you mean?" She was suddenly wary.

"Just that you aren't the only one who changed their name. John Patrick Blackheart is a much more fitting name for a cat burglar than Edwin Bunce."

"Oh, no," she groaned, hiding her face against his smooth silky chest.

"Oh, yes. Still want to marry me?"

She eyed him. "Can I marry Patrick Blackheart? I'll accept Francesca Berdahofski, but Francesca Bunce . . ."

"Changing my name was one of the few legal moves I made in my formative years," he murmured, kissing her lightly on the nose. "You can be a Blackheart, too, but you'll have to make it legal."

"Whenever you want, Blackheart. I have to warn you, though. I expect I'm out of a job. Phillip won't want his ex-fiancée as an administrative assistant."

"Kate's out of a job, too. I don't suppose you'd be interested in whipping Blackheart, Inc., into shape?"

"Along with Blackheart himself? That might prove very . . . challenging."

His mouth dropped onto hers, his tongue tracing the soft contours of her lips. "Why don't we start now?" he whispered.

"Because we're coming to the best part of the movie," she murmured limpidly. "And I want to see how Cary Grant manages those rooftops. Professional curiosity, you know. Just because you're giving up a life of crime doesn't mean that I intend to follow suit." Rolling away from him, she grabbed the remote control and turned up the sound.

A moment later the little box was wrenched gently from her hand, the television went blank, and the room was plunged into darkness. "I'll tell you all about it," he drawled. "If you come here."

"Well, it's a tough choice," she said on a low note of laughter. "But I guess they'll rerun the movie."

The End

CATSPAW II

Cast of Characters

John Patrick Blackheart—A retired cat burglar now running his own security firm in San Francisco. But was he *really* retired?

Ferris Byrd—Could she make a life with a man she couldn't trust?

Danielle Porcini—All she cared about was escaping her abusive partner-in-crime and wreaking a belated vengeance.

Stephen McNab—A cop with his own ideas of vengeance.

Senator Phillip Merriam—He was willing to do anything to gain national power, including selling out his own mother.

Marco Porcini—He possessed the cunning of a fox and the intellect of a soap dish.

"DO YOU EXPECT me to be Spider-Man?" Ferris demanded.

She and Blackheart were standing in a grove of trees on the west side of Regina's stately mansion, looking at the sharply angled roof four stories above.

"I expect you to follow my lead, dear heart. If the two of us can break in, then the place isn't as secure as it should be." He swung himself up into a tree and then began climbing.

She could hear the distant noise from the circus on the great lawn on the eastern side of the building; she could hear the muffled roar of the big cats. Ferris grimly reached for the first branch. "Are you up there?" she called. "I'm coming."

He was waiting for her, miles away from the safety of the thick-limbed oak tree, lounging indolently on the third-floor balcony.

"I won't let you fall. Jump! Trust me at least that far."

"I don't trust you, Patrick. I thought we made that clear."

"Come on," he said, and his hand closed over hers, yanking suddenly. Caught off guard, she had no chance to do anything more than shut her eyes and leap.

Chapter One

Vertigo
(Paramount 1958)

FRANCESCA BERDAHOFSKI, alias Ferris Byrd, stood in a pool of water outside her apartment, staring in frustration at the row of shiny new locks on the otherwise flimsy door. She shivered, sniffled, then sneezed, and for a brief moment leaned her forehead against the white-painted pine.

It was September in San Francisco, a cold, rainy September that made Ferris long for hot, barren deserts and doors without locks. All her doubts and uncertainties were pressing in on her, culminating in the frustration of the three new locks that she still hadn't managed to make work.

She pushed herself back, shoved her rain-drenched black hair away from her face, and began to search through her tasteful leather purse. She never could find her keys, and after a miserable day like today, starting with no coffee and a broken-down car, then tantrums among the socialites she was busy babysitting, and finally a diabolical cloudburst on the way home, it was clear that her rotten luck would hold.

No keys in her purse. While her apartment was usually a shambles, she kept her purse ruthlessly organized, and there were no keys lurking underneath the slim leather checkbook, the tiny flacon of Obsession, the Estee Lauder lipstick. There was only the piece of paper with the phone number of the garage written in blue ink. The garage where her navy-blue Mercedes was undergoing surgery. The garage that held her car, her car keys and the attached keys to her apartment.

Ferris Byrd, a woman of great self-possession who never cried, promptly burst into tears. She gave in to temptation and pounded on the unyielding door in mute frustration. The only answer was a thin, plaintive mew.

"Blackie," Ferris murmured mournfully to the cat on the other side of her door. "Why can't you be like your namesake and materialize through locked doors?"

Blackie's response was his usual huffy snarl, and through the thin door Ferris could hear thirteen pounds of alley cat stalk away from his mistress's voice.

"Go ahead, be like that," Ferris said bitterly. "Desert me in my hour of need." The unfortunate phrasing came a little too close to the truth of her current situation. Sighing, Ferris faced the unpleasant alternatives. She could either try to find a taxi and make her way to Guido's Imports to fetch her keys, or she could break into her own apartment.

Guido's Imports sounded appealing, but it was almost six o'clock, and Guido kept banker's hours. The big building on Canal Street would be locked up tighter than her apartment.

So breaking and entering it was. Not through the three shiny brass locks adorning her door. She could thank her conscientious fiancé for those. *Trust a retired cat burglar to know the best, most unpickable locks on the market. Of course,* he'd blithely told her that as far as he was concerned no locks were unpickable, but her talents as a cracksman or cracks woman were not as impressive. Besides, she'd mangled Blackheart's picklocks and he'd promised there was no need to replace them. And she'd believed him. Hadn't she?

If she was going to get into the apartment, it would have to be through the second-floor terraced balcony. And while she could always wait a few minutes in the wistful hope that the heavy downpour outside might abate, common sense told her it would be a waste of time. It was getting darker, the rain had been falling steadily for the last hour and a half, and with her luck it might even turn into a thunderstorm. The door wasn't going to open automatically, and she had no choice. It was time to renew her acquaintance with B and E.

She shrugged out of her peach silk raincoat and left it in a sodden pile outside her door. She'd never manage to scramble up the side of the old frame building with that flapping around her, and she was going to get soaked, anyway. She might as well make her attempt at scaling the building in the least encumbered condition.

She considered dumping her purse on top of the raincoat, then thought better of it. Her building wasn't the most secure place in the world; only her apartment was impenetrable. And her purse contained gold credit cards, too much cash and her birth control pills, none of which she cared to replace.

Slinging the thin strap over her head, she headed down the stairs and out into the rain, prepared to assault the fortress.

If anything, the rain had become even more relentless. The weight of it pulled at her loosely knotted hair, and she could feel sopping tendrils drip down her neck and over her high cheekbones like rats' tails. The water was running down her thin silk blouse, pooling in her bra, and her leather high-heeled shoes were squelching noisily as she moved around the outside of the building.

One of San Francisco's steep hilly streets ran along the side of the house, a blessing that Ferris was now heartily grateful for. Approaching her small balcony from the back corner of the building, her apartment was only a story and a half from the street, instead of the two and half that it was from the front.

The rain-swept streets were deserted, a fact that Ferris noticed with mixed feedings. On the one hand, she didn't particularly want an audience as she shinnied up the side of her building. On the other, maybe there would have been a Good Samaritan who shared the skills her missing fiancé had in abundance.

Don't think of him, *she ordered herself, gritting her teeth as the water poured in sheets down her back.* You'll just get madder. Think of a hot bath, an oversize glass of brandy and ice cream. Double Rainbow coffee, a whole pint of it, while you watch something soothing on TV Something that has nothing to do with retired cat burglars. Or practicing cat burglars, either.

The battered trash cans, Blackie's favorite home away from home, were lined up haphazardly in the alley behind Ferris's building, reeking of garbage and heaven only knew what else. Breathing through her mouth, she wrapped her arms around one smelly container and half carried, half dragged it around the corner, stopping under her second-floor balcony. She was cursing beneath her breath, sweating, her hands cold and slippery on the metal, her feet sliding around inside her wet shoes, so intent on her misery that she didn't notice the car parked opposite, didn't feel the gaze boring into her back.

She climbed up onto the rickety garbage can, scraping her knees on the dented lid. She got to her feet, bracing herself against the rain-slick siding, her ankles tottery in the slippery high heels as she stared down at her long, wet legs and shredded stockings.

"Wouldn't you just know it?" she demanded of the rain-dark skies. "The first time in fifteen years I dare to wear a miniskirt, and I end up climbing up a building in it. Hell and damnation."

The sky responded with an ominous rumble of thunder, and the lid of the can collapsed, sending Ferris into the pile of stinking refuse.

She practically catapulted out, beyond recriminations, beyond tears, beyond cursing. Upending the garbage can and scattering the ripped plastic bags of trash over the sidewalk, she kicked off her useless high heels and climbed back up, balancing on the upside-down can as she set one wet stockinged foot on her neighbor's windowsill. Clinging to the framework, she reached for the tendrils of ivy that cascaded down from her balcony, yanking hard.

A few wet leaves came off in her hands, but the vine held. Wrapping her arm in the thick, wet greenery, she hauled herself upward, her body swinging slightly, her purse slapping against her breasts, the ropelike vines cutting into her soft hands. She reached blindly with her feet, stubbing her toes against the wet wood, and pushed her way upward, slowly, painfully, the vine's support slipping slightly, the rain pouring down mercilessly all the while. The rim of her balcony was less than a foot beyond her reach, a tantalizing ten inches or so. If she could just manage one more boost up the clinging tendrils, she'd be home free.

She yanked, the vine pulled away from the wall, and for a moment she was swinging out over the garbage-littered sidewalk. She shut her eyes, uttering a little moan of terror. She hated heights, hated them with a passion bordering on mindless panic. Why in heaven's name hadn't she done the sensible thing and gone to a hotel for the night? Blackie would have survived without her.

She allowed herself a brief glance downward through slitted eyes. It seemed like an endless drop, and the garbage bags didn't look as if they'd provide too soft a landing, even assuming she was lucky enough to hit them. She couldn't go down; her only choice was to keep trying to go up.

She pulled again at the vines, pushing with her feet, and managed to gain another few inches, almost back to within a foot of safety. The miniskirt was tight, too tight, impeding her movements, and for half a moment she considered pulling it up to her waist and climbing the rest of the way in her shredded panty hose. But even with no witnesses she couldn't bring herself to climb around on the streets of San Francisco in her underwear, so she had to content herself with gritting her teeth, hiking the narrow skirt higher up her thighs and continuing upward.

Her pale, manicured fingernails were just inches below the edge of the balcony. She gave herself one last push, holding her breath as she released the vine and clawed for the edge of the terrace, determined to make it or die trying. Her hands caught the rim, slid for a second and then held, and with more panic than grace Ferris hauled her scantily clad body up and over, sprawling onto the wet slate surface, panting in fear and exhaustion, her eyes shut as the rain poured over her face and her wet curtain of hair.

She opened them a moment later and glared at her terrace door. She usually left it ajar, giving her erstwhile alley cat his freedom. But it had been a cold, nasty morning and Blackie didn't like the rain, so like a fool she'd closed and locked it.

She considered taking off her shoe and smashing one of the panes of glass near the locked door handle. But her shoes were down on the sidewalk in a welter of garbage, and she had nothing that would break glass but her own fist. And she wasn't quite desperate enough. Yet.

She could do it, of course, she thought, pulling herself to her feet and yanking her purse from around her neck. She could, for example, picture John Patrick Blackheart's enigmatic face in the glass, a face she hadn't seen in more than three weeks and of whose whereabouts at the moment she didn't have the faintest idea, and she could take her fist and drive it right into his teeth.

But that would hurt her far more than it would him. She didn't need a bloody fist and stitches, simply because she needed to take out on someone else the frustration and confusion of the last three weeks, the last few months, the last few hours and minutes.

She'd used a credit card on a terrace door before and succeeded, so she could do it again. Her bruised knees protested slightly as she knelt in front of the lock, her American Express card in hand, but she merely bit her lip, shoved her sopping hair out of her face, and applied herself. The American

Express card bit the dust and was soon joined by her gold Visa card, her Macy's card, and the one from Nordstroms.

Ferris looked longingly up at the glass, wondering if a karate kick might do the trick. She could limp for a while without greatly impairing her efficiency, if she wasn't called upon to climb any more buildings and break into any more apartments. And there was something very appealing about the notion of kicking the mental image of Blackheart in the teeth.

She pulled out her Daughters of the Pacific membership card. The plastic was sturdier than the others, and it was the symbol of her successful transformation, from Francesca Berdahofski, daughter of immigrants, always on the outside looking in, to Ferris Byrd, self-made, elegant and self-assured, as if born to privilege. Membership in the Daughters of the Pacific was hard to come by—one had to be proposed by three members, one's lineage had to pass muster, and one had to be voted on by the bluest blood of San Francisco. Even though Ferris knew how hollow such a victory, such a transformation of her life really was, she'd still secretly cherished the card and everything it stood for.

She slid it between the terrace doors, gently, coaxingly, as Blackheart had once taught her to do. The latch clicked, the door swung open, and thirteen pounds of smoky-gray, outraged tomcat raced out into the dusk, disappearing over the balcony without a backward glance.

"Glad to see you, too," she muttered, pushing the door open, letting the heat and light envelope her shivering body. She stepped inside, sneezed, and shut the door behind her.

Her apartment, never known for its neatness, was in a worse shambles than usual. Consisting of six rooms and three short flights of stairs, it was a rambling rabbit warren of a place that she would sorely miss if and when she moved out. She shouldn't be thinking *if*, not with piles of boxes stacked in every available space, waiting for their removal to Blackheart's less colorful, more spacious quarters. But when one's fiancé took to disappearing at odd times during the six months of their engagement, returning without a word of explanation, when he'd gone off again three weeks ago and hadn't been heard from since, when there'd been a string of robberies in Europe that had reminded suspicious authorities of the heyday of the Blackheart family, then she too could only begin to wonder, to fall victim to the kind of doubts no engaged woman should have to harbor.

There was a light burning in the living room. She didn't remember having left it on, but then she'd been in a foul mood that morning, having spent one too many lonely nights in her big bed, and she might not have noticed. She moved down the three steps, through the practically impassible dining room and up two steps into the living room. And stopped dead as her outraged green eyes fell on John Patrick Blackheart lounging casually on her sofa, a glass of brandy in one hand, her discarded raincoat folded neatly on the glass-topped coffee table in front of him.

"What the hell are you doing here?" she demanded, breathless with rage, surprise, and something else that was curiously, infuriatingly close to joy.

"How many times have you asked me that?" Blackheart replied lazily, not moving. "I suppose as many times as I've broken in to your apartment. At this point I've lost count. On the other hand, this was your first attempt, wasn't it? What took you so long on the balcony? That lock should have been a piece of cake."

Ferris dumped her purse onto the floor, ignoring the stray shiver that crept across her body. "You knew I was out there? Of course you did," she answered her own question bitterly. "Why didn't you let me in?"

At this point Blackheart did rise, his lithe, elegant body graceful as always in black denim, a black turtleneck and an ancient tweed jacket. He shed his jacket, dropping it onto the small couch, and advanced toward her. "I thought since you'd gotten that far, I shouldn't deprive you of the triumph of breaking in. After that scramble through the ivy like Tarzan's Jane, you deserved some sort of reward."

"You saw me climbing up the building?" she asked in a carefully restrained tone of voice.

No one had ever thought Blackheart imperceptive. He kept advancing, but his eyes were wary, as if he knew just how dangerous Ferris Byrd was at that moment. "It was very impressive," he said softly. "I think my favorite moment was when you pulled that ridiculous excuse for a skirt halfway up to your waist. Though your descent into the garbage bin had to run a close second."

"You just stood there and watched?" She wanted to make absolutely certain she was understanding him correctly.

"Actually I sat there and watched from my car. It was pouring rain, you know."

"Blackheart," she said through gritted teeth. "I am going to stab you."

"No, you're not, dear heart," he said, moving almost within range of her decidedly murderous rage. "You're going to let me get you out of those wet clothes and ply you with brandy and coffee, and then you're going to let me warm you up properly, and by the time we're finished you'll realize how pleased you are at having broken into your apartment without breaking any laws."

"Don't touch me, Blackheart," she warned, backing away.

"It's been too long since I've touched you, Francesca," he murmured, his voice low and beguiling and completely irresistible. He kept on coming.

"Whose fault is that?" She tried to summon up her earlier outrage, her anger and confusion, but all she managed was a plaintive little cry.

"Mine," he said, reaching for her, his body now within inches of hers.

She batted at him, but his hands were strong, too strong, catching her shoulders and bringing her, willingly enough, to rest against his lean muscled warmth. He didn't kiss her, simply held her against him, held her until the shivering stopped and her tight muscles loosened, held her until her arms slid around his waist and she tilted her wet face upward.

And then a sigh left his body, as if he'd been holding his breath, and his mouth dropped onto hers, lightly, teasingly, arousing her with such immediacy that she was once more lost, lost—and resentful of that fact.

But right then her mind wasn't working too well. He'd already managed to unfasten the buttons on her silk shirt, and now he was pushing the wet material off her shoulders and down her arms, letting it drop in a sodden heap to the floor. He found the zipper of her skirt, and with one deft move had managed both to unzip and slide it along with her shredded panty hose down her wet legs. She stepped free of her clothing, clad only in peach silk bikini briefs and a lacy scrap of bra, and was shivering again, this time with something other than cold.

Blackheart slipped his deft, beautiful hands up her sides, cupping the generous breasts that spilled from the inadequate bra, and his tawny-brown eyes were hooded, his breathing was rapid, and his lips were thin with longing. "I missed you, Francesca," he whispered. "I missed you damnably."

In response she moved her trembling hands under the fine cotton knit of his turtleneck and began to draw it upward, her knees weak, ready to pull him down onto the floor and make love to him then and there, when a sudden pounding on her flimsy door broke into her consciousness, wiping away any desire and replacing it with fear.

She jumped away from him as if burned, her green eyes looking up into his in a sudden panic she couldn't hide. His own expression was rueful. "Don't look like that," he said gently. "As far as I know, no one's after me. Go get your robe on, and I'll answer the door."

Ferris ran, slamming her bedroom door behind her as she heard Blackheart head for the front door. She was shaking all over, both with frustration and a sudden, incomprehensible reaction that had nothing to do with the moment, that simply brought back another time, six months ago, when a peremptory rapping at her door had shattered the tenuous relationship she and Blackheart had just managed to build up.

He was right, of course. No one was after him just now. No one should have been after him back then, either, but he'd still ended up in jail. When a man spent half his adult life committing crimes, he was more than likely to spend the other half paying for them, in little ways or big ones.

It was something she had to learn to accept; she knew that. It was just at certain moments, moments like these that all her good intentions vanished, and she felt vulnerable. And after thirty years of trying to protect herself, she didn't like feeling vulnerable one tiny bit.

She didn't pull on her robe. Now that Blackheart's hands were back where they belonged, she no longer felt so trusting. Before she went to bed with her long-lost fiancé she wanted to find out exactly where he'd been for the last three weeks and for that matter, where he'd been disappearing to for the last several months. Somehow she needed to pry that information out of him without displaying an unflattering amount of distrust.

She pulled on a faded pair of jeans and a t-shirt over her damp underwear, ran a brush through her wet tangle of dark hair and headed for the doorway. She was foolish to be so paranoid, she told herself. Whoever had come pounding at her door could only be a nosy neighbor or an importunate salesperson.

She opened the bedroom door and moved lightly toward the sound of voices that was coming from the living room. "Who is it, Patrick?" she murmured, then stopped short. She knew, she just knew that all color had drained from her face and her heart had skidded to a stop, just as her body had.

"How can I help you, officer?" she managed in a deceptively calm voice, noting with distant relief that Blackheart's beautiful wrists were free of handcuffs. He was glaring at her, however, his narrow, clever face suddenly cold and distant, and she wondered if he'd been able to read her mind, read her sudden dread and distrust.

"He's come about the littering, Ferris," Blackheart said in a gentle voice. If she'd had any doubts about his anger, they had now vanished. He never called her Ferris unless he was very mad indeed.

"Littering?" she echoed, giving the uniformed officer her full attention. He was tall, bland and beefy, towering over Blackheart's five feet eleven inches by a sizable margin, and he looked both stern and embarrassed.

"Yes, ma'am. Someone dumped some garbage cans onto the street outside, someone answering your description. I wondered if you had anything to say about the matter."

"Give it up, Ferris," Blackheart drawled. "Clearly there's been an informer on the job."

"Probably Mrs. Melton from down the hallway," Ferris said bitterly. "She always sees what she's not supposed to see."

"She was probably having as good a time as I was watching you break in," Blackheart murmured.

"Break in?" the policeman questioned.

"To my own apartment," Ferris hastened to explain, returning Blackheart's glare. "That's how the garbage got spilled. I had to use the empty garbage can to climb up onto my balcony. I'll go down and clean up the mess."

"The city would appreciate that, miss," the cop said stolidly. "I'll let you off with a warning this time, but I wouldn't want it to happen again."

"Neither would I," Ferris said wholeheartedly.

The officer turned to leave, then paused, peering at Blackheart's shuttered face. "You look familiar to me," he said.

"Do I?" Blackheart's own tone was unpromising. "I guess I have that kind of looks."

"You sound foreign, too. English?"

Blackheart wasn't liking this one tiny bit. "Half-English," he said briefly. "I'm not the one who dumped the garbage can, officer."

"Such a gentleman," Ferris said sweetly.

But the policeman wouldn't be distracted. "I never forget a face. I must have seen you somewhere, and it's going to bug me until I remember where and when."

"Then for your sake I hope you'll remember soon," Blackheart said icily. "Was there anything else?"

"I'd better go down," Ferris said hurriedly, eager to break up what might turn into a nasty confrontation. She grabbed her coat from the couch and headed toward the door. "I'll be right back. Why don't you make me some coffee, Black—darling?"

Blackheart's face darkened even more. "Why don't you remember to wear shoes, if you're going out among the garbage again?" he countered.

Ferris stared down at her bare feet, then back at the glowering cop. "I left a pair down there," she said, taking the policeman's burly arm and pushing him, gently but forcibly, through the open door. "I'll be right back."

"Take your time," Blackheart said softly. "I'll be waiting."

THE SLENDER YOUNG woman stood off to one side, leaning against the elegant seating that would soon be folded and packed in readiness for shipping across the Atlantic Ocean, through the Panama Canal to the west coast of the United States. She knew she was in the shadows; no one could see her expression as she watched the act in the center ring of the small, elite circus.

The Porcini Family Circus had been in existence for more than a hundred years. The current owner and latest to bear the name Porcini was high overhead, involved in his act. Marco Porcini was only an adequate aerialist, but he always managed to get the crowd to their feet, if not for his grace, then for his sheer arrogance. He would try anything, and the woman watching knew that if he ever fell, his reaction would be nothing more than astonishment.

She could hear the crowd ooh in anticipation. She looked up, way up, at the man who called himself her husband. She watched him as he edged his way across the narrow wire, digging her fingers into her palms, her heart pounding, her pale face beaded with sweat.

"Pretty dangerous tonight, eh?" Rocco, the old clown, had come up beside her and was following her gaze. "No net. Marco shouldn't count on having a charmed life."

"No," she said in a shaky voice. "He shouldn't."

"Don't worry, *cara,*" Rocco said, patting her affectionately on the shoulder. "He'll be all right."

And Dany Bunce, better known as Danielle Porcini, looked up at the man high overhead, and prayed that he might fall.

Chapter Two

Suspicion
(MGM 1947)

THE RAIN WAS pouring steadily, sliding down the neck of Ferris's rain-coat. Her high-heeled pumps were even more uncomfortable on wet, bare feet, and several of the garbage bags had split when she'd tossed them indiscriminately onto the sidewalk. Gritting her teeth, she struggled and shoved and pushed the unwieldy bags back into the battered garbage can, rolling it back into the alley with a furious clang, all under the watchful eye of her disapproving patrolman. Through it all she cursed Blackheart under her breath.

The temperature had dropped with the setting sun, and it took all Ferris's determination to keep from shaking with cold as she stomped back into her building, up the narrow flight of stairs, the simmering heat of her anger the only thing warming her chilled body.

Blackheart was gone. "I'll be waiting," he'd told her. A lie. How many other lies had he told her?

At least he'd left the front door unlocked. If she'd come back to a locked apartment, it would have been the final straw. She slammed the door, snarling with rage as she surveyed the empty living room, then slowly, carefully secured all three locks. Not that it would stop Blackheart if he decided to show up again, but it would slow him down long enough for her to hear him and be waiting with a cast-iron frying pan or something equally daunting.

Stripping off her sodden clothes as she went, she headed straight for the bathroom and a long hot shower, determined to wash away the chill of the early-evening rain and the stink of the garbage from her skin. There was no way she could wash away the tension and anger that were eating into her heart.

The phone rang, but she ignored it as she pulled on a soft yellow sweat suit and braided her wet hair. If it was Blackheart calling with explanations or apologies, she wasn't ready to hear them.

"Who am I kidding?" she demanded of her reflection in the ornate gilt mirror she'd found at a flea market. "Blackheart never apologizes and he never explains. It's up to you to see if you can live with that."

The reflection looked skeptical. She stared back at her alter ego. Francesca's green eyes were shimmering with anger, while Ferris usually managed to keep a cool distant expression in hers. Francesca's generous mouth was soft and pale and vulnerable, while Ferris kept hers carefully lipsticked and slightly compressed. Francesca's high cheekbones and thick dark hair made her look like a passionate gypsy; Ferris's beautiful bones and carefully arranged hair made her look elegant and cared for.

Ferris sighed, staring back at the woman in the mirror. "Who the hell are you?" she demanded wearily. "And what is it you want in life?"

But her reflection had no answers for her. She turned away, ignoring the renewed ringing of the telephone, and went in search of dinner. If Blackheart wanted to talk to her, he'd have to come back. No one in Ferris's large family could hold a candle to her when it came to stubbornness, and if Blackheart thought he could outlast her determination, then he was mistaken.

Curse him, he'd almost finished her brandy. And she simply wasn't in the mood for frozen gourmet dinners. There was no ice cream to speak of in the freezer, only three nearly empty Double Rainbow containers with frosty teaspoons of refrozen ice cream slimed into the bottom.

She settled for Rice Chex, carrying a huge bowl and her brandy snifter into the living room and sinking onto the love seat. She wasn't in the mood for the evening news, half afraid of what she might hear, and she hadn't bought a DVD player yet, despite her love of old movies. It simply didn't make sense when she was about to move in with and marry a man who owned the Cadillac of Blu-Ray players, but right then and there she would have given a great deal to snuggle down in her oversize bed with Alfred Hitchcock.

She looked down at the ring on her hand. She'd flatly refused to wear emeralds—they had too many unhappy memories. Blackheart had insisted that diamonds were too cold for her, but he'd settled for a large canary diamond in a beautiful, old-fashioned setting. She seldom took it off, but every now and then she wondered where he'd obtained it, and if it was left over from his ill-gotten gains.

She finished the mixing bowl of cereal, shoving the empty dish under the couch, then heard the footsteps approaching her door. *Not Blackheart,* she thought, listening, ignoring the sinking feeling of disappointment. He was so quiet that no one could ever hear him coming. He'd already taken years off her life by sneaking up on her. If he was coming back he wouldn't approach her door with that even measured tread; he'd simply materialize like the Cheshire cat.

She considered ignoring the polite knocking, but like another kind of cat, she was intensely curious. The brandy and cereal had gone some way toward soothing her temper, and the knowledge that Blackheart was back in town, albeit not with her, was an added relief. At least if he was in San Francisco he couldn't be in the great cities of Europe and couldn't be involved in the current rash of jewel thefts. Slowly, languidly she pulled herself from the couch and headed for the door.

The middle-aged man standing there looked like a jockey. He came up to her collarbone and not much farther, and he was slightly bowlegged. Instead of jockey's silks, however, he was wearing what looked like a chauffeur's uniform.

"Ms. Berdahofski?" he inquired politely in a voice tinged with the rich, meaty sound of a cockney accent.

No one but Blackheart could have sent him, she decided then and there, ignoring the rush of relief that swept through her. Everyone else still called her by her acquired name, and while she'd been trying to change it back, she was still too diffident to push it. "Yes," she agreed warily.

"I'm Simmons, ma'am. I have a car waiting for you. Compliments of Mr. Blackheart."

"What kind of car?" A ridiculous question, but she was stalling for time. She was also curious to find out how far Blackheart was willing to go to woo her.

"A Bentley, ma'am. The Rolls is being worked on."

She'd never ridden in either of England's fabled limousines. Even in her heyday, when she'd been engaged to State Senator Phillip Merriam, of the very moneyed California Merriams, she'd only managed Cadillacs and Lincolns. Phillip might have preferred British luxury or German engineering, but he knew where his constituency lay, and buying American was almost a second religion with him.

"All right," she said, throwing caution and hurt feelings to the wind. "Let me get my coat."

"I'll wait in the hall while you change, miss."

It was a gentle hint, but Ferris was having none of it. "He'll take me as I am," she said sweetly, "or he can do without."

The chauffeur allowed himself a small grin. "Blackheart's never been a fool, and I've known him for a long time. I'm ready when you are, miss."

The Bentley was a definite treat. Simmons settled her into the upholstered leather seat, handed her a sheaf of creamy-white roses, and began to open a bottle of champagne that had been left chilling in an ice bucket. He was oblivious to the rain pouring off his peaked cap, removing the cork with such efficiency that the quiet pop was barely audible. The champagne was Moet, the fluted glass he poured it into was Waterford, and the woven lap robe he tucked around her legs was cashmere.

The engine purred softly when Simmons turned the key, the minor noise quickly overridden by the lilting strains of Mozart as he deftly pulled into traffic. Ferris sat back and laughed out loud, taking a sip of the deliciously chilly Moet. "Is this a package deal, Simmons?" she inquired in her most caustic voice. "Or did Blackheart have time to arrange all this in just the last hour or so?"

"Blackheart wouldn't use a package deal, miss," he said, deeply offended.

"He's been planning this for a long time. Just had to wait till the moment was ripe, he told me."

"You mean he wanted to wait until I was so mad he had to use extraordinary measures to placate me. I'm not placated, Simmons. You can tell him so."

"Yes, ma'am." Simmons grinned at her reflection in the rearview mirror. "You like that champagne?"

Ferris noticed she'd drained her glass. "Love it," she said, reaching for the bottle and pouring herself another.

"Can't stand the stuff meself," said Simmons. "Give me a good dark ale any day, that's the ticket. None of the frenchified stuff. I never could understand how a decent lad like Blackheart could abide it."

"How long have you known Blackheart?" she inquired lazily, ignoring the streets of San Francisco speeding by beyond the smoked glass windows.

"Since he was a lad. His father used to bring him out to the racetrack when I was still a jockey. Blackheart senior used to like to play the ponies, and young Blackheart had a real gift for it. He's always been lucky, miss."

"Not always," she said, breathing in the rich, delicious scent of the white roses. "He spent six months in jail after he fell."

"Some would say it could have been a lot worse. They weren't able to pin a whole lot on him. There are people who think he got off too easy by half. But then, there's a lot of judgmental people around. I just likes to let things be. Live and let live, that's my motto."

"What was Blackheart like as a child?" she asked, unable to restrain her curiosity. "Did you know what his father did for a living?"

"Everyone knew. It was sort of a gentleman's agreement—no one ever mentioned it, but everyone knew. Not the toffs, I don't think. I can't believe they'd have kept on inviting him into their homes if they'd known he was going to rob them, but then, I can't be certain. The British upper classes are a strange lot, take my word for it. Blackheart was a good lad. A little wild, a little old for his age. He loved his old man, he loved his baby sister, and there it ended."

Ferris sat bolt upright, slopping some of the precious Moet onto the cashmere lap robe. "Sister? I didn't know he had any sisters."

Simmons's face darkened, and he ducked his head. "Just the one, miss. I don't remember what happened to her. Don't tell Blackheart I mentioned her. I don't think it's a very happy memory for him."

"Sorry, Simmons. I'm in a bad mood—I'm not going to make promises to anyone," she said firmly, draining the champagne.

"I understand, miss. But don't be too hard on Blackheart. He's going through a difficult time, if you know what I mean."

"No," she said. "I don't know what you mean. Explain."

Simmons had pulled the huge limousine to a halt outside Blackheart's apartment building. "We're here, miss," he announced, his cockney voice thick with relief.

"I could refuse to budge until you tell me more. There's most of the bottle of champagne back here, and I'm very comfortable."

"Please, miss," Simmons said, sweat standing out on his lined forehead. "Give me a break, there's a good girl. If you have questions, ask Blackheart."

There lay the answer, she thought, and the problem. She didn't want to ask Blackheart; she wanted him to volunteer the information. The few times she'd tried to elicit information from him, he'd slithered away from her questions like an eel, and it hadn't been until hours later that she realized he'd never told her a thing.

That would have to change tonight. He could ply her with champagne and white roses and Bentleys, he could put those beautiful hands on her, and she would remain adamant. No matter what he said or did, she wasn't going to give in to the almost obsessive longing that assailed her whenever she was near him, whenever she even thought about him. If there was to be any hope for their future, she was going to need some answers.

Simmons had opened the door and was standing there patiently, holding a huge black umbrella to keep off the pouring rain. She half expected him to whip off his jacket and lay it in the puddled gutter, but he contented himself with holding out a small-boned hand to help her out of the car.

Blackheart's building wavered and drifted behind the curtain of rain. Ferris looked up at the brightly lighted windows, wondering for the thousandth time whether she could ever feel at home there.

That was the least of her worries right now, she reminded herself as she slipped out of the car, the white roses still clutched in her hands, a twisting, nervous feeling in the pit of her stomach. She had to get through the next few hours first. After that, she could worry about the rest of her life.

DANIELLE LAY VERY still in the narrow bunk, clutching her stomach, breathing through her mouth as her body tried to adjust itself to the rolls and dips of the ocean far beneath her. She hated the sea, hated tiny dinghies, small sailboats, large yachts and massive ocean liners. Most of all she hated smelly diesel freighters that crawled across the vast, almost endless Atlantic Ocean, crammed with the contents of the Porcini Family Circus. There were elephants, tigers and lions in the hold of the ship, horses and monkeys and even seals. The smell on a hot day near the equator didn't bear thinking about.

There were acrobats and jugglers and clowns, aerialists and sword swallowers and bareback riders, all vying for space on the crowded freighter. Marco Porcini didn't believe in pampering anyone but himself, and the Star of Hoboken had clearly seen better days.

The ship rolled to the left, and Danielle emitted a small groan. They were nearing the Panama Canal on their interminable voyage from Madrid to the west coast of the United States.

She heard the door open, but didn't bother to look up. It could only be Marco—no one else would dare enter the one decent cabin the Star of Hoboken boasted without knocking.

"Get up, Danielle."

She didn't bother to open her eyes. "If I get up I'll die."

"I don't care. We want to use the bed."

At that point simple curiosity made Dany open her eyes. Marco Porcini was standing there, luxuriant black hair slicked down, bedroom eyes cold and assessing, thick-lipped mouth tightly compressed. Lurking behind him, looking both nervous and excited, was the new girl he'd hired to repair costumes.

Dany sat up, still clutching her roiling stomach. "Don't you think this will put the lie to our little farce of a happy marriage?" she inquired in her sweetest voice.

Marco smiled. "Of course not. Only if you were foolish enough to say something. And you are seldom stupid, little one."

If there was anything Dany hated it was to be called "little one." But if Marco could smile, so could she. "What about her?" She gestured toward the nervous-looking girl.

"She wouldn't dare. Would you, darling?" he inquired over his shoulder. The girl shook her head, biting her lip.

Dany swung her legs over the bunk, pausing for a moment as the room spun around her. For a brief moment she prayed that she would throw up all over Marco's shiny black shoes, but she'd thrown up so much in the last few days that there was nothing left in her stomach. She climbed off the bunk, gave the happy couple a weak smile, and headed out the door.

"And Danielle—" Marco called after her.

Dany paused. The girl had already gone into the cabin and was methodically, unemotionally stripping off her clothes. She was out of earshot, but even so Marco lowered his rather high-pitched voice. "If you behave yourself in San Francisco," he murmured, "if all goes as I've planned it, I just might let you go."

She stared up at him, for a brief moment allowing her hatred to fill her eyes. "You promised me," she whispered.

Marco shrugged. "We'll see how you behave."

She didn't move. "This is my last job for you, Marco. If you don't let me go," she said quite calmly, "I'll kill you."

"You could always try. Maybe you'll have better luck next time."

"Next time," Dany said, her voice fierce, "I won't miss."

BLACKHEART STOOD in the doorway of his kitchen, waiting. He'd seen her arguing with Alf Simmons, seen her hold her ground in the Bentley, and he could feel himself smiling ruefully. He should have known it wouldn't be that easy. Francesca wasn't the type to be dazzled into submission by limousines and champagne and roses. The candlelight dinner he'd planned probably wouldn't do the trick, either. He could tell by the defiant tilt of her head, even from the distance of his fifth-floor apartment, that she was looking for trouble.

Looking for answers would be the way she viewed it. Unfortunately this time the two were synonymous. And he was faced with the choice between two evils: having her furious and distrustful, suspecting the worst, or having her know, and thereby endangering any chance he had for success.

No. He'd made his decision, and he'd abide by it. Even if he had to put up with fury, sulks and a constant barrage of questions, he wasn't going to tell her until he was ready. The worst aspect of it all was her lack of trust, but that was always there, whether she had any reason for it or not.

It would have been wonderful, he thought, leaning against the doorjamb, if she'd simply trust him, took him at his word *No.* She didn't even have to get to that point, if she just knew he wouldn't do anything wrong and never felt the need to question.

But life wasn't that neat and comfortable. And in fact, he'd been doing a great many illegal things in the weeks he'd been away from her. She'd have too hard a time living with that, so instead she was going to have to live with her own damned lack of trust. He wasn't going to lie to her, he wasn't going to tell her the truth. They were at a stalemate.

That night, however, he had no intention of giving her a chance to ask those unanswerable questions. If it hadn't been for that damned cop, he would be sound asleep in her arms right now, instead of worrying about placating her. Tonight he needed her, needed her with something bordering on desperation. He needed her lush, sweet body, her warm arms wrapped around him, he needed forgetfulness and comfort and that almost unbelievable release that only she could offer. In bed they communicated perfectly, in bed she trusted him completely. And that was where he had every intention of taking her, as soon as he possibly could.

The damp weather was making his leg ache, reminding him of a bad fall and too many operations. He rubbed it absently, listening for the sound of the elevator, listening for the sound of her footsteps in the hallway. For a moment the brief, delicious vision of her scrambling up the side of her building in a miniskirt assailed him. And then he pushed himself away from the wall and headed for the door. If she was still waiting in the Bentley, he'd throw her over his shoulder and carry her upstairs. Three weeks was too damned long.

Chapter Three

Shadow of a Doubt
(Universal 1943)

"IT'S NICE TO SEE you dressed for the occasion." Blackheart's faintly British voice was a low drawl from across the candlelit room. Ferris held her ground just inside the doorway, feeling both vulnerable and faintly absurd, still clutching the bouquet of white roses like a Miss America contestant, wearing her pale yellow sweat suit and running shoes instead of a strapless evening gown and high heels.

She could see a table for two, set with crystal and china and silver candlesticks. She could smell the delicious scent of broiled chicken and could see the rain lashing against the windows outside, while inside all was warmth and comfort. She steeled herself against the insidious effect John Patrick Blackheart always had on her, but all she had to do was look at him to know she was fighting a losing battle.

Blackheart wasn't spectacularly tall, nor spectacularly handsome, nor even spectacularly kind. But he had a wiry, catlike grace that enabled him to leap tall buildings in a single bound, insinuate himself into the oddest of places, and sneak up on his fiancée when she least expected it. He wore his dark brown hair too long, the humor that twisted his sensual mouth was occasionally at someone's else's expense, and his tawny-brown eyes were distant, cool and assessing—except when they looked at her, as they were doing now, and then they warmed to an almost blazing heat.

"I didn't realize this was a formal occasion," she said, stepping into the room and closing the door behind her.

"It's whatever you want it to be," he murmured, his voice sliding down her backbone like a hawk's feather. "What happened to Alf?"

"I sent him home with the rest of the champagne, even though he said he'd rather have Guinness than Moet. We had an interesting talk about your childhood on the way over."

He didn't like that, not one tiny bit, she realized, but was making every effort to control his annoyance. "I expect it was very boring. Why don't you set those flowers down and come here?"

"Because I don't trust myself within touching distance of you," she said frankly, setting down the roses anyway.

"Don't trust yourself?" he said softly. "Or me?"

The room was very quiet. He'd started a fire in his fireplace, and the soft hiss and crackle of dry wood blended with the tap-tap of the rain against the windows. Ferris opened her mouth to speak, then shut it again. The moment of truth was at hand. It was a perfect opening for all the questions, all the doubts. All she had to do was ask.

"I trust you, Blackheart," she said.

He moved toward her then, his face in shadow, unreadable, his body taut with a tension she couldn't begin to understand. "No, you don't," he said, putting his hands on her, his devilish, wonderful hands. "But right now I don't care."

All her sanity and good intentions flew out the window at the feel of his hands on her shoulders. The heat burned through the fleece of her sweat suit, the scent of roses mingled with the wood smoke and coffee and cooking, and Blackheart was so close to her that she could feel the heat, the tension thrumming through him. *Neither do I,* she thought, half believing it. But she couldn't say the words out loud, couldn't give him that much solace.

Instead she slipped her arms around his neck and kissed him, her mouth soft and full of promise. He groaned deep in his throat, and then there was no longer any room for doubt, trust or conscious thought. He pushed her gently back against the wall, and in one swift movement he'd stripped the sweatshirt from her willing body. She kicked off her sneakers, the loose pants followed, and she stood there in a lavender silk teddy and nothing else.

"You dressed for the occasion, after all," Blackheart murmured in her ear, his hands possessive and dangerous on her suddenly heated skin.

She wanted to deny it. She made one last attempt, catching his long, clever hands at her waist and stopping their errant path along her sensitized body. "No, Blackheart," she whispered, her voice a raw thread of sound. "Please don't."

He was suddenly very still, his hands hard and motionless within hers. "No?" he echoed, his voice quizzical. "I've never forced a woman in my life, Francesca, and I'm certainly not about to start with you." Still his hands didn't move; he stayed where he was, inches, millimeters from her, his body a promise. And a threat.

She recognized the threat for what it was—a threat of mindless, almost frightening pleasure. The threat of losing herself, when she'd only just found herself. The threat of becoming so caught up in John Patrick Blackheart that she'd cease to exist.

"No?" he murmured, his voice like silk.

At that moment she hated him, hated the power he had over her. But most of all she hated herself for giving in to that power. "Yes," she said, closing her eyes and leaning against him, her slender body trembling. "Yes, Blackheart. Anything."

He hesitated for only a moment, and a distant part of her wanted to open her eyes to see his expression. Would it be triumphant or troubled? Or both?

And then he scooped her up in his strong arms, lifting her high against his chest. "Not anything, Francesca." His voice was rough with promise. "Everything."

He reached behind her and flicked off the lights, so that the living room was bathed in the fitful glow of firelight and candlelight. He set her on the big, comfortable sofa, following her down, his mouth catching, teasing hers, so that she could ask no more questions, make no more promises of a trust she couldn't deliver, voice no more doubts. Quickly, efficiently he stripped off his clothes, then his body covered hers.

She ran her hands up his arms, her fingers caressing the taut muscles, and she shifted beneath him, her body instinctively ready to accommodate his, her long legs ready to wrap themselves around him, her hips ready to rise in mute supplication. She kept her eyes tightly shut, but her hands were growing more and more fevered, clutching at him as she kissed him back with a kind of desperate frenzy that had only something to do with love.

He pulled his mouth away, and she could feel his breath on her upturned face, warm and sweet and tasting of brandy and coffee and Blackheart. "Slow down," he whispered. "This isn't a race. We can take our time. . . ."

But that was just what Ferris was afraid of. "No," she murmured. "I want you. Now." She tugged at him, trying to pull him on top of her, but he caught her hands in his, shifting to the side, holding her still.

"Open your eyes, Francesca." His voice was low, his tone inexorable. She tried to turn away, to hide her face against the rough cotton of the sofa, but his hand beneath her chin wouldn't let her. "Open your eyes."

She had no choice but to obey. She had no doubt he'd see the tears swimming in her eyes—the dim glow of the firelight would only make them shine. She had no doubt he'd see the fear and distrust there. Blackheart had always seen her far too clearly for her own peace of mind.

"Oh, Francesca," he whispered, his face in shadow, his voice weary and very, very sad. "What have I done to you? What have you done to yourself?"

She tried to summon up a smile, but it was a miserable failure. "We need to talk."

"Yes," said Blackheart. "But not now."

She could feel her heart beating at a rapid, headlong pace that matched his. His skin was a white gold in the firelight, shadow and light and dancing shadows gilding his flesh. "Not now," she agreed, her voice a mere thread of sound.

He reached down and unsnapped the teddy, pulling it away and sending it sailing across the room. His body covered hers, shutting out the light, and he entered her, driving deep with a swift, sure stroke that left her breathless.

She made a small, whimpering noise in the back of her throat, but she was wet, ready, desperate for him. Her hands clutched at him, fingers digging in, and her mouth met his in a sudden, frenzied seeking.

His hands framed her face, pushing the cloud of hair away from her tear-streaked cheeks as his mouth caressed, aroused and promised.

It had been too long. She convulsed around him almost immediately, her heart beating in spasms, her body rigid, and he held her, waiting, his hands impossibly tender, until she was past the first peak and ready for more.

He knew her body so well. He knew when to go slowly, to give her time to accustom herself to his presence. He knew when to go fast, to build up the tempo until she was ready to scream. He knew when to be gentle, when the softest of touches was exquisite pleasure. And he knew when to be rough, when gentle pressure wasn't what she needed at all.

There were times when she resented his control, but just then she was beyond rational thought. As he began to move again and began the inexorable buildup, she simply wrapped her arms and legs around him and held on, lost, as always, in the wonder and mystery of making love with John Patrick Blackheart.

But even Blackheart's control wasn't absolute. She could feel him tremble in her arms, feel the sweat that covered his back as he struggled to keep the pace of his driving thrusts steady. But it had been three long weeks for him, too, of that she had no doubt, and when the second peak hit her Blackheart was with her, rigid in her arms, his voice rasping in her ear, whispering something she couldn't hear as she found herself in that now-familiar darkness that was both haven and menace.

She would have fallen asleep if he'd let her. But when his heartbeat slowed to a semblance of normalcy, when his breathing was no longer labored, he pulled away, ignoring her clinging arms.

The lamp beside the couch glared as he switched it on. He sat at her feet, calmly ignoring his nudity, and stared at her, his eyes dark and shadowed. "All right, Francesca," he said, resigned. "Let's have it."

She lay there for a moment, wanting to postpone the inevitable. Finally she pulled herself into a sitting position, grabbing his discarded chambray shirt from the floor and wrapping it around her. Maybe he could have a discussion like this in the nude, but she was feeling vulnerable after the last half hour. She needed all the defenses she could muster, even if her only defense was a soft cotton shirt that smelled all too enticingly of Blackheart.

"Where were you?" The question came out accusingly, but she couldn't help it. "Why didn't you tell me where you were going? Why didn't you call me?"

He shut his eyes, leaning his head back against the sofa with a pained expression. And then he turned to look at her, his face remote and guileless. "I had business."

"Business."

He must have known her reaction wasn't promising. "In Europe," he added. "It came up suddenly, and there was too much involved for me to be in touch. Kate was supposed to let you know what was happening."

"Your secretary has never liked me and she never will," Ferris said flatly. "Where in Europe?"

"London."

"That's all?"

"I can show you my passport if you need proof," he snapped.

Ferris flinched. "I'm sorry. I didn't mean to cross-examine you."

"Didn't you?" His voice was cool. "What else did you want to know? I'm not going to tell you about the case. It's private information, and if you can't live with that . . ."

"I can live with that," she said in a low voice. "As long as it has nothing to do with me."

"It has nothing to do with you."

"Are you going to make a habit of that? Of just disappearing with no warning, no explanation?" She huddled deeper into the sofa, waiting for him to destroy her future.

He hesitated. "No," he said finally. "This was unusual. I wish I could tell you what was going on, but this time you're just going to have to trust me."

A simple enough request of a woman in love, Ferris thought miserably, hating herself. "Of course," she said, lying.

"You can tell me one thing," he drawled, and she knew enough to hate that tone of voice. "Exactly what did you think I was doing the last three weeks?"

"I hadn't the faintest idea."

"I don't suppose you were aware of the fact that there has been a rash of burglaries in Lisbon and Madrid during that time."

He couldn't see the guilty color stain her face—the bright pool of light beside him cast it into shadow. Didn't it? "I hadn't realized that," she lied easily. And then the question slipped out when she least expected it. "Did you have anything to do with them?"

She couldn't believe she'd actually asked him that. She sat motionless, waiting for the ax to fall.

Blackheart's reaction was surprisingly sanguine. "Such trust," he murmured. "No, Francesca. I didn't."

At least he still called her Francesca. If he were really angry with her he would have called her Ferris. He was looking at her quite calmly, expectantly.

"I'm sorry. I shouldn't have asked that."

"No, you shouldn't have."

She looked at him, guilt and something else twisting inside her, something she didn't want to examine too closely. She looked at him and didn't believe him.

"Is that all?"

"Yes," she said.

"Then let's go to bed."

She could think of a million reasons not to, but not one rose to her lips.

She just sat there, waiting, and he leaned over, brushing the wetness of tears from her cheeks. "Come to bed with me, Francesca," he said again, his voice low and loving. "We can work this out tomorrow."

"Tomorrow," she agreed, ignoring her better judgment. He held out his hand, and she placed her smaller one in his, noting its whiteness against his, his long, clever fingers, flat palm, strong wrist. She lifted his hand against her face, holding it there as she let out a pent-up breath. "Tomorrow," she said.

MARCO WAS LYING, Dany thought, shivering beneath the light raincoat as she leaned over the railing. He couldn't tell the truth if his life depended on it. But whether he intended it or not, this was going to be the last time she helped him. She'd been a miserable, sniveling coward for too long. This endless time on the ocean had done more than make her horribly sick. It had given her the chance to think, to realize that she didn't have to be a victim. After this last job was over she was going to walk away. America was a very big country—it should be a simple enough matter to lose one small female in its vastness. Particularly if that one small female had enough money.

She'd help him on this last job, for several reasons. The most important was that she needed enough money to escape. She wouldn't get very far on the pesetas she had rattling around in her pocket. America was big but it was expensive, and she needed her share, whether Marco gave it willingly or not.

She also had an old score to settle. A lifelong grievance that she'd finally be able to settle added to the allure of this last, dangerous enterprise, and she intended to take full advantage of that fact. When it was over she'd be gone, her purse full of American dollars, Marco Porcini would be richer but missing his helpful patsy, and her nemesis would be ruined. Her only regret was that she wouldn't be able to wait around and watch as John Patrick Blackheart got what he deserved.

But then, life was never that convenient. All that mattered was that life finally evened things out a bit. Blackheart would rot in jail, and Dany Bunce, better known as Danielle Porcini, would finally have revenge. It was enough to make her smile for one brief moment before the ocean shifted and her stomach shifted with it. Soon it would all be over. It couldn't be soon enough.

FERRIS SLOWLY opened her eyes. The rain had stopped, the bedroom was shrouded in darkness, and only the faint light of approaching dawn was to be seen over the city rooftops. Ferris looked at those rooftops and shuddered in memory.

She squinted at the bedside clock. Blackheart hated digital clocks, but the round dial with the small gilt hands was too difficult to see in the predawn light. She shifted slightly in the navy-blue sheets, turning to look at the man sleeping beside her.

He was lying on his stomach, his arms over his head, his long brown hair rumpled. Like all men he looked innocent and boyish in sleep, years younger than the thirty-eight that he admitted to. At some point during the endless, too-brief night she'd scratched his back, and a blush rose to her cheeks as she looked at the shallow red marks. She tried to remember when she'd done it, but the whole night had dissolved into a mindless blur of pleasure. But done it she had, during the second, or maybe it was the third time they'd made love. Probably the third, she thought. The second had been slow, gentle, languorous, reminding each of them that they were in love. The third had been full of resurfacing anger and doubt, and they'd taken it out on each other, ending spent and lonely in the big bed.

She put out a hand and ran it ever so softly along the smooth warm skin of his back. He barely stirred. She leaned down, resting her cheek against one shoulder blade, and he murmured something approving in his sleep, shifting to take her into his arms.

Instead she scuttled away, not without deep regret, and he settled once more into a sound sleep, barely aware of her absence as she slipped from the bed and padded silently into the bathroom.

The long hot shower did wonders to improve her equilibrium. As she surveyed her damp reflection in Blackheart's steamed-up mirror, she could almost convince herself that she was immune to her fiancé's charm, that the last few questions could be dealt with over coffee and something, anything to eat.

She suddenly realized she was famished. She could only hope Blackheart had something better than moldy bread and beer in his refrigerator. She knew for a fact that he'd left the chicken out all night, making it a dangerous possibility for breakfast, but if there was nothing else she'd risk salmonella for the sake of her empty stomach.

She grabbed Blackheart's navy-blue terry bathrobe and wrapped it around her, then searched for a comb.

He'd left his leather shaving kit on the back of the toilet. Without even a moment's hesitation she dived into it, searching for something to tame her thick wet hair.

At first glance she didn't notice anything unusual. Inside the large leather bag were the usual toiletries. Blackheart favored a single-edged razor, a shaving brush and soap, a British shampoo and an organic toothpaste. For some reason he'd left his passport in the bottom of the leather bag, and she stared it for a long moment, considering the value of trust versus the comfort of certainty.

She knew she shouldn't do it. She knew she was going to do it, anyway. She started to move a small zippered case out of the way of the passport, then stopped, staring at the thing in her hand as if it were a dead slug.

It looked like a manicure kit. When she unzipped it that was what she'd find, she told herself. When it came right down to it, she didn't need to unzip it to prove that he had never replaced the lock picks he'd sworn he wouldn't need again. She didn't need to check his passport to know he'd been to England and only England and nowhere near Madrid or Lisbon and the recent rash of jewel robberies. She could put everything back, walk out of the bathroom and take him on blind faith.

She unzipped the small leather pouch. She knew picklocks when she saw them—she'd broken half his previous set in an amateurish attempt at breaking and entering.

And it was with a curious deadness in her heart and no surprise whatso- ever that she opened his navy-blue passport and read the entry stamp from Madrid, Spain, dated two weeks ago.

"Learn anything interesting?" Blackheart inquired from the open door, his face an unreadable mask.

"Enough," said Ferris. "How many people have you robbed?"

He'd pulled on a pair of jeans but hadn't bothered with a shirt. She'd scratched his chest as well as his back, she noticed absently, and there were love bites on his neck. He opened the door wider, and there was no expres- sion on his face at all. "I lost count years ago, Ferris. Why do you ask?"

"Thief."

"You already knew that."

"Liar," she added, some of the ice cracking around her heart.

"That should come as no surprise either," he said coolly. "You want to tell me some more about how much you trust me?"

"Do you want to tell me you haven't robbed anyone these last few weeks?"

"You wouldn't believe anything I told you. You've made up your mind. Hell, I've faced more impartial judges in my time."

"I'm sure you have. You're so good at manipulating people."

"But not you."

"No," said Ferris. She took off the canary diamond ring and set it on the sink. "Not me. Goodbye, Blackheart."

He could have said something sarcastic, considering she was standing in his bathroom wearing his bathrobe and nothing else. But he didn't. "Good- bye, Ferris," he said, the phony name saying everything, and he shut the bathroom door.

Chapter Four

The Man Who Knew Too Much
(Paramount 1956)

FOR FIVE DAYS Ferris Byrd did nothing but drink coffee, pick at her food
when she remembered she was supposed to eat, and brood. Everywhere she
turned in her apartment she could see the piles of boxes, a nasty reminder of
her shattered plans. Blackie seemed to think she'd made a terrible mistake.
Not even Brie at the perfect stage of ripeness could tempt his finicky appetite. He showed up just long enough to hunch his shoulders at his mistress
with a perfect display of contempt before taking off into the streets once
more. And Ferris had nothing to cry into but her pillow.

At least she wasn't due in to work. In one of her more stupid moves, right
up there with falling in love with John Patrick Blackheart, Ferris had taken a
job as director of the Committee for Saving the Bay. *Babysitting socialites,*
Blackheart had called it, and he wasn't far off the mark. But with the termination of her engagement to Phillip Merriam had come the end of her job as his
administrative assistant, and the ensuing publicity of the whole Von
Emmerling affair had made her profile a little too high for the discreet sort of
employment she fancied. So she'd taken what she could get, herding a bunch
of good-hearted but basically inefficient women through their charitable
duties, fund-raising events such as balls, theater benefits and auctions. While
this raft of unpaid assistants managed to arrange dinner parties for
twenty-four and direct the running of mansions and their children's lives,
most of them had never held a paying job and they were unused to some of
the practicalities of life as most people lived it.

It was Ferris's job, as the only salaried employee, to herd her ladies
through these shark-infested waters, and to do so with tact and diplomacy.

Right then she didn't feel terribly tactful or diplomatic. Fortunately the
committee closed its offices at the drop of a hat, and September offered
horse racing in Santa Barbara, yacht racing in Santa Cruz, and changing leaves
any place one cared to look for them. So Ferris could spend five days holed
up in her apartment, coming to terms with the shambles of her life, and no
one would even miss her.

By the time Monday rolled around and Ferris, her social armor fully in
place, made it in to work, she'd moved from despair and anorexia to something far more satisfying: anger and gluttony. Everyone had heard, of course.

And everyone was very kind, very tactful, though Regina Merriam, Ferris's favorite person in the world and the major reason she'd once considered marrying her son, State Senator Phillip Merriam, had taken her to task about it.

Regina strode into Ferris's uncharacteristically neat office, her faded blue eyes blazing, her Calvin Klein suit hanging on her somewhat bony frame. "What's this I hear about you and Patrick?"

Ferris swallowed the jelly doughnut she'd shoved into her mouth and managed a disinterested smile as she wiped the powdered sugar from her face. "Word gets around fast," she said.

"Of course it does. Patrick's a particular friend of mine. As are you. Anything that concerns the two of you would be bound to reach my ears sooner or later."

"Sooner," Ferris grumbled. "It's only been five days."

"Ferris, are you certain you aren't making a very great mistake?" Regina said earnestly. "I can't believe there could be an insurmountable problem between you and Blackheart. You two are made for each other."

"No, we're not." Ferris's voice was very firm.

Regina didn't bother to hide her skepticism. "I'm assuming this breakup was your idea? I have too high an opinion of Blackheart's intelligence to think him capable of such a mistake."

"Thanks a lot."

"Blackheart's a man who recognizes true love when he sees it. He wouldn't let pride or misunderstanding get in his way."

"Neither would I."

"Then why . . . ?"

Ferris pressed a hand to her temple, leaving a trail of powdered sugar in her dark hair. There was no way she was going to tell Regina that Blackheart was on the prowl again. "I'm not going to offer any justification or explanation, Regina. We simply decided it wasn't going to work. Blackheart's free to pursue his own interests." *Cat burgling*, she added mentally. "As am I." She stared morosely at her jelly doughnuts.

Regina shook her head, clearly unconvinced. "I hope it doesn't take you too long to see reason. You're not getting any younger, darling, and fertility decreases after you're thirty."

"Regina!"

"Though I did have Phillip when I was thirty-seven. And look how he turned out," she added gloomily, twirling her perfectly matched string of pearls.

"Regina, Phillip is charming."

"I know. Charming, handsome, kindly, manipulative and shallow. The perfect politician. It's a good thing he never had to work for a living. Though I suppose he could always be a salesman."

"What would he say if he heard you talk like this?" Ferris was both amused and appalled by Regina's customary plain speaking.

"But he has. Many times. And he thinks I'm a meddling, hard-hearted old woman who ought to support him with the mindless adoration of his constituents. We still love each other dearly. I just wish he'd find someone like you to marry and give me grandchildren."

"He did," Ferris pointed out. "He found me."

"But you weren't in love with him. He needs someone with your combination of brains, ambition and warmth, but he needs it tempered by love. Someone to keep from taking the easy way out."

Ferris added guilt to all the negative emotions assailing her. "Regina, I thought I loved him."

"Of course you did. He's really very lovable. But he wasn't right for you. John Patrick Blackheart is. And nothing you say can convince me otherwise."

"I won't even try." Ferris reached for another doughnut and stuffed half of it into her mouth. "Did you have anything else you wanted to tell me, or were you just here to chastise me about my love life?"

Regina grinned. "I suppose I'll have to leave it to you to come to your senses. Or to Patrick. He can be very persuasive."

"Not this time." In fact he hadn't even tried. No phone calls, no notes, no sudden appearances in her apartment when she least expected it. Blackheart had taken the severing of their relationship with perfect equanimity, and she told herself that was relief burning in the pit of her stomach and at the back of her eyes. Regina was right, he was very persuasive indeed. If he'd had any interest in persuading her, she might have a very hard time resisting.

"As a matter of fact I did have something for you. I wanted to make sure the permits are all in order for our next fund-raising extravaganza. It's only eight days away."

"They're in order," Ferris replied. "My love life might be a mess, but at least I'm efficient. Why do you ask?"

"Efficient, yes, but you're getting forgetful in your old age," the ageless Regina said with a smirk. "Who do you think is arriving today?"

"I haven't the faintest—" Ferris smacked her forehead in disgust. "Of course. The Porcini Family Circus."

"All set for Circus Night for the Bay. We were lucky to get them, you know."

"I know we were. I still can't imagine why they offered. Not that it matters. Do you need any help on the reception?"

"All under control. Just show up tonight and smile." Regina reached out and snatched the final jelly doughnut from Ferris's grasp. "Circuses are supposed to be fun."

DANY SURVEYED her hotel room with profound distaste. She'd never been in America before, and what she saw she didn't like. Everything was very new, very clean, very plastic. She'd take a tacky hotel room in Paris any day—paint peeling, water-stained walls, lumpy mattress—rather than this soulless perfection.

She listened to Marco moving around in the room next door. The connecting door was closed, and she wished she dared lock it. It would have been an absurd gesture—Marco could get through the most challenging of locks with effortless ease. Hadn't she taught him everything she knew? The one-cylinder lock on this hotel door would be child's play.

At least she didn't have to put up with his so-called conjugal rights. To the curious eyes of the circus performers the adjoining rooms put up a perfect front. If most of them were also aware of Marco's interest in the voluptuous but cowed-looking wardrobe assistant, they turned a blind eye to it. Circuses were like one big family, but the family members learned discretion from the cradle.

Eight days. She had eight days left, and then she'd be free. One last hit, one last big score, then she would never have to answer to anyone again. All she had to do was play it cool, do her part, and it would be over.

At least Marco no longer touched her. It had been almost two years since she'd had to put up with his particularly nasty form of lovemaking, and God willing, she would never have to again. *Eight more days.*

THE QUEEN-SIZE bed in Ferris's bedroom took up almost all the floor space. She lay on her stomach on the tiny section of rug, fishing under the bed for her other black shoe, fighting her way through discarded panty hose, old magazines, empty tissue boxes and crumpled-up bags of Mrs. Field's Cookies, when her hand caught what felt like a high heel. She pulled it out, and then promptly threw it back under the bed. Instead of her black sandal she'd found a sparkly red shoe, reminiscent of Dorothy's ruby slippers, a gift from Blackheart in better days.

She pulled herself into a sitting position, crossing her legs, and let out a shuddering sigh. She shouldn't have left the shoe under there; she should have taken it and hurled it off her tiny balcony. With her luck that huge, humorless policeman would have caught her doing it, and she would have ended up in prison. The place where Blackheart belonged.

To hell with the red shoes. She wouldn't even remember it was under there. *And to hell with the black shoes, too.* She wasn't going to wrestle around in dark places looking for it anymore. Heaven only knew what nasty thing she'd come up with.

Back to the closet. She was already late for Regina's welcoming reception for the Porcini Family Circus, and she was feeling edgy, guilty and hungry. She'd have to find something else to wear, something that would go with the one matching pair of shoes she could find, and then get the hell out of there.

She was pawing through her closet when she heard the doorbell ring. Her immediate reaction was panic, a reaction she quickly squashed. "Don't be ridiculous," she muttered to herself, grabbing the first thing she could reach and pulling it down over her ice-blue camisole and tap pants. "No one's after you. If anyone's done anything wrong it's Blackheart, and you don't have anything to do with him."

She padded barefoot to the front door, shifting the clinging silk dress around her curves, curves that were getting a little curvier after two days of nonstop eating. She didn't even take the elementary precaution of asking who was there. With the impatient doorbell buzzing in her brain once more, she fiddled with the three stiff locks and flung open the door.

She'd been expecting Blackheart, she realized with a sudden wary disappointment. She should have known better, but deep in her heart she'd hoped he might show up and try to cajole her.

The man standing in her doorway was about as far removed from John Patrick Blackheart as a human being could possibly be. He was good-looking, as was Blackheart, in a sort of rumpled, world-weary fashion. He was somewhere in his mid- to late thirties, as was Blackheart, with sandy-colored hair and steely gray eyes. He was also holding police identification and a badge, something the most famous retired cat burglar in the world would never come close to possessing.

Ferris swallowed, her throat suddenly dry. "Can I help you?"

"I'm Police Detective Stephen McNab, Ms. Byrd," the man said in a pleasant, slightly raspy voice. "I wondered if I might talk to you for a few minutes."

"About what?"

"The man who was in your apartment last week when you were involved in an episode of littering. It took Officer Sweeney a few days to place him, but when he did he came straight to me."

"Why?"

McNab's mouth twisted in a grim smile. "He knew of my particular interest in John Patrick Blackheart, alias Edwin Bunce." He looked pointedly over her shoulder. "May I come in?"

"No."

"Ms. Byrd, I've done some checking." He had the patience of a saint, it seemed. Or the tenacity of a bulldog. "You were engaged to Blackheart for a period of six months, an engagement that came to an abrupt end when he returned from Madrid last week. I might mention that there was a spectacular jewel robbery in Madrid around the time Blackheart was in Spain. I don't suppose you know anything about that?"

Her blood had frozen in her veins, an odd sensation, when her heart and stomach were burning and churning in panic. "Not a thing." Her voice was wintry.

"And it had nothing to do with the termination of your engagement?"

"Do I have to answer these questions?"

McNab smiled again, but his light gray eyes were chilling. "Certainly not.

Not now. When I bring you in for questioning that might be a different matter."

"When?"

"If," he amended. "It would be a lot easier on both of us if you were helpful. May I come in?"

She couldn't help it. She felt like a lioness whose cub was being threatened. It didn't matter that she'd severed her ties with Blackheart, it didn't matter that he'd accepted his dismissal with too damned much grace. She wasn't going to stand by and let this rumpled, deceptively mild detective hound him. "You," she said, "may go to hell."

It was a mistake, she knew that from the broadening of his smile, the very real pleasure lighting his eyes. "You've been very helpful," he murmured. "If I had any doubts about Blackheart's involvement in the Madrid case, you've set them to rest. I don't suppose you care to comment on the Vasquez robbery in Lisbon? Or the Phelps Museum in Paris?"

She slammed the door in his face, her hands shaking as she secured the row of locks. She started toward the kitchen, in search of the comfort only ice cream could provide, when she heard McNab's raspy voice through a thin pine door. "Loyalty's a fine thing, Ms. Byrd. When it's justified. I'll be seeing you."

It took her half a pint of coffee fudge ripple before she felt up to facing the rest of the evening. The dress she'd pulled on in a rush would do—it was blue silk and the small spot of ice cream near the waist wouldn't show if she was careful. She wouldn't have to stay long, just spend enough time there to make sure the ladies of the committee and their husbands were enjoying themselves, and to make sure the Porcini Circus was set for the benefit performance next week.

They'd been a stroke of luck she was still thankful for. The committee had already made arrangements with another small European circus, when those plans had fallen through. The owner and star performer of the Mendoses *Cirque du Lyon* had been the victim of a vicious mugging that had left him laid up for at least three months. It was no time for them to start their first American tour.

But Marco Porcini had heard of his old friend Henri Mendoses' troubles and offered his own small circus instead through his agent, who also happened to be his wife. It would be no trouble—the Porcini Family Circus had been planning an American tour for years. They wouldn't mind the rush in the slightest. And the location of the proposed benefit should be no problem. The spacious grounds surrounding Regina Merriam's mansion should be fine, and no one would be bothered by the noise of the animals but the staid patrons of the adjoining Museum of Decorative Arts. Since Regina's family had built and endowed the huge, sprawling museum and given the land in the first place, not to mention the fact that both she and her son still sat on the board of directors, there should be no objections whatsoever.

It must have been her worries about Blackheart that had caused her groundless fears concerning the Porcinis. It had been luck, wonderful luck that had brought the Committee for Saving the Bay together with the Porcini Family Circus, just as it had been bad luck that Henri Mendoses had been set on by a pair of thugs. She couldn't rid herself of the feeling that things had been a little too convenient.

She was getting neurotic as well as forgetful in her old age. She needed to go to the party, to flirt with handsome lion tamers, if the Porcini circus came equipped with such things, and drink too much champagne. Maybe the handsome lion tamer would have to drive her home, and maybe she'd invite him in and have him make her forget all about Blackheart.

Who was she kidding? She didn't want anyone else showing her anything. She was planning to enjoy a nice healthy bout of celibacy, maybe for a year or two before she made another mistake like blindly trusting a convicted felon with her hand and heart. She'd even tossed her birth control pills in her certainty that she wouldn't be needing them. She couldn't afford to change her mind at this point.

She took one last, critical look at her reflection in the bathroom mirror. *Not bad,* she thought as she wiped the ice cream mustache from her upper lip. She'd left her dark hair loose around her elegantly boned face, her bright red lipstick had faded a bit from the ice cream, but her green eyes were as cold as the famous Von Emmerling emeralds she had once held so briefly. No one would ever guess she'd just broken her engagement to a man she loved with such passion that it frightened her.

Had loved, she corrected herself. *No.* Still loved. But it would fade, it would disappear, with time and his palpable lack of interest it would vanish. *You can't love a man you don't trust,* she told herself. And the brightness of her eyes was simply the reflection of the lights, not the brilliance of unshed tears.

In fact, the lion tamer was in his late fifties, a roly-poly Armenian with an equally roly-poly wife. No one even to tempt her, she thought as she glided through the crowds filling Regina's spaciously appointed downstairs rooms. She could drink as much champagne as she wanted, smile brilliantly, and take a taxi home. For tonight she didn't even need to remember her heart was broken, didn't have to think about Stephen McNab and his unsettling questions, didn't have to think about anything but the exotic, brightly dressed circus people mingling with the richest blood on the upper west coast of California. Just for tonight she didn't have to think about anything.

She'd drained her first glass of champagne and was standing there looking for a refill when a hand reached out from behind her, deftly removing the empty glass and replacing it with a full one. She turned with a smile of gratitude, a smile that died on her lips as she looked into Blackheart's fathomless dark eyes.

"Cat got your tongue?" he murmured, his expression wickedly amused and completely unrepentant.

She considered throwing her champagne in his face, but it would have been a waste of good Moet. She opened her mouth, to blister him with her anger and contempt, then shut it again. Over his shoulder, back by the doorway, stood two familiar figures deep in conversation. If she'd thought the person she least wanted to see was Blackheart, she knew now that she was wrong.

She didn't want to see Phillip Merriam, her ex-fiancé and Regina's only son, now that she was once more unattached. And she certainly didn't want to see S.F.P.D. Detective Stephen McNab's clear gray eyes boring into Blackheart's elegant back with an expression that could only be called determined.

She turned back to Blackheart with a despairing sigh. "If I were you I'd get the hell out of here," she said under her breath, giving him a completely false smile.

He was more fascinated than fooled by her affable expression. He could probably hear her grinding her teeth. "Why?"

"Because that man wants you," she replied grimly.

He turned and followed her gaze, looking into McNab's eyes with no expression whatsoever. "As long as someone does," he said sweetly. And without another word he walked away.

Chapter Five

Family Plot
(Universal 1976)

I CAN'T TAKE THIS, Ferris thought, draining her champagne and looking in desperation for a quick escape route. There were some things too difficult for even the strongest of humans, and being in a crowded, noisy room with Blackheart, Phillip and a burglar-hungry police detective was one of them. Not to mention the fact that it seemed as if half of San Francisco was watching her, watching her reaction to the presence of her two ex-fiancés.

The main exit was blocked by a surge of latecomers, and the French doors leading to the terraces were similarly inaccessible. That left sneaking through the kitchens. Not an unattractive alternative, since she'd already managed to finish the shrimp puffs within reach and she knew Mrs. Maguire, Regina's cook, would have another five dozen stashed out back. She set down her glass and began to slither through the crowd, doing her best to blend in with the other chattering magpies. She'd almost made it, the swinging door was just within reach, when Phillip's mellifluous, politician's tones reached her.

The curse under her breath was short and succinct, then she turned, giving him a brilliant smile that never faltered even as she realized he was still accompanied by McNab, and that fully half the occupants of the crowded room were avidly observing their little encounter.

"Hello, Phillip," she replied dutifully, reaching up to kiss his smoothly shaven cheek.

"You're looking radiant as ever. Breaking engagements must agree with you." There was just the faintest edge beneath Phillip's voice, an edge that surprised Ferris. It was unlike Phillip to let anything ruffle his carefully guarded emotions. He'd never shown any hint that she might have hurt him six months ago when she, or rather Blackheart, had severed their engagement. Apparently she'd been wrong.

"I've decided I'm not the marrying kind," she said with a light laugh. "Clearly I'm the love them and leave them type."

"I wouldn't say that. I think you just made a mistake."

Oh, no, she thought miserably, still keeping her smile firmly planted on her stiff face. *Don't tell me he's going to try to get me back.*

Leaning forward, Phillip slipped a smooth, perfectly manicured hand beneath her elbow, turning her in his companion's direction. "Let me introduce you to Detective McNab."

"We've already met," McNab said brusquely.

Phillip's smile was surprisingly cheerful. "Then you know why he's here."

"It's not really any of my concern." She tried to pull her arm out of Phillip's grasp, but his fingers tightened their grip.

"He doesn't think Blackheart's retired."

"How interesting." She began edging toward the kitchen door, but the shifting crowds had blocked her one and only exit, and she was trapped. She didn't know how completely trapped she was until she saw Blackheart within hearing distance, flirting with a newly-divorced redhead with seeming rapt attention. She knew by the tension in his shoulders that he was listening to every word of their conversation, even as he flirted. *Damn him.*

"You don't think he's retired, either," Phillip said with sudden acumen. "You've been so besotted with him that it could only take something of that nature to break you up."

"Phillip, I find this tiresome." In desperation she reached for another glass of champagne as it whizzed by on a silver tray. "Blackheart and I had several differences, none of them concerning his former line of work. Why should it matter to you?"

"Perhaps my hurt pride?"

"I wouldn't think Detective McNab would find the bruised ego of a politician to be of much help in an impartial investigation."

McNab was as fully aware of Blackheart's proximity as was Ferris. "I never said I was impartial, Ms. Byrd. I have every intention of putting John Patrick Blackheart exactly where he belongs. Which is behind bars for a good long time."

Even the eavesdropping Blackheart had his limits. Excusing himself from the redhead with his usual grace, he sauntered over to the threesome by the kitchen door. "It'll be a cold day in hell, McNab," he remarked pleasantly. "I've done nothing."

"Maybe not within my jurisdiction," McNab allowed. "But I know you, Blackheart, I know you better than you know yourself. Sooner or later you're going to slip up. You can't keep flying off to Europe, pulling a heist, and then coming back here expecting to be welcomed with open arms. It's a sickness with people like you, and sooner or later the craving will come over you and you'll try it again in your own backyard. In my city. And this time I'll get you."

Blackheart's yawn was perfection. "Have you always had such a well-rounded fantasy life, McNab? Or is it just part of a mid-life crisis?"

His casual pose might have fooled the others, but Ferris knew him too well, knew his body too well. She could sense the tension radiating from the corners of his dark brown eyes, could see the faint tightness in his thin-lipped mouth, could feel the anger and something else emanating from him, going straight to her heart with that inexplicable emotional telepathy that lovers sometimes had.

But they were no longer lovers. And he was lying, lying to everyone. Lying through that sexy mouth of his, lying with his eyes.

"Gentlemen," Phillip said smoothly, his fingers still clutching Ferris's arm. "Let's not have a quarrel in my mother's living room."

Blackheart's expression was no longer affable, it was downright dangerous. "Good idea, Phillip. If you just take your hands off Ferris there'll be no need to flatten you."

Phillip was an inch or two taller than Blackheart and much broader. "Try it," Phillip said, digging his fingers in harder.

"I should warn you, Phillip, that I don't fight fair, and I don't like people manhandling my ex-fiancée."

"She happens to be my ex-fiancée, too."

"For heaven's sake, let go of me, Phillip," Ferris snapped, yanking her arm out of his grasp. This time he let her go, but the tightness of his earlier grip had left red marks she could only hope Blackheart wouldn't notice. "I'm not an old bone to be fought over by a pair of pit bulls."

Blackheart laughed, some of the tension vanishing. "Hardly a pit bull. Phillip's more of an overbred Afghan. Big on looks and short on brain."

"What about you?" she couldn't keep from asking. For a moment his hard brown eyes softened, and they were alone in the crowded room.

"Nothing but an old alley cat, darling. Not worth the bother."

"There you are!" Regina's sonorous voice cut through the sudden hush, and Ferris greeted her intrusion with real relief. "I wanted to introduce you all to the Porcinis. We wouldn't be here tonight without their gracious offer, and I know you'll want to welcome them."

Danielle and Marco Porcini were more what Ferris had had in mind when she envisioned circus performers, she thought as Regina made her usual effortless introductions. Marco was tall, dark and handsome, the epitome of European allure. He practically glistened in the soft light, from his shiny black mustache, his perfect mane of hair to his small, white teeth and bulging biceps. If he'd been an unmarried lion tamer and Ferris even dumber than she was, she would have gone off with him in a flash.

But he came equipped with a small-boned, delicate English wife. Danielle Porcini had blue eyes and blond hair, a pale rose complexion, and no expression on her face whatsoever as she smiled and said all the right things. *Strange*, Ferris thought, momentarily distracted from her own troubles.

None of them, with the possible exception of McNab, had any illusion as to why Regina felt it necessary to introduce the Porcinis to the hostile little group by the kitchen door. As usual Phillip was suddenly all charm, and Ferris was tempted to remind him that Mr. and Mrs. Porcini couldn't vote. She bit her tongue, stealing a look at Blackheart.

She didn't like what she saw, didn't like it one tiny bit. He was staring at

Danielle Porcini and pretending not to. He was pale beneath his tan, and for Blackheart the rest of the crowd, herself included, failed to exist.

Madame Porcini seemed unmoved by his covert attention. Her eyes were on her husband, her delicate hand tucked into his burly arm. She treated the three men, McNab included, with impartial politeness, but it was as if part of her simply wasn't there.

Ferris felt such a sweeping of unfathomable jealousy wash over her that she was more than willing to hope the woman was a mental incompetent rather than a rational human being who might possibly succumb to Blackheart's wiles. As any rational human being would, she thought morosely.

And then Danielle Porcini's eyes briefly met hers, before moving back to her husband, and Ferris realized that far from being slow-witted, the circus owner's wife was one smart cookie indeed. Dangerously so.

"Ferris, I was just going to show Danielle the powder room. Would you do so for me?" Regina requested in the tone she occasionally used for royal decrees. Clearly she wanted to break up the unpleasant little scene in the corner, and she did so with her customary dispatch.

While part of Ferris was amused at Regina's highhanded disposition, another part was grateful. "Of course. Mrs. Porcini?"

As they made their way through the crowded room toward the hallway and the curving staircase, Ferris could feel any number of eyes boring into her back. It was an unnerving feeling, since she didn't for a moment suppose any of those interested gazes were particularly friendly.

The crowds thinned out as the two women slowly climbed the flight of stairs. Mrs. Porcini seemed unnaturally composed for someone so young, and without meaning to Ferris blurted out the first thing that came to mind.

"How old are you?"

The self-contained woman beside her smiled briefly. "Twenty-four. How old are you?"

"Thirty. I'm sorry, that was a very rude question. It's just that you seem older."

"I am," Danielle Porcini said briefly.

There was no response she could make to that. As she preceded the younger woman into the bathroom that was larger than half her apartment, she cursed the convention that women should accompany each other to the powder room. Mrs. Porcini made her acutely uncomfortable for many reasons, not the least of which had been the expression on Blackheart's face when he saw her. The young Englishwoman had appeared not to notice, but Ferris's misery and guilt hadn't blunted her powers of observation. Mrs. Porcini might never have seen Blackheart before, but she knew who he was.

Ferris sank onto a tufted velvet stool in front of the wall-size mirror and disconsolately surveyed her reflection. Her hair was still in place, but she'd managed to chew off the rest of her lipstick, and despite the artful application of foundation and blusher she looked pale, wan and depressed.

Would Blackheart regret what he'd thrown away? For all that she knew him so well, she couldn't read the emotions in his carefully shuttered eyes. He was still very angry with her, that much was certain.

Danielle sat down beside her, running a brush through her silvery-blond mane, her face perfectly composed. "An interesting group of men," she murmured in an indifferent tone of voice. "Tell me about them."

Ferris's instincts, already on edge, swung into overdrive. For a moment she considered telling the girl to mind her own business, then decided otherwise. She wouldn't tell her anything Danielle couldn't find out from anyone at the party. If *she* told her, she could control the information.

"They were an interesting bunch," Ferris conceded, tossing back her hair and admiring her own casual response. If Danielle Porcini could act, so could she. "Phillip is a politician, looking for more power than he's got. McNab is a cop, and that's about all I know."

"And the other man?"

You know as well as I do his name is Blackheart, sweetie, Ferris thought. "He's the most interesting one of all. His name is John Patrick Blackheart, and he's a retired jewel thief. You've never heard of him?"

"As a matter of fact, I haven't," Danielle said, and Ferris didn't believe her for a moment. "And is he friends with this McNab?"

"Sworn enemies, more likely."

Danielle Porcini smiled, a small, vengeful cat's smile that vanished as quickly as it appeared. But not so quickly that Ferris missed it. And her unease about the self-contained Madame Porcini increased tenfold.

BLACKHEART WAS in a foul mood, one of the foulest moods he'd ever suffered through in his entire life. Every time he turned around there was a new stumbling block, a new disaster or complication looming on the horizon.

There was no way out. He couldn't walk away from the incredible mess his life had become, for the simple reason that he hadn't made the mess. He might have contributed a bit in the past, but right now someone was diabolically intent on framing him for the recent rash of robberies plaguing the major cities of Europe. And he was damned if he was going to sit back and play the patsy anymore.

Of course Ferris immediately condemned him. A hanging judge if ever there was one, dear Ferris-Francesca. He was going to enjoy making her eat her words, having her crawling in abject apology when he was finally able to flush out the real thief.

But he was going to have to watch his step. He'd almost got caught last week when he broke into the Yendades town house to see if the thief had left anything incriminating that the police and Interpol might have missed. He couldn't really blame the police. When confronted with the exact modus operandi with which he'd operated for a good fifteen years, it was no wonder they weren't looking too far for another culprit. For a while he'd had very real doubts as to his ability to get back out of Spain.

But his passport was incontrovertible evidence. He hadn't been in Spain at the time of the robbery, any more than he'd been in Lisbon during the Vasquez robbery or anywhere near the Phelps Museum in Paris. Granted, he'd appeared on the scene as soon as he'd heard about it. And he hadn't been particularly cooperative toward the police. He couldn't change a lifetime of habit, and he never could, never would trust the police.

The final straw, the last insulting touch, had been the tarot card left behind at each scene. Very few people knew about that obscure part of the Blackheart family past. His grandfather and uncle had started their careers in the late twenties, when interest in the occult had been high among the British upper classes. It had been their particular conceit to leave behind a Knight of Pentacles at each scene, and Blackheart had done the same until the romance of the business had gone stale and he'd been more interested in simply doing the job and getting out safely.

Very few people knew about that telltale signature. The police had always been very circumspect about mentioning it, for fear they'd end up with copycat crimes. Clearly whoever was patterning crimes after the Blackheart family tradition had inside information.

Blackheart stared out over Regina Merriam's perfectly manicured grounds, across the wide expanse that would hold a circus tent, over to the impressive roofline of the Museum of Decorative Arts, the domed and angled roofs a perfect foil against the night sky. There'd been one link between all the recent robberies that had been plaguing Europe for the last couple of years, and Blackheart didn't know if anyone but himself was aware of it. Each time a robbery occurred, somewhere within an hour's journey of the crime the Porcini Family Circus was in residence.

He hadn't been sure it wasn't a simple coincidence until he'd heard of their benefit performance in his hometown. A benefit performance for a very moneyed charity. Most of the women volunteering for the Committee for Saving the Bay wouldn't go swimming without their diamonds. They wouldn't know how to dress down to attend a circus, and somewhere in that crowd of fifty or so employed by the Porcini Family Circus was someone who knew far too much about the Blackhearts and too great an interest in jewels.

He'd expected to have to cajole Regina into letting him take care of the security for the benefit. *After all*, it wasn't as if priceless jewels were involved in the performance. But he'd reckoned without Regina's romantic streak. If Blackheart and Co. were in charge of the security then they, he, would have no choice but to deal with Ferris.

He wasn't sure if that was an advantage or a drawback. On the one hand, he had every intention of enticing the skittish, distrustful Ms. Byrd-Berdahofski back into his arms, his bed, his life. On the other hand, things would be a lot easier if he could concentrate on one thing at a time and didn't have to worry about being framed for a succession of jewel robberies—not to mention the distinctly unpleasant sensation of having Stephen McNab breathing down his neck.

McNab hadn't liked it when Blackheart and Co. had received its license. He hadn't liked it when the company had prospered, and particularly hadn't liked it when he'd had Blackheart safely in custody over the theft of the Von Emmerling emeralds, then been forced to let him go when the real thieves turned up. He hadn't gotten it through his thick cop's brain that Blackheart had been completely innocent, and he probably never would.

Sooner or later it would all come together, Blackheart thought, more in devout hope than in certainty. He was already one step ahead of the game. He'd thought it would take days to find out who'd been following in his family's footsteps, and in the end it had been shockingly simple. He'd taken one look at Danielle Porcini's bland, distant face and seen his long-lost sister staring back. And if he was still shaken by the fact, even Dany herself didn't realize it. No one did. With the possible exception of his maddening, gorgeous ex- and future fiancée. He was going to have to watch his step.

THE FIRST THING Ferris wanted to do was to get the hell out of Regina's overcrowded house. Regina was in the front hall, and she'd have too many uncomfortable questions. McNab and Phillip were where she and Danielle had left them, by the kitchen, and Danielle Porcini was threading her way back toward them with the effortless grace of an athlete.

That left the terrace. It was a little cool for it to be a popular place, and unless she was mistaken a light rain was about to fall. Her silk dress would be ruined, but that was a minor price to pay for a quick getaway. She'd sneak out on the porch, climb over the railing and make her way across the grounds before anyone even realized she was gone.

In theory it was a wonderful idea; in practice she hadn't taken fate into account. No sooner had she slipped out the door, pulling it shut behind her, when a too-familiar voice purred in her ear. "Pussycat, pussycat, where have you been?"

"Damn you, Blackheart," she said with surprisingly little rancor. "I was trying to escape."

He was leaning against the stone railing, oblivious to the lightly falling mist, and it was too dark to read his expression. Not that she would have been able to guess what he was thinking, even in broad daylight. Blackheart was adept at keeping hidden what he wished to keep hidden.

"With the family jewels?" he countered, still not moving from his indolent pose.

"That's more your style, isn't it?"

"Not with my friends."

"That's right, you have your standards." She wanted to keep her voice lightly mocking, but an edge had crept into it. An edge of anger, but also of hurt and confusion. Why hadn't he fought for her?

"Indeed. By the way, I hate that dress. You look like you used to look before we . . . before. All elegant and refined and half alive. If it weren't for that blot of ice cream, I would have been afraid the real Francesca had gone for good."

"Only you would notice the ice cream," she mourned, staring down at the practically invisible stain. The light mist had soaked into the material, making it cling to her well-rounded figure, cling to the lavender silk underwear and the skin beneath.

"Only I would have been paying close enough attention," he agreed. "As I am now. Maybe I don't hate that dress, after all." He moved as he usually did, with speed and a kind of lethal grace that she was too bemused to fight. At one moment she was standing in the rain, in the next she'd been pulled quite firmly into his arms, the wet silk dress a thin barrier between his body and her own.

She was too surprised to fight him, too surprised to do anything but stand perfectly still in the circle of his arms, absorbing his quite remarkable body heat. He didn't kiss her; he just looked down into her rain-damp face, and his eyes were shadowed.

"What are you doing to us, Francesca?" he murmured, his mouth close to hers.

For a moment she wanted to dissolve in his arms, but she fought it, fought herself, fought him. "If you don't let go of me, John Patrick Blackheart, I will toss you through the French doors, and you'll lose another one of your nine lives."

To her surprise he grinned. "Right now I don't have them to spare, lady." And he released her, stepping back.

It was so cold without his arms around her. So cold and lonely. "Thanks," she said politely, and without another word she hiked her trailing skirts up to her thighs and scrambled over the wide stone railing, dropping lightly to the ground some four feet below. By then the rain had begun in earnest, and slipping off her high heels, she took off across the cold wet grass, running, telling herself she was running from the rain. But she was running from the man who stayed behind, watching her through the heavy curtain of rain.

Chapter Six

The Wrong Man
(Warner Brothers 1957)

FERRIS'S LATE MODEL Mercedes SL coughed, sputtered, and limped its way back to her apartment in the city. Her forty-thousand-dollar automobile didn't like the rain, the fog, or damp weather of any sort, and she was a fool to hold on to it in rainy, damp, foggy San Francisco. But by that time the car was so fully integrated with her invented self-image that she couldn't imagine herself without it, inefficient engine and all. Besides, it gave her something to curse, something to think about besides Blackheart as she drove home through the rain-slick streets.

It stalled two blocks from her apartment and refused to start again, but for once fate had the kindness to provide a nearby parking space on a downhill slope. She climbed out of the car and pushed, her feet squishing around in her wet high-heeled sandals, her hair hanging like a limp curtain around her face, her silk dress ruined. The parking spot was directly in front of a fire hydrant, but Ferris was beyond caring. She left the car at an angle, its elegant tail pointing out into the street, and she slammed the door with all her strength. She didn't bother to lock it. With luck someone would steal it, preferably before she got a parking ticket, and her worries would be over. At least one of them.

She would have left her keys, just to make sure any would-be thief didn't give up at the first little setback, but she didn't fancy shinnying up her building again. If someone wanted her Mercedes, they'd simply have to work for it.

The rain turned into a downpour as she hiked the two blocks to her apartment, cursing and muttering under her breath. She was too physically miserable to think about Blackheart, to think about the strange undercurrents in Regina's odd assortment of guests. She still hadn't figured out how McNab had managed to show up. The *A* list of the Committee for Saving the Bay didn't include cops, even if retired and semiretired cat burglars figured high on the list of desirables. He was awfully chummy with Phillip Merriam, but then, a politician on the stump was everyone's friend.

Still, it seemed as if there was more to it than that. She might almost have suspected Phillip of bringing him, but then her former fiancé had no motive. Unless he was holding a grudge.

Her three locks gave easily enough, a small consolation on a miserable night. Slamming the door behind her, she stood in the middle of her living room and yanked off her clothes, dropping her sodden dress into a wastebasket, kicking her muddy shoes across the room, stripping off her lavender underwear and walking naked through the twisty little apartment, past the piles of boxes into her bedroom.

Blackie had gone out on his nightly rounds. Ferris shut the terrace door, shivering in the chilly night air, grabbed her flannel nightshirt and had started back toward the kitchen when something caught her eye.

If she hadn't been so miserable, both physically and emotionally, she would have realized someone had been in her apartment. She had only a moment of uneasiness before irritation and a reluctant amusement washed over. Blackheart hadn't let go as easily as she'd thought.

She'd left her bed a rumpled mess. It was now neatly made, the pretty pastel sheets smooth. And sitting in the middle of the bed was a familiar-looking bag. Mrs. Field's Cookies. She didn't even have to open the bag to find out they were the coco-macs.

She and Blackheart had shared half a dozen of them on their walk around San Francisco after he'd initiated her into the art of cat burglary, centuries ago. They'd eaten them on picnics, on drives, in movies and for breakfast. Most of all they'd eaten them in bed.

She should take the bag and hurl them off the terrace. But then McNab would probably show up and bust her for littering again. She'd had too many sweets that day—she should throw them out. Run them under water first, to blunt temptation.

But then she hadn't eaten much at Regina's. And after almost a week of not eating, surely she could afford to eat a cookie or two. She'd throw the rest out, of course she would.

By the time the ten o'clock news was over she'd finished the bag. Her pastel sheets were littered with crumbs, her stomach was complaining at the sudden influx of sugar, and she was very close to tears. The taste of those damned cookies was forever linked in her brain with the taste of Blackheart. He couldn't have chosen a more insidious punishment. Or was it a bribe?

Crumpling up the bag, she tossed it under the bed, flipped off the light, and nestled down among the sheets, ignoring the crumbs as they dug into her skin. *Six cookies.* Wasn't there an old legend about that? Someone had gone down into hell, eaten six pomegranate seeds, and ended up having to spend six months of every year in bed with the devil.

She'd already done her six months with Blackheart, a six months that had felt uncomfortably akin to demonic possession. Had she just committed herself to another six months? Was it worth fighting?

With a moan she rolled over, burying her face in her pillow. It was too late and she was too tired. Tomorrow she'd recognize what she'd done, pigged out on too many cookies and Blackheart's fiendish sense of humor.

Maybe tomorrow she'd send him a pint of Double Rainbow ice cream.

Maybe, if she had any sense at all, she'd forget it. Ignore the cookies, ignore Blackheart. The caloric gift was probably just his way of saying goodbye. If it wasn't, she certainly couldn't be won over by a sugar buzz. Answers were what she needed, and answers were just what he wasn't going to give.

At least she had no reason to see him again. Regina might have invited him to her party, but there'd be no reason to run into him from then on. Why, with any luck she wouldn't even see him for months and months and months. With any luck she'd have enough time to get over him.

Because it had only taken one look at him, one touch of his hands on her body, and she'd known she was just as in love, just as obsessed as she'd always been. And God only knew how long it was going to take her to forget him.

"WHO WAS HE?"

Dany stared at the pale face in the mirror, ignoring the reflection of the blustering man behind her. Marco had had too much to drink, and he'd been further stimulated by the obvious, idiotic admiration of all the fawning females at the big house tonight. She could see by the glitter in his eyes that he was in a dangerous mood, and if she had any sense at all she'd watch what she said.

But when had she ever had any sense? "Who was who?" she countered, taking off her crystal earrings and dropping them onto the plastic counter in front of her.

He moved swiftly, the drink scarcely slowing him down at all, but she'd been watching, and she was able to tense herself when he grabbed her, his thick arm going around her neck, snapping her head back. His breath smelled of whiskey and garlic, his body was sweaty and muscular, but she controlled the shiver of fear that had started deep within her.

"You know who. The man who was looking down your dress and trying not to."

"My brother?"

The arm tightened for a moment, and she choked before he lessened the pressure. "Don't be too brave, little one. As you may remember, I have a temper."

"Not my brother, then. He didn't know who I was," she added smugly.

"No," Marco agreed. "The great Blackheart has been overrated. But we're not talking about your obtuse half-brother, are we? We're talking about the other man."

"The cop."

For a moment she wondered whether he'd snap her neck. It might almost be a relief. There wasn't an ounce of joy or pleasure in her life, and hadn't been for years. Maybe it would be better to end it here than to carry through her intricate revenge and then hope to find some better sort of life.

Marco released her, stepping back. "A cop," he echoed flatly. "What did he want? What did you tell him?"

"Nothing, I told him nothing. I'm in this just as deeply as you are."

"Don't forget it," Marco snarled, sobering up. "That still doesn't explain what he wanted."

Dany smiled. "To look down my dress."

Then he hit her. Not as hard as he could; it was an openhanded blow that knocked her back against the bed. She knew how to fall, how to relax her muscles and roll with it. She lay on the bed, staring up at him, veiling the contempt and hatred that threatened to consume her. She knew from bitter experience that hatred only managed to excite him.

It was a close thing. Marco stood there, weaving slightly, his eyes hooded, contemplating his alternatives. There was a dead silence in the room, broken only by the sound of his breathing. "Don't push your luck, *cara*," he murmured finally. "I get tired of your smart mouth. Did the cop have any suspicions?"

Her face tingled from the blow. She'd been hit so often that she'd developed a second sense about how much damage he'd done. This one wouldn't even leave a bruise. Just a little stiffness around the jaw. "The cop was interested in Blackheart," she replied, keeping her hatred banked and out of her carefully neutral voice. "He wanted to know if I knew anything about him, and I think he was attracted to me. But as far as I could tell he didn't have any suspicions about either of us."

Marco nodded, apparently satisfied. "Attracted to you, eh? No accounting for tastes. Maybe American men like flat-chested little man-eaters."

Dany sat up, careful not to make any sudden moves that might ignite Marco's temper. "Somehow I don't think there's a future in it."

Marco laughed, his good humor restored. "True enough. I can't see an American cop and a thief having a good time together. Unless it's in the police car on the way to jail."

"If I go to jail, Marco, you go too." She was pushing it, she knew, but she had her limits.

Fortunately Marco's temper had vanished. "No one's going to jail, Danielle. No one but your long-lost brother. Think of that when you get sullen, little one. You're about to get your fondest hope. Revenge."

"Yes," she said, wishing she could feel better about it, wishing she could forget the little tendrils of doubt that were curling inside her, wishing she could simply have looked up into Stephen McNab's eyes and believed what she saw reflected there.

"You're not having second thoughts, are you?" Marco was headed toward the connecting door.

Dany could hear the muffled sound of someone moving around behind that closed door, and she knew that for now she was safe. "Not when I'm so close," she said.

"Cheer up. In a few days you'll be rich, you'll have your revenge, and you'll be rid of me."

"A lovely thought," she said, pushing her hair out of her face. "Your friend is waiting."

For a moment he hesitated, his dark eyes running over her body with an expression she'd learned to dread. "I might send her away."

"No, Marco."

It was a mistake. He liked a fight. His mouth widened in a smile, and his hand left the doorknob. "No?" he echoed.

It took all her self-possession to shrug lightly. "As you wish."

He frowned, and she knew from bitter experience that her capitulation was like a bucket of ice water on the coals of his desire. "Not this time, *cara.* But soon."

Over my dead body, she thought, smiling faintly at him. "As you wish," she said again. And her smile broadened as he slammed the door behind him.

Until she remembered McNab. She'd been left alone with him in the crowded room while Phillip Merriam had been enticed into showing Marco the layout of the mansion. She'd already been uneasy—she wasn't used to casual conversation with a policeman, nor was she used to the banked admiration in his chilly gray eyes. Most of the men she met knew she was Marco's property, and they knew of Marco's temper. McNab had known, and he hadn't said a word that was less than proper. But she'd seen the look in his eyes.

A stray shiver washed over her body, and for the first time she wished she'd taken some whiskey herself. Now wasn't the time to lose her nerve, and the blank expression on Blackheart's face when he'd met her had only strengthened her resolve. Not only had he forgotten her very existence, he hadn't even recognized her when she turned up.

He'd remember her eight days from now, when she'd be very rich and long gone. And maybe McNab would remember her, if he wasn't too busy reveling in his triumph at finally having nailed Blackheart to the wall.

She should be happier about the whole thing. She should be delighted that things were happening at last. She looked across the room at her reflection in the mirror, the imprint of Marco's hand red across her pale face, her blond hair hanging down, her mouth trembling. She summoned forth her coolest, most controlled expression. And then watched in horror as her reflection crumpled into silent, ugly tears.

FERRIS BREEZED into her office, a wide smile on her carefully lipsticked mouth. The rain and despair of the last few days had lifted, almost as if by magic. When she woke the next morning the sun was out, a crisp breeze had blown the last of the clouds away, and with it all the doubts and depression that had tormented her. Suddenly anything was possible.

She'd washed the crumbs from her skin, dressed in a green silk suit that matched her eyes, and stepped out into the morning air with nothing short of a swagger.

Her car was where she'd left it, and no one had given her a ticket. It started right up, running smoothly as she drove across town to the office. Life was suddenly back under her control, something that hadn't happened since she first set eyes on John Patrick Blackheart. Her life was once more her own, and she had no reason to see Blackheart and fall under his spell again. A new life spread out before her, and she was ready to greet it with open arms.

She was halfway through her second cup of coffee, completely preoccupied with the papers she was leafing through, when something landed on her desk with a disrupting thump. She looked up, only mildly irritated, to find Blackheart's partner, Trace Walker, staring down at her with gloomy disapproval.

"Trace," Ferris said politely, leaning back and setting down her coffee mug—next to the bag of Mrs. Field's Cookies Trace had delivered. "What can I do for you?"

"Now isn't the time to go into it," he growled. "I told Patrick I'd drop these off on my way to the Merriams' place."

The moment she'd set eyes on Trace, she'd felt her ebullient mood begin to ebb. It now vanished with a crashing thud. "Merriams?" she echoed very cautiously. "Why would you go to the Merriams'?"

"Preliminary security check. Patrick's going to meet me there."

"Why do we need security for a damned circus?" It had to be another of Blackheart's devious excuses to torment her. There was no need for anything but glorified gatekeepers.

Trace drew himself up to his full six feet three or four, and his beefy, handsome face was forbidding. "I expect you'll have to ask Regina about that. She and Patrick made all the arrangements."

"You can bet I'll ask Regina," Ferris snarled. "We don't need Blackheart and Company's specialized services and you know it as well as I do. We certainly don't need to waste the committee's hard-earned money on expensive security when simple security guards will do just as well."

"If you can find simple security guards," Patrick's smooth voice broke through her rage. "Most of the ones I know are reasonably intelligent."

Trace's imposing bulk had shielded Blackheart's characteristically silent approach, but then, Ferris had been in such a towering, noisy rage that she might not have noticed, anyway.

She picked up the bag of cookies and hurled it at his head. "Get out of here, Blackheart!" she snapped, all her newly-won self-control vanishing.

Blackheart caught them deftly, snaked around his partner and pushed him out the door, then closed it behind him, sealing himself in the spacious office with his furious ex-fiancée. "Tsk-tsk," he said reprovingly. "Such a temper, Ferris. One would think you cared."

She just glared at him. No one in the world could strip away her calm, her defenses, as John Patrick Blackheart could. She was overreacting as always, but she couldn't help it. Just moments ago she'd thought her life was back in her control and that she was beyond caring. All he had to do was appear, his lean, black-clad figure lounging in her best chair, and she knew she was a long way from being over him.

"I don't care," she said. "I just don't see the need to waste our limited resources on your very substantial fees."

"We're donating them."

"Don't be absurd. Half of your work is for charity functions. You can't afford to work for free."

"All in a good cause." Blackheart's smile was bland. She might almost have believed him, if it weren't for the shadows lingering in his cool brown eyes, the cynical twist of his mouth—and the fact that she desperately wanted to believe otherwise.

"All right," she said. "We never turn down donations."

"Good." He tossed the cookies back onto the desk in front of her.

"The *committee* doesn't turn down donations. I do." She picked up the battered bag and dropped it into her trash basket. Turning back to Blackheart, she gave him her most professional smile. "I'll arrange for one of my assistants to accompany you out to Regina's. I'm certain it won't take much of your time."

"Guess again."

"I beg your pardon?"

"This is a bigger job than it appears. And I don't believe in working with assistants,"

Ferris controlled the urge to scream again. "Blackheart, it's a circus, for heaven's sake. Not some priceless collection of diamonds."

"Or emeralds," he reminded her softly. "Nevertheless, there are still substantial jewels involved. Not to mention Regina's collection of artwork."

For a moment she forgot they were enemies, forgot that he'd betrayed her and broken her heart. "Have you ever stolen works of art?" she asked with nothing but simple curiosity.

"Never. Jewels were the family tradition, and besides, they were far more portable."

"So at least Regina's collection is safe from you." She'd pushed him too far, she knew it the moment the words were out of her mouth, but her anger was still too fresh.

He just stared at her for a long moment. "Nothing is safe from me," he said. "And no one. Remember that." He rose, his indolent grace deceptive. She knew the fury that was vibrating through his body. "I'll meet you at Regina's in an hour."

"I don't think I can make it."

"Be there." His voice was a silken threat, one she didn't quite dare to fight.

She half expected him to slam her door as he left, but he closed it very, very quietly. She stared after him, prey, as always, to conflicting emotions. On the one hand she regretted making him so angry. She didn't for a moment believe he would rip off Regina or any of their friends.

On the other hand, the angrier she made him, the farther away she'd drive him. And if she was to have any hope of recovery, she needed to drive him very far away indeed.

She'd go out to Regina's and accompany him over the grounds, if that was what he insisted on. She'd prove to him that he couldn't goad her into a fury. Then maybe he'd leave her alone.

In the meantime she was suddenly, astonishingly hungry. With one furtive glance at the now-empty hallway beyond her glass-doored office, she reached into the wastebasket and retrieved the now-mangled bag of cookies. And leaning back, she began to nibble on the broken pieces.

MCNAB WAS IN A very bad mood. Not only was John Patrick Blackheart being an exemplary citizen, but his ex-fiancée had proved a complete washout. So far, at least. The only one interested in helping him was State Senator Phillip Merriam, and when it got to the point where a cop had to trust a politician, then things were in pretty bad shape. Particularly since this politician had an ax to grind.

On top of that there was Danielle Porcini. Married to that walking sweat gland, barely meeting his eye, moving through the noisy crowds at Mrs. Merriam's with a self-possessed calm that he didn't quite believe. As a cop he counted on his instincts, and they were telling him something wasn't right about the young Mrs. Porcini.

That wasn't his only reaction to the circus owner's wife. While she hadn't been the prettiest woman in the room, the richest or the friendliest, there was something about her that spoke to him on a very elemental level. Which was incredibly stupid on his part. It had been three years since his civilized divorce, and if he'd had any doubts as to whether a sane woman could survive being married to a cop he'd found out otherwise. No woman could put up with the hours he put in, the obsessions that ruled his life when he was on a hot case. The smartest thing he could do would be to put her out of his mind, considering that she came equipped with a very large husband. If he could just get rid of the feeling that there was more to her than met the eye.

First things first. The first thing on his agenda was catching John Patrick Blackheart in the act of robbery and putting him behind bars for a long, long time. And the second was to figure out exactly what the Porcinis, Danielle in particular, were doing. If those two goals happened to coincide, so much the better. But he knew what his first priority was, and he was getting so close that he could taste it. He was going to nail Blackheart to the wall. Then he could think about his love life.

Chapter Seven

Notorious
(RKO 1946)

IN THE CLEAR, beautiful sunlight Regina Merriam's acres and acres of manicured lawns looked more like a battle zone. The Porcini Family Circus came equipped with a huge tent, several smaller ones, trailers, motor homes, trucks and cars, and a brightly arrayed sea of humanity swarmed over the grass. Ferris parked her car up by the house, brushed the last cookie crumb from her mouth and carefully reapplied her pale lip gloss. Blackheart hated pale lips. She smiled smugly at her reflection, her joy in the perfect day returning. If her pleasure was augmented by the upcoming battle with Blackheart, she didn't have to admit it, even to herself. But as she crossed the graveled drive to the front door she was humming tunelessly to herself, and even the distant roar of what had to be some sort of caged jungle cat couldn't dent her cheerfulness.

Regina greeted her arrival with uncustomary relief. Her silvery hair was falling in wisps around her shoulders, her faded blue eyes were edged with cheerful desperation, and her silk blouse was coming untucked. "Thank goodness you're here," she said. "They're driving me crazy."

Ferris did her best to sound callous even as she gave Regina a reassuring hug. "It's your fault. We don't need Blackheart and Company for something as straightforward as a circus."

"Who said anything about Blackheart and Company? They're the least of my worries. It's Nelbert Securities that's giving me a migraine headache."

Ferris let out a soundless whistle. "What in the world are you doing with the two biggest security companies crawling all over your house? I don't imagine Blackheart was too pleased to run into one of Jeff Nelbert's minions roaming your hallways."

"It's Jeff himself. And it's not my fault—Phillip arranged for them without consulting me."

"Fire them."

"I can't. It's *The Hyacinths.*"

"You've lost me."

"That damned little painting Henry bought a few years before he died. It happens to be a Van Gogh," Regina said in a mournful tone. "You must remember what happened to his painting of irises a year or two ago?"

"Vaguely."

"It sold for somewhere around forty million dollars, and it was painted during the same period. I don't want to be sitting in a house with what might conceivably be one of the world's most valuable paintings. Ever since the iris sale I've been making arrangements to get rid of it. I'm donating it to the museum—that way I can simply walk down the hill and see it, if I have a mind to. Nelbert's in charge of museum security, and he's busy taking measurements, making plans. So I have to suffer."

"You're giving it away?"

Regina shrugged. "I don't need the money—I have more than enough to keep me comfortably, and Phillip has his own substantial income. Besides, think of the publicity if I put it onto the auction block. People, nasty criminal types, might start wondering what other treasures I had tucked away here, and then there'd be no peace."

Blackheart had appeared beyond Regina's shoulder, his expression guarded. "So instead you have to put up with nasty criminal types crawling all over the place, trying to keep your treasures intact."

"Patrick, don't even think such a thing!" Regina protested.

"I thought I'd better say it before Ferris could open her mouth. At this point I can read her mind."

You always could, she thought. "He's already assured me he wouldn't touch works of art. Too bulky, right?"

"Right. Of course, *The Hyacinths* is actually quite small. I could tuck it into a briefcase and walk right out with it and no one would be the wiser." He smiled faintly at Ferris. "It's worth considering."

"He's teasing you, my dear," Regina said kindly.

"He's wasting my time." Ferris gave him a withering stare, one that left him noticeably unmoved. "I'm going back to the office." She turned to head out the door, but his hand had already caught her arm, his long, clever fingers digging in with just a trace too much force.

"I want to show you my security precautions first, dear heart." The edge in his voice was so subtle that only Ferris noticed it. "Then you can run back and hide in your office."

"Go along, darling." Regina waved her away, much cheerier than when Ferris had first arrived. "I'm sure I can manage to withstand Jeff Nelbert's overwhelming personality, if you can manage to withstand Blackheart. Can you?"

"Ferris has a will of iron," Blackheart drawled, tugging her toward the stairs. "She can withstand anything."

I only wish that were true, Ferris thought mournfully. Even the impersonal touch of his hand on her arm was melting her brain at an alarming rate. "Why are we going upstairs?" she inquired in her calmest voice, once they were out of sight of Regina's fond eyes.

Blackheart grinned at her, momentarily lighthearted. "I have several suggestions."

"I'm sure you do."

"I wouldn't jump to any conclusions if I were you. Distrust is not an aphrodisiac. Regina was thinking of having a dinner before the circus, with a guest list of some one hundred and fifty people. The only criterion for an invitation is money, something like five hundred dollars a plate, which leaves us in a bind. Anyone with the price can get in, and five hundred dollars is a small enough investment when you think of what someone could get away with. So I thought I'd use your considerable expertise to go over the house and see where the problems lie."

"My considerable expertise?"

"You have a natural talent for breaking and entering, darling. You're a born thief. I'm counting on you to be able to figure out how an amateur burglar would think. I tend to be too convoluted in my planning. No one is as good as I am, and I might expect something too complex in the way of a heist."

"As good as you are?" she echoed. "Or were?"

They were at the top of the curving staircase. The upper hall was deserted, the morning sunlight streaming through a vast, multipaned skylight and sending shadows spearing around them. "Don't push it, Francesca," he said. "Or I'll think you have a reason for wanting to goad me."

"I'm not about to make off with Regina's jewelry collection, if that's what you're thinking. You'll have to look elsewhere for a suspect. Like in a mirror."

For a minute his hand tightened on her arm, then he released her, forcing a laugh. "You have a definite talent for making me crazy. No, I don't think you're going to rob anybody. I think you're unable to leave me alone, so you taunt me to get a reaction."

The truth was like a slap in the face, robbing her of her defenses. "I can leave you alone," she managed to say after a moment. "There's no reason for me to be here. For that matter there's no real reason for you to be here, either. It's not as if you're guarding some specific, priceless object. Why don't you leave me alone?"

"You might find this difficult to believe, but I didn't con my way into this job simply to be near you."

She ignored the shaft of pain that shot through her. "I believe you. You know as well as I do that what was between us is over."

"Goading me again, Francesca," he murmured.

She ignored it. "But what I don't understand is why you talked Regina into letting you do it."

"And the reason you don't understand is that you jump to conclusions, you don't consider alternatives, and you're so damned quick to judge." His voice was bitter. "Come along, Ferris. We'll look at *The Hyacinths*, we'll be charming to Nelbert, and we'll go over the kind of locks and alarm systems

Regina has in place. And then you can run away."

"How about if I run away now?" Her voice was low, almost pleading. But if she was hoping for pity from Blackheart, it was a waste of time.

"I'll catch you and bring you back. I'm not going to let you go, Francesca."

"You won't have any say in the matter."

"You don't think so?" She had her dignity, and she was not going to run away from him like a coward. She pulled free of him, giving him a brittle smile. "Try to stop me." She turned on her heel and continued down the stairs, resisting the impulse to run. She could feel him watching in the silent hallway, but right then her defenses were rapidly slipping. One minute more and she would either have thrown him over the balcony or ended up kissing his knees.

"Coward," he called after her, and she gritted her teeth.

"Thief," she shot back over her shoulder, and continued on her way, refusing to look back one more time.

BLACKHEART LEANED against the railing, watching her stalk away from him. The streaks of sun from the skylight made patches of light and shadow as she moved, and he had the strong urge to spank her. *Thief, indeed.* It was nothing she hadn't already known. He rubbed his knee with a surreptitious touch. He'd twisted it, keeping his balance when she'd shoved him, and after three operations and years of physical therapy it still wasn't perfect, and never would be again. All because of another woman scorned, he thought, remembering Prudence Hornsby's red-faced rage when she'd locked him in the basement after catching him stealing her ugly but quite valuable jewels.

It was just as well Francesca walked away. She was too distracting. He hadn't needed her there that day—it would have been better all around if he let her immure herself in her office until this whole mess was sorted out and could devote his full attention to her.

But he never did have much sense, particularly where Francesca was concerned. It was bad enough sleeping alone, not having her grumbling over his coffee, his apartment and his peripatetic existence. He could survive a few weeks, even months of celibacy if he knew Francesca would be there at the end of the wait. But doing without her entirely, even her distrust and baiting, was a little more difficult. He'd take an insult from Francesca over a dozen sweet words from anyone else, and she probably knew it.

At least he had no doubt at all that she was still just as much in love with him as she'd always been. She was fighting it, fighting it with all her strength, and he couldn't get rid of the nagging fear that if he did leave her alone and concentrate on his myriad problems, she might just manage to get over him. He wasn't romantic enough to think that true love would conquer all and last forever. True love needed to be nourished and encouraged.

"Is she worth the trouble?" Jeff Nelbert had crept up on him. Blackheart betrayed no surprise, but inwardly he cursed. The day that a cigar-smoking, two-hundred-and-forty-pound Jeff Nelbert could sneak up on a retired cat burglar of Blackheart's talents was a sad day, indeed.

He turned to face his greatest rival, his expression bland. "None of your damned business." Nelbert was a paunchy, aggressive, not very ethical individual, but he was a born salesman, and that arcane talent had brought him too far in the security business for Blackheart's peace of mind. Blackheart disliked and distrusted the man, but right then he didn't have the energy to waste on a minor irritant like Jeff Nelbert.

"Heard you two had a falling-out." Nelbert licked his thick, pink lips. "I thought I might have a crack at her. She has the cutest little . . ."

Blackheart found the energy. "You'll keep your sweaty hands off her," he said with his friendliest smile, "or I'll tie your tongue in knots and dump you into the bay. She's mine."

"I don't know if she agrees with you on that. Word has it she dumped you, and no one can figure out why. If two people ever looked like they were in love it was you two. The only thing I can guess is that she must have caught you doing something you shouldn't have. And I'm betting it was something our friend McNab would want to hear about. Am I right?"

"You're an idiot, Nelbert."

Nelbert's grin widened. "That answers my question. But don't worry, Blackheart. I know when to keep my mouth shut. When someone makes it worth my while, that is."

He could toss him over the railing without much difficulty, Blackheart mused. The splat he'd make on the marble floor beneath was too nasty to contemplate, however, so he merely shrugged. "You're swamp algae, Nelbert. Go protect *The Hyacinths* and leave us poor working stiffs alone."

"Sorry, old boy. *The Hyacinths* are your responsibility as long as they're here. They don't become my problem until they hit the museum next week. And you can be sure I've got an alarm system designed that not even you could break through."

"Is that a challenge?"

"Let's just call it a friendly warning. You've got problems enough in this life, Blackheart. Keep away from *The Hyacinths.*"

FERRIS WANTED nothing more than to head to her car and drive like crazy straight back to her office, or even better to her apartment, shutting herself away from the disparate emotions that were assailing her. *Damn Blackheart!* Did he want her, or didn't he? Was he still stealing, or a victim of circumstance? Had he lied to her, or was there some reason for his mysteriousness?

No reason was good enough. If he'd ever really loved her, wanted to marry her, then there was nothing he couldn't tell her. She was wasting her time trying to drum up excuses, when her emotional energies could be much better spent turning her life in new directions.

And she had no doubt whatsoever what her first move should be. The Committee for Saving the Bay would do very well without her—half the volunteer help had exceptional organizational skills. Anything they didn't know how to do, they could hire someone to take care of.

Her second move would be away from San Francisco. Maybe up to Seattle, though she wasn't sure if she could stand all that rain. Or the mountains—Colorado, maybe northern New Mexico. Away from the bay and the fog that came in on little cat's feet or however that cursed poem went.

Seven days. Seven days until the circus, their next big fund-raising event. She'd give Regina her notice and make her plans. And in seven days she'd be gone.

So why didn't she feel the weight of the world lifting from her shoulders? In seven days she'd never have to see John Patrick Blackheart again.

"Because you're still in love with him, you stupid fool," she muttered. "And you have exactly seven days to get him out of your system." She squared her shoulders, that small physical gesture telling her, reminding her that she wasn't powerless. In the meantime, she had a job to do.

She could see Danielle Porcini's lithe figure down by one of the Winnebagos. The least she could do was make sure the Porcinis had everything they needed. The committee expected to make a great deal of money from the benefit, and Ferris was both puzzled about and grateful for the Porcinis' generous offer. Besides, she was also curious about the mysterious Mrs. Porcini.

She threaded her way through the preoccupied crowds of circus people, local electricians, circus-struck socialites and yuppies on their lunch hour, her attention centered on Danielle's disappearing back, when a strong, thick-fingered hand caught her arm, pulling her up short.

"Ms. Byrd." Marco Porcini displayed an enviable set of teeth in a grin that reminded Ferris of the big bad wolf. "Or may I call you Ferris?"

"Certainly." She tugged surreptitiously at her arm, but Marco didn't seem to notice. She was getting tired of being manhandled, she thought wearily. If anyone was going to clamp onto her arm she'd just as soon it were Blackheart. "How may I help you?"

He lifted his moist eyes for a moment, staring in the direction Danielle had taken, and then all his attention was centered on Ferris. "You were looking for my wife?"

If Marco was adept at phony smiles, Ferris was no amateur. She curled her lips obligingly. "I wanted to see if you had everything you needed."

"Why not ask me?" He lowered his voice an octave, the breath hissing out of him as if he were a snake. A garlic-laden snake at that, Ferris thought, controlling the urge to wrinkle her nose. He'd been working out—he was wearing a mesh tank top despite the cool, damp weather, and his bronzed muscles were glistening with sweat.

"All right," Ferris said gamely. "Do you have everything you need?"

"There's a problem in the caravan."

"Caravan?"

"This thing." Porcini slapped the side of the Winnebago. "If I could just show you . . . ?"

At thirty years of age Ferris was old enough to know better. In retrospect it was just one more thing she could blame on Blackheart. If she hadn't still been so addled by her encounter with him up at the mansion, she would never have walked blindly into the Winnebago with an oversexed aerialist at her back.

The closing of the door behind them blocked out the bright daylight. Ferris reached out for a light switch, and found Porcini instead.

In a matter of seconds he'd wrapped his sweaty arms around her and maneuvered her onto a convenient bunk, his well-muscled body covering hers.

Her first thought was sheer annoyance. She would have to pick today of all days to wear linen. It was going to end up rumpled and sweat-stained. Her second thought was the beginning of concern. Marco Porcini was very strong indeed.

"Would you like to let me up?" she inquired politely as his mouth nibbled, no, gobbled at her neck.

He wrapped his meaty hand in her hair, pulling it free from its pins. "You've been begging for this, *cara*," he muttered. "I've seen you watching me."

Ferris laughed. She couldn't help it, even though she knew it wasn't the most promising defense. "I've been watching your wife, Marco. Not you."

"Why?" He lifted his head, staring down at her in disbelief.

"Your wife reminds me of someone." The moment she came up with that, she realized it was true. In addition to Danielle Porcini's unnatural calm, there was a curiously familiar air about her, one she couldn't place.

With a suddenness that was as welcome as it was unflattering, Porcini lost interest. He climbed off her, headed for the door and flung it open, letting in the daylight. Ferris pulled herself upright, brushed back her hair and tried to straighten her pale green jacket around her.

"You're mistaken," Marco said, not bothering to look at her, the impressive muscles in his shoulders noticeably tense. "My wife doesn't look like anyone but herself. You couldn't have seen her before. She's lived in Europe all her life."

"But I must have seen her."

"She's spent the last year in Lisbon, Paris and Madrid," he growled. "If you were there, if you saw the circus, then perhaps you might have seen her perform."

Lisbon, Paris, Madrid. Why did those cities sound familiar? "I've never been to Europe."

"And she's never been to the States before. That answers your question.

She's a stranger." He started down the three short steps of the vehicle. "Close the door behind you," he ordered, disappearing into the crowd.

Ferris stared after him. "Curiouser and curiouser," she said aloud. She looked around the tiny, shipshape little RV, but it was still spotless, no sign of habitation marring its plasticity. What had managed to discourage Marco so quickly, when he'd been so intent on a conquest? And why did those three cities sound so familiar?

It wasn't her problem, she reminded herself, deliberately leaving the Winnebago's door open as she stepped out onto the grass. She only had a week to go, and then she wouldn't have to think about circuses, benefits or semiretired cat burglars. *Seven more days.*

SEVEN MORE DAYS, Dany thought. Surely she could make it that long. The unnatural hush of the Museum of Decorative Arts crowded in on her, adding to her uneasiness. After the ceaseless noise of the circus, coupled with Marco's constant litany of self-praise and abuse, she should have welcomed the thick silence. It just went to prove that anyone could get used to anything. As her leather-shod feet moved silently through the marble halls, she found herself longing for noise, for a chattering family of tourists, a noisy security guard, anything.

But the Museum of Decorative Arts wasn't a major tourist attraction in San Francisco, and there was scarcely a security guard to be seen. Something was going on in the west wing, something to do with a new painting, but that was the least of Dany's worries. Paintings held no interest for her, not even a priceless Van Gogh. She paused for a moment, wondering what the silly Americans were doing putting a Van Gogh into a museum devoted to decorative arts, then dismissed the question. Understanding the natives of her new home would take time, a commodity she would have in abundance in seven days.

In the meantime, the rest of the world could worry about Van Gogh. Directly ahead of her was something far more inspiring, and a great deal more portable.

They sat there on their marble and gold bases, four jewel-studded, ridiculously ornate eggs. For a moment Dany had the fancy that they had been laid there by a fantastic jewel-encrusted bird, some mythical beastie committing its last act before vanishing into the mists of time.

Absurd, of course, Dany thought with a sniff. The eggs hadn't been laid by some extinct creature. Unless you could call Peter Carl Gustavovitch Faberge extinct, which, since he died sometime after the Russian Revolution, you probably could. But he left behind these eggs, four of some twenty or thirty.

Dany stared at them, her palms damp, her mouth dry, her heart racing in anticipation. She might not want to steal them, but since she had no choice in the matter, her instincts were clicking into place, and that old, dangerous excitement was taking over. No wonder Blackheart had done it for so long.

The exhibit was in a small room, one of many sectioned out of a huge hallway. She looked overhead, assessing the security system. It was basic, no frills, tricky enough to be a challenge, predictable enough to ensure eventual success. Timing was everything. Once the Van Gogh was in place and the security beefed up, then they might remember that the Faberge eggs were worth a tidy bit on their own.

Of course, they'd be long gone by then. Gone by the time the Van Gogh made its stately trek from the mansion up the hill. And she'd be gone with them.

Seven days, she thought again, rubbing her damp hands on her khaki pants. *And no one even suspects.*

"Lovely, aren't they?" a voice murmured in her ear. "It makes one understand why some people are thieves and some are cops. Make your fingers itch just to look at them, don't they?"

Slowly Dany turned, expecting Blackheart, preparing herself for a confrontation she both anticipated and dreaded. Instead she found herself looking up into Police Detective Stephen McNab's cool gray eyes. And for the first time in years, she was lost.

Chapter Eight

Stage Fright
(Elstree Studios 1950)

IT WAS A VERY strange emotion, Dany thought, still silent, looking up into the face of a man she could fall in love with. A man who was the sworn enemy of everything she'd worked for, everything her energies were directed toward at that very moment. The question was, did he suspect?

She glanced back at the Faberge eggs with a careful nonchalance that betrayed nothing more than curiosity. "They certainly don't incite any latent criminal tendencies on my part," she said with great truthfulness. Her criminal tendencies were nothing if not overt. "I mean, what could you do with them? Sit and gloat, I suppose. They're a little too fat to sit on a mantel, assuming one even has a mantel in one's flat. Chances are the kids would knock them over and they'd smash, and then where would you be? A few hundred thousand dollars in the red. Do you have any children?"

The question came out before she even realized it had been in her mind. McNab didn't seem the slightest bit surprised. "Approximately three hundred and fifty thousand dollars in the red, per egg, according to the last price paid at auction. No."

"No?"

"No, I don't have any children. Do you?"

"I'm not even . . . planning to have any," she amended quickly, about to betray the speciousness of her married state.

"Why not?"

"Too much responsibility. You can't help but let them down, and then where are you? Better not to take a chance of ruining some young kid's life."

"Did someone ruin your life?"

Dany tossed back her silvery-blond mane and laughed. Only a very observant man would know that laugh was hollow, but McNab had struck her as very observant. "Do all Americans have such intimate conversations with strangers?" she countered.

"We do tend to be an outspoken race. Why are you here? Don't you have work to do with the circus?"

"Is this a professional inquiry, Detective? Do you think I'm planning to pop the eggs into my handbag and walk out with them?" She could feel the adrenaline buzzing through her veins. This was what she would miss, the excitement of taking absurd risks and getting away with it.

"Stephen," he corrected. "And no, it's not a professional inquiry. I might be more concerned if you were watching them set up the new security system for Mrs. Merriam's Van Gogh, but I don't think anyone's going to bother with the eggs."

"Just out of curiosity, why?"

"Too hard to fence. And as you said, if you don't have a mantel you're just plain out of luck." There was a glint in his wintry-gray eyes, but his expression was suitably grave. He was laughing, secretly amused, but Dany wasn't threatened. As long as there was that light in his eyes, he couldn't suspect her of any worse crime than that of a married woman flirting with a police detective.

"Wouldn't the Van Gogh be even harder to sell?"

"Indeed. But one would go to a lot more trouble for something worth forty million than for a Faberge egg."

"Well then," Dany said, smiling easily, "I'll be certain to steal the Van Gogh if I feel a sudden larcenous streak coming on."

"You do that," Stephen said calmly. "In the meantime, can I buy you a cup of coffee?"

"I don't think my husband would like that." Her eyes were demurely lowered, her tone chaste. "I'd better get back to him and tell him about the Van Gogh. Who knows, he might decide thievery is a better profession than owning a circus.

"He might, at that. It certainly pays better than police work. Well, if you won't join me, I suppose I'd better get back to work, too."

"What are you doing here, for that matter? Just taking in the works of art, or were you planning to pull off a heist on your own?"

"You know, I never thought of that. Police pensions being what they are, I certainly ought to keep all possibilities in mind. But I don't think *The Hyacinths* is the answer. So there's nothing left for me to do but make sure the security system conforms to city regulations."

"Isn't that some minor bureaucrat's job?"

"I hate to tell you this, Mrs. Porcini, but I am a minor bureaucrat."

"Call me Dany," she said suddenly, impulsively. No one had called her Dany for more than fifteen years.

"Dany," he agreed. "Besides, if anything gets taken from this museum, it's my butt on the line. So it behooves me to make sure security is everything it should be, particularly when it comes to the Van Gogh. But I wish she'd left it to some other city, one not in my jurisdiction."

"Cheer up. Maybe someone will steal it when you're not on duty."

"Somehow that doesn't make me feel better." Beneath the lightly spoken banter something else was shifting, stirring, something incredibly enticing and too dangerous to bear. "Have coffee with me," he said again, his voice deep and warm, like no voice she had ever heard before. He held out his hand, a good hand, with long, well-shaped fingers, a narrow palm, and strength that wouldn't fail her.

She wanted to put her hand into his. She wanted to turn her back on the Faberge eggs, once and for all. But there had been too many years, too many lies, and there could be no future at all for a cop and a thief. "Marco would rip your head off," she said with a laugh. "He's a very jealous husband. I'll see you around." And she took off, her high heels clicking lightly on the floor in her haste to get away from him.

"Yes." McNab's voice followed her, just reaching her ears as she made her precipitous escape. "You will."

IT WAS AFTER SEVEN when Ferris let herself into her apartment. The sun had already set, and shadows filled the twisting line of rooms that made up her apartment. Blackie was in residence, waiting with regal feline disdain to be fed and released from bondage. Ferris kicked off her shoes and headed for the kitchen, dumping her bag of Mrs. Field's Cookies and the *pasta primavera* from Willey's Deli onto her spotless counter.

She held herself very still. Nothing in her apartment was ever spotless—it went against the very grain of her nature. And Blackie had gone out that morning, refusing her enticements to return inside, and the early-morning chill had precluded leaving the terrace door open even a crack.

She knew all the rules—any single woman living alone in a city knew them. *If you suspect your apartment has been broken into, you don't wait around looking to see what has been taken. The perpetrator might still be lurking inside a closet. You run, and call the police from the nearest public phone.*

Of course, those rules applied to single women unacquainted with John Patrick Blackheart's peripatetic ways. Besides, he had already gone, and the apartment was empty. She knew that as well as she knew her own name—whichever one she happened to be using—and if she felt a wrenching regret, she told herself it was only because she wanted to scream at him.

"I bet you welcomed him with open arms," she accused her haughty alley cat, dishing him up a generous portion of herring in sour cream that hadn't been in her refrigerator that morning. She peered into its barren depths, wondering if Patrick had left her any other tokens of esteem, but nothing but Diet Coke, yogurt and Sara Lee Cheesecake, her usual staples, met her eyes.

There must be something else. Fond as Blackheart was of his namesake, he wouldn't have broken into her apartment and left nothing but herring and clean counters.

He'd made the bed, too. Not with the pastel flowered sheets she'd been using; he'd managed to unearth the maroon ones that reminded her far too clearly of him. "Damn him," she muttered under her breath. There was no way she'd be able to get a decent night's sleep in those sheets. She should have thrown them out, not hidden them under a pile of towels.

Of course, she thought, dropping onto the bed and folding her arms under her head, in the normal course of events those sheets would have stayed hidden. It wasn't her fault that she'd fallen in love with a cat burglar who made himself at home in her apartment, rummaging through her linens to his heart's content—

She sat bolt upright, staring ahead of her. The one thing her tiny bedroom held, beside the queen-size bed, was an oversize television set, its top usually cluttered with empty ice-cream dishes, old magazines, discarded panty hose, single earrings, and anything else that a normal person would throw out. All that had been ruthlessly removed, and Ferris had no doubt she'd find everything in the trash. In its place was a sleek, black, beautiful Blu-ray player, a twin to the one she'd coveted in Blackheart's apartment.

Two DVDs sat on top of the black metal. She was almost afraid to look, but curiosity overruled caution. The first was obvious. *To Catch a Thief.* It would be a cold day in hell before she watched that one, she thought, dropping it into her overflowing wastebasket, knowing perfectly well she'd retrieve it before she took the trash out. Still, the gesture was satisfying.

She picked up the other box. *Spanish Dancing*, it read. The woman on the cover was wearing red shoes just like the ones Blackheart had given her, the ones that were hiding somewhere under her bed. Holding the DVD in her hands, she sat back and burst into tears.

NO ONE KNEW he was there. The house was empty, with only the servants sound asleep in their beds. He looked at *The Hyacinths*, reveling in the wash of sheer color and beauty that had somehow sprung from a madman's mind. He could see the tiny pinpricks of red light from the security system, a system only three people could legally circumvent. It didn't matter who took the blame when the painting disappeared. The only issue of any importance was that no one would suspect him. If he could pay off an old score or two into the bargain, then so much the better.

If life were only just a tiny bit simpler. Someone was going to take this painting and lock it into a vault, gloating over it in deepest privacy, never allowing anyone else to marvel at its beauty. Decades, generations later it might resurface, after enough time had passed to cloud its dubious passage from the Merriams' San Francisco mansion. He wondered briefly if the painting was insured. Certainly not at forty million. But if Regina Merriam could afford to give forty million away, she could certainly afford a loss on her insurance.

And speaking of her, she'd be back anytime now. He'd have a hard time explaining his presence in her upper halls with nothing but moonlight and the occasional beam of infrared to keep him company. He'd better get out, fast. He'd be back soon enough.

DANY KNEW MARCO was watching her, much more closely than he had in recent months. There was no way he could have the faintest idea what she'd planned, but his watchfulness disturbed her. He hadn't seen her meeting with Stephen McNab. He'd sent her over to scout out the museum while he was busy at the circus grounds—otherwise he would have gone himself. Wouldn't he? So it couldn't be misplaced jealousy. Of course, he did have a dog-in-the-manger air about him. Even if, *thank heavens*, he didn't want her, he didn't want anyone else to have her.

But he'd been so busy preening before a crowd of fascinated women that he wouldn't have had time to notice if Stephen McNab had shown a flattering amount of interest. He couldn't possibly have guessed her plans. She'd been very outspoken about her decision that this would be the last job. Marco was the sort who believed only what he wanted to believe, and if her future didn't fit in with what he wanted, then he would ignore them.

But she'd been very careful. There were no plane or train tickets, and her tiny horde of cash was so well hidden even Marco couldn't find it. Not that it would take her very far. She was counting on her share of the money from the eggs to keep her, not in style for a few months, but in modest peace and safety for years. She'd grown up making do on very little. She could survive for years on her ill-gotten gains.

Marco was sitting on the bed in the crowded little caravan, watching her. She had never thought she'd look back on that antiseptic little motel room with nostalgia, but anything was better than these close quarters, closer even than their cabin on the old freighter. This time she had nowhere to run.

"I want to know," he said suddenly, his voice breaking through the silence like a rusty saw blade, "what you told the cop."

Damn, thought Dany. So much for thinking she was safe. "Not a thing. We talked about the Van Gogh."

"I'm going to have to remind you of something, little one," Marco growled, flexing his fingers. Marco had very strong hands. "You belong to me. Until I let you go, whether I want you or not, you're mine."

Her response didn't matter. If she meekly agreed with him, he'd hit her anyway. She had nothing to lose.

She met his gaze with blithe indifference, her chin held high in defiance. "I don't belong to you, I have never belonged to you, and I never will."

She hadn't taken into account the fact that if she angered him, he'd hit her even harder. The force of the blow knocked her backward and she fell against the side of the van.

"Go to hell, Marco," she said, her voice muffled from her split lip.

He was advancing on her, meaty hand upraised, his face contorted in rage, when her calm voice stopped him. "Don't you think my new boyfriend will notice if I'm bruised?" she taunted him.

"You think your handsome cop will come to your rescue? He's more likely to slap you in jail, once I get through talking. And what about your long-lost brother? You think you can count on him for anything? You never could before."

"I can count on myself. And I can count on you to remember the bottom line and not jeopardize your career because you don't like the way a man looks at me. If the cop has the hots for me, so much the better. He's less likely to think I'm up to something if he wants me."

"Maybe," Marco said. "But he's more likely to want me out of the way."

"It's only seven days. Don't you think I can string him along for that short a time?"

"I don't trust you, Danielle."

"That makes us even. I don't trust you. But you should remember that you can't get the eggs without me. You don't have time to train anyone new. And I can't get the eggs without you. So we're just going to have to keep on with this unpleasant partnership for one more week."

He nodded in reluctant agreement. "Just don't push it. I might decide it would be worth the risk to do without you."

She was so close, so very close to everything she'd ever worked for. She'd be a fool to risk it for the sake of taunting Marco, for the sake of McNab's beautiful gray eyes. "You do your part," she said, "and I'll do mine."

Marco nodded. "Now all we have to worry about," he said in a dream voice that sent shivers down her back, "is the very nosy Ms. Ferris Byrd. A small accident, don't you think? Something to incapacitate her for the next seven days?"

"Why?" Dany breathed.

"She's just a little more observant than I like. I prefer women who lie back and keep their eyes and mouths shut."

"I'm sure you do. What has Ms. Byrd said to make you nervous?"

Marco smiled. "I don't think I need burden you with that information. You have too much to worry about already."

Dany was growing more and more distraught. *Damn Marco.* If he couldn't hit her, he still knew other ways to get to her. "What are you going to do to her?"

"Something creative, little one. Something creative."

FERRIS HAD STRANGE dreams that night. It was little wonder. She'd spent the evening crying, crying until runnels of mascara streaked her face, crying until her cheeks were bright red and her lashes bleached white from the salt water of her tears. She lay on her back and let the tears race down her face and drip into her ears. She lay on her stomach and cried into the maroon sheets. She wandered through her apartment, hiccupping and sobbing, occasionally flopping onto the love seat to beat against the pillows until she remembered the first night she'd made love with Blackheart, starting on this love seat and ending in her bed. She'd jumped up, bawling anew, and sobbed her way into the kitchen, into half the Sara Lee Cheesecake, which wasn't improved by the added salt, and then on into her oversize bathroom. But her bedraggled reflection wasn't the sort of thing to cheer her up, either.

Blackie offered no comfort at all, demanding to be let out and away from his howling mistress. That was the difference between dogs and cats, Ferris thought morosely. A dog would cuddle up to you, licking your face and sharing your distress. A cat simply shrugged his elegant feline shoulders and stalked away. Maybe she should trade in this model Blackheart, too, for something affectionate and malleable. Maybe a Peek-a-poo, one those peculiar crosses between a Pekingese and a toy poodle.

Once the tears subsided, she considered resorting to brandy to induce a decent night's sleep. But she didn't want to get into the habit of it— Blackheart had already had far too devastating an effect on her. He wasn't going to turn her into a secret tippler besides.

So she drowned her sorrows in Diet Coke and ice cream. She took as long and as hot a shower as she could stand, pulled on her softest, oldest flannel nightgown, and climbed into bed. And fell asleep watching *To Catch a Thief.*

When she awoke in the drizzly gray light of a rainy predawn, she had a smile on her face and a warm, delicious feeling in her body. It took her only a moment to remember she had nothing to smile about. She sat up, pushing the hair out of her face, grimacing at the rain falling on her slate terrace. The television screen was black. That was odd. She thought she'd fallen asleep just as Cary Grant went swimming in the Mediterranean. She must have gotten up sometime during the night and turned the set off.

It was a shame she'd had to wake up. Whatever she'd been dreaming had been both comforting and definitely erotic. Maybe it hadn't even been about Blackheart, she thought hopefully. Anything was possible in this world. Though not very likely.

Ferris suddenly sniffed the air. It smelled like roses. She'd bought flowers a few days ago in a vain effort to cheer herself up, but they'd been scentless daisies, and they were sitting, brown and dried out, in a vase in the living room. Slowly she turned her head. There on the pillow next to her lay a single white rose.

She reached out for it, her hand trembling slightly. And on her finger was the canary-yellow diamond engagement ring she'd thrust back at Blackheart days ago.

She stared at it for a long moment, considering whether she should once more bathe herself in tears. But she'd cried enough to last for a good long time. Looking down at her replaced engagement ring, she began to laugh.

MARCO WAS ACCUSTOMED to getting up early. If he slept too much, his body grew slow and sluggish, and he couldn't afford to have anything happen to his body. His talent was a gift, and he had to treat it with the respect it deserved.

He started with a hundred push-ups, then moved into the weights. This was the time he could think and plan the best, when his body was being pushed to its limits and no one was around to disturb him with their idle chatter. He stood there in the early-morning drizzle, curling two hundred pounds of metal weights against his bulging chest, and thought about the future. And of how he was going to kill Ms. Ferris Byrd.

Chapter Nine

Spellbound
(Selznick International 1945)

JOHN PATRICK Blackheart, ne Edwin Bunce, was sitting on Regina Merriam's flagstone terrace overlooking the early-morning bustle on the circus grounds, waiting for his Francesca. She might be having a little trouble recognizing that she was, in fact, his, but sooner or later he'd be able to convince her.

Leaving her this morning had been one of the hardest things he'd ever done. She'd been lying there in the maroon sheets, the blank television screen bathing the predawn room in an unearthly light, and he could see dried tears on her elegant cheekbones. The flannel nightgown was endearingly sexy, more so than one of her silk and lace confections, and he'd wanted to strip off his clothes, crawl into bed with her and just hold her in his arms.

She would have woken up screeching. *Maybe.* He couldn't take the chance. Even worse, she might have cried some more, and then his resolve would have vanished. And he couldn't tell her what was going on. He couldn't incriminate his own sister, but that was the only way he could exonerate himself. If McNab proved to be as tenacious and tricky as Blackheart suspected he was, it was going to be a close-run thing. And if he told Francesca what was going on, she'd have no familial qualms. She'd sacrifice Danielle Porcini without a second thought in order to keep him out of jail, and he couldn't let her do that.

Besides, he knew better than anyone alive that Dany couldn't have pulled the Madrid job herself. She wasn't tall enough for some of the reaches, even if she used the best of equipment. He had no doubt at all that she'd been instrumental in planning—there was simply too much Blackheart brilliance in the three recent robberies that had been placed on his doorstep. *And who knows how many before?* he thought wearily, shivering in the chilly morning air. His sweet little long-lost sister might have been active for years.

But she hadn't been active alone. With any luck at all he could pin everything on her accomplice, and get her out of reach of McNab's long arm. Now he just had to figure if the identity of her accomplice was as obvious as it appeared to be.

If he was going to save his sister's neck without putting his own onto the chopping block, he was going to have to be very busy. As long as no one knew of his relationship with Danielle Porcini, they'd have no reason to suspect anyone involved in the circus. Blackheart and Company's considerable reputation was behind the Porcini Family Circus, guaranteeing their trustworthiness. If he blew it, he'd blow it for Trace and Kate as well as himself. His partner and his wife were as dependent on the well-being of Blackheart and Company as he was. Not to mention any future with Francesca.

"Damn," he said out loud, his voice soft and bitter above the distant sounds of wild animals. "What did I do to deserve such a mess?"

"You tell me."

It wasn't Francesca. If he knew his slothful darling, she was probably still buried under the covers, unaware of the ring back on her finger.

Instead Dany Bunce stood there, dressed in black chinos and a black turtleneck, her blond hair tied back, her blue eyes cool and mocking.

He hadn't seen her since she was six years old. He'd been eighteen, their father had just died in a fall from a slippery copper roof, and he was embarking on a career in the family business. He couldn't take care of his six-year-old half-sister. Both their mothers were dead—his of cancer when he was a child, hers in a car crash in Nice. The only solution was his aunt and uncle in the Lake District. The Eustace Bunces were stoutly disapproving of the family business. Uncle Eustace was a farmer, Aunt Prunella a dedicated farm wife who'd already raised three docile children. They were the best able to cope with a half wild toddler. If they weren't adept at showing affection, at least they'd instill conventional, comfortable values. And the farm was beautiful.

He'd just about forgotten her existence. And now here she was, a defiant expression in eyes that weren't much different from that angry six-year-old's. Clearly the Bunces' conventional values hadn't taken hold.

He'd been sitting in a tipped-back wrought iron deck chair and didn't bother to change his position or his expression. He also chose to ignore her provocative statement. "Can I help you? Mrs. Porcini, isn't it?"

His sister smiled, showing very straight, very white teeth, either the result of orthodontia or the good Bunce genes. "Call me Dany," she said affably, and her blue eyes were waiting, daring him to react.

If she thought she could fence with him and win, she would soon find she was way out of her league, Blackheart thought, keeping his face smooth. "Dany," he agreed.

She moved over and perched on the wide stone wall, very lithe, very graceful. She would have been good, Blackheart thought, very good indeed. Who had she been working with?

"I was interested in the Van Gogh. Detective McNab said there was a painting here worth millions of dollars. I wondered if I might see it."

"Why ask me?"

"Aren't you in charge of security? I'd think you'd be very wary of anyone messing with a priceless painting that's your responsibility."

"I thought you wanted to look at it, not mess with it," he said.

"I expected you to be a bit paranoid. Anyone in your position might be."

"Oh, I'm never paranoid. Extremely distrustful, but never paranoid. Certainly you can see the Van Gogh, if you so desire. But not right now."

"Why not? Do you want to check out my background first and make sure I'm a decent security risk?" Her cool blue eyes were assessing.

Feisty little creature, isn't she? thought Blackheart, half amused, half irritated. He could still see traces of that six-year-old glaring at him. "We ran standard security checks on everyone connected with the circus before you even arrived in the States." Which went to prove how worthless those security checks had been. They'd turned up nothing more exciting than one of the knife throwers having spent time in jail for spearing a rival. No mention of Madame Porcini's clouded past, or anything that might point to her accomplice.

She absolutely grinned at that point, and he resisted the urge to throttle her. "And you discovered we have spotless reputations?"

"Something like that. You'll still have to wait. Regina sleeps later than the working classes, and I don't think she'd care to have people traipsing through her third-floor hallway."

"Is that where she keeps it?"

He was getting tired of this, mortally tired. Dany Bunce had no more interest in the Van Gogh, no matter what its vaunted worth, than he did. The question was, what did she want? She wasn't here for a family reunion. Unless he was greatly mistaken, she was out for blood. His. Those robberies in Lisbon, Paris and Madrid hadn't pointed to John Patrick Blackheart's famous modus operandi by accident. She'd framed him then, and she probably had every intention of framing him again. But how? And how was he going to protect himself, Francesca and his self-destructive half-sister?

"Come back in a couple of hours, and I'll have someone show you exactly where she keeps it. We'll even acquaint you with the security system, in case you're interested."

"I'm not."

"Oh, you never can tell when a knowledge of heat sensors and infrared lighting can come in handy. Life is full of possibilities. In the meantime, don't you think you ought to be getting back to the business at hand?" He nodded toward the organized chaos of activity out on the south lawn. "Don't you need to practice, warm up, something like that?"

"I'm no longer a performer. I used to be an aerialist, but now I work strictly in a business capacity."

"Why? Did you fall?" He didn't like that idea one tiny bit. A fall had killed their father, a fall had nearly crippled him. He didn't want to think of his larcenous baby sister tumbling down, down. . . .

She smiled sweetly. "I'm scared of heights." She slid off the wide stone wall, dusted her black chinos, and moved toward him. "What about you, Mr.

Blackheart? Are you scared of heights?"

"Nope. I love them. It runs in my family."

She blinked, her only reaction to his veiled taunt. But she was persevering and game. "I heard you were once a famous cat burglar. Is that true?"

He reached up, caught her cheek between his thumb and forefinger and pinched, just hard enough to leave a red mark. "That runs in my family, too."

She jerked away from him, startled, her mouth open to say something, anything. Even the truth might have been a remote possibility. And then saw something over his shoulder, and her mouth curved in a smug, engaging grin that was a twin to his father's, and her eyes lighted with malicious amusement. "What a happy childhood you must have had, surrounded by such a colorful family. Let me know when I can see the Van Gogh." And she sauntered away, down the wide expanse of slate terrace.

He watched her go for a brief moment. If he'd had any doubt why she hated him, she'd just put that to rest. Her life with the Eustace Bunces must have been hell. And she was determined to pay him back for that.

He sighed, leaning back and shutting his eyes for a moment. And then he remembered that something had caught her eye and stopped her from incriminating herself. And that something, someone, had opened the French doors and stepped out onto the terrace behind him.

He didn't turn to look. The faint whiff of perfume was new, unfamiliar, a spicy, defiant scent unlike Ferris's usual Cabochard. But he knew it was his beloved Ferris-Francesca behind him, knew it even before she dropped the big canary-yellow diamond ring into his lap.

"I hope I wasn't interrupting anything," she said in a voice that was even chillier than the autumn morning. "But you misplaced this, and I thought it should be back where it belonged as soon as possible."

"So did I," he said calmly. "That's where I left it."

"Stay out of my apartment, Blackheart. No secret visits, no gifts or bribes, for me or my cat. Leave me alone. Concentrate on your little circus girl."

At that he turned and looked up at her, a wide smile of genuine delight on his face. "You're jealous," he said, amazed. Ferris was never jealous.

She was looking particularly gorgeous that morning, he thought with a resigned sigh, knowing that he shouldn't touch her. She must have raced after him without bothering to put on her yuppie armament. Her thick black hair hung loose and wavy around her unmade-up face. The faded jeans she was wearing had seen years of service, and they hugged her long legs and wonderful hips as he longed to. She'd taken time to wear a bra under the cotton sweater, but if he pulled her into his lap and slid his hands up under that sweater he could probably unfasten it in record time. With another resigned sigh he closed his eyes again, shutting out the enticing picture she made, resting his folded hands strategically over his lap.

"Blackheart," she said in a weary voice that a less intelligent man might almost have believed, "I wish you every happiness in the world. Run away with Mrs. Porcini, pray that her husband with the bulging biceps doesn't catch up with you, and live happily ever after. Just leave me alone."

Blackheart's eyes flew open, her words triggering a sudden memory. "They're not really married," he said abruptly. That was one thing the security check had picked up, something he'd disregarded as of no importance until he'd seen the face that went with the name Danielle Porcini. There was no record of any marriage ceremony, legal or religious, between the two circus members.

"Then I hope you'll be very happy." Her footsteps made angry, clicking noises as she walked away from him and the French door slammed behind her.

He caught up with her in Regina's deserted living room. There was no one in sight, the lights were still off, and the spacious, empty room was filled with shadows.

When he put his hands on her shoulders she didn't fight him. She had enough sense not to. Any resistance and he would have pulled her into his arms against his taut, needful body. As long as she stood, quiescent and watchful beneath his hands, he couldn't do anything more than hold her there.

"How did you get in here? Are any of the servants up?" *Stupid question,* he mocked himself. He was just wasting time, prolonging the brief contact his body and soul were crying out for.

"What if I told you I broke in?" Her voice was hushed, solemn.

"I'd be charmed."

"Too bad. Regina gave me a key years ago."

"Back when you were on your first fiancé," he countered. If he made her mad enough, she might struggle.

"Second," she corrected him. "I was engaged to my high school sweetheart. You ran a distant third, Blackheart."

"Then how come I was the only one able to get you into bed?"

"Is that how you viewed it, Blackheart? 'Getting me into bed'? Well, now that you've accomplished such a remarkable feat, I would think the challenge would be gone. Time to move on to greener pastures. Maybe you can find another twenty-nine-year-old virgin to seduce."

She was getting very angry indeed. *Good,* he thought, sliding one hand up her shoulder to cup her neck. He could feel the pulse pounding beneath her delicate skin, and he wanted to feel that pulse beneath his lips. "I didn't seduce you, Francesca," he whispered. "I fell in love with you."

"Don't." The word was a quiet, helpless moan. But she wasn't pulling away from him, she was swaying toward him, and the muscles in her shoulders had gone from tense and stiff to soft and warm and weak, and he slid up his other hand, cupping her face, his thumbs gently brushing her pale, lipstickless mouth. Her green eyes were lost and pleading, and he knew he could drown in those eyes, drown in her body, lose himself forever in the sweet delight of her smooth flesh.

She was the one to bring their mouths together. In the lonely hours and days that followed he would remind himself of that, cherishing that small, temporary act of trust. Her soft, warm lips touched his, for no more than a brief instant. And then his self-control vanished, he slanted his mouth across her, and she opened for him. He held her there, kissing her with all the longing and despair that were ripping through his shaking body.

For a moment she struggled, and he knew he should let her go, when her arms escaped the prison of his body and slipped around his neck, pulling him closer. He could feel the softness of her breasts through the sweater, the hardness of her nipples, the sweet warmth of her hips pressed up against his, and he groaned deep in his throat. Surely this was worth more than honor, family, safety, anything at all?

He'd gotten his hands under her sweater, just as he'd wanted to since the moment he'd seen her, and he'd just managed to unfasten her bra when a bright light flooded the living room, streaking through their temporary insanity like a lightning bolt from an angry god.

She tore out of his arms, as he knew she would, and he turned to rage at the intruder, frustration and fury wiping out the last tiny bit of common sense he possessed.

The sight of Regina Merriam, her thick white hair in a plait down her back, her designer silk dressing gown reaching the floor, her usually kind, serene face creased with worry, brought back a measure of sanity.

He looked at Francesca. She was out of reach, halfway across the room, surreptitiously fumbling with her bra clasp. He wanted to go to her, to brush her awkward hands away and take care of it, but he knew his touch wouldn't be welcome. He stayed where he was, watched her flushed, miserable face, and cursed his sister with all his heart.

"I don't suppose this is a reconciliation?" Regina asked in a sorrowing voice.

For some stupid, romantic reason Blackheart held his breath. But Francesca shook her head, her long dark hair hiding her face. "Just another mistake. I seem to be making a lot of them nowadays. I hope we didn't disturb you, Regina?"

"Not at all. I was just coming down to share coffee with Blackheart when I heard the two of you. I'm sorry I interrupted."

"I'm glad you did."

Damn her, if she could be cool and unconcerned, so could he. "Yes, it was probably just as well," he drawled, taking a small, perverse pleasure in her sudden start.

Regina looked from one to the other, her sorrow now shadowing her face. "Why don't you both join me for coffee? Surely we can at least share some decent morning conversation?"

"Could I have a rain check?" Ferris pleaded, pushing her hair back and looking calm and very determined. "There's something I want to find out."

Blackheart was a man who'd lived on his instincts for far too long not to listen to them when they were shrieking at him. "What's that?" he demanded.

"Mrs. Porcini," she said. "I can't get over the feeling I've met her before. I wanted to discover if that's possible. I thought I'd ask her where she'd been for the last five years."

If Regina hadn't been there listening, he would have let out a string of curses that would have turned the air blue. If Regina hadn't been there he would have threatened, yelled, coerced, kidnapped her before he let her literally go down among the lions, with her jealousy blinding her to far more dangerous possibilities.

As it was, he had to make do with a veiled warning. He knew his Francesca. Anything more overt would only fuel her determination. "Circus people are a funny breed, dear heart," he murmured. "I don't think they like answering personal questions about their pasts."

He should have known it would be a waste of time. "Oh, I can be discreet, Blackheart. I just want to warn her about you."

"She doesn't need a warning. She already knows."

Wrong again. His ex-fiancée's smile was bitter indeed. "I'm so glad to hear you confide in someone. I still intend to talk to her. See you."

She left without a backward glance. He watched her go, then turned to meet Regina's stern gaze. "Patrick, my boy," she said, "you blew it."

"Regina, my girl," he responded wearily, "I'm afraid you're right."

FERRIS DIDN'T KNOW who told her Danielle Porcini was looking for her. A clown passed a message from an acrobat who'd gotten it from an elephant handler who'd gotten it from a seamstress. But Mrs. Porcini was down near the cages that held the big cats, waiting for her.

If Ferris hadn't been still shaken by her encounter with Blackheart, she would have been more observant. If her mouth weren't still tingling from the feel of his kiss, if her knees weren't weak, if her bra weren't hooked awry . . . If only her brains didn't fly out the window the moment that man touched her—the moment that man even looked at her.

If onlys were a waste of time. And she wasn't jealous of Danielle Porcini, truly she wasn't. If the lady was unencumbered, she'd be only too happy to hand Blackheart over to her. But the lady came equipped not only with a large husband type—even if Blackheart said they weren't really married—but that police detective, McNab, had been far too interested in her. He already had reason enough to want to nail Blackheart. It certainly wouldn't be too smart to add sexual jealousy to the potent mix.

The early-morning sun had just hit the lions' cages, and the stench, even in the vast green outdoors of Regina Merriam's south lawn, was almost overpowering. She wasn't too happy with the noise, either. It seemed as if all the circus people were busy someplace else. She could clearly hear cute little kittylike purrs, nasty little kittylike growls, and the ominous sound of claws clicking on a metal floor.

"Mrs. Porcini?" she called. Her voice came out with just the tiniest bit of a tremor. "Danielle?"

The Porcini Family Circus has too many big cats, she thought nervously, edging around one of the cages. She could see at least six lions, two tigers and a couple of pure white cats she couldn't even begin to identify. They were watching her just as she was watching them, and they all looked very hungry.

"Danielle?" she called again, her voice now absolutely wobbly. Her shoes were silent on the soft, squishy ground as she turned another corner, but her heart was beating loudly enough to alert even the sleepiest tiger. It was a lucky thing the cages were locked. There was no one close enough to come running if she called for help, and the huge white cat in front of her looked as if he was positively clamoring for a taste of Ferris Byrd.

She heard a noise behind her and whirled, but there was nothing, just the back of another cage. "Danielle?" she tried once more, her voice a plaintive whisper this time.

Then she froze. Slowly Ferris turned to her right, telling herself that it could only be Danielle Porcini.

She was wrong. Standing there, its evil, colorless eyes trained on her defenseless throat, was the hungry white beast she'd been eyeing warily just moments before. It had made no noise in the wet grass. Huge, clawed paws were just as silent on the damp earth as Ferris's sneakers. It didn't growl. It didn't have to. The cage door was open, and the cat was moving slowly, inexorably, toward its breakfast.

Chapter Ten

Dial M for Murder
(Warner Brothers 1953)

FERRIS CONSIDERED screaming. Considered, then rejected the notion. She had seen no one anywhere near the animal cages. The pure white cat was moving steadily closer, but if she startled it there was no telling what it might do. One shriek, one leap, and Ferris Byrd would never have to worry about John Patrick Blackheart again.

"Nice kitty," she said, surreptitiously taking a step backward. The nice kitty growled low in its throat.

Ferris considered crying. Considered, then rejected the notion. She didn't want to die a coward. When they found her, she wanted her expression noble and unblemished by tears.

The early-morning sun had risen higher in the sky, burning through the cool damp mist and beating down on her head. Ferris shivered, wondering if she dared run for it.

"Don't move." The voice came from directly behind her, and Ferris swiveled her head to look into Danielle Porcini's pale, sweating face. The hungry cat growled again. "I told you not to move!" Danielle snapped.

Ferris turned back to look at the animal that was still moving slowly toward her. "What the hell am I supposed to do?" she muttered under her breath. "Stand still and become this lion's Big Mac?"

"Tiger," Danielle corrected. "Albino tiger."

"Just tell me one thing." Ferris's normally husky voice had risen several octaves. "Is it going to eat me?"

"I don't know."

"Some help you are."

"We have two albinos, Simba and Tarzan. Tarzan'll tear your throat out as soon as look at you—he's a born killer. Simba is a sweet old pussycat."

"Don't tell me," Ferris begged. "You don't know which one this is."

"I don't spend much time around the big cats."

The albino tiger certainly looked ferocious. It was yawning, displaying a very nasty set of teeth, one that made Jaws seem nothing more threatening than a grouper with an overbite. A few more steps, a very few more steps, and he'd be within touching distance. In chewing distance.

"Big cats?" Ferris echoed, resigned. "Unfortunately I have. At least the human variety. I don't mean to sound hysterical or anything, but don't you think you might go for help?" There was just the trace of an edge in her voice.

"I don't want to make any quick moves, in case it's Tarzan. The wrong move, and it'll be all over."

"You're so comforting," Ferris said feelingly. "So we're just going to stand here like this?"

"I don't think so. He's getting closer."

Ferris looked directly into a pair of colorless feral eyes. "Well, if you aren't going to help me and there's no knight in shining armor nearby, it's up to me." Slowly, carefully, she held out a shaking hand. "Nice kitty," she whispered, her voice a raw croak. "Nice kitty."

The tiger took another step closer, opening its massive jaws. Ferris shut her eyes, unable to watch as she held out her trembling arm. "Nice kitty," she said hopefully. "Nice Simba."

The jungle cat growled deep in its hairy throat, moved closer and sent his long, wet tongue lapping against Ferris's hand.

"It's Simba," Danielle announced, her voice rough with relief.

"Nice kitty," Ferris said again, this time with real enthusiasm. "Want to go back into your nice cage?"

He was still licking her trembling fingers with the air of a connoisseur, and Ferris thanked heaven she hadn't taken the time to wash her hands after she'd given Blackie his herring in sour cream. If she could just get this oversize alley cat back into his cage, she'd bring him a whole case of the stuff.

Danielle moved into view, and Ferris noted with distant surprise that she looked just as shaken as Ferris felt. "Come on, Simba," she said, giving a huge shoulder a push. "Back into your cage."

The tiger allowed himself a snarl, then ignored the rude interruption as he sought out Ferris's other hand. There was a limit to her self-control, as well as to her ability to keep standing. She wasn't going to be able to remain a salt lick for a jungle cat for much longer, and as innocent as Simba appeared, she wasn't too sure how he'd react if she landed in a dead faint at his feet.

"Simba," she said, pulling her hand away from his voracious tongue and holding it out in front of him like a carrot before a horse. "Into your cage, Simba. Good pussy, come on. Come with mama."

"Ferris—" Danielle interrupted.

"Shut up," Ferris murmured in a low, throaty growl meant to appease the hungry beast in front of her. "Come on, pussy. Come get breakfast." She backed toward the empty cage, and Simba followed, eyeing her fishy hand with feline determination. She had no choice but to back up the ramp, back into the awful-smelling cage herself.

It was a horrifying moment; her back was against the bars as Simba filled the doorway, blocking any chance of escape. In the meantime, though, Danielle had found something foul-smelling and particularly destined to appeal to animal appetites, and was busy dumping it through the bars into his dish. Simba ignored the shaking hand of his captive, and sauntered past her to the dish of rancid red meat, swishing his tail as he went.

In two seconds Ferris was out of the cage, the door locked and barred behind her. She slid down the ramp and collapsed onto the wet grass, forcing herself to take slow, deep breaths as reaction set in. Her skin felt too tight, prickling all over her body, her heart was too big for her chest, and her breath was strangled in her lungs. A small, strong hand reached behind her neck and shoved her head down between her knees. "Calm down," Danielle said briskly. "It's over."

Ferris considered throwing up in the grass. The smell of the animal cages wasn't contributing to her peace of mind or the state of her stomach, but she hadn't the energy to move. She just sat there, her head between her knees, and breathed through her mouth.

It was a long time before she could lift her head. Danielle Porcini was kneeling in the grass beside her, her own face pale. "Feeling better?"

"A little bit. What are you doing here, anyway? Just come to watch the results of your little ambush?"

"My ambush?"

"You set me up. I was told you were waiting for me down by the big cats. Instead, I find I'm about to be first course."

"I didn't even know you were here on the grounds. Why should I want to meet you down here? Why should I want you dead?"

"You tell me. Maybe it has something to do with the fact that I know you from someplace."

If Danielle had seemed wary before, it was nothing compared to her expression now. "I've never seen you before the party two days ago."

"Maybe. And maybe I've never met you before. But there's something about you that's driving me crazy. Maybe I saw your picture in the newspaper. Maybe you remind me of someone. Maybe I saw you someplace where you shouldn't be, and you need to get rid of me before I remember where it was."

Danielle's laugh was cool enough to be believable, if Ferris's instincts hadn't been razor sharp after what she'd just been through. "That's all very interesting. But I didn't know you thought I looked familiar. You hadn't bothered to mention it to me, had you? Even if I had a deep dark secret to hide, there's no reason for me to try to kill you. And if it was me, why didn't I lock the cage behind Simba and leave you two alone? He's a nice cat, but even the nicest ones get hungry."

"Maybe you thought it would take too long."

"You still haven't answered my question. Why would I try to kill you if I didn't know you thought I looked familiar?"

"Because I was stupid enough to tell someone else."

She flinched, an expression so brief Ferris almost thought she'd imagined it. "Well, if I really am an international terrorist or a murderer or something, then it must be my accomplice who tried to kill you. Who did you tell?"

For a moment Ferris thought she might really throw up. Sickness washed over her as she remembered her words to Blackheart, taunting him with having seen Danielle Porcini before. He couldn't have, he wouldn't have

The sickness vanished. She might have been weak-minded, besotted and foolish on many accounts, but she couldn't have been that far-off. She couldn't have fallen in love with a man who was capable of murder.

And then she remembered the other person. "Actually I did say something to the man pretending to be your husband. And he certainly showed a great deal more distress than you do."

"Marco wouldn't feed you to the tigers," Danielle scoffed, her blue eyes worried. "He'd be more likely to seduce you into silence."

"That's what he was trying to do. Although seduce might be too polite a word for it. When I mentioned you looked familiar, he let go of me immediately."

"Marco is impetuous. Aren't you going to ask why we pretend to be married? You see, I'm being perfectly honest with you—I won't try to deny it."

"Perfectly honest," Ferris echoed. "I'm sure you have a wonderful reason all ready."

"It makes the red tape easier when going from country to country."

"Does that mean your passport identifies you as Danielle Porcini?"

"Don't be so eager to find trouble where none exists. Women keep their maiden names in Europe as well as the States, Ferris. My passport is legal."

"What is your maiden name?"

"Thatcher."

"And Maggie's your mother?"

"She was a little strict, but very loving."

"I thought you were going to be honest with me," Ferris shot back.

"I will. I'll warn you away from Marco. I don't think anyone let the tiger out of the cage to kill you. If anyone wanted to, they'd have the sense to release Tarzan, not Simba. Maybe someone wanted to have you keep your nose out of things that don't concern you. But for your own sake, keep away from Marco. And if you have any sense of self-preservation at all, I'd keep away from Patrick Blackheart, too, if I were you."

A blinding, jealous rage swept over Ferris, one that left her feeling stupid and shaken. "You want them both."

Danielle smiled. "In a manner of speaking. They're nothing but trouble, but it's trouble I can handle. I gather you broke your engagement to Blackheart. It was the smartest thing you could have done. Keep away from him."

"I was thinking of taking him back," Ferris drawled, her face bland, her eyes filled with rage.

"You're too smart for that. You wouldn't want a man who didn't want you. Don't go looking for any more heartbreak, Ferris. I give you a friendly woman-to-woman warning. Go for that nice politician that hangs around you. But keep away from my men."

Ferris rose, brushing the grass from her jeans. Her hands were still trembling, though this time it was from fury rather than fear. "I'll keep your warning in mind. Thanks for the help with Simba."

Danielle rose also, her smaller, lithe body incomparably graceful. "I was going to say anytime, but I trust there won't be another chance. You strike me as a woman of sense. Use it, and pay attention to my warnings."

"What are you doing down here, Danielle?" A blond, scantily dressed giant with a Teutonic accent strolled into view. Walking beside him, placidly enough, was another albino tiger, a twin to the beast now safely locked in the cage.

Danielle was eyeing the cat warily. "Just talking with a friend, Franz. What's Tarzan doing out without a restraint? You know as well as I do how dangerous he could be."

Ferris stared at the white beast, at the colorless eyes and sleek body. She knew before Franz opened his mouth what he would say.

"I'm not an idiot, Danielle. I wouldn't let out a killer like Tarzan. This is Simba." And he rubbed the friendly tiger behind the ears.

FERRIS SANK INTO the soft leather seat of her Mercedes, shutting the door behind her. She managed to get the key into the ignition, but that was where her energy failed her. There was no one in the parking area in front of Regina's mansion. In the long walk from the animal cages, with a hundred curious eyes following her calm, measured stride, she had held her head high and her shoulders back. Now, for the first time, she had no audience. With a low, miserable moan she let her head fall onto the steering wheel and shook.

She heard the rattle at the passenger door and looked up—into Blackheart's angry face as he tugged at the locked door. "Go away," she said, loudly enough for him to hear it through the closed windows. And she locked her own door for good measure. She dropped her head back onto the steering wheel, hoping for once he'd do as she asked, but it was a vain hope. She heard the rasp of metal, and looked up again to see him calmly inserting one of his new picklocks into the passenger door lock.

She should turn the ignition and roar away from there, leaving him in the dust. She even managed to reach out her still-shaking hand to do just that, then let it drop onto her knee. She had no energy for a confrontation, but even less for a wild ride home. She wasn't calm enough to drive yet. She had no choice but to put up with Blackheart.

The door opened, and he slid in beside her. It had started to rain again, a steady drizzle that obscured even the house directly in front of them, and his dark hair was beaded with drops of rain. In the murky light she could see the tenderness in his eyes, the gentleness in his demoralizing mouth, so before she could give in to the comfort she so badly needed, she went on the attack.

"It's reassuring to see you carry your burglar's tools wherever you go." She tried for an arch tone, but it was somewhat diminished by the raw shakiness that lingered. "You still want to tell me you're retired?"

"I don't want to tell you a damned thing. Come here." He didn't even give her time for a protest, but simply reached out and hauled her shaking body into his arms, over the gearshift and the emergency brake, over the half-filled can of Diet Coke and the crumpled bag of Mrs. Field's Cookies. He wrapped his long, strong arms around her, shoved her face against his shoulder and held her there, one deft hand stroking her long hair.

She lay in his arms stiffly, without moving for countless seconds. And then, sighing, she sank into him, her bones melting, her body flowing over him as she gave up fighting. At least for the moment.

He was so warm, and she was so very cold. She could hear the steady thudding of his heart beneath her, racing just slightly, as if something had frightened him. His hands were tough but gentle, brushing the hair away from her face, holding her trembling body in the shelter of his arms, and for a short while she allowed herself the luxury of believing that as long as he held her, everything would be all right.

The mindless state, delicious though it was, couldn't last forever. The heavy downpour lessened, her own throbbing heart slowed its tumultuous pace, and sanity, with its evil twin, uncertainty, returned.

She pushed away from him, and he let her go, not moving to stop her as she made her ungainly way back across the gearshift and the emergency brake and junk food trash. Once she was back in the safety of her own bucket seat, her hands firmly on the leather-covered steering wheel for the sole purpose of giving her something to hold on to rather than Blackheart, then she could toss her hair back over her shoulder and meet his gaze directly.

"Better now?"

She could be gracious. "Yes, thank you."

He looked as if he wanted to grab her again, but was controlling the urge. "You want to tell me what happened?"

"Not particularly."

"Let me rephrase that. You are going to tell me what happened."

It would have been useless to argue. Besides, she needed to talk to him. "I went looking for Danielle. Someone told me she was waiting for me down by the animal cages. I went down there to find her, and someone let one of the tigers out."

"Who told you she was there?"

"I don't remember. One of the clowns, I think, but he told me an acrobat had gotten the message from someone else."

"All right. What happened next?"

"Danielle showed up, together we lured the tiger back into the cage and locked the door, and then I came back up here."

"Somehow I think I'm missing something."

She managed a wry smile. "Actually I was wondering where you were. Like a fool, I kept expecting you to show up at the last moment and rescue me."

"Francesca . . ."

"And actually you did. I still had some of the herring you brought for Blackie on my hands. The tiger licked my fingers and followed me into the cage. So you've done your good deed for the day, and now you can go. . . ."

"Shut up, Francesca." He didn't pull her this time; he climbed across the barrier and put his arms around her, drawing her face close to his. "You're all right now?"

He was too close for her peace of mind. Her equilibrium had been restored, at least to a working level, and she had no excuse to move closer. "I'm fine, Blackheart. I just want to go home and change."

"You should do more than that. You should leave town."

"Sounds like an excellent idea. I'm sure you'd be happy enough to see me go. Unfortunately I can't leave until after the circus benefit."

"To hell with the circus benefit. A dozen women at the committee could do what you're doing."

"Yes, I know just how dispensable I am. Nevertheless, I have a responsibility, and I'm not going to shirk it just so you can chase after Danielle whoever she is without me watching."

He sank back into his own seat with a snort of disgust. "Is there any way you can control your jealousy long enough to see reason?"

"I'm not jealous. Maybe you have no carnal interest in Danielle. But you're interested in something, something that makes you carry your picklocks around with you. And I'm not going to go away, and I'm not going to stand idly by while you give in to your baser urges."

"The only thing my baser urges want is you, Francesca. Go away, dear heart. Somewhere deep in that flintlike heart of yours there must be a spark of feeling left for me. Give in to that spark, just for two weeks. Go away, and when you come back everything will be over and I can explain."

"Trust is a two-way street, Blackheart. Tell me now."

He looked at her for a long moment. "I can't."

"And I can't go away. So it looks as if we're at an impasse."

"That's what it looks like," he said wearily. "Just do me one favor."

"If I can."

"Keep away from animal cages. I'm not the only person you can't trust."

HE ALREADY HAD a buyer. A man of untold wealth and spotless reputation would pay anything, anything to own *The Hyacinths*. He didn't care where it came from, he didn't care that no one would ever know he owned it. He didn't care that he was paying possibly more than it would get at current inflated auction prices. He wanted it with an obsessive passion and he would stop at nothing to get it.

Fortunately there was nothing the buyer needed to do but come up with an enormous supply of untraceable bills and bearer bonds—and wait for him to do the dirty work.

And fortunately for him, the dirty work wasn't all that dirty. Taking *The Hyacinths* from its current location in Regina Merriam's third-floor hallway would be child's play. He had a key to circumvent the alarm system, he had an accomplice, and he had not one but two possible scapegoats. The way his luck was going, there was no telling where it might end. Possibly beyond his fondest dreams. Although his dreams were pretty grandiose already.

He almost wished he didn't have to wait. He almost didn't trust the utter simplicity of it. He wanted to get it over with, to make certain it really was as easy as it appeared to be. But his buyer wasn't ready, his accomplice wasn't ready, his alibi wasn't ready, and his scapegoat wasn't quite ready. Eager or not, he'd have to wait. And gloat, in anticipation. Things would only be getting better.

Chapter Eleven

Psycho
(Paramount 1960)

THE DAMNED RING was back on her finger. Ferris stared down at it, her eyes still blurred with sleep, and cursed. Last night had been bad enough. She's somehow managed to put in most of a day at work, had crawled home and sat in her huge old bathtub until the water cooled and Blackie drove her crazy with his incessant mewing. She'd fed him herring, shuddering in memory, and had gone to turn on the television.

A DVD of *Mary Poppins* was sitting on top of the player. She'd stared at it, mystified. The mind of John Patrick Blackheart worked in mysterious ways, but right then she needed something mindless and soothing. A Walt Disney musical, complete with animated foxes and the like, should hit the spot, and there'd be nothing to remind her of a certain cat burglar.

Wrong. Two thirds of the way through the movie, when she'd been lulled into a comfortable acceptance, the entire cast started dancing over the roof-tops of London, leaping from building to building with the expertise of a dozen cat burglars. She watched, throat dry, heart pounding, even the glossiness of a Disney extravaganza unable to calm her fear of the dizzying heights. *Damn Blackheart,* she thought miserably, unable to simply press the button and turn off the machine. *Damn his black heart.*

She sat up, the morning light filtering around her, and peered at her digital clock. Later than she'd thought—after ten. It was a good thing the office was closed—the way things were going she'd be out of even her menial job. Becoming irresponsible wasn't the way to start a new life.

It had never been in her nature to be irresponsible. So why was she still lying in bed, when anyone else would be up and accomplishing things? Maybe she didn't feel like accomplishing anything. Maybe she just wanted to sit in her lonely bed and feel sorry for herself.

She tugged at the ring. It was too tight on her finger—she'd need soap to get it off. How had Patrick managed to slip it on while she still slept? Maybe he'd used Krazy Glue—she wouldn't put anything past him.

She looked around her uneasily, then breathed a sigh of relief. She'd stripped the maroon sheets off the bed and replaced them with pink flowered ones that had never seen Blackheart's irresistible body. With his ability to cloud her mind and walk through walls, she wouldn't have been surprised if he'd managed to change the sheets under her sleeping body, but the pink ones were still in place. Then she smelled the coffee.

"Hell and damnation," she said.

"Is that any way to start a morning?" His voice floated in from the kitchen. He appeared in her doorway, a cup of steaming coffee in his hand.

Ferris didn't know which vision had the stronger emotional effect on her—Blackheart in his black denims and ancient tweed coat or the cup of perfect coffee that only he could make. She'd been making do on instant, and she missed Blackheart's coffee almost as much as she missed the man himself.

"If that coffee's for me, bring it here," she grumbled, still tugging absently at the ring. "Otherwise go away."

"It's for you." He sank onto the bed beside her with his customary grace, the coffee barely sloshing the sides of the full cup. "And don't tell me to get off the bed. You don't get the coffee unless I sit here."

"I may be an idiot where you're concerned, Blackheart, but my price is a little bit higher than a cup of coffee." She could smell it, the aroma dancing across the air to tease her nostrils and make her mouth water.

"Not the price of my coffee," he countered. "Lighten up, Francesca. I said sit here, not let me have my wicked way with you. Stop tugging on the ring, drink your coffee, and listen to me."

Certain things weren't worth fighting. She took the coffee, absorbing the caffeine with a contented sigh. "That's where I get into trouble. Listening to you. You're tricky, Blackheart."

"I know you don't trust me, Francesca. You've told me so in as many ways as you can manage. Right now I don't give a damn. Your lack of trust is your problem, not mine."

"Is it?" The coolness in her voice would have chilled a less stalwart soul than Blackheart.

He leaned back on the bed, away from her. "I'll say it just once, Francesca, and then we'll drop it. It's not me you don't trust. It's yourself. You're afraid of being in love with me, afraid of losing yourself. So you manufacture excuses, when deep down inside you know perfectly well that if you listened to your heart, you'd know that you can trust me. You'd know that I love you and that you love me, and if we have that then everything else can be worked out. But as long as you're too much of a coward to listen, it's a waste of time. Besides, I have more important things on my mind right now. Your neuroses can wait."

She'd gone through a dizzying range of emotions during his short speech, moving from annoyance to melting love to absolute fury. She would have thrown her coffee at him, but at that point the coffee was worth more to her than the man. She drained it, shoving the empty mug under her bed and glaring at him. "All right. Then let's talk about more important things than my puny little neuroses. You slimy, conniving, black-hearted—"

"Ah-ah-ah," he reproved. "You don't want to use those nasty words, do you, dear heart? You might have me convinced you really care."

"You're so egocentric, you'll believe anything you want to believe." She was tugging fretfully at the canary diamond again. He reached out and covered her hands with his.

"Stop yanking at it," he said. "If you just stopped eating so many cookies, it would probably fall off."

"You've been sending me the cookies!" she snapped, outraged.

"That's because you were getting too skinny. Eating your heart out over me, I suppose. I thought I'd better fatten you up." Before she realized what he was doing, he'd levered his body across hers, his hands cupping her rounded hips. "I don't know, maybe you could do with a few more cookies. I like you with a few extra pounds."

"Go drown yourself, Blackheart." She tried to push him off, but it was a half-hearted effort, and they both knew it. She squirmed, then realized with sudden astonishment that he was completely aroused.

"Yes," he said. "You do have that effect on me."

"Tough."

"Yes," he said, lowering his mouth to hers. "Tough." He kissed her, long and deep, pushing her back into the pillows, kissed her with lips and tongue and teeth and soul until she was feverishly kissing him back, her hands trapped beneath their bodies, her hips reaching up to him, her body straining for his. Once more it was starting, the dark midnight of desire that wiped out thought and will and any lingering trace of sanity, and with the last ounce of effort she yanked out her hands from beneath them, bringing them up to his shoulders to push him away.

For a brief moment her fingers clung to him, to the thick tweed and the tense shoulders beneath, clung and kneaded. And then she shoved, taking him off guard, so that he fell back onto the bed beside her.

He just lay there for a moment, breathing deeply, his chest rising and falling, his eyes closed. And then he opened them, turning to look at her, and there was a wicked gleam in their brown depths. "You can't blame me for trying," he said. "Or maybe you can. You have the ability to blame me for all sorts of things, whether I've done them or not."

"Have you?"

"Have I what?"

"Done them? Did you rob the people in Madrid and the museum in Paris and the people in Lisbon? Have you been breaking into places? Have you been breaking the law and lying to the police?"

He said nothing, looking up at her, his face expressionless, wiped free of desire, irritation or any emotion at all.

"Please answer me." To her inner disgust her voice was cracking. "I can't stand this uncertainty. Tell me the truth."

"The truth, Francesca, wouldn't end your uncertainty," he said briskly, sitting up and withdrawing from her, physically, mentally, emotionally. "You want any more coffee?"

"I want answers."

"You'll have to find your own." His voice was colder than she'd ever heard it, and she knew with sudden despair that she'd gone too far. Past the point of no return.

All right, she thought, drawing her defenses back around her like invisible armor. *I can survive. I can survive anything.* "Did you just come to make me coffee and harass me?" she demanded. "Or was there something you wanted?"

He paused in the doorway, and a blessed glint of humor lit his somber eyes. "Loaded questions again. If you think this is harassment, you ain't seen nothing yet. And I thought I made it clear there was something I wanted."

"Stop it!"

He shrugged. "All right. Yes, there's something I need from you. A little help for old times' sake, and I didn't know who else to ask. Surely you can be noble enough to do me one small favor."

"One small favor? All right, Blackheart. For old times' sake I'll do you one small favor. What is it?"

His face was wreathed in an innocent smile. "Do a little roof-hopping and housebreaking," he replied. "What else?"

DANY WAITED UNTIL the door to the Winnebago slammed, waited until she was sure he was well and truly gone. She lay in the narrow bunk, unmoving, not quite daring to believe she was alone at last. He'd been whistling something cheerful and jaunty, and the grating sound of that tuneless little song died away as Marco moved across the grounds.

She'd been such a complete fool. Hadn't she learned anything in the twenty-four hard years she'd been on this planet? Hadn't she learned you don't threaten and provoke a wild beast, no matter how tame it seemed? Hadn't she learned not to hope for happy endings?

She pulled her aching body out of the bunk, her fingers clinging to the edge as dizziness swept over her. She shook her head to try to clear the mists, but the pain was so intolerable that she fell back against the hard mattress with a wordless moan. She lay there, and for the first time in the last long, horrible day, she cried.

The salt tears stung her face, reminding her that she couldn't spend the day in bed feeling sorry for herself. She'd gotten herself into this mess and was simply paying the price for her own stupidity. This time she was able to get to her feet and totter across the narrow aisle to the miniature bathroom, holding on as she went.

She hadn't meant to look into the mirror. She waited until she'd finished her shower, waited until she'd drained the water reservoir and stumbled back into the tiny bathroom. And then she caught sight of her reflection, the swollen jaw, the raw scrapes from Marco's knuckles, the black eye. It was going to take five pounds of makeup to cover it this time, she thought wearily, swallowing three ibuprofen and praying that they'd work quickly. If only she could cover up what he'd done to her body.

She stared at her reflection in the mirror. Yellow covered the red marks, green toned down the purple bruises, and a heavy matte makeup did an adequate job. She'd have to stay out of bright sunlight and away from curious eyes, particularly those of Stephen McNab. What a fool she was, to think he was comfort and safety! Stephen McNab was the long arm of the law, and if he knew what she'd been doing for most of her adult life, he'd slap her in jail so fast her head would spin. *No.* There was no one she could turn to, no one who could help her. Only her own wits could do that now.

Ferris Byrd was going to have to use her own wits, too. She'd done what she could to protect her, and had probably put her in worse danger. There were times when Dany wasn't sure if Marco was quite sane. But it wasn't a question of sanity. It was a question of a not too bright, not too civilized creature feeling threatened. And when stupid creatures were threatened, they reacted violently.

She was going to have to be very careful, Dany thought, pulling on a turtleneck shirt that covered the bruise at the base of her throat. Five more days and she'd be free. In the meantime she had to go out into the sunny morning and hope that no one looked too closely. And that she didn't run into the eagle-eyed Stephen McNab.

"I DON'T WANT to be doing this," Ferris said.

Blackheart had his back to her. They were standing in a grove of trees on the west side of Regina's stately mansion, and her ex-fiancé was looking upward, way, way upward, to the sharply angled roof four stories above.

"Then why are you here?" he countered, not bothering to turn and look.

He didn't need to. He knew as well as she did that she was dressed in black denims and a turtleneck, with ballet slippers on her feet and her dark hair tied back with a dark bandanna, ready for his particular brand of work. He knew that panic would lurk in her eyes despite the determination on her lips. And he knew she'd have no argument against the indefensible. He asked, and she was here. It was as simple and as stupid as that.

"Do you expect me to climb up the side of the building like Spider-Man?" she demanded. She could hear the distant noise from the circus on the great lawn on the eastern side of the building, could hear the muffled roar of the big cats.

"I expect you to follow my lead, dear heart. If the two of us can break in, then the place isn't as secure as it should be."

"What do you mean, if the two of us can break in? I thought we'd be a formidable combination."

He glanced back at that, his expression inscrutable. "So did I," he said. "But you're not viewing this from a distance. We've got one experienced cat burglar, but one who is sadly out of practice, whether you believe it or not. Not to mention that he's hampered by a game leg. And we have a woman who's a base coward, terrified of heights and terrified of love. It seems to me a baby gate could keep us out."

"Blackheart . . ." she warned.

"Follow me, my love." He swung himself up into the first branch of a tree, then began climbing. "Unless you're too chicken."

"I'm too old to fall for dares," she said, looking up at him as he disappeared into the branches.

"I double dog dare you, Francesca," his voice filtered down. "Hurry up, or you won't know where to go when you reach the top."

She who hesitates is lost, Ferris reminded herself grimly, reaching for the first branch. She wasn't as tall as Blackheart, nor as limber, and it took her a couple of tries to swing her body up and over the thick limb. She was just as glad she didn't have an audience. "Are you up there?" she called. "I'm coming."

"I know you are," she heard him say. "I'm waiting."

"I know you are," she muttered under her breath, hauling her body upward, mentally cursing the last few batches of Mrs. Field's Coco-Macs.

He was waiting for her, all right. Miles away from the dubious safety of the thick-limbed oak tree, lounging indolently on a third-floor balcony. She stopped her relentless climb, clinging to the branch for dear life, refusing to look down at the ground miles below her, and glared across the vast space. "How did you get there?"

"I jumped." He leaned over the thick stone parapet that was waist high and held out his hand. It was an eternity away from her reach. At least eight inches.

"Forget it," she said. "I'm going back down."

"If you go back down you'll have to look. And I'd advise against it."

She knew he was right. She considered a brief peek at the grass and gravel beneath her and thought better of it. "I think I'll just stay here," she said, clinging more tightly to the branch.

"It'll probably rain this afternoon. Don't you think you'll get wet?"

"That's all right. Then I won't have to worry about a shower."

"What about food?"

"I need to burn off a few of those cookies you've been plying me with. I'll be fine. Just send the fire department to extract me in a few days."

"Francesca," he said, his voice stern. "Come here." He reached out, crossing the space, and could almost touch her. "I won't let you fall. Trust me at least that far."

"I don't trust you, Patrick. I thought we made that clear." Slowly, carefully she pried one hand away from the tree branch and put it into his.

His long, strong fingers closed over hers. The leap would only be a couple of feet, and she'd land on the terrace with its nice high wall protecting her.

He wouldn't let her fall. Would he?

"Come on," he said, yanking suddenly.

Caught off guard, she had no chance to do anything more than shut her eyes and leap. When she opened them she was standing safely on the balcony, Blackheart's arms wrapped tightly around her.

She pushed him away, brushing the clinging bark and leaves from her black clothes. "Well," she said briskly, "that was simple enough."

Blackheart's smile was devoid of cynicism. "Wasn't it, though? The next part will be even easier."

"We're going into the house and climbing the stairs, right?"

"Wrong. We're climbing up the outside of the house to the roof and going in through the attic."

"The hell we are!" Ferris protested, heading for the door.

His hand caught her before she'd gone two feet, spinning her around to face him. "Don't chicken out now, Francesca. I'll make a little bargain with you. If you can climb up the rest of the way without any more whining, then I'll let you go."

"You'll let me go back downstairs?" she said, not quite understanding.

"No. I'll let you go completely. No more breaking in to your apartment, no more leaving little gifts, no more cookies or movies or pickled herring. Just prove to me you're brave enough to do it, and I'll trust you to manage the rest of your life on your own."

She just stared at him. This was what she wanted, wasn't it? Finally to be free of him? Wouldn't she be willing to climb the Matterhorn for that freedom, never mind something as puny as Regina Merriam's stone mansion? "All right," she said breathlessly. "You've got a bargain."

His own smile was grim. "I thought I might. You first." He gestured toward the edge of the balcony.

She peered over it dubiously. "You want to tell me how we're going to manage this, or am I supposed to make it up as I go along?"

"No whining, Francesca, or the deal is off. Just be glad we're doing this in broad daylight and not the dead of night." He came up behind her, his body warm and solid, and she wished, longed for the chance to lean back against him and close her eyes, close out the dizzying heights and the miserable agreement she'd just made. His arm reached beside her, pointing. "It's not as bad as it looks. There's a stone ledge at least eight inches wide that will get us as far as that deep-set window, and you should be able to hoist yourself up the rest of the way."

"And if I can't?"

"There are boxwood below. They should cushion your fall."

Her reply was brief and colorful. "Why don't you go first?"

"I thought I should be there to catch you if you fall."

"I hate you, Patrick. You know that, don't you?" she muttered, climbing out onto the parapet.

"I know that, dear heart," he said gently, following close behind her, his strong hand within inches of hers.

Ferris edged out onto the narrow parapet, her sweaty hands clinging to the stones jutting out from the building. Once out on that narrow ledge there was no going back. With a deep intake of breath she put her brain on automatic pilot and began to climb, always aware of Blackheart close behind her.

Halfway up she realized she wouldn't fall. Blackheart wouldn't let her. Logic told her that there was nothing he could do to stop it if she started to tumble, but logic had nothing to do with it. He was behind her, his sheer force of will forcing her up, up, and that will would keep her safe. Even the dangerous slickness in her hands dried up in the soft autumn breeze that was playing around the angled roofs of the Merriam house, and as she reached up for the copper gutter she only allowed herself a brief moment to hope that Regina kept her gutter intact. Even that thought vanished. Blackheart would have checked it first, before he brought her out here.

She pulled herself up, landing on the roof with little grace and a great deal of relief, sprawling along the greenish metal and watching as Blackheart levered himself up and over.

"You did it," he said, his eyes alight with something she couldn't read.

"Yes, I did. Why?"

"I thought it was to get me to leave you alone."

"I'm not talking about that. Why did you want me to do it? No lies or evasions, Patrick. Why did you make me climb up here?"

"Because I wanted to be alone with you?"

"No."

"Because I hoped you'd fall and take my terrible guilty secret to the grave with you?"

"No."

"Because I wanted you to realize you do trust me, after all?"

"That's it," she agreed. "But you promised to leave me alone if I did it."

He grinned in the glorious sunlight. "Francesca, dear heart," he said. "I lied."

Chapter Twelve

The Thirty-Nine Steps
(Lime Grove 1935)

AT LEAST HE DIDN'T make her climb down the skylight window, Ferris thought as she followed him through the dormer window into the musty attic. She wouldn't have put it past him. She knew for a fact that he was more than slightly partial to the old caper movie, *Topkapi,* and he loved the scene where the robbers were lowered through the skylight. While Blackheart hadn't been into fantasy games in the past, she'd still been holding her breath. After what he'd just put her through, she wouldn't have been surprised at anything.

He'd proven his point, unpleasant as she found it. She did trust him, and in recent weeks she'd forgotten that elemental fact. Not with jewels, not with worldly goods, but with her life, with her well-being, even with her love, she trusted him. She just didn't know how she was going to live with that knowledge.

She landed on the dusty floor with a soft thud, her ballet slippers pinching her feet slightly. There were dust motes in the late-morning sunlight, shifting shadows, and an odd assortment of science-fiction-type lights over to one side. "What's that?" she demanded, heading across the attic in its direction.

"The security system for the Van Gogh." Blackheart barely glanced at it.

Ferris stopped short. "It looks impressive."

"Trust me, it isn't. That wouldn't stop a determined teenager. For one thing, three people have keys to the system, and that's two people too many. For another, the technology is antique. That form of infrared detection went out several years ago."

"Who has the three keys?"

"It doesn't matter." Blackheart was poking around the boxes and trunks stacked by the doorway. "Any self-respecting thief could circumvent it, anyway."

"Is there such a thing as a self-respecting thief?" She was momentarily distracted.

Blackheart turned and grinned at her, and even in the murky light she could see the flash of his white teeth. "What do you think?"

"I think you're conscienceless. You still haven't answered my question.

Where are the keys?"

"Regina has one, Phillip has the other," he said, turning back to his investigations.

"Need I ask where the third one is?"

"You needn't. It would probably take me less time to go through it without the key than with it, but yes, I have the third key. After all, I set up the system several years ago."

"An outmoded system."

"It wasn't outmoded then," he replied with great patience.

"What the hell are we doing up here, Blackheart?"

"I told you—we're double-checking the security. We have less than a week to worry—after that it's Nelbert's problem. I just don't want anything to happen in the meantime." There was a row of doors at the far end of the cavernous room, and Blackheart systematically began opening them, pawing through shallow closets filled with old clothes, boxes and trunks.

Ferris moved closer, drawn by a glimmer of deep blue silk, and within moments she was looking through an array of evening gowns dating back to the beginning of the last century. The heavy stone Merriam mansion had survived the earthquake and fire of 1906, so it was entirely possible that some of these gowns came from that era. They were made for women shorter and far more buxom than Ferris, but the richness of the materials shimmered across her hands, and she was assailed with a sudden weak-minded and entirely feminine longing for something as beautiful as this to wear.

She turned to find Blackheart watching her, his expression guarded. He said nothing, closing the door of the closet he'd been delving into and advancing on her. She didn't know what she expected, and instinctively put up her hands to ward him off.

"Get into the closet," he ordered tersely.

"Blackheart, this is neither the time nor the place."

"Someone's coming, you idiot. Get into the closet." Without waiting for a further protest he shoved her in, following her and pulling the door shut behind them, pushing the silks and satins back on the rod with a ruthlessness that caused Ferris to cry out in protest. The noise didn't get very far. He slammed his hand over her mouth and pushed her back against the partition. The dresses closed around them, still smelling faintly of faded roses, and they were alone in the cramped darkness, Blackheart's hand across her mouth, listening, listening.

At first she didn't believe him. It wouldn't have been beyond his capabilities to manufacture an intruder, just to give him the chance to back her into the closet. But a moment later she heard the sounds that had alerted him. After years of midnight invasions, Blackheart's ears were more finely tuned than those of a normal human being, and the footsteps, the muffled voices just outside the attic door were clearly not just an excuse for him to put his hands on her.

Slowly he released her mouth, but not his grip on her. His other hand was around her waist, holding her still, and she didn't dare squirm as she so desperately wanted to. Her fear of heights didn't extend to dark, enclosed spaces. She felt warm, cozy, and inexplicably excited in that cramped darkness with only Blackheart's heated body beside her, and she had to mentally slap herself for thinking what she couldn't help thinking.

There were three voices and presumably three sets of footsteps to go with them, though Ferris's hearing wasn't sophisticated enough to be certain. "As you can see," Jeff Nelbert's thick, fruity tones lectured, "this security system is laughable. Nothing compared to what I've set up at the museum for *The Hyacinths*, but then, Blackheart got into the business through the back door in more ways than one. One couldn't expect him to have the professional expertise I have."

Blackheart's low growl was inaudible to anyone but Ferris, plastered against him in the dark closet. She smothered a laugh against his shoulder, wishing he'd move away, wishing there was room enough to breathe without inhaling the scent of faded roses and sexy, impossible John Patrick Blackheart.

His mouth was somewhere just above her ear, his hand had reached up and loosened her hair, and yet all his attention seemed focused on the voices outside the closet door. She only wished she could be as single-minded.

"What makes you think Blackheart's going to go for the painting?" There was no mistaking Stephen McNab's deep tones, and if Blackheart's taut body started in surprise, it didn't stop his lips from nibbling on her sensitive earlobe.

Ferris stretched and preened like a stroked kitten. Her skin suddenly felt hot and very sensitive, and she wished those interfering voices from the attic would go away and leave her in peace with the man she loved.

"It's his only chance," Nelbert replied, his two-hundred-plus frame shaking the sturdy attic floor as he moved across the room. "He knows once it's gone from here and under my protection in the museum, he'll have a snowball's chance in hell of getting his hands on it. He's got to act fast, and he's going to use these circus goings-on as a cover up."

"Maybe," McNab said. "I'd like to believe it, but Blackheart's never had any connection to stolen artwork. It's hard to believe he'd change his MO so late in the game."

"Don't you believe it? What makes you think he hasn't done artwork before? Look at how hard it was to pin any of the jewel robberies on him. He could have been responsible for half the art thefts in Europe and those idiots at Interpol would have no idea."

"Maybe." Ferris could tell by the sound of McNab's voice that he was clearly unconvinced. She could also tell that he didn't like Nelbert that much, but then, nobody did. She wasn't able to make any more deductions because Blackheart had slipped his hands under her turtleneck shirt. "It wouldn't hurt to check."

Blackheart's mouth grazed her ear. "It's hot in here," he whispered, a bare thread of sound, one that would reach no farther than the tasseled silk wedding dress in front of them. "Why are your nipples hard?"

She turned to glare at him, but his mouth caught hers, kissing her with a complete dedication that in no way diminished the attention he was paying to the conversation in the outer room. She knew that, she hated it, but she kissed him back anyway, pressing her hips up against his, noting without surprise the extent of his arousal, wishing those noisy people would just go away.

"Listen, Detective—" A new voice entered the fray, one surprising enough to make Blackheart release her mouth and listen. "We wouldn't be wasting our time if we didn't think there was something that merited your attention. I'm well aware of how overworked and underpaid our police is. I'm simply concerned about my mother's safety."

Blackheart's response was nothing more than an obscene, sibilant whisper in her ear.

"What makes you think your mother's in any danger?" McNab countered stubbornly, and Ferris found her feelings for the tenacious policeman warm several degrees. "Blackheart's never been involved in any form of assault. Cat burglars seldom are—it goes against their self-image. I'll tell you again, I don't believe Blackheart's going to change his ways this late in the game. He's not going to turn to art theft and he's not going to beat up old ladies."

"Are you willing to stake your career on that?" Phillip Merriam demanded. "And my mother's safety?"

There was a pause. The two in the closet listened intently, and Ferris was aware of an intense, sudden dislike of charming, noble Phillip Merriam.

"I'm not willing to risk anyone's safety without good reason," McNab said finally. "Maybe you're right. After all, you're the one who got the tip. And a painting like *The Hyacinths* isn't just a work of art, it's the heist of a lifetime, and when it comes to gall Blackheart has no bounds. Don't worry—we'll be watching."

"That's all I ask, Detective," Phillip said smoothly, all belated affability. "That's all I ask."

They waited in silence, shrouded by the silk wedding dress. As they listened the footsteps faded away, the heavy clang of the metal door at the top of the stairs reassuring them they were once more alone.

Blackheart, thorough as ever, reached for her again, but she was one step ahead of him, pushing through the wall of clothes and out into the dusty attic before he could make her forget everything once more. "What's going on?" she demanded, keeping her voice down in case their visitors were still within earshot.

Blackheart shrugged, strolling over to get a closer look at the blinking, winking monolith that constituted the Van Gogh's security system. "Sounds like I'm about to become an art thief. Except that our friend McNab is going to catch me in the act. What does it sound like to you?" He seemed no more than casually curious, but Ferris knew he was intent on her answer.

"It sounds to me like a setup."

His smile across the expanse of the attic was beatific in the midday light. "Why, Francesca, you do trust me."

"No, I don't. I just agree with McNab. You're not about to start ripping off paintings this late in your career. If you steal anything, you'll steal Regina's jewels."

"She doesn't have any to speak of," he murmured absently, still watching her.

"You'd know that, of course."

"Just force of habit. When you've spent as many years as I have in the business, it's hard to let go of instincts. Besides, I've done security for Regina often enough to make it my business to know what's of value in this house."

"You don't need to keep explaining," Ferris said mildly.

"The hell I don't. You're enough to make a saint paranoid."

"You're no saint."

"No, it sounds more like I'm a fool. And a patsy."

"I can't imagine why Phillip would think you'd be planning on robbing his mother. He's usually such a fair, sensible man."

"Is he? Maybe he's got something else on his mind."

"I don't think he's pining for me, if that's what you're suggesting. He was very gracious about our engagement."

"Which engagement? Yours and his, or yours and mine?"

"Don't be obtuse. His and mine, of course. So I don't think his brain is clouded by latent jealousy. Especially now that you and I are no longer involved."

"Aren't we? What were you doing in the closet with me?"

She could only hope the shadows obscured the blush that rose to her face. "Kissing you," she said flatly. "Small enclosed places turn me on. Anyone would do in a situation like that."

If she'd hoped to goad him, and she had, it was obviously a waste of time, for he laughed, suddenly cheerful. "I'll keep that in mind. So if Phillip isn't intent on revenge, why is he setting me up and using Nelbert to do it?"

"Nelbert's obvious. He's your biggest competitor and he's always been jealous of Blackheart and Company. McNab doesn't even need an explanation—he's determined to nail you. Maybe they've tricked Phillip into thinking you're a danger."

"I'm not overly impressed with politicians' intellects, but Phillip isn't that much of a dunce. He's no one's dupe. If anyone's pulling the strings, he is."

Ferris couldn't rid herself of the suspicion that he just might be right. And since she could think of no motive for it but her own involvement with both men, she immediately denied it. "You're the one who's paranoid, Blackheart. Clearly you have nothing to worry about. If you're not going to steal *The Hyacinths* and sell it to the highest bidder, then you don't have to worry about what those three conspirators were doing. If they're busy watching the Van Gogh, you won't even run into them."

"No, I can steal Regina's jewels in relative peace and safety," Blackheart drawled.

"I thought she didn't have any jewels."

"Just testing. Do you want to go back over the roof, or would you prefer the steps?"

"Wouldn't we run into those three if we followed them into the house?"

"Maybe. Does that make a difference?"

"Not in the slightest. I'm not going back onto that roof for love or money."

"We can take the stairs," he agreed. "Regina knows what we're doing, anyway. If we run into the three musketeers we can refer them to Phillip's mother. That should put the fear of God into them." He moved to the door, holding it open for her. There was no sign of anyone on the stairs leading down into the third-floor hallway and *The Hyacinths,* and no sound of voices filtered upward.

"You don't like Phillip, do you?" she asked curiously, moving past him down the stairway. "I thought you two used to be friends."

"Amiable acquaintances," Blackheart corrected her, shutting the attic door behind them. "Polite relationships like that don't stand up to sexual jealousy on either side. The first time I saw him put his hands on you, I wanted to murder him."

That violent statement shouldn't have started a small fire of pleasure burning in the pit of her stomach, but it did. She stopped on the bottom stairs, not even noticing the glowing, jewellike colors of the priceless painting, and looked up into his face. "Did you really want me that much?"

He put out his hand and she couldn't move, mesmerized by the light in his warm brown eyes. "I did," he murmured, his voice low and beguiling, the kind of voice that could seduce a mother superior. "I still do." His fingers lightly touched her cheek, the rough texture of his skin sending tremors of heat across her face.

"Patrick," she whispered, her husky voice equally beguiling. "I—"

"I didn't realize you were around here." Phillip's smooth voice came booming into their concentration, shattering it like a crystal figurine.

Blackheart raised his head, and his expression was frankly inimical. "You weren't supposed to," he said.

Phillip's response was the epitome of the professional politician: a hearty laugh, a genial smile, and all the charm that was second nature to him. It was hard to remember that that same cheerful voice had been implicating Blackheart only moments before. "I hadn't realized you two were talking to each other. Is there any hope for a reconciliation? I know it would make my mother very happy." An edge slipped into his voice, so slight that Ferris doubted he was even aware of it—anger for her, anger for Blackheart, anger for his mother? She opened her mouth to say something, but Blackheart's hand caught hers and his fingers closed tightly over her palm, silencing her.

"No," Blackheart said flatly. "Ferris tells me I'm a lost cause. She's just been kind enough to help me check out some of the security on the house."

Phillip's blue eyes took on a slightly glassy tint. "I wouldn't think there'd be anything worth that kind of trouble in the place. Mother disposed of most of her silver and jewelry years ago. Said they were too valuable to have sitting in the house. I believe she donated the proceeds to some AIDS organization. That's my mother, the bleeding heart. There's nothing anyone would want left in the house."

"Except the Van Gogh," Blackheart murmured.

"Except the Van Gogh. But then, artwork isn't really in your line at all, is it, Blackheart?" Phillip said smoothly. "It's the glittering colors of emeralds and rubies that excite your larcenous instincts, not the jewellike hues of a painting."

"Oh, I don't know, Merriam. A man shouldn't be too set in his ways. A moment of avarice, a moment of anger, and a lifetime of rules can get swept away. Can't it?" Blackheart's voice was low and his tone taunting. Ferris listened with growing confusion. She tried to pull her hand away from his, but his grip was unrelenting. There was something going on between Blackheart and Phillip, something she didn't understand, but whatever it was she didn't like it. Something was simmering beneath the surface, and she didn't want to accept the obvious answer.

"You tell me, Patrick," Phillip said, his affability never faltering. "You're the expert on breaking rules. And laws."

"Maybe. Maybe not. Where's your mother?"

"Going to tell on me?"

"What are you two talking about?" Ferris had had enough of this fencing. She yanked her hand free from Blackheart's grip, moving down the last few steps and confronting Phillip.

"Tell her it's nothing to worry her pretty little head about," Blackheart suggested helpfully. "I'd like to see her deck you."

Phillip reached out a hand. By sheer coincidence his smooth, well-manicured fingers brushed the same spot on her face that Blackheart's rougher hand had. "I wouldn't think of saying such a thing," he murmured. "Ferris and I understood each other. We had a civilized relationship, based on mutual respect and caring. We could have it again."

The touch of his flesh left her unmoved, except for a faint regret that it wiped away the memory of Blackheart's touch. She swallowed, taking a step backward against Blackheart's waiting body. "You're very sweet," she said, searching for the right words. "But I think you're too good for me."

Blackheart's laugh was mocking. "Don't you believe it, dear heart. Your golden senator has feet of clay."

Phillip ignored him. "I'm sorry," he murmured. "More than I can say."

His eyes met Blackheart's for a brief, telling moment, and once more Ferris thought there was something more going on than she was aware of, something dark and wicked gliding beneath the surface. "I'll tell Mother you're looking for her."

They watched him go, his broad shoulders and golden head disappearing down the next flight of stairs. "A graceful exit," Blackheart drawled.

"Do you have to be such a rat?" Ferris snapped, guilt and regret for what couldn't be slashing through her.

"Sorry, darling. We don't have a civilized relationship based on mutual respect and caring. We're rather savage about it, don't you think?"

"Don't, Blackheart." But the words were murmured against his mouth as he hauled her back into his arms. His actions fitted his words. There was nothing civilized about his kiss, nothing civilized about her response. His hands threaded through her thick hair and held her still, his mouth caught hers in a bruising possession.

This time she didn't hesitate. This time she shoved him with all her strength, catching him off guard so that he fell back against the attic steps. Seconds later she was gone, speeding down Regina Merriam's broad marble staircase without looking back.

Blackheart watched her go. Slowly, ruefully he picked himself up off the stairs, shook himself off, and smiled. "Run, Francesca," he whispered. "You can't run away from yourself." And with a jaunty little whistle he followed his erstwhile love down the stairs.

DANY MANAGED very well for most of the day, staying in the shadows, keeping her head down, her voice lowered, locking herself into the Winnebago with the accounts and keeping her back to the sun when anyone came to disturb her. At least Marco had made himself scarce. She had no illusions that he might be feeling remorse. His only regret might be that someone would notice the bruises. And while she was tempted to wash off her makeup, she controlled herself. That kind of petty revenge would only make things worse. A few more days, and she'd be home free.

She'd had more than a few curious looks, of course. Rocco, the old clown, had been around long enough to know what was going on, and without saying a word he went out of his way to be kind. He brought her coffee and fresh pastries and kept people away from her. If he hadn't gone for an early supper, she would have made it safely through the day.

But there was no faithful Rocco guarding the tiny door to the van at five-thirty in the afternoon, no one to stop Stephen McNab from sticking his head in.

He couldn't have chosen a worse moment. She'd let the room grow dark, not bothering to turn on a lamp, and as she sat there in the shadows, the account books no longer visible, she allowed herself the rare luxury of crying. Her head ached, her ribs ached, her entire face felt raw. And she felt alone, as she had always felt, alone and a stranger in a world of other people's friends.

She saw McNab silhouetted in the doorway and held herself very still, hoping he wouldn't realize she was in there. But her body betrayed her with a watery hiccup. McNab hit the lights, flooding the Winnebago with a bright electric glare, and his startled eyes met hers.

"What in God's name happened to you?"

Chapter Thirteen

The Lady Vanishes
(Lime Grove 1938)

"GO AWAY," DANY said, turning her face away. McNab paid no attention, slamming the door behind him and advancing into the cramped quarters. She was cowering behind the tiny built-in table, but he simply swept the papers out of the way, reached in and hauled her out.

He was quite a bit taller than she was. Quite a bit stronger, too, but she knew instinctively that unlike Marco he'd never use his strength to hurt anyone. Instead, with great gentleness, he caught her chin in one large hand and forced her to turn her battered face up to his.

His swiftly indrawn breath told her just how much of her makeup must have washed off during her bout of tears. "Porcini?" he demanded in a sharp voice, and she quickly revised her earlier opinion. He would never use his strength to hurt *her*, but she wasn't sure Marco would be safe.

"I fell," she said, repeating the lie she'd told Rocco. "I was working on an old acrobatic routine and I didn't warm up properly. You don't know circus people—bruises are part of the business."

"And do they sit in the dark and cry about them?" McNab's harsh tone was at odds with the gentleness in his hands.

"I fell, Detective."

"Stephen," he corrected her. "And you must have fallen into Porcini's fists. We arrest wife beaters in this country, Dany. You don't have to put up with that kind of abuse."

"I don't know much about American law, but I imagine you can't arrest him if I don't lay a complaint. And I'm not going to do that." She felt calmer now, a coolness overlying her desperation. She was very close to blowing the whole thing. And she wanted to do just that, wanted to lay her head on Stephen's broad shoulder and tell him everything. Then she'd be the one in jail, she reminded herself.

"Why not? Do you love him that much?"

"I hate him."

"Then why don't you leave him? Divorce him? We can get a restraining order to keep him away. You don't have to stay with a brute like that."

"I can't get a divorce," Dany said. "We're not married."

She was unprepared for his reaction. She expected disgust and anger, not a sudden, unexpected grin of delight. "That makes life easier. Get your things."

"Why?"

"You're getting out of here. At least for a couple of days, until lover boy manages to control his temper."

"Where am I going?" She eyed him warily.

"Well, there are any number of shelters in the city for battered women. You'd be safe there. But I thought you might come with me."

"Where?" she asked again.

"I have some time off coming. We could go north. And don't jump to any conclusions. I'm not trying to get you into bed. That's the last thing you need, after what you've been through. I just think you need to get away for a while."

"How do you know what I need?" she muttered under her breath.

"I beg your pardon?" Luckily Stephen hadn't heard her.

"I said I'll go with you. For a couple of days. Just so I can have time to think."

"Are you sure you won't swear out a complaint . . . ?"

"I fell," she said firmly, heading for the door.

"If you say so. Don't you want to bring any clothes?" He stood still in the middle of the caravan, dwarfing its already cramped confines.

"I have a suitcase packed and stowed over by the tack tent. I like to be ready to leave at short notice."

"Do you? I wonder why?"

For a moment she faltered. What in the world was she doing, turning to an enemy for help? Stephen McNab didn't realize he was the enemy; he thought he was the only friend she had. How would he react when he found out the truth, as he was bound to, sooner or later? His determination to nail Blackheart would be nothing compared to his fury with her. She'd have to burrow very deep into the American heartland to get away from him.

If she had any sense at all she'd stay. Marco wouldn't dare hit her again, not if he hoped to carry off the job with her assistance. Stephen McNab was too enticing, with his world-weary air and absurdly kind eyes.

But she was ready to be enticed, ready for kindness, for anything else a couple of days in hiding with Stephen McNab might bring. "You'll find out why," she said. "Sooner or later. Let's get out of here before Marco gets back."

"I wouldn't mind having a few words with your friend Marco."

The thought of such a confrontation made Dany dizzy with horror. "Let's get out of here before I come to my senses," she said.

That moved him. "All right. Maybe we'll be lucky and run into him on our way out."

But they ran into no one at all on their trip through the dusk and across the trampled lawns to McNab's beat-up Bronco. Not an acrobat, not an illusionist, not an animal trainer, not a soul saw them leave. Except Rocco.

He watched them go, then headed into the mess tent, a smile wreathing his weary old face. He was a man who knew how to keep a secret—a man who would enjoy seeing Marco Porcini squirm.

THERE WERE NO presents in Ferris's apartment that evening. She told herself she was deeply grateful, as she fed an indignant Blackie a can of Seafood Surprise. As she soaked her weary muscles in her oversize bathtub and tried to forget the number of times Patrick had kissed her that day, she told herself she was glad he was finally leaving her alone. She told herself she could start concentrating on the rest of her life and forget about old memories and lingering desires. And pushing a disc into the DVD player, she climbed into her bed and sat back to watch *To Catch a Thief.*

The first thing she did the next morning was to check her ring finger. The canary diamond hadn't been replaced. It was still sitting where Blackheart had left it, on top of the television. She told herself she was very, very happy as she stomped into the kitchen, her lavender silk kimono trailing around her boxers and tank top. She told herself life was going to be splendid as she made herself a horrible cup of instant coffee, searched in vain for any kind of milk product that hadn't soured, and tossed out several stale doughnuts she'd ignored in favor of cookies in the last few days. And it was only because she stubbed her toe on the step up into the dining room that she sank to the floor and began to howl like a spoiled three-year-old.

There were no deliveries to her office at the Committee for Saving the Bay's headquarters. No phone calls, no summons to the circus setup on Regina's spacious grounds. Nothing.

By three o'clock she was ready to scream. She'd been able to accomplish one thing during the day, clearing up a minor glitch involving the license for the circus performance. But for the rest of the time she'd pushed papers around on her desk and waited for someone to call.

If she'd ever had any doubts about the worthlessness of her job, that endless day put them to rest. She wasn't needed there, she was wasting her time and energies. At three-fifteen she wrote her letter of resignation, effective the day after the circus performance, at three forty-five she had copies in the mail to the five trustees who were nominally her employers, and at three fifty-seven she was on her way home.

No one called her that night. She brought Blackie herring and Brie, but even he didn't show up, clearly not trusting his distracted mistress. She unplugged the phone at nine-thirty, tired of staring at its sleek lines and begging it to ring. She'd stopped by a store and bought three movies, two comedies and a gangster film. She climbed into bed with a large snifter of brandy and watched *To Catch a Thief.*

There was no canary diamond on her finger the next morning. On a Saturday there was no work, either. The rain was pouring down, sheets of water lashing against the windows, turning the middle of the day into a lightless gloom. By two o'clock Ferris knew that one more moment in her apartment and she'd start screaming. Digging out her peach silk raincoat, she pulled it on over her jeans and sweater, grabbed her purse, and headed out into the rainy afternoon with one thought in her mind. There was more than one way to skin a cat.

DANY LIKED AMERICA, she decided as she sat curled up in the window seat of the old cabin and watched the rain. She liked the rawness, even the tackiness of the new towns that seemed to have sprung up overnight around the more elegant areas of San Francisco and Marin County. She liked the log cabin Stephen had brought her to, a place off in the woods up north of Santa Rosa in Sonoma County, with running water and electricity but not much more, not even a telephone. She liked eating hamburgers and pizza and spaghetti, the limit of Stephen's cooking, and she liked his oddly polite way with her. In the last day and a half he hadn't touched her. He'd taken care of her like a kindly uncle, and yet there was nothing avuncular about the way he looked at her. She'd been waiting, longing for him to make a move, a gesture, but he'd done nothing but wish her a polite good-night at her bedroom doorway before retiring into his own room. And while Dany told herself it was all for the best, she was beginning to long for those big, strong hands of his to touch her, anywhere, just touch her. She needed to remember what love felt like after all the years of abuse.

It had been a curiously peaceful time, considering how little they'd talked. She'd responded to his gentle probing about the past with evasions and outright lies, spinning him a story about her upbringing that was culled directly from Christopher Robin and the Pooh stories. Stephen had stopped pressing her, and had responded to her own questions with equal reticence. All things considered, she knew as little about him as he knew about her. She knew he had two brothers, that he'd grown up on the east coast, and that he'd always wanted to be a cop. But she knew nothing else.

Not that it mattered. She wouldn't have minded if he'd had a wife and six kids stashed away in one of those towns they'd passed through; she wouldn't even have minded if he was on the take. It would have equalized the sides a bit, making both of them cheating liars instead of just one of them. Herself.

She leaned her forehead against the glass, staring out into the afternoon rain. They'd have to go back soon, she knew that, though he hadn't said anything about it. He was intent on catching John Patrick Blackheart, that much she knew instinctively, and Marco was busy baiting the trap—the trap to catch her half-brother and make him the scapegoat, while they got away free and clear.

She thought about Blackheart for a moment. He wasn't what she'd expected, but then, twenty-one years was a long time ago. She didn't hate him as she'd thought she would; as a matter of fact, she had to work to raise any kind of anger at his desertion. After all those years, it suddenly no longer mattered.

She just wished he'd had enough family feeling to notice that she looked slightly familiar.

She was a fool to brood. Everything was moving along at its preordained pace, and it was too late to stop what had been set in motion long ago. She'd made her choices; now she had no option but to ride along to the bitter end. She should just be glad she hadn't ended up in bed with Stephen McNab. After more than two years of celibacy it might have proved her emotional undoing. She was far too attracted to the man as it was, attracted in a spiritual, emotional way as well as on a simple physical level.

She could hear him splashing about in the kitchen. He'd refused to let her cook or do any housework, insisting that she needed time to relax and think. *All right,* she'd thought, but it had been impossible to relax with Stephen so near and yet so far. She drew back, looking at her reflection in the rain-spattered glass. The bruises were fading—a light application of makeup would cover up the worst of them without her having to skulk about in the shadows. It was time to go back, before she did something unforgivably stupid.

She got up, stretching lazily, and put another log onto the fire. There was a slight chill in the air, but the vast fireplace proved more than adequate to the task of heating the cabin. The smell and crackle of the fire added to the coziness, and for a moment she considered curling up on the rug in front of it and taking a nap. *That's what a sensible person would do,* she reminded herself. But when had she ever shown any sense?

Stephen McNab had just finished shaving himself at the kitchen sink, the only sink the cabin boasted. There were a stall shower and a toilet in a small alcove off the back, but every day he'd shaved in the kitchen, and she'd studiously avoided the room while he was busy. He couldn't have heard her approach—she had the ability to move in complete silence, and bare feet on a wooden floor didn't make much noise, anyway. But he knew she was there, and he turned, dropping the towel he'd used to dry his face. His expression was wary.

His shirt was lying on the wooden counter next to the sink. Dany managed a shy smile, trying to avert her eyes from his chest. "I thought I might make some coffee," she said. "I was feeling sleepy."

"You should take a nap," he said, turning to reach for his shirt.

"Oh, Stephen," Dany whispered in muffled horror. "What happened?"

Stephen McNab had a beautiful torso. Lean and wiry, he made Marco's bulging muscles look overblown in comparison. But Marco didn't have any scars marring his artfully tanned flesh.

Someone had done something very nasty indeed to Stephen McNab—but long enough ago that the scar had faded into a thick white line that traveled from his back, around under his arm and ended up by his right nipple.

"Sorry," he said, pulling on his khaki shirt and starting to button it. "I know it's not pleasant to look at."

"No," she said, crossing the kitchen before she had time to think and stopping his hands. "It's not that. It just must have been so painful."

He kept his hands still beneath hers. The bright kitchen light glared behind him, and outside the rain was pouring, sending shifting blue shadows through the windows and into the corners of the small room. "It was a long time ago, Dany. It doesn't matter."

"But you could have been killed."

"That's what my wife thought."

She hadn't really wanted to hear that, Dany reflected numbly, dropping her hands and letting him continue buttoning the shirt. "What happened?"

He was busy tucking his shirt into his jeans, stalling for time. "I had just made detective, and I wasn't too bright. I made the wrong enemies, pushed where I wasn't supposed to push, and someone decided to teach me a lesson. Unfortunately I'm not a quick learner. He's in jail, and I'm alive and well."

"And your wife?"

Stephen sighed, his wintry-blue eyes almost black in the glaring kitchen light. "She said she couldn't stand watching me take chances and eventually end up getting killed. She said I had to choose between her and being a cop."

"And?"

"I'm still a cop."

"I'm sorry, Stephen."

"Don't be. We were just kids, anyway. High school sweethearts aren't supposed to spend the rest of their lives together. At least we didn't have any children."

"Did you want them?"

"Not then."

"Do you still miss her?"

He shook his head. "I hadn't thought of her in months. Years, maybe. Until I met you."

Damn, Dany thought. *God's punishing me, all right. Here I am, falling in love with a man who's any thief's natural enemy, and on top of that I remind him of his ex-wife.* She backed away, plastering a phony smile onto her face. "You'll have to find someone else who reminds you of her," she said brightly.

"Dany," he said in a weary voice, "Lucille was a redheaded Valkyrie with a fanatical devotion to makeup and clothes and doing as little as possible. She was a prom queen who never grew up or faced the consequences of the choices she made, and when the going got rough she took off. Does that sound like you?"

Yes, she thought miserably. *I don't want to face the consequences of the choices I've made. I want to live happily ever after.* "Why did you say I reminded you of her?"

"I didn't. I said I started thinking about her when I realized I wanted someone else. More than I'd ever wanted anyone, Lucille included, in my entire life."

Dany shut her eyes, taking a step backward. "This won't work. You don't know anything about me, and if you did, you wouldn't like it. It's doomed before we even begin."

If she expected an argument, she didn't get one. He just stood there, looking at her in the bright kitchen light. And then he reached over the sink and flicked the switch, plunging the room into a shifting, shadowy darkness. "Maybe," he said, his rough voice curiously caressing. "We'll never know until we find out."

"Stephen . . ."

"He didn't rape you, did he?" It wasn't a question. It was more that he wanted to verify a suspicion.

"Marco? No. He hasn't touched me for over two years. Except to hit me."

"I thought you fell," Stephen taunted her gently, moving toward her across the shadowy room. She held her ground, her heart pounding in anticipation—and regret. She shouldn't do this; she knew better than he did how hopeless it was. But she couldn't resist. His big hands caught her narrow shoulders, pulling her gently toward him. "I've been afraid to touch you, for fear you'd been hurt too badly to want me. But you do, don't you, Dany?"

"Want you?" she echoed. "I shouldn't."

"But you do." His mouth touched hers, gently, brushing against her lips, teasing them open. "You do, don't you?"

She slid her arms around his waist and up under his loose shirt, her hands grazing the rough texture of that terrible scar. "Yes," she whispered against his mouth. "Yes."

BLACKHEART'S STREET was half-empty on that Saturday afternoon, and his battered Volvo station wagon was nowhere in sight. Ferris jiggled the set of keys that she'd tucked into her jeans pocket and hoped that Blackheart hadn't changed his locks. He'd have no reason to. He would never suspect, after her high-and-mighty exit from his life, that she might want to break in when he wasn't around.

If he had changed the locks there was no way she'd get in. The one person you couldn't steal from was another thief—Blackheart's locks were impenetrable to any normal human being. Maybe the thief in Europe would be able to handle them, but not someone with her limited expertise.

She didn't know when she'd come to the conclusion that there really was a thief in Europe, and it wasn't Blackheart still plying his trade. It might have been when he kissed her in the closet. It might have been when she followed him out over rooftops, risking life and limb to prove heaven only knew what. Sometime during the last few days she'd realized that Blackheart hadn't reverted to his former ways.

But he'd still been lying to her, covering up. He knew far too much about the thefts in Madrid, Paris and Lisbon, but he wasn't about to tell her until he was good and ready. And she wasn't about to wait any longer. She was going to go through his apartment, inch by inch, and when she finally came up with the answers she was seeking, she would curl up on his couch and wait until he came home, so that she could confront him with it.

She had the presence of mind to call his apartment from a pay phone at the end of the block. She had absorbed certain tricks of the trade; whether it was from Blackheart himself or from the various caper movies she'd been watching was a moot point. There'd been no answer, and the way was clear. She just had to hope she had enough time to find what she was looking for before he put in a reappearance.

She went to the kitchen first. There was just enough coffee left in the pot to make a mug—she put it into the microwave and drank it black, savoring every drop. She had to give Blackheart credit—he was neater than she was. Not by much—he went in for artless clutter and piles of books as much as she did, but he seemed to have a slightly better sense of order.

She strolled into his living room, past the overstuffed couch where she'd spent far too much time, and headed straight for the desk. If he'd locked it, she could use her credit card, she told herself, her hand on the drawer pull, her eyes glancing at and then dismissing the old photograph of Blackheart and his father, dressed for business in tails.

She stood there for a long moment, considering. This was her future at stake—surely unethical things were necessary, even justified when it came to her only chance of happiness.

Maybe. Maybe not. If she opened the drawer and started pawing through it, she'd be just as untrustworthy as she'd accused Blackheart of being. Even if the end of uncertainty lay just beyond that closed door, she couldn't do it. She dropped her hand, moved away and sank onto the sofa.

"I'm glad you changed your mind." Blackheart's voice drifted to her from the bedroom door. "Why are you here? Looking for proof of my guilt?"

"No," she said. "I wanted to find out who you were covering up for."

A cynical grin twisted Blackheart's face. "A step in the right direction, but not the confession of undying love and trust I was hoping for. Go away, Ferris, and come back when you've made up your mind."

She didn't move. "Go away, Ferris," he said again, moving toward her. "Or I'll make sure you don't want to leave."

Ferris ran. It wasn't until she was halfway home that she remembered the picture on the desk and realized something she'd never noticed before. John Cyril Blackheart, alias Seymour Bunce, Blackheart's father, looked very familiar. And it wasn't his compelling son who resembled him. It was Danielle Porcini.

Chapter Fourteen

I Confess
(Warner Brothers 1952)

STEPHEN SLEPT heavily, his face in the pillow, one arm stretched out, holding her loosely even in sleep. Dany regretfully edged out from under its protection, climbing from the bed and tiptoeing into the deserted living room. The rain had stopped sometime during the night, and now in the chilly predawn light a faint mist was rising from the short grass around the cabin. It was going to be a long, cold walk into town.

She didn't even dare take the time for a shower. She didn't really want one. This was all she was going to have of Stephen McNab—fate and history wouldn't allow her more, and she had no intention of washing away the scent and feel of him before she had to.

So many times during the last twelve hours she had wanted to tell him the truth. Never had she felt so open, so vulnerable, her defenses and her secrets crumbling around her. So many times she'd bitten her lip to keep from doing just that. His determination to catch Blackheart was so all-consuming that she had no doubt at all if she told him who she was and what she was really doing in California, he'd let go of her, jump out of bed and start reading her her rights.

So she kept her mouth shut, except to kiss him. And when the night began to vanish, a fitful daylight crept over the hillside and dreams were over, she knew she had to escape. She didn't believe he'd let her go that easily, that he'd just assume she'd changed her mind about being involved with him and leave her alone. She was going to have to come up with an excuse, something plausible to keep him away while she finished her job with Marco. Then by the time she was gone, he might be able to summon up some gratitude that he hadn't become more involved.

She shivered as she stepped onto the porch. The temperature wasn't that bad, but the chill came from deep inside her soul. She wished she could tell herself she was being noble, but she didn't even have that solace. Denying herself Stephen McNab now was simply anticipating his horrified rejection. As a defense against heartbreak it wasn't much, but it was better than nothing.

Her sneakered feet were quickly soaked by the heavy dew on the grass as she crossed to the rough dirt road. She shivered, pulling her thick sweater closer around her, and headed down the road.

He caught up with her five minutes later. The battered Bronco pulled up beside her, the passenger door slammed open, and he sat there in the driver's seat, glaring across at her, dressed in jeans, an old sweater and nothing else, his bare feet on the brake. "Get in."

"Stephen . . ."

"Get the hell in. We'll discuss this when you're in the car."

"I really don't think I'd better—"

"I'm bigger than you, Dany. A lot. You're getting into this car."

He'd do it, too, she thought. He was angry, not the cold, biting rage he directed at people like Marco and Blackheart, but a hot, heavy fury. If she stalled he would grab her, then he'd hate himself for it. It was one thing she could do for him, she thought, climbing into the front seat and keeping her head lowered, and at the same time she could enjoy the pleasurable torment of a few more minutes of his company. While she thought very fast of a plausible excuse.

He turned the Bronco around on the narrow road, each turn of the steering wheel accomplished with much more force than necessary. Leaning forward, he flicked on the heater, blasting her damp, chilled legs with blessed warmth. The Bronco kept moving, past the empty cabin, on up the winding road toward the top of the mountain.

"I don't think much of one-night stands, Dany," he said after a while, his eyes trained on the road, his profile grim.

"I don't either." Her voice wasn't much more than a whisper, but he could hear her.

"Then why?"

She deliberately misunderstood him. "I couldn't help it. I'm very attracted to you."

"That's not what I was talking about, and you know it. I mean why did you run?"

"I don't suppose you'd believe me if I said I hadn't enjoyed myself."

His laugh was humorless. "No. I was there, remember? And I don't think attraction and enjoyment are the operative words in this situation. This wasn't a yuppie mating ritual."

"We had sex, Stephen."

"We made love, Dany. There's a big difference." They'd reached the top of the hill and a small turnaround with a graveled parking space. Stephen pulled up the edge and parked, but left the motor running so that the heat still surrounded them in a cocoonlike warmth. "What's going on, Dany? Don't you think you can trust me enough to tell the truth?"

It was Dany's turn to laugh, but all she could manage was a dry, mirthless chuckle. In her ears it sounded definitely on the watery side, and she bit her lip, hard. "It's not you who can't be trusted."

"Are you feeling guilty about Marco? The man is pond scum—he doesn't deserve any loyalty or consideration."

"Stephen . . ."

"You don't owe him anything. I don't want you going anywhere near him again—he's too dangerous. I think you need police protection. Twenty-four hours a day. And I'm offering it free of charge. Move in with me, Dany. I promise you, you won't regret it."

"I can't." This was worse than she'd anticipated. She'd expected an inquisition, not enticement. She leaned against the door, away from him, hugging herself in her misery. "I just need to go back. My job's there, my friends are there. This was very nice. . . ."

"Nice?" he echoed, clearly affronted.

"All right, it wasn't nice!" she exploded. "It was wonderful, heavenly, the best thing that ever happened to me. But it's doomed! Hopeless! Can you get that through your thick cop's head?"

She'd been hoping to anger him, but his gray eyes merely narrowed as he watched her. "Why?"

"Take me back, Stephen."

"Why?" he persisted, his voice softer now, less demanding. He reached out his big, strong hand to gently stroke her tear-damp cheek. "I hate to tell you this, Dany, but I'm falling in love with you. So you can at least tell me why we're doomed."

It was the last straw. No one in all of her twenty-four years had ever told her they loved her. Something inside her burst, a tiny bubble of anger and hope, and she turned to him, her eyes filled with despair. "Because I'm a thief, Detective McNab. Any cop's a natural enemy. My real name is Danielle Bunce, and I've spent the last four years in Europe as an accessory to a cat burglar. On top of that, I'm John Patrick Blackheart's half-sister." She leaned back and closed her eyes, breathing deeply, waiting for those words she'd heard so often on the telly. "You have the right to remain silent," it began. She couldn't remember the rest, but it didn't matter. She was about to hear them.

What she heard in the cab of the Bronco was absolute silence. Just the sound of the engine, the noisy whirr of the fan as it spun heat around them. And the steady breathing of the man beside her.

When she could stand the quiet no longer, she held out her slender wrists in front of him, keeping her face averted. "Where are the handcuffs, Detective? I won't put up a fight."

But it wasn't cold metal closing around her wrist. Warm, long-fingered flesh was encircling her, pulling her over the bench seat and into his lap. "Damn," he muttered. "You don't make things easy, do you?" And he kissed her.

It was a while before she surfaced from that kiss, but when she did, she was more confused than ever. "You can't, Stephen," she said breathlessly. "I'm everything you despise. Didn't you hear what I just told you? Didn't you . . . ?"

"Hush," he whispered. "I heard you. And you're not everything I despise. I told you, I'm falling in love with you, and you could be a chain saw murderer and it wouldn't make any difference to me. We can work it out."

"Stephen . . ."

"I've spent my entire law enforcement career watching scum make deals and get off with a slap on the wrist. For once plea bargaining is going to work in my favor. Do you have any warrants out on you?"

She just stared at him. "As far as I know, no one has ever suspected my involvement. Or my partner's."

"That's a different matter. You can turn state's evidence, get off with a suspended sentence, but Blackheart's going away for a long time." The grim satisfaction in his voice did little to help her state of mind.

She pulled away from him, and he let her go, watching her as she scrambled back to her side of the car. Here would be the perfect revenge that she'd always sought. Stephen assumed Blackheart was her partner—she could incriminate him and disappear.

But the stupid thing was, it no longer mattered. Whatever Blackheart's reasons for abandoning her had been, they must have felt justified at the time. She no longer needed her pound of flesh, not when her own heart lay shattered and bleeding on the ground. "Sorry, can't help you," she muttered, staring out the window.

"Can't?" he said. "Or won't?"

"There's nothing I can tell you that will help you in your vendetta against my half-brother," she replied with absolute honesty.

As usual Stephen was more alert than she'd hoped. "He's not your partner, is he?" he asked in a quiet voice. "Does he even know you're his sister?"

Dany's only reply was a strangled sound that was half a negation, half a sob.

"He doesn't," Stephen said. "So that leaves Marco." Leaning forward, he threw the gears into reverse and began backing around. He headed down the hill at a reasonably sedate pace, and the brief glance Dany stole at his strong, world-weary profile told her only that he was deep in thought.

When they reached the cabin again he turned off the engine, staring out the windshield with an abstracted air.

Dany couldn't stand the silence any longer. "What are you going to do? What next?"

He turned to look at her then, and the tenderness in his eyes twisted her newly vulnerable heart. "I'm going to take you back into the cabin and prove to you that you don't have to be frightened of me. And then I'm going to try to figure out what I can do without incriminating you."

"And if it's impossible? If there's no way you can do anything without sending me to prison?

"Did you ever see The Maltese Falcon?"

"I beg your pardon?"

"An old Humphrey Bogart movie—a real classic. He's a private eye and the woman he loves is a murderer who killed his best friend. Problem is, she loves him too."

"What does he do?" She was fascinated despite herself.

"He tells her he'll wait twenty years till she gets out of prison."

"What does she say?"

"Something along the lines of 'Go to hell.'"

It surprised a laugh out of her. "So what happens?"

"I don't know. That's where the movie ends."

"You can turn me in, Stephen. The most they'll do is extradite me back to Europe. If I tell the truth, I'll get off lightly for helping them nail . . . my accomplice. If I insist I'm innocent, they probably don't have enough to convict me on. So it's all right. Start the car, let's drive back to San Francisco, and you can arrest me."

For a long moment he didn't move. She could see his big hands clasped on the steering wheel, so tightly that his knuckles were white with strain. And then he sank back, sighing. "Can't arrest someone without a warrant," he said, pulling the keys out of the ignition and flinging them into the under-brush surrounding the cabin. "And there's no evidence on which to issue one. You're stuck."

"Stuck?"

"Here. With me."

"Stephen," she said, desperation making her normally rich voice high-pitched. "You can't turn your back on everything you believe in. For pity's sake, take me in and arrest me!"

He was already out of the Bronco, walking around to her side and opening the door. "Sorry, babe. The only place I'm taking you is to bed." And scooping her up into his arms, he carried her up the creaking front steps of the cabin, kicking the door shut behind them.

FERRIS BYRD WAS very, very angry. After days of stupidity, she'd finally put two and two together and come up with a nice neat package of four. Patrick's long-lost sister had appeared on the scene, probably with a burglar friend in tow, and Blackheart was doing everything he could to save the girl from her folly. *Including lying to and misleading his fiancée,* she thought bitterly. Her last, lingering doubts had vanished. Blackheart hadn't taken to a life of crime once more. He'd taken to a life of chivalry, *curse him.*

She sat in her messy apartment, staring out the windows into the foggy San Francisco afternoon. While Ferris sat on the living-room love seat and thought, Blackie had come in, eaten the Brie and disappeared again. She welcomed the quiet, welcomed the distant noise of the traffic, welcomed the cocoon of fog that surrounded her apartment. She sat alone with her dark and shifting thoughts, her hands clenched into angry fists.

She knew she should be reasonable. She knew she should be relieved at finally understanding what lay behind Blackheart's mysterious behavior. *After all,* she had six brothers and sisters, countless nieces and nephews, a vast, sprawling, affectionate family. She of all people should understand blood ties.

But she didn't. All she knew was that Blackheart had sacrificed her and her love, and was well on the way to sacrificing his career and possibly even his freedom for a spoiled, amoral young woman who had appeared out of nowhere to wreak havoc and destroy their lives.

She wasn't going to let it happen. She wasn't going to roll over and play dead, sit back and wait to see if Blackheart could pull it off. This was her own future at stake, not just her erstwhile lover's. She'd spent enough time crying, enough time eating. Now it was time for action. And the first thing she was going to do was confront Danielle Porcini and find out what the hell she thought she was doing.

The memory of Tarzan, the albino tiger, suddenly shot into her brain, and she hesitated. That had been no accident—someone had tried to kill her. Could it have been Blackheart's sister? Blackheart himself?

The absurdity of the last question made her laugh out loud, the sound soft and comforting in the shadowy living room. No matter what Blackheart's transgressions, and they were many, he would never hurt her. He loved her, she could at least accept that, and it made everything else, every danger, every tall building she had to leap, worth it.

But what about Danielle? Her appearance at the time had been fortuitous, to say the least. But she'd also helped Ferris lure the carnivorous beast back into the cage. It would have been a simple enough matter to leave her there, to lock her in and come back after her screams had died away.

No. Danielle's appearance hadn't been coincidence, but it hadn't been murderous, either. She'd known Ferris had been in trouble, and she'd come to save her.

So whom did that leave? Dany's mysterious accomplice, the current cat burglar himself. And there was really no mystery to it at all. Marco Porcini might not have the brains to plan and carry out the complex robberies in Europe, but he had the agility and strength. And Danielle Porcini had brains in abundance—not to mention her knowledge of the family business.

Was there a family tendency toward burglary, some sort of recessive gene or ingrained trait that was passed from generation to generation? Was she going to give birth to a passel of baby cat burglars?

The very thought boggled her mind—because she had no doubt whatsoever that she was going to marry John Patrick Blackheart, ne Edwin Bunce, and give birth to their children. Maybe if he changed back his name and they produced a small handful of little Bunces, they might break with the family tradition. Or maybe they'd better make sure at least one of them became a lawyer, so she or he could bail the rest out of jail.

Ferris stretched out on the love seat with a sigh, relaxing for the first time in days. Now that she at last had a very good idea of what was going on, she could handle it. Whatever Danielle and Marco Porcini were here to steal, Blackheart would stop them. She was just going to have to make sure her once and future fiancé didn't succumb to temptation and steal it himself.

He needed her. He needed her to drill some sense into his head, to make sure he didn't take the fall for his sister. He needed her almost as much as she needed him. And if she found her need for him frightening, threatening, she was no longer going to fight it. She'd simply have to learn to live with her fear.

At least she didn't have to worry about Regina. The Porcinis hadn't been anywhere near that blasted Van Gogh, and the painting wasn't due to be moved until after the circus benefit, when the Porcini Family Circus would be packing and moving to the next stop on their American tour. *No,* it was something else, and Regina, at least, was safe.

IT TOOK DANY TOO long to find the keys where he'd tossed them. Even in the glinting early-afternoon sunlight they were hard to find, and she wasted precious time searching through the long grass surrounding the cabin.

Stephen was in the shower. She knew he took long showers—she'd already taken one with him, and while he didn't have her as a distraction just now, he still was a man who took his time once he got into the stall.

Still, she couldn't count on anything. The rest of the day had been spent in bed, glorious, endless hours that had apparently left Stephen sure of himself and their relationship. Once the pleasure faded, it had only filled her with despair.

She couldn't do it to him. She couldn't allow him to turn his back on everything he believed in, just because he imagined he was in love with her. She'd learned over the long hard years that she wasn't worth loving, and she certainly wasn't worth a man destroying his life over her.

Never before had she put someone else's needs ahead of her own. Never had she made any sacrifice for a greater good—the greater good had always been what suited her. But not this time. This time she was going to be sickeningly noble. She was going to do one decent thing to counterbalance the years of anger and selfishness. She was going to abandon Stephen up at this cabin, without a vehicle, without a telephone, miles and miles away from the nearest town. She was going back to Marco, going through with the job, then she'd be gone.

Someone else would be working in Stephen's place when he didn't show up. Someone else would be to blame when the Faberge eggs turned up missing from the museum. And while Stephen would be filled with anger and regret, his life wouldn't be destroyed. It was the least she could do for him; it was the best she could do for him.

The keys suddenly glinted in the sunlight. She pounced on them, then sprinted for the Bronco, terrified that Stephen might curtail his shower and come in search of her. But her luck held. Five minutes later she was several miles down the road. And Stephen was still singing in the shower.

In three hours she was back at Regina Merriam's sprawling estate, darkness closing around her. She'd abandoned Stephen's Bronco on the other side of town, taken a taxi back and was making her solitary way across the grounds, when she thought she heard someone moving behind her.

A frisson of fear raced down her backbone. She couldn't forget Tarzan's evil, colorless eyes as he'd stalked Ferris. Someone, the same someone who'd loosed him on Blackheart's ex-fiancée, could have set him free again.

"Don't be ridiculous," she told herself. "Marco doesn't even know you're back."

She'd been certain she was safe from him. Even though she'd disappeared for days, he'd be too relieved to have her back in time for the job to even touch her. He wouldn't dare jeopardize the steal of a lifetime out of rage for someone he didn't even want.

So why was someone watching her, when she couldn't see anyone at all on the deserted grounds? Why could she hear the muffled sound of footsteps every time she walked? Why—?

Darkness descended as a blanket came down over her, smelling of something sharp and acrid and very dangerous. She struggled, but a pair of strong arms had encircled her, holding the enveloping material over her, forcing her to breathe in the fumes that were making her lightheaded and dizzy. The body holding her was short, squat and unfamiliar. And the voice in her ears was unknown.

"That's right, me girl. Take a little snooze," the cockney voice murmured into her ear. And then the blackness closed in.

HE DIDN'T LIKE creeping around in his socks, but he couldn't rely on his tread being as light as Blackheart's. The last thing he needed was for the old woman sound asleep downstairs to wake up and hear an intruder wandering around her third-floor hallway. Around her precious Van Gogh.

He didn't need to be there. He was tempting fate by coming back for one last look, one last gloating appraisal before they set their plan in motion tomorrow night. He was risking everything, but then, he suspected that was half the fun. This was his first dip into a life of crime, and he was finding it strangely exhilarating. No wonder Blackheart had so much trouble giving it up.

He could have had a thousand plausible excuses for being there, but he'd used not a one of them. He had a key to the house, but he hadn't used it either, sneaking in through an unlocked window in the downstairs pantry.

He'd left his shoes just inside and had crept through the house, up the flights of curving stairs to the third-floor landing, his heart pounding, his palms sweaty, the adrenaline rushing through him.

The Hyacinths glowed in the moonlight, and he stared at the painting, knowing that in the future this was one flower he'd pay attention to. He'd have dozens of them planted around his house as a private joke, a silent toast to his one, extremely lucrative venture into crime.

"Tomorrow," he whispered to the painting, a promise from an impatient lover. And turning, State Senator Phillip Merriam silently made his way back down his mother's stairs.

Chapter Fifteen

Frenzy
(Pinewood 1972)

FERRIS SLAMMED herself back against the cage, hoping there wasn't an inquisitive white tiger behind her. She'd come in the back way, over the unguarded museum wall, to see if she could find Danielle Blackheart Porcini without running into her accomplice. She had every intention of confronting her future sister-in-law, though she wasn't quite sure what that would accomplish. Perhaps if Danielle knew her secret was public knowledge, she might give up her current plans. If she proved stubborn, Ferris had no qualms about decking the little wretch. She was a good four inches taller and probably twenty pounds heavier, and even if Danielle was an accomplished aerialist, she still would be at a disadvantage. Maybe all those cookies would come in handy, after all.

The one person she didn't want to run into was Marco Porcini. She didn't know which would be worse, being the recipient of his nondismissable attentions or being fed to a tiger. She might prefer the tiger, but she'd prefer to avoid both. Dinnertime seemed as good a time as any. She was counting on Marco being in the dinner tent, counting on Danielle keeping a low profile, as she had during the past three days. According to Regina, the lovely Madame Porcini hadn't left the Winnebago since Tuesday. Ferris had every intention of bearding the lioness in her den, to use an unpleasant figure of speech, and pointing out a few home truths to her.

But the Winnebago was empty. Ferris had hidden back in the shadows, uncomfortably close to the animal cages, and waited, jumping every time she heard a big cat growl, her palms sweaty, her heart racing. *Damn the Porcinis, and damn Blackheart.* She'd much rather be home and in bed, watching *To Catch a Thief* for the umpteenth time. But if she didn't do something now, she might as well spend the rest of her life looking at that movie. And she had every intention of catching her own particular thief, for life.

She heard Danielle approach, and breathed a silent sigh of relief, edging around the corner of the Winnebago with a stealth that would have done Blackheart proud. So quiet was she, in fact, that the dark figure behind Danielle didn't even notice he had a witness. Ferris watched in horror as a small, wiry figure dropped some sort of heavy cloth over Danielle's head. There was a brief struggle, then the woman's body went limp.

Her assailant hoisted the dead weight to his shoulder with some difficulty and headed toward the back boundary of the estate. There was something familiar about the way he moved, the way he held his head, the tuneless whistle that came to her ears as she followed him. But it wasn't until she saw the Bentley that she was able to place him.

He dumped Dany's body into the back seat, breathing a sigh of relief that was audible even to Ferris's distant ears. "You just stay sleeping, me girl," said Alf Simmons, Blackheart's old friend and occasional chauffeur. "And everything will be just fine."

Thank heavens, he'd parked only a short distance away from Ferris's Mercedes. The moment the Bentley began its stately journey from the parking lot, Ferris raced for her own car, yanking open the unlocked door and diving for the ignition.

It didn't start. She shrieked, a short, colorful imprecation that compressed all her despair and determination into a few four-letter words. She turned the key again, her hands shaking, and this time it caught. The lights of the Bentley were already fading in the distance, and she pulled out of the museum parking lot with a screech of tires and a silent condemnation of her upscale vehicle.

"Tomorrow," she muttered, "I'm trading you in for a Corvette."

In response the Mercedes sputtered, but Ferris was having none of that. Jamming her foot down hard on the accelerator, she took off after the Bentley, driving with her customary disregard for the rules of road safety.

Either Alf was unused to this sort of work and didn't notice that he had a very determined driver tailing him, or he knew and didn't care. When she finally lost him, they were within three city blocks of his final destination, and Ferris knew the area well enough to make it the rest of the way on her own, ending up behind the Bentley, slamming to a stop and jumping out just as Alf Simmons opened the back door of the limousine.

He looked up, startled, ready to shield his unwilling passenger, when he recognized Ferris's pale face in the lamplight. "Oh, no," he said, shaking his head. "'Is nibs isn't going to like this, not one tiny bit."

"Is she all right?" Danielle's well-being wasn't of prime concern to Ferris at that point, but she hoped the girl was at least still breathing.

"Fine. Just gave her whiff of stuff to put her out while I brought her here. She'll have a hell of a headache, but then, that's not me problem."

"No," said Ferris, looking up at Blackheart's windows. "That's her brother's."

"You've got a head on your shoulders, I've always said so," Alf Simmons said admiringly. "Patrick didn't think anyone knew."

"Patrick's problem is that he thinks he's smarter than everyone," she said. "But he's not smarter than I am. What are you supposed to do with her?"

"Bring her upstairs and keep her out of harm's reach until Patrick can get her safely out of the country." Alf glanced in at the unconscious girl. "I think he was going to lock her in the bathroom."

Ferris's brain was working double time. "I'll tell you what. You take her to my place, and I'll go up and talk to Blackheart."

"Are you nuts? He's paid me to do a job, and when a Blackheart hires you to do something, you do it."

"You're not scared of him, Mr. Simmons?"

"The boy's got a nasty temper when he's crossed."

"But I'll be the one dealing with the boy," Ferris reminded him, pushing past and kneeling on the leather seat. For a moment she remembered a ride in that very car, with the scent of white roses and the bubbles of her favorite champagne tickling her nostrils. Ruthlessly she shoved away that sudden weakening, and reaching down, took Danielle's thin shoulder and shook her.

The drugged woman batted at her, murmuring something. "Wake up, Danielle," Ferris said ruthlessly, hauling her into a sitting position. "Wake up."

Danielle's blue eyes opened, slowly focusing on Ferris's determined face. "Go away," she said, and fell back against the seat.

Ferris was having none of that. "Come on, lady. Wake up." She yanked her upright again, giving her an enthusiastic whack across the cheek.

That did the trick, a little more effectively than Ferris could have wished. Danielle's eyes shot open as she winced, and in the artificial light overhead Ferris could see the fading bruises adorning her pale face.

"Sorry," Ferris muttered.

"Where am I?" Danielle asked groggily. "What's going on?"

"You're going to my place for a while. If you promise to go quietly and stay put, Alf won't drug you again."

Danielle shuddered. "I think I'm going to be sick."

The beautiful Bentley probably had never seen such rude behavior, but it served Alf right, Ferris thought. "There's a silver ice bucket you can use," she suggested.

"What do you want from me?"

"Not a damned thing. I just want to keep your brother from getting into any more trouble."

"My brother?" Even half-drugged and very nauseous, Danielle managed a creditable confusion, Ferris thought to herself. "I don't know what you're talking about."

"Yes, you do. Now are you going to go quietly or is Alf going to have to drug you again?"

"No more drugs," she said, shuddering. "I'll go peacefully."

"Word of a Blackheart?" Ferris knew she was pushing it.

There was something akin to fury glittering in Danielle's eyes. "Word of a Bunce," she snapped.

Simmons pushed Ferris out of the way. "That's me girl," he said cheerfully, putting a cashmere lap rug over Danielle's legs. "You come along peacefully and we can talk about old times."

"Old times?" Danielle echoed.

"Don't tell me you've forgotten your second cousin Alfred? For shame, girl." Straightening up, he closed the heavy door of the Bentley, taking long enough to favor Ferris with a broad wink. "Better go deal with his lordship up there. The two of us will be fine."

"Are you really their cousin?"

"I am."

"And you aren't a cat burglar?" Maybe there was hope for her offspring, after all.

"No, ma'am. In my spare time I'm a bookie." And with a tip of his hat he climbed into the driver's seat and took off into the night.

BLACKHEART DRAINED his glass of whiskey, looking longingly at the bottle that was more than half-full. He wanted another drink, needed it, but wasn't about to give in to temptation. He needed his wits about him right now. Everything was coming together, all the tiny little bits and pieces, and he couldn't afford to let even a tiny part of his brain be marginally impaired.

Where the hell were they? He'd sent Alf out hours ago. It should have been a simple enough matter. According to reliable reports, Danielle had been hiding out in the Winnebago for the last few days—Alf wouldn't have had to search around for her. If his sister had any Blackheart blood at all in her veins, she'd put up a hell of a fight, but Alf was experienced in these matters. He should have been back here at least half an hour ago. Where were they?

He wasn't really looking forward to confronting his long-lost sister with the gloves off. He wasn't thinking very fond thoughts of her at that moment. She'd cost him his fiancée, his peace of mind, and was well on her way to costing him his freedom. McNab had been watching him, sitting there and waiting like a hungry blue spider, waiting for him to slip up. The irony of it was that now Blackheart was in more trouble than he'd ever been, at a time in his life when he was most guiltless.

Much as he'd like to wring his sister's pretty little neck, he wasn't going to do that. But he was going to find out exactly what she and that thick-brained accomplice of hers had planned. It seemed embarrassingly obvious to Blackheart, so obvious, in fact, that he couldn't believe they were planning it. But no one else seemed to have noticed, so perhaps it was only his professional expertise that made their target so glaringly conspicuous.

But he needed verification. He needed to know when, he needed to know how, if he was going to foil Marco Porcini effectively and not end behind bars himself.

As if that weren't enough, he also had Phillip Merriam's convoluted stratagems to take into account. While Blackheart couldn't believe the bland and noble senator was really going to try to lift his dear mama's priceless Van

Gogh, everything, including the usually infallible word on the street, pointed to the fact that that was exactly what he intended to do. And he expected Blackheart to take the fall for it.

Apparently destined to star as scapegoat in not one but two robberies, Blackheart was getting just a little bit irritated—not to mention missing his Francesca. Celibacy didn't sit well with him, but he had no interest in any of the other available females around. He wanted his woman, and no one else.

In the meantime, though, he was going to have to content himself with persuading his little baby sister to keep out of the way, and then he'd work from there. It was all coming together—it couldn't last much longer. Still, there were moments like these when he would have given anything to find Francesca waiting at his door.

He heard the pounding on his door with a grimace of irritated relief. *Back at last.* Alf probably couldn't manage the key with an unconscious female over his shoulder. Setting down his empty glass, Blackheart crossed his lonely, dimly-lighted living room and flung open the door.

"What kept you . . . ?" The words trailed off. Francesca stood there, an answer to an unconscious prayer.

She was dressed the way he liked her best, in faded jeans and an old cotton sweater, her upscale clothes packed away with her discreet gold jewelry, her perfect makeup and her alligator shoes. Her black hair was loose around her face, her green eyes glittered with apprehension and vulnerability and the traces of anger, and her mouth was pale and tremulous. On her left hand was the canary diamond.

He just stood there, momentarily blocking the door, too bemused to even think of an excuse. Any moment Alf would return, Danielle's comatose body over one shoulder, and then there'd be no way he could get rid of Francesca.

"What are you doing here?" His voice was surprisingly rough. He wondered if she could hear the longing in it. Longing for her.

She met his gaze with a semblance of calm, but her voice was huskier than usual, and he could see she was nervous. He wanted to put his hands on her, to calm her nerves, to make her think of something else entirely, when her words stopped him. "I had Alf take your sister to my place. She promised to wait until she heard from me."

He'd been a fool to underestimate her. He'd been a fool to ever let her go, even for a few weeks, just to protect her if things turned out badly. "How long do you think she'll wait?" he asked abruptly.

"Till tomorrow, at least."

It wasn't a conscious decision. It was inevitable, overwhelming and right. "Good," he said. "Then we've got all night." And he pulled her into his arms, shutting the door behind them.

If he was expecting a fight, she wasn't the one to give it to him. She went willingly, gladly, flowing into his arms like a hummingbird to a flower, without a word of protest. Her mouth was warm and sweet beneath his, tasting of surrender and delight, and she leaned against the door, kissing him back, sliding her hands up under his turtleneck, running them along his back, her fingers touching, caressing, exciting him beyond belief.

He yanked her sweater over her head with more haste than deftness, unfastened her jeans and shoved them down her long legs. The dim light in the hallway cast strange shadows around them, and as his mouth trailed along the slender column of her throat, he could hear a muffled laugh beneath his lips.

"Are we going to do this again?" she murmured. "We've made love in your hallway once already. Why don't we use the bed?"

He lifted his head to look down into her eyes. There was a dreamy expression on her face, a smile hovered about her pale mouth. "Are we going to make love?" he inquired huskily, pressing himself against her body.

"Maybe I'm jumping to conclusions," she said, her voice catching somewhat as his hands brushed the soft, full breasts that were still confined in a lacy bra. "Maybe you were just planning to put me into the shower?"

"We've done that already, too. We probably shouldn't repeat ourselves. What about the kitchen counter?"

"What about the bed?" she whispered, her lips brushing against his, slowly, tantalizingly. "We're out of practice."

"Practice makes perfect." He lifted her, wrapping her legs around his waist, and carried her into the bedroom, laying her down on the bed with infinite gentleness. He stripped off his clothes in the semidarkness and followed her onto the queen-size bed, his hands reaching for her with a sureness that felt impossibly right. It didn't matter whether she trusted him or not. It didn't matter what she knew, what she didn't know, what she thought she knew. All that mattered was that she was here, now, lying in his bed, her wonderful green eyes glittering in the shadows.

Her hands on his body were the same, that heady mixture of wonder and delight. In their six months together she'd never lost that sense of astonishment, of discovery, and he hoped she never would. Twenty-nine years of virginity had made her particularly appreciative of sensual delights, and he could only hope that after fifty years of making love with him, she'd still retain that fresh attitude. He had every intention of being around to find out.

Her mouth was growing bolder, moving down his chest, kissing, nibbling, her hands sliding down his rib cage, trailing down to capture the heavy solid heat of him, her fingers deft, arousing him to a point dangerously near explosion while her mouth teased his navel, his hip bones.

She'd never before touched him with her mouth, and he hadn't pushed her, never even suggesting the faint edge of disappointment he'd felt when she'd come close, achingly close. He wanted, he needed her mouth on him more than anything he'd ever needed in his life, but he bit his lip, hard, rather than beg.

She moved her mouth away from his stomach, looking up at his rigid face in the half light. Her eyes were heavy-lidded, a sensuous smile curved her mouth.

"Don't you like that?" she whispered, her voice a throaty enticement in the darkness as her fingers stroked his cock, caressed, bringing him closer and closer.

"Come here," he said, his voice a raw demand as he wrapped his hands around her upper arms, ready to haul her up and over him.

"Not yet," she said. And put her mouth on him.

His hips arched in sudden reaction. He couldn't help it: he put his hands on her shoulders, holding her there, terrified that she'd pull away. But she didn't. He'd had a brief, conscious fear that during their time apart someone else had taught her this, but that unworthy thought vanished beneath her clearly untutored, achingly delightful ministrations.

He knew he wouldn't be able to bear much more of this, and wasn't sure if Francesca was ready for the logical consequence of her actions. "Dear heart," he said, his voice strangled, pleading. "Come here."

She lifted her head, releasing him from the warm, enveloping prison of her mouth, and he almost cried aloud with the anguish of that sudden desertion. "Didn't you like it?" Her voice was low, uncertain.

"Like it?" His laugh was a bare thread of laughter. "Francesca, darling, I could die from the pleasure of it. But I want all of you right now." This time when he pulled her she came, sliding up his length and over him, her hips settling over his as he reached up and joined them, slipping into her with a deep, savage thrust that she greeted with a shimmering, inner tremor. If he'd had any fears that he'd been taking advantage, her body set them to rest. She'd never been so ready, so responsive.

She was so right for him. So tight, so warm, so attuned to his body that he wondered how he'd survived so long without her. She sank down onto him, whimpering softly in delight, and he felt himself expand, filling her, every inch of her, until Ferris-Francesca and all her doubts disappeared, until Blackheart dissolved, until they were just one in a joining that grew more powerful, all-encompassing, until it swept over them, a triumphant destruction, a destructive triumph, a beginning that was an end and a beginning again.

He could feel her face, wet with tears or sweat or both, pressed against his chest as the tremors slowly left her body. He could feel his own face damp, with sweat or tears or both, and he wondered how he'd survive if she left him again—if she lifted her weary head and told him she still didn't trust him.

"Oops." Her voice was soft, muffled against his chest, and he felt her sudden stillness with a sinking feeling. *Here it comes,* he thought.

He was nothing if not resigned. "Oops?" he prompted. "Is that your way of telling me you made a mistake?"

She lifted her head, looking into his eyes, and there was a rueful expression on her face. "A major one," she said. "I stopped taking the pill."

"Oops," Blackheart said. "Why?"

"Without you around, there was no need for it," she said simply.

"But what if you met someone else?" He knew the answer to that one, but he wanted to hear it from her lips.

"Give me a break, Blackheart. If it took me twenty-nine years to find you, it'll probably take me half a century to find a suitable replacement. I'll be too old to get pregnant by that time, so why fill my body with chemicals?"

"That makes sense. This way you can just keep it full of healthy stuff like Diet Coke and cookies."

"Exactly. Don't worry, though. It's the best possible time in my cycle. If I do get pregnant, it'll be something close to a miracle. And then I'll just simply have to accept my fate."

"Accept your fate?" he echoed, not liking the sound of that.

Her smile lighted the darkened room with its sheer, childlike pleasure. "Maybe I should have said embrace my fate. Wholeheartedly." Gently she pushed him back against the pillows, and there was a mischievous expression on her face. "The damage has already been done. Want to tempt fate again?"

He reached up, sliding one hand behind her neck and pulling her down to his mouth. "And again," he said against her lips. "And again, and again."

REGINA MET THE bland, ingenuous expression in her son's blue eyes across the silver coffeepot, her expression troubled. "I'm so glad you could join me for breakfast, darling," she said, pouring him a cup and adding the sugar and cream he liked. "I haven't seen enough of you recently. How's the campaign going?"

"Wonderfully. I'm up three points in the polls, and we've still got almost two months till the election."

"Isn't this very expensive?" she inquired in a careful voice. "I keep seeing your face on television when I least expect it. It's very unnerving," she added with a soft laugh.

"That's the way campaigns are run nowadays, Mother." He laughed his well-practiced, genial laugh. "We're running at a slight deficit, but things should improve. I'm expecting a major contribution."

"From whom?"

He frowned for a moment, clearly having forgotten that his mother was a sharp old lady. "A Dutch paint company," he replied, a tiny, smug smile twisting the corners of his mouth.

And Regina, remembering a day some thirty years ago when her only son had taken her pearl necklace to buy a new bicycle and then lied about it, was filled with a sudden dread.

Chapter Sixteen

To Catch a Thief
(Paramount 1955)

"I THINK I MISSED your coffee almost as much as I missed you," Ferris said with a sigh, leaning against the refrigerator door in Blackheart's kitchen and drinking deeply of the rich brew. She was wearing an old T-shirt of Blackheart's and her jeans, and she felt weary, replete and ridiculously happy. It was almost over. The worst part was past, the time without Patrick. Never, never would she willingly go through that again.

"Thanks a lot." His tone was ironic as he devoted his attention to the croissants heating in the toaster oven. "If I'd known that was all it would take to get you back, I would have shown up every morning with a thermos of the stuff. I should have realized you weren't a woman to be bought with diamonds."

"Nope. Mrs. Field's Cookies and a great cup of coffee should do it." She pushed away from the refrigerator, coming up behind him and putting her arms around his waist. "Don't let me be stupid again, Patrick," she whispered, pressing her cheek against his back.

He turned in her arms, threading his own around her, but his expression was wry. "I don't think I have any say in the matter, dear heart. If you persist in ignoring your instincts and listening to your fears . . ."

She stiffened. "I think trust goes both ways. You refused to confide in me, you still haven't explained."

"And I'm not going to. Not until it's over. There are just too many little threads that could unravel and end up tripping everything up."

This time she pushed away from him, hard, and he ended up against the counter. "I thought we came to an understanding," she said, her tone dangerously angry.

"Not exactly. We came to a climax, several of them, as a matter of fact. But that doesn't mean that all our troubles are over. The fact remains that you still don't trust me. Or if you do, it's only after you've received concrete proof. You couldn't pay attention to your own instincts, you were so busy running away. . . ."

She was about to run again, to storm from the kitchen in a rage, when his words stopped her. "You'd rather have a confrontation?" she demanded. "Fine." And stepping back, she swung at him. But he caught her, his hand fastening on to her wrist and holding tight. They stood there, immobile, and then he slowly, deliberately pulled her toward him. She went, hating herself, feeling herself once more vanishing into a vast, impenetrable cloud of love and desire where everything she was disappeared. She couldn't fight it, wasn't even sure she wanted to. She pressed her body against him and put her head on his shoulder, shuddering lightly.

"Why do we always do this?" she whispered.

"If I told you, you'd try to hit me again," he murmured into the silken cloud of her hair. He reached a hand under her chin, tipping up her head, her mouth to reach his. "Let's stop talking." His lips covered hers.

He tasted of coffee. He tasted of love. She shut her eyes, willing this to go on forever, when the insistent buzzing broke through her concentration. Lifting her head, she cast a questioning look at the toaster oven, but Blackheart shook his head.

"The front door," he said, releasing her.

"Don't answer it," she pleaded. "It'll be nothing but trouble. If it's not someone to arrest you, it'll be someone to arrest me. Let's just hide in the closet or sneak out the back."

Blackheart grinned. "The only way to sneak out of here is up the fire escape and over the rooftops. Are you game?"

"For you, yes."

His eyes narrowed. "Francesca, I could almost believe you do trust me, after all."

"I . . ."

This time he silenced her. "Not now. Wait till we get rid of our intruder."

She trailed after him to the door. "Don't answer it." He opened it anyway. Standing in the doorway was a rumpled, hostile-looking Stephen McNab. "What did I tell you?" Ferris demanded. "We're doomed."

McNab didn't even waste a glance at her. Shouldering his way past a willing enough Blackheart, his flinty-gray eyes searched the apartment. "Where the hell is your sister?"

"For God's sake!" Blackheart exploded. "Does everyone know we're related?"

"Everyone who counts," Ferris said smugly. "Why do you want Danielle?"

"I don't think that's any of your business," McNab said in a cold voice. "Where is she?"

"I haven't seen her," Blackheart replied with complete honesty. "Do you happen to have a warrant, Detective?" His voice was silkily polite. "Because if you don't, I suggest you leave. The city of San Francisco frowns on police harassment."

"I'm off duty," McNab growled. "This is personal."

"You mean you don't want to arrest Danielle?" Ferris questioned.

"The only person I want to arrest is Blackheart. It doesn't look as if I'm going to have the chance."

"No, it doesn't, does it?" Blackheart said cheerfully. "So tell me, McNab, what personal interest do you have in my sister? As head of the family I think I have a right to question your intentions."

"Don't push it, Blackheart," McNab warned, his eyes mere slits in his angry face. "For one thing, your sister stole my car."

"Did she? How enterprising of her. That makes her the first Blackheart in history to go for something other than jewels. Are you going to arrest her, McNab?" he inquired politely. "Or simply deport her?"

McNab glared at him. "I'm going to marry her." And without another word he slammed out of the apartment.

Blackheart stared at the tightly shut door. "That's all I need," he mourned. "A cop for a brother-in-law."

"Who says Danielle will go along with that?"

Blackheart shrugged. "I suggest we ask her. That is, if she's still waiting meekly at your apartment."

"She'll be there," Ferris said, sure of no such thing.

"I hope so. I have a few things to say to my long-lost sister," Blackheart said grimly. "And I'm tired of having to chase around after her."

"She's the one who committed the robberies, isn't she?"

Blackheart just looked at her. "You figure it out, dear heart. I'm not going to tell you." And without another word he headed for the shower.

THERE WAS NO SIGN of the Bentley outside Ferris's modest, two-and-a-half-story apartment building. They'd driven over in Blackheart's aging Volvo station wagon, barely speaking, and Ferris was sorely tempted to say something—until she noticed the expression on Blackheart's face, the muscle working in his jaw, the darkness of his eyes. She kept her mouth shut, following him up the stairs to the second-floor hallway, struggling with a new realization. Blackheart, the bold, brave cat burglar, Blackheart, who always knew what he wanted and seemed to know what everyone else wanted besides, Blackheart the invincible was afraid. Unsure of himself, wound up and afraid.

The last icy little part of her wounded heart melted. For some reason she'd never thought of him as vulnerable—it was only Francesca-Ferris with her troubled background and her confused future who was vulnerable. If Blackheart could care so much about a sister he hadn't seen in decades, it proved he was human, after all, and not the invulnerable man of steel she sometimes feared he was.

"Do you want me to wait out here?" she asked, her voice low and husky, completely devoid of her previous sulky manner.

He looked at her in surprise, not expecting the sudden softening on her part. "What makes you think she's still here?"

"She's a Blackheart. Or maybe she's a Bunce, I don't know. Either way, she's here. Do you want me to go get some coffee or something?"

For a long moment he looked at her, his tawny eyes dark and enigmatic. And then he leaned over and kissed her, a brief, hard kiss. "I want you with me," he said.

The living room was empty. From somewhere in the distance Ferris could hear the sound of voices, and it took her a moment to place them. Grace Kelly and Cary Grant, bickering throughout eternity, as *To Catch a Thief* played on the Blue-Ray.

Danielle was sitting curled up in the middle of Ferris's big bed, dressed in jeans and a sweater, looking vastly different from the elegant creature she usually resembled. Her eyes were faintly red-rimmed, any makeup washed off long ago. In her arms, purring like a docile house pussy, sat Blackie, the smoky-gray alley cat.

Danielle was watching her brother, a wary expression on her face, a stubborn thrust to her lower lip. Blackheart stood motionless beside Ferris, and she found herself holding her breath.

"You look about three years old with that pout," he said finally.

"I feel about three years old," Dany said.

The light in the bedroom was filtered by the foggy day, but Blackheart was nothing if not observant. His eyes narrowed. "Who hit you? If it was that swine McNab . . ."

"McNab? What made you think of him?" She looked startled, hopeful and worried.

"He showed up at my apartment, demanding to know where you were. He said you stole his car."

"Borrowed it," Dany amended with a shrug.

"He also said he was going to marry you." Blackheart moved into the room, his lean body tense and edgy. "Which is, as far as I'm concerned, the worst thing you've done to me. I can put up with being implicated in crimes I didn't commit, I can put up with being framed for your latest clumsy attempt, and I can put up with my professional reputation going down the tubes. I can even contemplate the idea of an undeserved jail sentence with a fair amount of equanimity. But the thought of having Stephen McNab as a brother-in-law is too much."

A small, wistful smile curved Dany's mouth. A mouth that was almost a twin to Blackheart's, Ferris noticed with belated surprise. "Don't worry, I'm not going to marry him. It wouldn't work. And I expect I'll be the one who's going to jail, not you. And I'm sorry, though that doesn't do much good. Does that improve matters?"

"No," said Blackheart. "I want my sister back."

Dany dissolved into hiccuppy sobs, Blackheart took her into his arms, and Ferris wisely tiptoed out the door, closing it behind them. Blackie made it out just in time, having a typical feline disdain for heavy emotion, and followed his mistress into the kitchen, his spiky gray tail switching back and forth.

"All right, I've been ignoring you," Ferris murmured, searching through the refrigerator for guilt food. "I've had problems of my own, you know."

Blackie jumped onto the counter, his bulk landing with a heavy thud, and his only response was a haughty meow. "Yes, I know," she said, dishing out the last of the herring and opening herself a Diet Coke. "You don't care about my problems, you only care about your stomach. What I want to know, cat of mine, is why you were cuddling up to a stranger? The only other stranger I've seen you tolerate is Blackheart. Do you have a certain affinity for cat burglars?"

Blackie shoved his face into the herring, ignoring her. Ferris levered herself up onto the narrow counter beside him, swinging her long legs. "Who can blame you?" she murmured, half to herself. "I have a certain affinity for them myself."

She was halfway through her soda when Blackheart emerged from the bedroom, Dany trailing behind him. "What makes you think everyone knows what we're going for?" Dany demanded, crowding into the tiny kitchen with them. "The Van Gogh is the logical target. When something like that is available, why would anyone go for the eggs?"

"Eggs?" Ferris echoed.

Blackheart opened her refrigerator, clucked in disgust and closed it again, leaning against the counter, brushing against her with that casual gesture that bespoke complete ease with another's body. She only wished she could be so nonchalant with his. The feel of his arm against her was reminding her of last night all too vividly. "Dany and her heavy-fisted accomplice were planning to steal the Faberge eggs from the museum. They naively assumed that everyone would be watching the Van Gogh. What I've been trying to point out to her is that McNab, even in his besotted condition, is no fool. He knows that if a Blackheart is around and in a larcenous mood, that Blackheart is going to go for jewels. And the most bejeweled things in San Francisco at the moment are the Faberge eggs. Ergo, Blackheart's sister is going to go for the eggs."

"McNab never asked me what our target was."

"Did he have time?" Blackheart countered. Dany's response was a surprising blush, and Blackheart swore. "I guess I'm going to have to put up with a bloody policeman for an in-law. He's going to have to make an honest woman of you."

"I'm not going to let him compromise his principles for me," Dany said nobly, her eyes filling again with tears.

"Fine," said Blackheart, taking the can of Diet Coke from Ferris's hand and drinking. He shuddered and handed it back. "Then you can compromise your principles for him. After all, you're a thief, born and bred, and you're planning to give up your wicked ways. I'd think you'd let him meet you halfway."

"Do you miss it?" Dany asked the question Ferris didn't dare put.

Blackheart placed an arm around Ferris's waist, drawing her closer.

"Francesca keeps me distracted whenever I get a larcenous urge. I'm certain you can count on McNab to do the same for you."

"Maybe," Dany said, reaching forward to stroke Blackie's thick gray fur. If there was one thing Blackie hated, it was affectionate gestures when he was pigging out, but he lifted his sour-cream-dappled face, looked at Dany, and purred.

"I know what you're getting as a wedding present," Ferris said sourly. "Let's hope McNab isn't allergic to cats."

"I don't know," Dany said. "I hardly know anything about him. It would be a ridiculous mistake to marry him."

"It seems to me, sister mine, that you've made a great many mistakes in your life. This one just might turn out well."

"You're forgetting about Marco. He's not going to let me go without a fight."

"He's not going to have a choice in the matter. He can't pull off the museum heist alone, can he?"

"No."

"And at this point you haven't committed any crimes on American soil?"

"Except for stealing McNab's car."

Blackheart dismissed that minor technicality with a wave of his hand. "And you managed to confuse the European authorities thoroughly. As long as you stay in this country, safely married to your cop, you should manage to live happily ever after. I think we can count on McNab to take care of Marco."

"Make him see reason." Dany turned to Ferris for support. "There's no future for a thief and a cop."

"Blackheart believes what he wants to believe. Unfortunately, he's usually right."

"Maybe." Dany didn't sound so sure. "But I don't think so. Not this time. I'm going to take a shower, if that's all right."

"Go right ahead," Ferris said. "Blackheart and I will still be here, arguing."

"We're not arguing, we're planning," he corrected her as Dany disappeared. "And all we have to worry about—" his voice was a silken purr "—is trapping Ferris Byrd's thieving ex-fiancé."

She jumped, looking into Blackheart's tawny eyes. "I thought you said you were no longer thieving?"

"I'm not. You happen to have more than one former fiancé."

"Don't be absurd!" Ferris protested, sliding off the counter. Unfortunately Blackheart helped her down, easing her body alongside his in a manner calculated to make her brain melt. They were alone in the tiny kitchen, and in the distance they could hear the muffled sound of the shower. She also noticed he'd said she had two former fiancés. If she wondered where they stood after last night, he'd just obliquely answered the question—still at an impasse.

"Phillip wouldn't steal anything. He doesn't need to—he inherited a fortune from his father."

"He also has substantial campaign debts and a very tight race with a Hispanic congressman from San Diego. He needs more television time, and that's very, very expensive."

Ferris stared at him in disbelief—a disbelief tempered by the fact that she'd learned to trust Blackheart. If he said a notorious straight-arrow like Phillip Merriam was straying off center, he was most likely right. "What's he going to steal?"

"What else? His mother's Van Gogh."

"That's ridiculous! He wouldn't steal from his own mother. I don't believe you."

"Don't you?" It was a mild enough question.

Ferris hesitated. "I suppose I do. But why would he take such a risk? Couldn't he just ask his mother for the money? Why would he jeopardize his reputation and his career like that?"

"I've been doing a little checking in the last few days. He's borrowed everything he can, legally. And Regina, bless her heart, supports Congressman Diaz. Not to mention that she wouldn't sacrifice a treasure like the Van Gogh for the sake of her son's ambition. She wants it to belong to the people, and that's what will happen to it, if Phillip doesn't get there first."

"I still can't believe he'd take the risk," she said stubbornly.

Blackheart put a hand under her chin, forcing her eyes to meet his. "You know as well as I do how seductive danger can be. Your bland and boring Phillip is just about to be deflowered. Unless, of course, we stop him."

"Why would you be willing to do that? There's no love lost between you and Phillip. I wouldn't think you'd care what happened to him."

"I don't. But I do, however, have a fondness for Regina, and Phillip's disgrace would be hers. And there's one other little problem. Phillip's planning to frame me for the theft."

"Don't be ridiculous!"

"He had me recheck the security system yesterday, when you and I both know he went over it with Nelbert and McNab not three days ago. He made sure I left my fingerprints all over everything. He's also asked me to meet him at the house tonight at midnight, to discuss certain events in Madrid. I'm sure I'm supposed to arrive and discover the painting missing, with even more clues leading directly to me. If it weren't so obvious, I might be irritated. But with a clod like Nelbert helping him, he was bound to be fairly basic in his planning."

"Nelbert's in on it, too?"

"You can't trust anyone nowadays," Blackheart said with a soulful look. "Nelbert is as sleazy as they come. He's just managed to keep a lower profile than I have in my past indiscretions."

"That's a polite term for breaking and entering."

"Oh, I'm always polite," he said.

"So what are we going to do about it?"

"We aren't going to do anything. Tonight's the night of the circus performance. I'll be there anyway, but instead of watching the pickpockets and housebreakers, I'm going to keep my eye on the good senator. If I can't catch him in the act and stop him, then I deserve to take the fall for it."

"And what will I be doing?"

"You'll be circulating among the crowds, doing what you do so well."

"What's that?"

"Being charming. Of course you reserve that charm for everyone but me."

"Maybe I keep my charm for those who deserve it."

"Maybe," said Blackheart, pulling her into his arms, his mouth very close to hers. "And maybe you trust me enough not to have to charm me. Maybe you know that your very presence on this earth is charm enough for me." He brushed his lips over hers, a brief, glancing caress, one she reached for, pressing her mouth against his, deepening the kiss.

His hands slid down her back, catching the seat of her jeans and pulling her up tight against him. She could feel his arousal, feel the taut, hungry heat of him, and she moaned deep in the back of her throat.

"I wish your sister wasn't here," she whispered against his shoulder when he finally broke the kiss.

A sudden irritated expression crossed his face, and he released her abruptly. "How long has it been since you heard the shower?"

"I wasn't paying any attention." She followed him out of the kitchen, down two steps into the dining room and up another two to her bedroom. "She couldn't have left, Blackheart. She would have had to go past us."

Blackheart had already yanked open the bathroom door, exposing the empty room beyond. He swore, sharply and succinctly. "Do you think a Blackheart has to worry about things like front doors and stairs? If *you* can climb up your balcony and break in, it would be child's play for Dany to escape that way." He climbed across the bed that filled the small room, yanked open the terrace door and stepped out into the fitful sunlight. "Damn!"

She'd followed him, leaning against the open door, watching him out of somber eyes. "Where do you think she's gone?"

"That's one question," he agreed. "The other one is why?" He came back into the bedroom, no longer interested in the rumpled bed or Ferris's heated body. "I think, dear heart, we may be in for a rough ride."

Chapter Seventeen

Sabotage
(Lime Grove 1936)

THE EVENING WAS a zoo in more ways than one. Ferris threaded her way through the glittering, absurdly bejeweled crowds at the circus, a perfect smile plastered to her face, her eyes darting into shadowy corners, alert for the reappearance of Dany Bunce. There was no sign of her, though she kept running into a glowering Stephen McNab. Clearly his luck was as bad as hers, or he would have worn a more pleasant expression.

She was leaning against the side of the grandstand, watching her old friends the white tigers go through their paces, when she felt someone breathing down her neck. She looked up into the detective's steely eyes with the unflinching courage born of complete desperation. "I haven't seen her," she said, forestalling his obvious question.

"If I find you have anything to do with her getting away, I'm going to put you in the slammer along with Blackheart," he growled. The sound was fiercer than her old friend Tarzan's theatrical roars from the center ring.

Ferris thought about it for a moment. "I might prefer that," she said finally. "If you're going to arrest Blackheart on trumped-up charges, I'd just as soon go along with him."

"They won't be trumped up. I'm going to nail him for grand larceny, breaking and entering and obstructing justice, and I'll get you as an accessory."

"You can also charge me with littering," she added politely.

"Don't push me."

"Don't push me," Ferris countered. "Blackheart hasn't done any of those things in years, certainly not within your jurisdiction, and he paid for his earlier crimes."

"Six months in jail is not paying for more than fifteen years of crime."

"Are you a cop, McNab? Or are you God?"

He didn't say anything for a moment, his jaw working in rage and frustration. He was able to swallow it, a shudder leaving his body. "I need to find her," he said in a quieter voice. "I can't let her disappear. I need her."

"Do you think there's much of a future for you if you hound her brother into jail?" She refused to feel sorry for him.

"Her brother can do anything he damned well pleases. He can knock over Fort Knox for all I care. I'm not on duty tonight, and I'm not on his case anymore. It's somebody else's problem."

Marco Porcini was beginning his high wire act. Ferris looked up and shivered. "I'll do what I can. So, as a matter of fact, will Blackheart."

It must have galled him to accept aid from his nemesis. But he swallowed his pride. "I'll be around if you see anything."

She nodded, her attention on Marco's muscular form. She felt rather than saw him leave, so enrapt in watching the strong body overhead that she couldn't pull her eyes away. She didn't want to look. Even the sight of someone braving such great heights made her heart pound and her palms sweat in empathic fright. The net beneath offered no comfort. She watched Porcini's slippered feet dance along the high wire and wanted to throw up.

She heard a murmur of appreciation from the crowd, a ripple of laughter, one that she couldn't identify. Marco was doing nothing more than dancing lightly on the wire, nothing to encourage such a reaction. The reaction was growing, and Ferris reluctantly pulled her eyes away to the side, where a clown with oversize shoes, a gigantic purple wig, glowing nose and preposterous figure was making his way up the rope ladder to the high wire.

"What are you doing?" Blackheart breathed in her ear.

"Damn!" She turned her complete attention to the man who'd materialized behind her, grateful for the distraction. "You do creep up on a person, don't you? I was doing what you ordered me to do. Watching the circus and keeping an eye out for suspicious behavior. You told me I wasn't allowed to help you with your trap. For that matter, why aren't you lying in wait near the Van Gogh?"

Blackheart shrugged. "Nothing was happening. And I didn't order you. I suggested you might be more constructive down here. Particularly since I planned to go in over the roofs. It was hard enough for you in the daylight. Trust me, you wouldn't have liked it at all tonight."

"Did you go in over the roofs?"

"Actually, no," he admitted, keeping a wary eye on her. "But I might have had to. I still might have to, and you know you don't want to do that. You can barely stand to watch Porcini." He glanced up, and Ferris followed his gaze. The clown had reached the opposite end of the tightrope, and with a great show of incompetence and trepidation the figure started edging out onto the taut line.

Porcini reacted with theatrical rage, gesturing the clown to go away. The audience was in stitches, Ferris's palms were soaking, and she pulled her attention away from the spectacle. "No, I wouldn't want to climb over the roofs," she agreed.

"So why are you dressed like that?"

Ferris looked down at her black silk jumpsuit, an outfit that effectively covered her from wrist to ankle. An impressive expanse of pale breast was visible, but she only had to do up a couple of buttons to cover up even that amount of white flesh. "Don't you like it? It cost a small fortune."

"It's also brand-new. I know your clothes well enough to know you just bought it, and I know as well as you do how effective an outfit that would be for a cat burglar. Forget it, Francesca. You're not going to have anything to do with the festivities tonight."

"Why not?"

"Because I don't want you getting hurt."

"Why not?"

"Don't be obtuse. You know why not," he growled. "Even if there's no future for us, I want you to be alive and well enough to enjoy a future with someone else."

Ferris's fear of heights vanished, replaced by a new apprehension. "There's no future for us?" she echoed.

He pulled his eyes away from the act overhead for a brief moment. "Is there?"

It was her turn to look away to the figures of Porcini and the clown. They were engaged in some sort of mock struggle and the audience was eating it up. "Blackheart," she said, her voice raw with emotion, "I—"

"Oh, my God!" It wasn't a shout, it was a strangled gasp of horror as Blackheart effectively forgot her existence. "That's Dany up there."

Just at that moment Porcini lost his formidable balance. Clutching at Dany he fell, yanking her off the wire. Then losing his grip, he tumbled toward the net. Instinctively tucking himself into the proper position for falling, he landed smack-dab in the middle of the net.

The net should have rebounded, sending him into a standing position. It didn't. With an ominous rending sound it pulled free from one of its supports, sending Marco hurtling to the sawdust floor.

Throughout the tent, the laughter had been replaced by frightened screams. But Marco rolled into the sawdust, performed a somersault and ended standing, his arms held overhead in the age-old demand for applause.

He got it in spades. The crowd went wild, delighted at being tricked for a moment into actual fear. They seemed to have forgotten the figure still up on the wire, clinging with gloved hands, swinging over the broken net.

The silence fell, as one by the one the audience remembered and looked upward. Ferris could feel Blackheart, taut and sweating beside her, could hear his whispered words, part threat, part encouragement. "You can do it, you can do it. You stupid idiot, climb up there."

Dany swung her leg around. The oversize shoe fell off, tumbling to the floor, and her leg missed the wire. She tried again, one hand slipping and then grabbing again, and the audience gasped. One more try and she was up, sitting on the wire, looking down at the cheering spectators with pantomimed surprise.

She then proceeded to crawl on her hands and knees across the wire, exaggerating every step to the delight of the crowd. When she reached the platform at the end of the line, Marco was waiting for her, a huge, toothy grin on his sweaty face, a murderous glare in his eyes.

Blackheart started toward the base of the pole, when McNab suddenly appeared out of nowhere. "I'll take care of this," he said in a determined tone of voice.

Blackheart let him go. "Do you think he's a match for Porcini?" Ferris questioned, watching as Marco half dragged, half carried the penitent clown out of the tent, with McNab just behind them.

"I wouldn't be standing here if I didn't."

"Maybe you can't resist me?" she suggested lightly. "That certainly was a terrific act, wasn't it? They had the entire audience going. I didn't realize Dany still performed."

"It wasn't an act."

"I beg your pardon?"

"What you just witnessed," Blackheart said in a glum voice, "was attempted murder. By my sister, of a man who doubtless deserved it. I just hope McNab didn't catch on."

"Patrick." Regina Merriam joined them, perfectly dressed as always in blue silk, her mane of white hair neatly arranged, her face perfectly made-up. "And Ferris. I wondered where you two were. Wasn't that simply marvelous? I had no idea the Porcinis were so talented."

"They are quite different, aren't they?" Ferris said, casting a worried glance at Blackheart's troubled expression. And then she noticed Regina wasn't looking terribly happy, either. As usual she'd put a calm face on things, but Ferris had known her long enough and well enough to realize something was wrong.

"Are you feeling all right?" Blackheart managed to pull himself out of his abstraction.

"As a matter of fact, I was a little worried about something," she confessed with a contrived laugh. "I know you'll think I'm silly, but I'm concerned about the Van Gogh. It moves to the museum tomorrow, and I can't help thinking that this would be the perfect time to take it."

Ferris felt her heart twist at the sight of her old friend's desperate dignity. "Are you worried about the Van Gogh, Regina?" she asked gently. "Or about Phillip?"

Regina shut her eyes for a moment, leaning back against the grandstand. When she opened them, they were glittering with tears. "Does everyone know but me?"

"Only Francesca and I have guessed," Blackheart said gently. "Don't worry, Regina. We won't let him do anything foolish. I promise you."

Regina smiled through her tears. "I think I must have spoiled him. He was always so charming. It was easy to give him anything he wanted. He's just used to having everything."

"Maybe. I may just teach him a lesson or two tonight," Blackheart said.

Regina nodded. "I think it might be long overdue."

"You stay down here, Regina," Ferris said, pressing the thin hand that suddenly felt frail. "I'll make sure everything's all right."

"I knew I could count on you both," she said simply. The grounds were almost deserted as Ferris followed Blackheart out into the night, heading toward the mansion. She had to run to keep up, and her high-heeled black sandals sank into the damp grass with each step. "Wait a minute," she gasped, struggling along.

"I don't want you involved in this," he snarled, not slowing his pace. "I told you that. This thing could turn ugly, and I don't want you in the line of fire."

"Why didn't you tell Regina that? She would have kept me with her."

"I wasn't about to tell an old lady her son might be dangerous. It's hard enough for her to deal with the fact that he's turning larcenous."

"I hadn't thought of that." She stopped for a moment, pulled off her shoes and threw them into the bushes, sprinting to catch up with Blackheart's elegant figure. He was wearing evening dress, as were most of the men tonight, and Ferris couldn't help but think that a tuxedo was the perfect outfit for a society burglar.

"Well, think of it. And know that if Phillip does anything to hurt you, then Danielle won't be the only Blackheart capable of attempted murder."

"I can go back."

His arm caught her, tugging her along. "At this point I think you're safer with me," he said, resigned. "Just watch out for Nelbert. He's even stupider than Phillip, and a great deal more ruthless. Keep quiet and do as I say. Understood?"

"Yes, sir."

They went in through the terrace door. The house was dark. Most of the servants were down at the circus, and only Nelbert's hired security guards were in sight. It was child's play for Blackheart to move past them, the work of two seconds to go through the solid lock on the terrace door. And then they were creeping through the darkened house, up the long, curving stairs, Ferris fully as noiseless as the more experienced Blackheart.

They stopped on the second-floor landing. Fitful beams of light were filtering downward from the third-floor landing, and Ferris could hear the muffled sound of voices. Without ceremony Blackheart pushed her against a wall and clapped a hand over her mouth. "They're early." Barely a trace of sound issued forth, and Ferris wondered if she was getting adept at reading lips. He removed his hand, still keeping his body pressed against hers, and the light in his eyes came from determination and an unholy excitement.

"What if they have guns?" She mouthed her response.

Blackheart shrugged. "Then duck."

"How reassuring." It was hard to be icy when you were speaking in something softer than a whisper, but her irony managed to reach Blackheart anyway, and he grinned.

"Listen, angel, you chose to come along," he taunted her. "If it makes you feel any better, I don't think either of them are armed. Phillip is too smart for that and Nelbert is too dumb."

"There are just the two of them?"

"Maybe."

"Maybe? Don't you know?"

"Someone else just came in downstairs. One set of footsteps. It could be a maid, or it could be an accomplice. I'm not taking any chances."

"I don't hear a thing," she protested, not making a sound.

"That's because you don't listen." He tugged at her, pulling her under the curve of the winding stairs. "We'll wait here. The Hardy Boys will be down before long, carrying their ill-gotten gains. They're lucky *The Hyacinths* is so small. It would have served Phillip right if it was the size of a Bierstadt."

"How big is a Bierstadt?"

"Room size." The footsteps directly above them signaled that the thieves were on the move. "When they get down here you stay put. I'll confront them."

"With what? The force of your personality? Blackheart, this is danger-ous!"

"Sweetheart, just because they won't be carrying guns doesn't mean I'm similarly inclined." Reaching down to his ankle, he pulled out a very small, very nasty-looking little gun. "And yes, I have a permit. It's very legal."

"I wasn't going to ask that. I was going to ask if it was loaded."

"There's not much use in having a gun if it isn't loaded. First rule of firearms, darling."

"What's the second?"

"Don't brandish it, if you're not willing to use it."

"And the third."

"I already told you that one. Duck."

They stood there, huddled under the stairs for a time that stretched on endlessly, listening to the steady advance of the felons from the floor above, the accomplice from the floor below. In actuality it couldn't have been more than a minute and a half, but the time stretched and pulled like a rubber band until Ferris was ready to scream.

Blackheart was in total control, only the glitter in his dark eyes betraying just how much he was enjoying all this, Ferris thought bitterly. He waited until the last moment, until beyond the last moment, when the shadowy figures were almost ready to start down the second flight of stairs.

"I think you've gone far enough," he said calmly. His hand reached out and hit the light switch, flooding the landing with light, and as he stepped into the hallway, his nasty little gun was pointed directly at the center of Regina's priceless painting.

Phillip swore, dropping the picture, frame and all, onto his toe. Nelbert backed away, an ugly expression on his ugly face, and began fumbling under his coat.

Ferris decided it was time to contribute to the situation. "He's going for his gun, Blackheart," she said, stepping out of her hiding place.

"Get back, damn it!" Blackheart swore, diving for Nelbert before his hand could emerge with the gun. The force of his one hundred eighty-some pounds, catapulted against Nelbert's two hundred forty, was enough to knock the larger man off balance. He began to tumble down the stairs, grasping for Blackheart. Blackheart stepped neatly out of reach, watching with no reaction at all as Nelbert fell down a total of seventeen stairs to end lying in a crumpled heap at the bottom. He was moaning slightly, reassuring anyone who happened to care that he was still alive.

Regina was standing there, a rueful expression on her face. She looked up at the tableau above her, and an expression of utter sorrow darkened her faded blue eyes. She started up the stairs, holding on to the marble banister like a woman whose life had been shattered. In one day she'd aged twenty years, and Ferris was sorely tempted to toss down her witless son after his accomplice.

Blackheart looked up too, into Phillip's expressionless face. "Put the painting back, you jackass," he said mildly. "You've done enough harm for one night."

"You don't understand," Phillip whined. Golden, handsome Senator Phillip Merriam whined. "It costs too much to get elected nowadays. I have to have the money."

"I want you to withdraw from the race, Phillip." Regina's voice was cold, her tone determined as she reached the second-floor landing.

"Mother . . ."

"I want you to withdraw from the race, or I will turn you over for prosecution."

"You wouldn't!" He gasped.

"I would." She cast a beseeching glance at Blackheart. "Can you dispose of that—that trash downstairs?" She gestured toward Nelbert's lumpish, groaning figure.

"Certainly. Are you planning to file charges?"

"That's up to Phillip. What's it to be?"

"Can't we talk . . . ?"

"No. Your decision."

Phillip hung his elegant blond head. Ferris almost thought she heard a snuffle of misery. "I'll withdraw," he said sulkily.

Regina nodded, satisfied. "In that case, just dump his accomplice someplace and leave it at that. I doubt Mr. Nelbert will be interested in pursuing our acquaintance after this fiasco."

"What about the painting?" Ferris asked. It was lying facedown on the carpet, no way to treat a masterpiece.

"Do you suppose you could put it in the museum on your way home? Just leave it inside the door. If someone else comes along and takes it, they're welcome to it."

"Certainly." Blackheart gingerly picked it up, eyeing the glowing colors with a mixture of admiration and distrust. "Come along, Francesca."

For a moment she didn't move—she stood there staring at the shell of what had once, years ago, seemed her most attainable dream. With a tiny, imperceptible shake of her head she followed Blackheart down the stairs, passing Regina's upright figure with a brief, sympathetic touch on the arm.

Trace Walker materialized from the shadows, a questioning look on his bland, beefy face. "Take care of Nelbert, would you?" Blackheart requested of his partner. "We've got something to do."

"Sure thing. Do I have to be gentle?"

Blackheart grinned. "Use your judgment."

They were halfway across the lawn, almost at the circus area, when Ferris spoke. Blackheart had grabbed a raincoat from a hall closet to drape around the masterpiece, and he strode along carrying his burden, seemingly lost in thought.

"What's going to happen to Phillip?" she asked, wishing she hadn't been so precipitate about tossing her shoes. The grass beneath her stockinged feet was damp, sending a chill up her back.

"Do you care?" Blackheart didn't slow his pace.

"For Regina's sake. And yes, for his sake. I was once rather fond of him."

"Pretty tepid emotions to base an engagement on. Do you always agree to marry someone on such mundane grounds?"

"Not always." She wasn't about to offer anything more, and he wasn't about to ask.

"I expect Phillip will run in the next election, and probably win it," Blackheart said, answering her previous question.

"Patrick, the man's a sleaze with no moral judgment whatsoever, a liar, and more than willing to frame someone else for his misdeeds."

"Yup," said Blackheart. "At that rate there's no telling how far he'll go."

"You're such a cynic."

"I know," he said, unrepentant. "There's just one thing that's worrying me."

"What's that?"

"Where the hell is McNab?"

Chapter Eighteen

Rope
(Warner Brothers 1948)

IT TOOK BLACKHEART less than a minute to crack the heavy locks that guarded the entrance to the Museum of Decorative Arts. He clicked his tongue in professional disgust as he undid the final bolt. "We're going to have to do something about these locks," he muttered.

"We? I thought Nelbert Securities was in charge of the museum." Ferris shivered lightly in the breeze that was picking up. There was only the barest sliver of a moon that night, a good night for going a-burglaring, Blackheart had always told her. The noise and lights from the circus seemed far away, almost on another planet, and Ferris devoutly hoped everyone that mattered was down there, including Marco Porcini, McNab and Dany. She had the unpleasant suspicion that they were all much closer than that.

"You don't seriously think Nelbert's going to keep the job, do you?" Blackheart countered, following her into the darkened main hallway. "Even without formal charges, word will get out, and very quickly. Nelbert's washed up in this town, as well he should be."

"And you think you'll get the job?" She shivered again. She'd never liked the museum. Regina's robber baron father had constructed it to house his collection, and it had been designed after an Italian castle dating from the early fifteenth century. It was built of massive stone, cold and damp and eerie, and the entire feeling of the place was oppressive.

"We're the logical choice." Blackheart headed for the checkroom, dumped the raincoat-covered painting behind the half door and turned to face her. "Regina already had me double-check Nelbert's arrangements for the Van Gogh, and I also did a once-over on everything else. Including the Faberge eggs."

"Do you think they would have been able to take them?"

"I have no doubt at all they would. And I'm not sure we're out of the woods yet. I won't rest easy until I find out where McNab and my sister have gone."

A strange noise had been worrying away at the back of Ferris's brain. For a moment she'd been considering large, evil rodents, then she realized what the sound was. "I don't know about Dany," she said gloomily. "But I think we've found McNab."

He was propped up against a massive marble column just inside the Egyptian room. There was blood on his forehead, and he was moaning groggily.

"What happened?" Blackheart demanded with more tension than sympathy, pulling him up by his lapels.

McNab slapped his hands away. "What do you think happened? Porcini blindsided me. I followed them in here and just when I was about to arrest him, the lights went out. Damned fool."

"Porcini?"

"Me. I should have paid more attention. But he was hurting Dany, twisting her arm, and I got so mad I couldn't see straight."

"They're here?"

"They're here. They've gone after the eggs. He was dragging Dany, and she was putting up a hell of a fuss, but I imagine he was able to make her do what he wanted. Dammit, she was crying."

"Well, if she'd tried to push me off a tightrope, I might want to twist her arm, too," Blackheart said fairly.

Ferris glared at him in the shadowed room. "What are you planning to do about it?"

McNab struggled to his feet, swaying slightly. "I've got to find Dany."

"First you need to call in reinforcements," Blackheart corrected him. "There's a crime being committed, and someone's going to have to arrest Porcini."

"But what about Dany?"

"We'll have her safely away by the time your backups get here. Just tell them to be quiet." McNab still didn't move, and Blackheart gave him an overenthusiastic shove. "Go ahead. I'm going to do something about the alarm system."

"Why?" Ferris had the temerity to ask.

"Because I don't want the alarm going off if somebody makes a false move. Whether I like it or not, I'm in this just as deeply as Porcini and Dany, and it's my neck I'm saving, too."

"All right, I can accept that," Ferris said. "What do you want me to do?"

"I want you to go back to the cloakroom and hide down behind the counter. Keep your eyes on the Van Gogh at all times, and don't move until you hear my voice."

"The hell with that. I'm not going to sit passively by, doing nothing."

"Watching the most valuable work of art in the city isn't doing nothing."

"I'm not—"

"You are!" His grip on her arm was viselike, just short of bruising, and she had no choice but to allow herself to be hustled ignominiously back to the cloakroom. He shoved her down onto the floor, glowering at her. "Stay put. It will all be over in a few minutes."

"Go to hell, Blackheart."

He grinned, and once more she recognized the reckless excitement that was throbbing through his veins. "Only if you're there, dear heart." And he disappeared into the vast darkness of the museum.

Ferris hadn't even seen where McNab had gone to call in reinforcements. It didn't matter. She wasn't going to sit there and babysit an oil painting that no one seemed to want, no matter how much it was worth. The stone floors were icy beneath her stockinged feet, and the shadows and dark shapes looming up made her skin crawl. She had only the faintest recollection of where the fabulous jeweled eggs were kept, and in the dark they'd be harder still to find, but she was damned if she was going to sit and cower while everyone else had all the fun. She'd suffered too much already. She was going to see this thing through to the end.

At the center of the museum was a great hall that had once been filled with armor, stuffed elephants, Rodin sculptures, and anything else that wouldn't fit into a smaller room. That hodgepodge had mostly either been tossed or relegated to other spaces, and the great hall had been divided up into fifteen or twenty smaller rooms, their partitions reaching halfway up the stone balconies on either side. The Faberge eggs were in one of the twenty, but Ferris couldn't even begin to guess which one.

Unfortunately she didn't have to.

"There you are, *bella.*" A burly arm snaked around her neck, pulling her back against a strong, sweaty body. "I thought you might show up sooner or later. Where's the boyfriend? He's not going to do you much good, any more than that stupid cop could stop me. There are some things that are just meant to happen, and this is one of them."

"Let me go!" At least, that was what she tried to say. With his muscled forearm across her throat, the words came out in a muffled oomph.

Even someone of Marco's self-absorbed intellect could figure out what she was saying, given the circumstances. "I'm sorry, but I need you," he said, half carrying, half dragging her up a flight of stairs. They, like almost everything else in the damned building, were stone, and banged against Ferris's shins as she flailed and kicked.

When they reached the top he flung her forward, so that she sprawled facedown on the equally hard floor of what was doubtless one of the balconies overlooking the great hall. She stayed there for a moment, absorbing the impact of the unforgiving stone, trying to figure out how she was going to get out of this current mess.

Marco locked the balcony door behind them, then crossed to the railing and began fiddling with something Ferris couldn't see. "Now if your lover had just left well enough alone, we wouldn't be in this predicament. There was a heat sensing device surrounding the doorway to the room with the eggs, and it would have been a simple enough matter to use some fire extinguisher to pass through. But no, he had to add infrared. Therefore—" he reached down and hauled her to her unsteady feet "—we have to go in from the top."

A wire stretched across the vast, cavernous expanse of the great hall, reaching to the opposite balcony. Even in the shadowy darkness Ferris could see Dany's absurd white clown's face at the other end, standing by the wire. "I hate to say this," Ferris whispered, "but what's this 'we'?"

"But you're going with me, of course. Otherwise, how can I trust my lethal ex-partner not to loosen the rigging? Daniella!" he shouted across the room. "See who I have with me! Your brother's girlfriend decided she would help me out. Not that I gave her much choice, you understand. But if you unfasten the rope you don't just send me to my death. You send her, too. *Capisce?*"

"I understand." Her voice was dull, its tone accepting.

"So you will make sure the rigging stays taut, won't you, *cara?* Once I get the eggs and make it safely back to the other side, then you will be free. I'd love to teach you another lesson, but I'm afraid I don't have the time. But don't worry. Your handsome cop will arrest you, and you'll have plenty of time in American jails to think about all the mistakes you made—the biggest of which was thinking you could fool me."

He climbed up onto the balcony, balancing lightly over the great drop beneath him, and Ferris began to sweat. He'd changed from his spangled spandex into a loose-fitting jumpsuit, and he looked fully as graceful as Blackheart ever had. And then, to Ferris's absolute horror, he reached down and hauled her up onto the wide stone balustrade beside him.

"I'm afraid of heights," she said through chattering teeth.

"That is a great deal too bad. Because you're coming with me."

"Where?" she demanded, mystified.

"Out there." He gestured to the taut wire in front of them as if it were a boulevard.

"I can't. I'll fall."

"Perhaps. But not if you're careful. Don't worry, I don't intend to make you walk it yourself. That takes years of practice to perfect. I'll simply carry you. As long as you keep perfectly still and don't struggle, we should be fine. Otherwise I'll drop you. And it's a long ways down."

"You can't do this."

He jerked her arm, hard, and tossed her over his shoulder with effortless disdain. "I'm about to. I've done high wire acts with trained chimpanzees who don't weigh any more than you do. If they can survive, I expect you can. If you fall, just close your eyes and pray."

Ferris was already doing just that, praying with all her might as Porcini stepped out into space.

"Ferris, I'm sorry," Dany called in a low voice. "I didn't mean to get you into this."

Keeping her head down and her eyes shut wasn't helping matters, so Ferris lifted her head to look at the clown across the vast expanse that was slowly diminishing—too slowly. "Why did you run?" she asked, her voice a raw thread of sound. Porcini's shoulder was digging painfully into her stomach, and her fear strangled the breath in her throat, but if she was about to die she might as well die enlightened.

"I couldn't let all of you risk your futures for me," Dany replied miserably. "Particularly Stephen. I love him. I couldn't let him destroy himself over me."

"But we could have helped you," Ferris said earnestly.

"If I were you, *cara*," Marco wheezed into her ear, "I wouldn't shift around too much. I was mistaken—you're a little heavier than a chimpanzee." He stopped where he was, looking around him. A huge marble column stood nearby, some relic of an ancient temple. The flat, pitted top of it was perhaps twenty-four inches square.

With a sickening whoosh of air Porcini swung her limp body over his head and deposited her on the top of the column. For a moment she clung to him in panic, but he pulled away, and she felt her balance begin to give, could see the floor, miles away, looming up to meet her.

She pulled back, overcompensating for a moment so that she swayed backward. Finally she held still, clinging to the tiny bit of space like an angry cat, doing her best to control her rapid breathing, her trembling limbs, her very heartbeat.

"Now you be a good girl and stay there, *cara*. And if Danielle obeys my orders and doesn't try to murder me again, everything will be just fine." He looked across at the clown figure waiting on the opposite balcony. "Are you ready, Danielle? Send me the rope."

There was no further hesitation. Though Ferris's brain was fogged with fear, she could just make out the rigging Danielle was sending toward Marco's waiting figure. A rope and pulley sort of affair, sliding across the taut wire. Marco looked calm and alert, as casual as if he were standing on a boardwalk and not a thin line of wire. He caught the pulley when it reached him, tested it for a moment, then dropped off the wire, letting himself down the rope toward the room twenty feet below.

Ferris found herself holding her breath. The best thing in the world would have been for him to fall, but right now, in her precarious position, she didn't want to see anyone fall. She had the horrible certainty that if Marco fell, she'd fall too, in some sort of sick empathy.

She could just see him beyond the partition. He was within ten feet of the floor, within ten feet of the beautiful, intricate eggs that Ferris hated with a very real passion, when the building was flooded with light.

She blinked, swaying on her tiny platform, for a moment unable to see a thing. She heard McNab's voice, strong and sure and very angry. "Nice of you to drop in, Porcini."

Marco had already begun to scuttle back up the rope like a fat black spider. A few more feet and he'd be out of their reach, with the only hostage available a stupid fool stuck on the top of a Grecian column.

McNab reached into his coat and pulled out the biggest gun Ferris had ever seen in her life. "If you don't want a bullet right where it would hurt most, Porcini, you'll get your thieving, woman-beating butt down here," he drawled.

Marco ignored him, shinnying up the rope at an astonishing speed. Without further hesitation McNab cocked the pistol, and the sound of gunfire echoed through the stone-walled building.

Marco shrieked, tumbling to the floor. He landed as well as he could, an aerialist used to falls, but the stone floor knew no forgiveness, and he lay there, moaning, the rope still clutched in his hand.

A wave of relief washed over Ferris. McNab hadn't shot Marco; he'd somehow managed to hit the dangling rope.

"Fancy shooting," Blackheart murmured, hauling Marco upright.

"I'm considered something of an expert," McNab said modestly. "I'd better read him his rights." Quickly he did so, saying the familiar television words that went straight through Ferris's brains. All the while Marco remained silent and sullen, glaring at his two captors.

"I think I hear your reinforcements," Blackheart mentioned.

"Damn," said McNab. "You realize he's going to get deported? He'll have a nice cushy ride back to Madrid to stand trial."

"Cheer up. Spanish jails aren't noted for their pleasant atmosphere."

"True enough. There's just one small problem," Stephen said politely.

"What's that?"

"If I hit him, I might jeopardize his arrest. Police brutality and all that. And he really needs to be hit for what he did to Dany."

"Oh, allow me," Blackheart volunteered courteously.

"Be my guest."

Blackheart advanced on the larger, quivering Marco. The blows were swift, efficient and downright dirty. "This one is for my sister," he said between his teeth. "And this is for trying to feed my lady to the tigers."

A second later Marco was back on the floor, groaning very, very loudly. The two men ignored him, just as they ignored the two women overhead who were watching them. "I never thought I'd have you for a brother-in-law," McNab said, shaking his head.

"We all have to make compromises in this life. My sister is worth it."

For the first time McNab looked up, into Danielle's white-painted face. "You know," he said, "I believe she is."

"Blackheart." Ferris's voice was plaintive. Now that the worst danger is over, she could react to her own predicament with at least a touch of asperity. "Would you consider getting me down from here?"

His grin was absolutely heartless. "I'd consider it. However, it's nothing more than you deserve. I told you to stay put."

"I know."

"What kind of future will we have, if I'm not able to trust you?"

"I know," she said miserably.

He didn't move for a long moment. "I guess you suffered enough. I'll get you. Stay right there."

"I'm not moving," Ferris said fervently.

She had a perfect view of the proceedings. She got to watch a moaning, whining Marco being carted away by uniformed police, she got to watch McNab race up to the balcony and pull a weeping, repentant Dany into his arms. She would even have allowed herself a sniffle or two of sympathetic pleasure, if the rest of her attention hadn't been concentrating on Blackheart as he climbed onto the wide stone railing with, she had to admit, even more consummate grace than Marco Porcini. The tightrope wire lay in front of him, thin and deadly.

"Maybe you shouldn't do this," she suggested uneasily. "I can stay here awhile longer. Why don't you go find a crane or something?"

"Nonsense, dear heart," Blackheart said, climbing out onto the wire with surprising skill. "Sooner or later you're going to have to admit you trust me. I can't think of a better way for you to prove it."

"Blackheart," she moaned, hiding her eyes. If he was going to fall to his death on her account, she didn't want to watch it.

He stopped long enough to catch the end of the rope and pulley, then continued. Before climbing out onto the wire he'd taken off his shoes and socks, and his long, narrow bare feet clung to the wire with almost as much self-assurance as Marco's had. "What I liked best," he murmured in a conversational tone as he was about to reach her, "was when Marco kept comparing you to a trained chimpanzee. I'm surprised you didn't clobber him."

"I didn't dare. We both would have fallen."

"I've never known you to refrain from a self-destructive act when your temper is up," he said, stopping beside her. There was a space of some eighteen inches between them. Had they been on nice, level ground it would have been no trouble at all. Or even four feet up in the air. But halfway up in the stratosphere, such a distance was too far to cross.

"I'm not moving, Blackheart," she said fervently. "You can't make me."

"I'm not going on without you."

"Blackheart, Marco was used to lifting weights. A trained chimpanzee, an angry woman was nothing more than a challenge to him. You aren't used to it."

"Now's as good a time as any to learn."

"I don't want to die."

"Neither do I. Come on, dear heart. Just one tiny step. I'll catch you."

"I'll knock you over."

"I trust you, Francesca."

What could she say? He was standing there, seemingly at ease on the thin, coiled wire, watching her tenderly. "Damn you, Blackheart," she muttered, slowly, carefully straightening from her semi-crouching position on the top of the column. "Maybe some things are worth dying for." And without another word she took the step.

He caught her, rocking back under the unexpected weight, and for a moment they swayed there, the wire quivering beneath them. When it finally held steady he moved his hands from their tight grip on her upper arms, slid down to hold her hand, and started edging across the rope.

"Just move very carefully," he said. "And don't look down."

Ferris looked down. Moaning, she jerked her head back up, and spied their destination—the far side of the great hall. "Why don't we go back the way you came? It's shorter." Her tone was still plaintive.

"You'd have to go first." He kept moving, a fraction of an inch at a time, and she followed him, trying to forget about the rooms beneath her, about the Rodin sculpture that could crush her fragile bones, the crusaders' pikes that could skewer her. "Besides, I have something better in mind."

They were halfway across the room. The police had left with their prisoner, and Dany and McNab were nowhere in sight. They were alone on the wire in that shadowy old building. Blackheart still had the end of the rope in his hand as he halted, looking downward.

Ferris allowed herself a brief, terrified glance. They were directly above her favorite exhibit, a bedroom transported direct from a Venetian villa. She looked up again at Blackheart, and she didn't like the meditative expression on his face. "Why have we stopped?"

He put an arm around her waist. "Hold on to me," he whispered in her ear, his eyes alight with pleasure.

"Why?" Even as she questioned she obeyed, wrapping her arms around his narrow waist and holding tightly.

"Because," he said, and jumped.

Her scream echoed through the building, cut off as the rope stopped their precipitous descent a scant four feet from the green damask-covered bed. Blackheart let go of the rope, and the two of them dropped onto the bed. A cloud of dust rose around them.

"I hate you," Ferris said passionately, sneezing. "I despise and detest you, I'll never trust you again, I—"

"You love me," Blackheart said, odiously sure of himself. "And you'll never distrust me again. So let's stop arguing and take advantage of this bed."

"I could scream," she suggested fiercely, not about to be cajoled, despite the fact that Blackheart was busy undoing the rest of the buttons on her black silk jumpsuit.

"You already did. No one heard you, no one came to your rescue."

"They might if I tried it again."

He'd pushed the clothing down from her shoulders, temporarily imprisoning her arms. "With our luck they might. Don't scream." He covered his mouth with hers.

It took her less than five seconds to help him rid her of the rest of the jumpsuit and another seven seconds to take off his clothes. Then they were naked in the huge Renaissance bed, lost in pleasure, in passion, in love. He was hard and strong and pulsing within her, and she wrapped her arms and legs around him, holding him tightly, rising, falling with him, lost and floating through heights that knew no limits.

When it was over he collapsed on top of her, hot and sweating as she was, panting, heart racing in tune with her own. It was a long moment before either of them spoke, and when Blackheart did, it was disarmingly prosaic. "This isn't really a mattress we're lying on, is it?"

"I don't think so. Cardboard boxes, maybe. You're just lucky we didn't land on wood," she said sleepily, nuzzling his damp hair.

"It was only a four-foot drop at that point. We would have ended up with a few bruises."

"I think you gave me a few, anyway," she murmured. "I do, you know."

"Do what?" He knew the answer as well as she did, but was waiting to hear the words.

"Do trust you. I was wrong to think you'd lie to me. I trust you almost as much as I love you."

"Almost as much?" he echoed.

"Nobody could feel anything as much as the love I feel for you," she whispered against his shoulder.

"In that case, maybe you'd better marry me, after all. You don't seem inclined to give up the ring, and I hate to tell you this, but I didn't bring any protection tonight, either. I really didn't expect we'd end up like this. I don't suppose you did anything . . . ?"

"Nope. I guess you're going to have to make an honest woman of me," she said with a sleepy smile.

"When?"

"How about tomorrow?"

"It'll take three days to get the license. Are you going to change your mind?"

"No. Three days will be fine. Somewhere along the way I figured something out."

"What was that?"

"You're right. It wasn't you I didn't trust. It was me. I would get so lost whenever I was with you. I felt I was disappearing. It frightened me."

"And what changed your mind?"

"Oh, I didn't change my mind. I do tend to disappear when I'm with you. Ferris Byrd and Francesca Berdahofski cease to exist. What I didn't realize is that instead of being me alone, I become joined with you. The two of us are one, stronger than me alone. I don't lose something, I gain it. So I don't have to be so frightened."

"Very wise," he murmured, his mouth brushing hers. "Does that mean we get a happy ending?"

She grinned up at him. "You bet, Blackheart. Happily ever after."

Epilogue

Mr. and Mrs. Smith
(RKO 1941)

"DON'T TELL ME," said Stephen McNab. "I don't want to hear it."

"Of course you do," his wife of eight months declared. "You want my brother to be happy."

"Not particularly," he muttered. "However, I've gotten rather fond of Francesca during the last few months. I suppose for her sake I won't begrudge him."

"Noble of you," Dany McNab said.

"Yes, isn't it? So tell me. Mother and child safe, I suppose? Father recovering from the trauma of it all?"

"Don't be so snotty. You'll probably be going through it before too long yourself."

Momentarily distracted, Stephen pulled his wife onto his lap and indulged in a few brief minutes of passionate necking. "All right," he said finally. "Tell me the details—I know you won't be able to concentrate on more important things until you do."

"Francesca had a baby girl, Catherine Emilie, with lots of dark hair and greeny-blue eyes. She weighed eight pounds even, Blackheart was with them, and everyone is very happy. You're an uncle, Stephen."

"Great," he said morosely. "She's not going to grow up to be a cat burglar, is she? I know bad blood when I see it."

Dany grinned. "Who knows? You'll have to provide a sterling example for her."

"Catherine Emilie," Stephen murmured, trying it out. "What are they going to call her?"

"What do you think?" Dany murmured. "They're going to call her Cat."

The End

About the Author

Anne Stuart is currently celebrating forty years as a published novelist. She has won every major award in the romance field and appeared on the *NYT* Bestseller List, *Publisher's Weekly*, and *USA Today*. Anne Stuart currently lives in northern Vermont.

Made in the USA
Lexington, KY
25 May 2015